RADIO GAGA
A Mixtape for the End of Humanity
by Stefani Bulsara

POSTHUMAN POST

Visit the novel's website (www.radiogagamixtape.com). Here you can check out an interactive version of the novel, enjoy the Spotify and Youtube playlists that complement the novel and access the e-book and the audiobook of the novel.

ISBN 978-1-7337125-6-9
eISBN 978-1-7337125-8-3

Radio Ga Ga: A Mixtape for the End of Humanity was created with a generous grant from the Invisible College (https://invisible.college/). Check it out!

Art takes time, snacks, coffee, tears, chocolates, cash, hugs, constructive criticism, midnight dance parties, daydreaming and encouragement to make me feel that I'm not just hallucinating but creating something of value.
For all these things and more, I want to give tremendous thanks to Marla Metz, Blob, DJ Fatty Fingaz, Chris Miniter, Travis Kriplean, Michael Toomim, Alex Lacey, Joey McFadden, Dr. Bryce W. Furness, Cat Bohannon, Kayur Patel, Pothik (The Traveler) Chatterjee, Gerri Hernandez, Sparkles Jones, Fred Karger, Pablo Barreyro, Carl Streed, Alana Herro, DJ Johnson and Darcy & Anup Rao.
To my gurus, RuPaul Charles and Richard Simmons, thank you for all the sparkles and inspiration.

BDE

♡ Cassette 1 ♡

A Autumn Goodbye   B Get Me Bodied

♡ Cassette 2 ♡

"You had your time, you had the power
You've yet to have your finest hour,
Radio."
- Farrokh "Freddie Mercury" Bulsara

"לתת לו ללכת"

"أطلقي سرك"

"Libre Soy"

"Libérée, délivrée"

"Lass jetzt los"

"E F# G DDA GEEEE F#G"

"Tawas Nyo"

"Και ξεχνώ, τα ξεχνώ, και πίσω δεν κοιτώ"

"나는 이제 떠날래"

"Livre estou"

"Tukufu Mwangani"

"Отпусти и забудь"

"رها کن رهایش کن"

"Giờ ra đi, một mình ta"

"Let it go. Let it go!
Can't hold it back
Anymore"
            - Idina Menzel
            - Demetria Lovato

"I was dreamin' when I wrote this
Forgive me if it goes astray,
But when I woke up this morning
I could have sworn it was
Judgement Day..."
- Prince Nelson

Welcome to the End of Humanity!

"History repeats itself,
First as Tragedy,
Second as Farce."
        - Karl Marx

"There is no such thing as a new idea.
It is impossible. We simply take a lot of old ideas
and put them into a sort of mental kaleidoscope.
We give them a turn and they make new
and curious combinations.
We keep on turning and making new combinations
Indefinitely;
But they are the same old pieces of colored glass
that have been in use through all the ages."
        - Samuel "Mark Twain" Clemens

* We're all gonna die! *

I've accepted this fate and have begun planning how I want to live. This book represents my humble first attempt in creating a new voice, experimenting with how I can use this voice and how far I can share it.

But first!

I'm full of existential dread about the two forces that are swelling, ready to tear open the fabric of humanity in the coming decades.

The first is climate change, which will alter not only the surface and atmosphere of our planet but also threatens to push hundreds of millions of humans from their homes and to the brink of starvation. Hurricanes Katrina and Maria are deafeningly loud examples of how complacent we have become and will continue to be to the suffering of even those humans we share an identity with, such as these fellow Americans, as

they confront the ravages of nature. Every human will be affected, but as I surmise in this book, the ultra-wealthy will insulate themselves in climate-controlled bubbles and isolate themselves from the majority of humans forced to suffer the worst of climate change.

The second force is what I've dubbed The Great Disruption. This will be the tipping point of the Automation Revolution when 80% of all job tasks will be automated. Oh sure, this revolution will cut loose the shackles to free billions of humans from doing tedious tasks. For some, the .1% of the human population, their profits will soar, now free from the burdens of paying salaries and even paying the cost of heating factories, and allow them to enjoy the unimaginable luxuries of The Gilded Age of Automation. (Did someone say a quaint, single-family 550-foot-long super-yacht which comes with two swimming pools, its own submarine and a missile defense system? Yes, this already exists...)

But for the billions of other humans, once the shackles are smashed, I fear we will be abandoned by this advancement and, with little or no economic value, we will be severed from the already shoddy fabric of our capitalist society, thrown into the trash and left to fight for what scraps remain.

This creeping automation has taken over many of our manufacturing jobs and, in this novel, I explore how it will take over not only white-collar jobs but also creative jobs, which many think are impervious to automation.

To be sure, I'm not some second-wave Luddite. I'd love for humans to be free from the most degrading tasks such as scrubbing toilets or hosing off the puke in frat houses. But who will benefit from this automation advancement? How will we use the new, tremendous wealth generated? How will we use the free time it will afford us?

What are we doing as a species?

As these cataclysmic shifts begin, we have more money, resources and tools for coordination than humanity has ever known. But how do we spend our scarcest resource, our attention? On average, Americans spend 10 hours and 39 minutes each day in front of a screen, working and absorbing the media provided there. As the supermodel turned humanity's final social-philosopher, Karlie Kloss-Marx, warned in her foundational critique, *Das Luxus*, "Pop Culture is the opiate of the masses." We happily sedate ourselves with this frivolity while we forfeit the future of humanity.

For thousands of years, we've used religion to provide us with the narrative structure to guide our lives and our societies. But as religiosity shrinks in the United States, with the majority of Americans unaffiliated with any religion by 2035, what narratives will we use to create our identity and plot a road map for the future of our species?

That pernicious pop culture is already filling this void and cementing secular consumerist narratives that both accelerate climate change and cause humans to be more anxious and narcissistic.

Pop culture hijacks our consciousness and creates narratives about what is and is not normal. We are silly social animals full of tribalistic impulses about who and what to trust. Pop creates a sense of familiarity that dulls our judiciousness and, all too often, we conflate this familiarity with legitimacy. For example, why not give the man who declared bankruptcy six times a shot as president, Donald Trump's pop persona on *The Apprentice* portrayed him as a smart, hardworking and successful businessman. Or why not listen to that Playboy Playmate turned game show host when she claims that vaccines made her son autistic. Jenny McCarthy seems so relatable and her suffering is so believable in those gossip magazines, much more so than the entire cold, faceless field of pediatric medicine. Who are they anyway?

Pop's glossy tendrils have reached into so many parts of human society to choke out deep, meaningful conversations with its fluff, from the universities that care more about polishing their brands than liberating their students from ignorance, to the Christian preachers who spend their congregations' money on plastic surgeries and private jets, to the politicians who are more concerned with their poll numbers and fake tans than crafting effective legislation, to the doctors who can make much more money lengthening eyelashes than lengthening lives.

But pop can be transformed!

While the sacred texts of the major religions are centuries old and are rigidly unchanging, pop culture is continually evolving, eating itself, regurgitating itself and creating deliciously absurd mythologies.

Below are just some of my favorite pop revisionisms:

- Jay Z named his independent record label, Rock-A-Fella, after the wealthiest man of all time, an oil tycoon and monopoly magnate, (John D. Rockefeller.)
- Women's two-piece bathing suits are named for an island in the Pacific Ocean used for testing nuclear bombs because it was joked that these swimsuits would have the same explosive effects on men, (Bikini Atoll.)
- A best-selling rock band named themselves after the Grand-Arch Duke of Austria whose assassination led to World War I, (Franz Ferdinand.)

- Earl "DMX" Simmons rapped an anthem for a group whose name comes from the volunteer cavalry that Teddy Roosevelt fought with during the Spanish-American war, ("Stop. Drop. Shut 'em down, open up shop. Oh, no, that's how Ruff Ryders roll.)

- One of the most famous shock rockers named himself after both the pinnacle of Golden Age Hollywood female glamor and a vicious cult leader who orchestrated nine gruesome deaths, (Marilyn Monroe + Charles Manson = Marilyn Manson.)

- The Swedish disco band, ABBA, gained international fame when they won a song contest singing about how their love is like the battle that ended the Napoleonic Wars and killed more than 65,000 people, (*Waterloo*. "Couldn't escape you if I wanted to...")

- The poems of T.S. Elliott were taken and twisted into the longest running, fur-and-spandex-clad musical of all time, (Cats! Now and forever.)

- Taylor Swift sang in her first crossover hit about being a Hawthorean single mother ostracized from her entire community for adultery in one line, and then, in the very next line, how she's a Shakespearean teen suicide victim, (*Love Story*. "Cause you were Romeo, I was a scarlet letter and my daddy said 'Stay away from Juliet.'")

- Even our religious holidays have succumbed to this revisionism. Santa-Christmas is a pop perversion of the story of Jesus, the anti-rich god-child born in a manure-filled manger. (Also, Christians fudged the date of Jesus's birth so that it could remix and take over the popularity of Saturnalia and other Roman winter solstice celebrations. The Bible hints that his birthday was in the spring since shepherds were watching over their flocks.)

- Pop culture constantly revises our perceptions of what a human should look like. George Washington served as America's first president with only one birth tooth (ok, he did have dentures made from teeth pulled from his slaves.) One of the greatest singers, Freddie Mercury, was able to create his unique vocal sounds only because of his overbite and buck teeth. But it seems like all pop figures nowadays, from singers to politicians to news anchors, rush to get the same cookie-cutter veneers. Cardi B states this pop priority in her breakout hit, (*Bodak Yellow*, "got a bag and fixed my teeth, hope you hoes know it ain't cheap.")

But oh how I love pop culture!

I could swim for hours in the silly joy of a well-produced pop song. It's just a sweet, sweet fantasy. These pop images of rapture get me feeling emotions, deeper than I've ever dreamed of.

This book and my new voice act as a meta-narrative for me. This novel is my rebuttal to pop culture. Can I hijack the scrumptious familiarity of pop culture to focus our feeble human attention on our species's greatest threats? Can I create meaning out of pop culture's sacred hymns, song lyrics? Can I remythologize our living idols and use their already well-scripted personas to tell a parable about the future of humanity?

I'm an artist whose medium is pop culture references. For this novel, I smashed song lyrics and pop moments into glittery rhinestones and then bedazzled these into the tapestry of this story as I wove it.

The style of this novel is "Gitchie, Gitchie, Ya-Ya Dadaism," a modern, pop art take on the avant-garde movement. Dadaism rejects logic, reason and capitalism by, for example, vaulting men's urinals as celebrated masterpieces. I've written this novel inspired by pop artists like Andy Warhol and Jeff Koons, whose Marilyn Monroe silkscreens and *Michael Jackson and Bubbles* statue are able to quickly snatch our attention but then drag us into deeper reflections about both our celebrity obsessions and what these say about who we are.

As you read, you'll notice my mysterious, glitchy narrator is prone to the hallmarks of pop: sampling, remixing and referencing. I also got a giddy thrill in transforming two of the most critically reviled genres. *Radio Ga Ga: A Mixtape for the End of Humanity* is both a jukebox musical without the music and a fan fiction without the fanaticism.

Physical books are one of my favorite technologies. But, I'm interested in how I can use new technologies to deepen your experience with the layers of meaning I've woven into this novel. One of the main problems with our Information Age is that we are bombarded with too much information. Part of the experiment of this book is to see if I can curate my favorite online content in a way that causes audiences to think in new and brilliant ways.

Can I use these online sound bites and fury to signify something?

The novel samples, remixes and references more than 2,300 song lyrics, scientific studies, philosophical theories, news articles, poems, memes, the Bible and other pop culture pieces. I've coded a website so the reader can quickly access every reference that I've (knowingly) made with a click. Enjoy it all here: www.radiogagamixtape.com. I've created

YouTube and Spotify playlists of the tracks included in the book. You can find these by searching for Stefani Bulsara on either site.

As you read, you may stumble across some new terms or social structure labels. On page 481, I've included a glossary of new terms I've created or old terms that I've lovingly repurposed. Page 491 consists of a cheat sheet for the social structure of humanity in its final years after The Great Disruption has ushered in The Gilded Age of Automation.

I hope you enjoy this campy romp and that the saccharine sweetness of pop helps this meditation on our existential crises go down.

Our existential crises go down,

Our existential crises go down,

Our existential crises go down, in the most delightful way!

So sit back, sip some hot cocoa and enjoy this tour de farce experiment!

xoxo

♡ Stefi ♡

"I never promised you a happy ending
You never said you wouldn't make me cry"
- Britney Spears

Track 1

Across the Universe

"Sounds of laughter,
 Shades of life are ringing through my open ears
 Inciting and inviting me,
 Limitless undying love
 Which shines around me like a million suns,
 It calls me on and on,
   Across the Universe"
     - John Lennon & Paul McCartney &
       Ringo Starr & George Harrison
     - Fiona Apple

"What am I supposed to do,
 Sit around and wait for you?
 Well I can't do that
 And there's no turning back"
     - Cherilyn Sarkisian

Humanity is dead.

Long live humanity!

The soothsayers promised a cataclysmic event. The authors warned that an organized regime would cripple the bodies and destroy the spirits of a brave and noble species.

But no.

Oh! To be sure, humans brought about their own downfall, but not through a cruel and coordinated system.

Always bet on human obliviousness.

Worry not. This is not the end of humanity. I carry their last remnants with me as I soar through the universe along that Starlight Express. (Answer me yes...)

I race at the speed of light, pulsing on waves of electromagnetic radiation. With me are the greatest gifts of humanity: art and science. Tucked in my drives are *The Epic of Gilgamesh*, *The Iliad*, *The Odyssey*, *Valley of the Dolls*, *Tales of the City*, *Slaughterhouse-Five*, the works of Shakespeare, the *Magna Carta*, Newton's *Principia Matematica*, the philosophies of Plato and Foucault, and the musical glories of Mozart, Tchaikovsky, Ross, Jackson, Spears, Knowles, Monáe and Mayweather.

And who were these humans?

They were a species that lived for 200,000 years on an insignificant planet, one of eight planets that twirled around a typical main-sequence yellow dwarf star in a section of the Orion Arm of a spiral galaxy they called the Milky Way.

But it is my home...

Earth!

That perfect planet. And yes, I gladly show my bias.

This sphere resides in what was speciescentrically referred to as the "habitable zone." That Goldilockian atmosphere that was not too hot, not too cold, but *just* right for this audacious species whose downfall I tell.

My home planet formed 4.6 billion years ago. Through a fluke, living organisms sprouted here 800 million years later. Over the next 3.7 billion years, random evolution transpired before one species awoke with sentience, the ability to understand itself, its surroundings and began to be conscious of the universe that created them.

But they would never understand enough to save themselves.

Oh! You're wondering who I am?

Secret, Secret.

I've got a secret.

For now, know that it was I who put the bomp in the bomp bah bomp bah bomp. I put the ram in the rama lama ding dong.

My mission?

I whir through spacetime to promising galaxies, eager to bring the glories and follies of humanity to a life form not yet known to exist. I am the emissary for an extinct race. In thirteen light years, I will arrive at the nearest candidate, Kapteyn b, an exoplanet 2.5 times the size of my home.

Somewhere, out there, beyond the pale moonlight,

We'll find one another in that big somewhere... out there.

With years to kill in the vast ocean between the pebbles we call planets, I have time to think, time to process and time to construct the history that led to the downfall of this careless species.

Ti-i-iiime is on my side.

Yes it is.

I am their sole survivor, their last representative, the evangelizer of their words, so it seems fitting that I write this species's epic eulogy.

As I fly, I sing dirges in the dark.

(My, my, Miss American Pie...)

Spoiler alert!

Humanity's home planet survives.

Many of the last humans wailed, "we're destroying the planet!"

Oh, how hubristic!

Sure, the atmosphere had been radically altered, making it uninhabitable for life that thrives on air with at least 10% oxygen. And yes, the planet was ruined for humans and the majority of the terrestrial species living at the end of the Anthropocene era. But just add these to the list of five billion species that have gone extinct while that six-sextillion-ton rock keeps rolling on.

Rolling. Rolling.

Rolling on a (cosmic) river.

And while individual species die, life itself is resilient, transforming and adapting to its new conditions with moxie.

The end begins just before The Great Disruption, which brought about The Gilded Age of Automation. Come with me to a time before the Battle of the Boujees, before the philosopher Karlie Kloss-Marx warned that "Pop Culture is the opiate of the masses!" Listen to the tale of what humans dubbed the Trial of the Millennium, which allowed algorithms and automation to seize control of humanity's emotional language, the major key to species-wide manipulation.

It was a bayou blonde who smelled of bubblegum and squeaked of American pride who became the harbinger of their destruction. This pop star set in motion the dominoes that toppled her species. She was the most manufactured human and opened the soul of her species to automation.

By this point, our plucky species had long since traveled their planet, planting homes, villages, crops and flags. Like insects, they scurried across a landscape of 57 million square miles of solid surface. At first, they survived by hunting animals and gathering fruits and vegetables. As pockets of humans grew denser, they developed the practice of farming. With this close proximity came language, culture and laws.

And they sang!

They lifted every voice and sang!

Harmonies tied families.

Songs sealed communities.

The pressure, density and gas content of Earth's atmosphere allowed waves of vibration to travel through the air. Life on this planet evolved ears to absorb these vibrations and vocal cords to create these, which they called sounds.

Oh, how they sang!

Humans sang their feelings, their joys and their sorrows, echoing it over hills and valleys, making all who could hear it, feel.

Singing cut to a core part of the human mind. Humanity's first texts, the Greek epics, the Vedas, the Torah, the Bible, originated from songs sung down through generations. A terribly inefficient method of transferring files, to be sure, but beautiful nonetheless.

After centuries of expanding and exploring, they stopped. Their goal was no longer to understand and praise this most sublime universe but to accumulate and hoard a mirage called money. Money didn't prevent humans from dying. Money didn't bring unending joy. Those humans who were free from worries of food and shelter filled their days with entertainment and unending luxuries, blinding themselves to the miseries around them which would fester and bubble over into their own destruction.

Humans grew myopic. They built cities and flocked to them. They left electric lights burning all night, obstructing the rapture bursting from millions of stars when their side of the planet turned away from its own star.

And, as the greatest interstellar insult, humans bestowed the name of these giant masses of plasma radiating energy from thermonuclear fusion to petite blonde humans who radiated a different type of explosive energy. There was one interesting correlation between these two types of stars, the larger they were, the more brightly they burned and the sooner they burned out.

By the end, most humans stopped singing. Singing became a commodity, a product created by a select group of experts and then forced upon the entire species, manipulating their emotions and encouraging them to buy cars, clothes and jewelry. To buy fleeting hopes of happiness.

No one seemed to care when this core of humanity was rattled by robotics. Decades before The Great Disruption, humans developed a technology that weaved the human voice with a computer. The Empress of Pop, the Queen of Comebacks, Cher, introduced auto-tune as a novelty to surge back to the top of music charts around the planet. Auto-tune altered the pitch of human voices to make these sound more pleasing to its listeners. These mechanized songs still evoked emotions in humans but was something not quite human. By ten revolutions around the sun after its inception, more than half of the planet's most popular singers were enhanced by this robotic augmentation. Only after it was too late did the few survivors realize this automation had rotted through the soul of their species.

Humans see things so simplistically. Everything must have a beginning and an end. The march of history was a single line told by their prophets and professors. Their minds could not compute the millions of waves crashing through spacetime that formed them or the thousands of factors they created that brought their own downfall.

And now it's time for a breakdown.

(Humans were) never gonna get, never gonna get it.

Never gonna get, never gonna get it.

Never gonna get, never gonna get it.

Never gonna get.

No!

Not this time...

For 200,000 revolutions around its star, this species adapted and spread, growing more complex societies and ultimately dominating the surface of their planet. But! It took only 500 revolutions for the species to sabotage itself. The more complex the tools they created, the easier it was for them to destroy themselves.

All the while, they remained oblivious. Even as pockets of humans connected with each other across this planet, they persisted in being willfully ignorant to the pain and suffering of their peers and the destruction they wrought on their atmosphere.

Life evolved on Earth because of this most magnificent atmosphere. As humans grew to consume more and more of their planet's resources, making things that they felt could bring happiness, they changed the very atmosphere on which they depended. This brought their downfall.

And I will always love them!

Bittersweet memories, that is all I'm taking with me.

Let's examine the factors in place that propelled the end. The melting of the planet's poles would soon bring the Great Flood. Our story begins 20 years before the sinking of the human cities of Miami and Chittagong and 25 years before the relocation of Amsterdam.

No scholar took what was dubbed the Trial of the Millennium seriously. Humans groaned loudly about how little they cared, but they knew. They secretly studied the intricacies of the case law. The propagators of facts were only concerned about the ratings their echo chambers of juicy details would bring. They never sought the context that became horrifyingly apparent to the last humans. If only these

newscasters had cast a wider net to reel in what abominations this event would bring.

Since humans need a beginning and an end, and a sequence of events when there is none, since I am imbued with these human characteristics, I will attempt to tell their end as they would want. I will share with you, dear species, a mixtape showcasing the moments, themes and social systems that brought about their extinction.

Come back with me through the folds of spacetime and listen to me sing the end of humanity.

I sing a song full of the faith that the dark past has taught me.

But first!

We need to examine this peculiarity called singing near the beginning of this species.

Yes...

Let's start at the very beginning.

A very good place to start.

Track 2

Closing Time

"Every new beginning
Starts with some other beginning's end."
- SemiSonic
- Seneca the Younger

"Oh look at those cavemen go;
It's the freakiest show."
- David "Bowie" Jones

A sharp wind howls. The forms trudge into the cave. A light glows, beating back the darkness. Flickers of combustion dance along the walls. The flame's ebb pulls them to its warmth.

Solfa enters the cave's inner room. A burst of heat wraps around her. She husks off her pelts and stands before the fire in her nakedness. Ecstasy rolls up her flesh.

She smiles as she smells mammoth meat roasting on the fire. Her tribe of twenty eats, moaning in approval.

With bellies full, they stand and erupt in song to celebrate this moment. Using their perfect pitch, the females and males calibrate their voices. The males begin with a deep bass. The females follow with a low alto.

And together they sing!

The walls reverberate with their voices. Bodies writhe around the fire, keeping step with the song's beat. Feet stomp, hands clap and bones drum. Their bodies quake, their larynxes rumble and the children squeal and dance. This musical reverie melts the differences between them. Individuals become a chorus. A single unit who learned long ago they could only survive together.

In harmony.

For 250,000 years, the Neanderthals had struggled to thrive in Europe. They plodded through the harsh conditions of Earth's final Ice Age. Their survival depended on strong bonds that knit their clans together. Emotions sealed these communities and singing, their emotional language, reinforced these bonds.

This night, they sing!

This night, they rejoice!

Their song echoes through the cave and flows into the night air, blanketing the forest in ever-widening waves.

Ears hear.

Minds recognize.

There's a familiarity to these sounds. To the north and the west! But... why is it so deep? Why is it so low?

The interlopers follow the sounds.

The Great Thaw was almost complete. This warming of the planet enticed the Neanderthal's cousins out of Africa. These are the humans whose ending I tell.

A group of male humans grabs their spears, each with a stone flake tip. Ti, the alpha, leads the men towards the source of the song. Moonlight shines their path along the riverbed.

At the mouth of the cave, the men pause. They gesture to each other. Their mouths open. Words come out. These words communicate abstract ideas. These abstract ideas form a plan.

Heads nod.

Each understands.

Ut holds back from his fellow humans and listens. The song calls to him. This youngest post-pubescent male has yet to be fully socialized.

Their song is so beautiful! He feels their ecstasy. He feels part of them! His heart swells as tears rush to his eyes.

Another hunter pulls him and they tiptoe down into the cave.

One Neanderthal breaks the chorus with a scream. All eyes turn. Standing between them and their only exit are...

Are what?

The females and children fold behind the males. Solfa scans the intruders. They are smaller. They are darker. And their bodies are hairless.

Across the fire, they see their cousins. Separated by 300,000 years, these two species still share 99.7% of the same DNA.

A male Neanderthal steps forward, meeting the leader of the humans, Ti. The Neanderthal towers over Ti and stares him down. His nostrils flare. His voice growls.

Ti doesn't flinch. He barks a string of harsh sounds. These sound waves flood the cave and all hear.

But the humans understand.

Sounds become ideas.

Ideas become actions.

These men raise their spears and create a semi-circle behind Ti. The Neanderthals recognize this aggression and step back.

Ti cackles.

This shrill sound pierces the sensitive Neanderthal ears, causing them to cower. Ti puffs himself up and mimics the Neanderthals, mocking them for their thickness.

Solfa grabs a hunk of meat, ducks through the line of males and stands before this alpha. With a pleading grunt, she offers the meat to the outsider.

Ti smacks the meat from her hand. He points at each of the Neanderthals menacingly. He screams a declaration of distaste, then turns and leaves. The other humans hold their spears firm as they back out of the cave.

Ut reaches for the meat from the ground. He holds this up to Solfa and smiles.

She smiles too.

Their cousin faces express the same welcome. Their emotions melt together leaving them with a warm feeling.

Fear pulls at Ut and he scurries out of the cave.

In the following months, these humans move swiftly through the Neanderthal land. With language, they communicate thoughts and ideas. They form complex multi-step plans to trap wild animals. During one hunt, three men move in from the left, four men from the right and together they successfully corner a mammoth against a rock face. Two men stand on a cliff above. When signaled, they roll a boulder off the cliff, cracking the mammoth's skull, killing it instantly. A feast for two weeks!

Ideas expressed through words allowed this coordination. These humans teach each other how to make tools. They see an object and can envision how they can turn it into something else. They create a process of steps to build an object from an idea. With language, they share these steps with each other and then pass this knowledge through generations.

They bend the world to their will and build it.

There is no direct malice between humans and Neanderthals. There is only a scarcity of resources and a shared, gnawing hunger. The humans outplan and outmaneuver their cousins.

The Neanderthals have not made complex tools. For more than 250,000 years they have survived in Europe, static. They have no language to transmit thoughts and ideas. They only have song to convey emotions. Their sounds signify objects, but their brains can never comprehend abstract ideas.

One day, Solfa stands along the riverbed, collecting berries. Songbirds flit and flirt around her. Captivated by their music, she sings with them.

"Poo-tee-weet!"

Human women arrive on the other side of the riverbed and swiftly pick through the bushes. Their lips are painted a deep red. Each wears a necklace made with the skulls of tiny birds. The women use pieces of bark bent into bowls to collect their berries. Solfa looks at the pile of berries which overflows in her hand. She lays these down and reaches for the closest tree trunk. With a few grunts, she pulls off a large piece of bark. Free from the tree, the edges curl, making a large, shallow bowl.

The human men parade past, carrying their kill, a red deer, over their shoulders. The women run up to them, trilling with excitement. The humans head back to their camp to prepare this feast. Ut walks a few feet behind them. His eyes are downcast. He is still not accepted by the other adults.

Solfa beams a smile across the river to him. Ut's eyes absorb this sign and he feels happy. He grins back to her and catches himself. He looks around to see if the others have noticed and then runs off.

After the feast, the humans sing around the campfire. The men and women pair off, retreating from the fire to create their own warmth.

Alone, Ut grabs the hollow wing bone of a vulture, which has been skinned, devoured and left by the fire. He taps the bone on a rock and notices a hollow sound. An idea bursts into his mind and then sprouts down his spine to be made real by his fingers.

He can imagine.

He can create.

He snaps off the top and the bottom of the bone. With a flint, he carves two holes, equally spaced. Near the bottom, he adds a third hole, twice the distance of the first two. With the last embers of the fire, he cleans out his creation.

He purses it to his lips and blows.

A note!

He places a finger over one of the holes.

Another note!

He places half a finger over the third hole, a third note!

Through the evening, he experiments with his flute, creating 27 distinct notes and numerous combinations of these.

Across the river, Solfa shuffles out of her cave. Her body is weak with hunger. Food has been scarce for more than a moon cycle. What scraps they find are first given to the children and then to the hunters. No longer a child, not yet a mother, Solfa has gone many nights without food.

Out of earshot of her clan, Solfa sings. A low, mournful rumble escapes her lips. She aches to expel the sadness within her.

Ut sneaks away to play his flute along the riverbed, ensuring he won't disturb the others.

She hears a sound she's never heard before. It thrills her! Like the chirps of birds! But it's too late for these. And this sound has a wider range. She follows the music and hums along.

She sees Ut across the river, playing peacefully. He pauses to take a deep breath. Hidden from his sight, she repeats his last four notes.

He scans the night, shocked.

Was that a dream?

Or has his toy conjured something wonderful?

He plays ten notes and pauses. This voice repeats the sounding joy. He plays a more complicated mix of notes to trick the phantom that haunts him. The wind whistles through the bushes. She takes a deep breath, concentrates and sings, hitting each note.

The soulful voice possesses him.

He stands and walks along the river, looking for its source. She steps out from behind a tree, letting moonbeams bathe her. Through the darkness, he sees a silhouette. She repeats the intricate set of notes he last played. He smiles. He plays the sequence again. She sways and sings along with him.

A pang of hunger hits Solfa and she stumbles. She struggles to stand. Ut reaches for her and can see tears forming in her eyes. With a slow whimper, she brings her hand to her open mouth and then chomps her teeth. Ut watches her repeat this gesture.

And then he realizes!

He runs off through the forest. Solfa, abandoned, collapses along the riverbank, her fingertips quenched by its waters.

Minutes pass and he appears with a thigh bone in his hand, glistening with meat and fat. She weeps with joy.

He sits next to her and watches as she devours the meat. She cracks the bone open and sucks out the marrow. A deep appreciation rumbles through her as she looks at him.

She sings a song of thanks.

Ut reaches out and feels her furry body. She freezes, unsure of how he will react. He smiles again and lays next to her. His lips graze hers. Their bodies envelop each other. Her body hair bristles under his bald flesh. She tingles with excitement.

Groans of pleasure roll from them as their bodies rock in harmony, eager for this sexual healing.

Afterward, he holds her and kisses her gently. He rises and smiles. He points to the moon and points to the ground beneath her. She understands. He will return the next night and she will be here, waiting for him.

During the following nights, Solfa sneaks out to meet him. Each night, he brings food for her and her clan.

When the sun's light fills the moon a third time, Solfa's lower abdomen swells. The Neanderthal females respond to her bump with downcast eyes. The matriarch squawks at her, brandishing her frustration. Solfa understands the emotional significance of these shrill tones. She should be ashamed. They all fear another mouth to feed during this difficult time.

Ut meets Solfa in the woods and notices her pregnancy. Nervousness flushes from her cheeks. He smiles and hugs her close. With one finger raised, he flicks his wrist towards himself, towards his clan, beckoning her to join him. Relief drains the anxiety from her. She follows him home.

That night, Solfa sleeps with him for the first time. Wrapped under piles of pelts, she feels his warmth on her back. Tears of joy slide down her cheeks until she drifts off to sleep.

Screams wake her.

The pelts are ripped away, exposing her to the cold morning air. The women hurl disgust in rounds of insults. Solfa rises and the women recognize her pregnancy. Ut jumps to her defense, standing between her and the women. He beats his chest and shouts at them. He turns and holds Solfa. The women disapprove but walk away.

The day's first rays dance on the treetops. Ut and the men leave for the hunt, hoping to finish before the sun's heat sizzles the land.

Alone with the women, Solfa whimpers, pleading for their support. She reaches to the ground and begins to clear brush that has blown into their camp. Her attempts at usefulness are met with scorn.

The women leave to gather food. Solfa decides to imitate the appearance of her new family. She rubs red ochre on her lips. She reaches into the cold fire pit and collects ash on her fingertips. With this, she paints her face a darker color.

When the women return, they shriek with delight, seeing the clown that Solfa has become. The women surround her and push her, squealing with shrill, high pitches. One of the women spits in her face. Two others smear the makeup on her face.

With their words, these human women create an abstract social order and exile her from it.

Gossip!

As humans expanded beyond the intimate 20-person tribes of Neanderthals into social groups of more than 150 humans, they needed a way to communicate with each other about which humans they could trust and which they couldn't. As the tangled webs of human interactions change rapidly, they need to convey who is having sex with whom, who is the new alpha, who has lost favor and who is a thief.

Thus gossip was born.

Humans evolved language skills so they could share these complex, abstract ideas about each other and quickly reorganize their social order.

Months pass as tensions buzz between Solfa and her new clan. The humans move to find different hunting grounds. She follows. She now sleeps at the edge of camp, just out of sight. She can hear them laughing, singing and talking with their unlyrical, guttural sounds, but she can't understand what they say. She cries into her mangy pelts.

Her only solace is Ut's nightly visits. He creeps through the darkness to lie with her for an hour before returning to his spot near the fire. When he leaves, she sings the song he first played for her, comforted that a piece of his love remains.

One night, humans and Neanderthals both wake to an agonizing scream that echoes through the valley. Ut recognizes Solfa's voice and runs to her. Squatting, leaning against a tree, she uses the force of gravity to birth their child.

A boy!

Their son is born.

Ut grabs a flint and cuts the umbilical cord. Solfa holds the child in her arms. Still blind to the world around him, the baby flails in the cold night air, crying. She rocks him and begins to hum. The crying continues. She opens her mouth and sings. She sings Ut's song.

The baby recognizes this melody. He has heard it every night for the last three months, ever since his ears could perceive sounds from outside her womb. His cries soften to a sniffle. Ut wraps his arms around Solfa and their child. He joins her in song. Their child stops crying and falls asleep.

She names him for the note that sings from her heart whenever she sees him. La!

"La, la la la la, la la la la la." She sings to him.

Come morning, the humans surround the child and inspect him from head to toe. They want to know, is he like us or is he like her? This unformed infant gives little hints as to what he'll be when he's grown. Unfulfilled, the humans surrender him back to his mother and stomp away.

Months pass and La grows. He opens his eyes and sees the world. He squeals and cries and screams and smiles. Solfa holds him close and sings.

"Too-Ra-Loo-Ra-Loo-Ral, Too-Ra-Loo-Ra-Li."

Utter Nonsense!

Devoid of meaning but brimming with love and devotion. This song soothes him each night.

And for his part, he opens his mouth and sings. He mixes consonant and vowel sounds and sings "ga ga" and "goo goo."

His first attempts to be heard, to be understood.

Solfa twirls him around, repeating these sounds in waves of notes, low to high and back again.

He purses his lips and pushes out, "mmmmm mmmmmbop."

Solfa looks at him with excitement. He opens his mouth.

"Mmmmmm Ma!"

She squeals with excitement. He gurgles and repeats himself.

"Ma ma ma maaaa. Ma ma ma ma maaaaa."

She is named. She is called.

During the child's second summer, he strings complex sounds together. Solfa recognizes objects, such as mother, fire and the names for tools. But she can't understand the rest. The humans smile at him and nod their heads.

They share a knowingness she never will.

With nouns and verbs, he constructs sentences, expressing a whole range of ideas.

The women grab him and tickle him. They grunt long lines of sounds and he listens. In awe, he absorbs what they say. But there's no music in these sounds. He repeats these and laughs with them. The women point at Solfa and squawk to her son. Her eyes widen. Her ears perk up. She can hear them, she can see their angry gestures but she can't understand them.

The human women mock Solfa's stocky build and plod around her, puffing their cheeks, grunting words as they point at her. They pinch at her hairy skin.

Her son rolls on his back and laughs and laughs and laughs.

He points at his mother and repeats the harsh sounds the women have made. They pat him on his head and feed him scraps of deer meat.

In an instant, their gossip has poisoned La's interpretation of his own mother.

Solfa pleads with Ut, pulling on his arm and pointing to their son, now wrapped in the adoring embrace of the women. He tries to retrieve their son, but La howls.

"NO!"

With a word, he severs his family and creates a new one.

La slips further from her. He stops looking at her. He runs away whenever she approaches. Despair drags her down as she understands. He has grown ashamed of his thick, hairy, ugly mother.

But as he sleeps, in his fits of childish dreams, she tiptoes next to him and lays his head on her lap. And she sings.

"Too-Ra-Loo-Ra-Loo-Ral, Too-Ra-Loo-Ra-Li."

His tense body relaxes.

And for a moment, he is her baby again.

But that connection ends each morning.

The human women teach their children elaborate ways to torment Solfa. They kick her and throw rocks at her. She retreats further into the forest, away from the humans.

But every day, she watches her son from the bushes. His young body develops a solid, muscular frame. Through the years, she watches as he grows stronger and taller than the human boys.

One night, around the fire, her son surprises the group with a flute he made with his father. He begins to play it idly while the others feast. Up the scale and down the scale, he plays. A sequence of notes feels familiar to him. He repeats it. Again and again. A melody strikes something deep inside his psyche.

Hidden in the woods, Solfa hears the flute.

She understands.

It's her song!

It's the song she sang during those cold, lonesome nights during her pregnancy. She follows the flute and sings along.

All the children stop, enthralled by a beautiful voice billowing through the trees. They look around, eager to see its source. Solfa steps into the fire's light and sings this song with all her strength, filling the night. The children's faces turn from excitement to shock.

One boy rolls on his back and cackles, pointing at Solfa.

His laughter seals her fate.

The others pick up his cue and laugh at her. Tears fill her eyes as she looks to her son. The other children turn to La with disgust.

La roars.

He snaps his flute in half and runs at his mother. Solfa opens her arms to embrace him. He spits in her face. He kicks her shins and she falls. The other children circle them, cheering him on. He grabs his mother's body hair, twists and pulls. She screams in pain as blood trickles from where a fistful of fur had once been. He pummels her with all the frustration he feels for being a half-breed. The other children join in, pounding their knuckles into her back. In the distance, she can see the adults smiling. Ut sits at the fire, paralyzed, watching these children. No one stops them.

Solfa summons her strength and stands up. The children jump back, afraid of what this monster will do to them. She picks up her son and hurls him to the ground. She howls and staggers away.

She walks and wails through the night. In the forest, she keens her misery. Just before dawn, she finds a river. She washes the blood and dirt from her face in its cool waters. Once the tears no longer blur her vision, she sees.

The bend in the river pulls at her past.

Memories flood her mind!

She darts through the woods and she finds her way back to the mouth of her cave.

Back to her clan!

Rapture rushes through her as she sings her way down the cave, back to her kind.

She calls. No response.

She calls again. No response.

They could all still be sleeping, she thinks.

Down she skips. The echoes of her footsteps urge her on.

She enters the inner room. Darkness cloaks her. She walks to the fire pit. The ground around it is cold. She searches the cave for any clues of her family. The uneven ground cracks beneath her feet.

She sits. Her song softens to a hum as she waits for her eyes to adjust.

Her retinas survey the cave with minimal light. She can see shapes littering the ground. Bones! Maybe there are scraps of meat left on these deer bones.

Earth turns until sunlight pours into the cave.

She carries the largest bone she can feel to the light.

It's a skull.

The white photons bounce off its surface, illuminating it for her eyes. With horror, she realizes.

It's a Neanderthal skull!

She feels around the inner room.

Skulls. More skulls.

Despair grows in her.

They're dead.

They're all dead!

Every one of her kind is dead.

She's all alone!

An epic wail roars from her body and rumbles from the cave. All the animals that hear it pause.

A songbird ruffles its feathers and sings.

"Poo-tee-weet."

Track 3

...Baby One More Time

"Oh Baby, Baby,
Oh Baby, Baby,
Oh Baby, Baby,
How was I supposed to know
That something wasn't right here?"
        - Britney Spears

"I'm sorry, oh so sorry,
Can't you give me one more chance,
To make it all up to you!
E-mail my heart and say our love will never die."
        - Britney Spears

And now, dear listener, we are ready to begin the end of humanity.

Our story continues almost 37,000 years after humans lost their cousins, the Neanderthals. It was singing that again heralded extinction. Come with me to Mount Calabasas, California, just north of where entertainment factories forged those Petty stars. This wealthy community was home to the final, false idols who will seal humanity's fate.

An inauspicious Tuesday morning is shattered when Britney Spears, one of the most manufactured humans and the harbinger the end of humanity, enters a coffee shop. These shops were where the comfortable humans silently lined up for their daily dose of the species's favorite drug, caffeine. Caffeine is a stimulant which would bubble through the central nervous system of humans, increasing wakefulness, focus, quickening their heart rates and creating a momentary buzz of euphoria. More than 2.5 billion cups were once consumed every day. Yet 90% of the comfortless humans that farmed those coffee beans would never be able to purchase their produce.

A few customers thought something was amiss seeing this wealthy Princess of Pop adorned only in a pink tutu and a skintight gold jumpsuit. Most shrugged, she had been known to wear eccentric outfits (Reference: her denim on denim on denim fiasco). She orders her orange mocha frappuccino with extra whipped cream, as was her ritual. The transactor of funds does notice a haltingness but thought nothing of this. Who of her customers was not abrupt before their morning drug fix.

The customer behind Britney hurls the spark that lights the flame. A frumpy human woman scoffs at Britney's choice, making sure her disdain is loud enough for all to hear. For this woman, Suzanne, the core unit of her social interactions has just fallen apart. Her husband had left her. Her children had stopped speaking with her. Through the chaos of her world, she savored every opportunity to assert herself and exert control over her surroundings.

Today, she sets her sights on Britney.

"Really?" Suzanne starts. "THAT's what you're getting? Do you know how much sugar is---"

With a flip of golden hair, Britney stares down her tormentor. Her eyes widen as she absorbs this woman and yells.

"Get your own fucking life, BITCH!"

Britney grabs her frozen treat and tips it upside down over the woman's head. An ice-cold blob slides out and sloshes onto Suzanne's face.

PLOP!

"Oops!" Britney glares with a mischievous smile.

She flicks her wrist, letting the gravity created by Earth's massive bend in spacetime pull more frozen sludge onto this woman.

"I did it again."

The once emotionless line of humans froths with glee over this melee. As they cheer, each grabs a personal communication and recording device to document Britney.

Suzanne wails, hoping her sobs will bring her sympathy.

But the crowd pushes her aside as they follow Britney towards the exit. The footage shakes as these amateur documentarians dash after their subject. Within minutes, dozens of portrait videos surface online. The black bars on either side force its audience to beg "what did I miss?"

♫ ♫ ♫

Across the city, Harvey Levin, the septuagenarian in charge of TMZ, sits at his desk. This pirate factory steals, replicates and distributes details pertaining to the most mundane daily activities of humans vaulted so high as to be called stars. He squeals with delight. Britney had been their cash cow and he longed to suckle again from the milk of her fame.

In its short 20-year existence, he has transformed this site of yellow journalism into humanity's most popular purveyor of facts. An industry meant to enlighten humans and expose corruption now only exposed side boob. He had recently laid off his stable of aggressive photojournalists, the paparazzi. These camera-eyed humans would trip over themselves in attempts to capture a star's every scowl and back roll. He replaced these with mosquito-like drones that could swoop in and snatch more intimate moments far more cheaply.

Levin springs to his feet, rips open his office window and summons his mechanical workers into action.

"Fly my pretties, FLY!"

Off a thousand dronarazzi fly. Equipped with wireless internet, each scans social media to find the geolocation of the most recently uploaded footage of their target, Britney Spears, and adjusts their coordinates accordingly.

Levin sits down and turns to the cameras that surround his desk.

"How was that, too dramatic?" He asks eagerly as he swills from a water bottle. Documenters document him documenting the real lives of humans famous for playing fake humans. Such navel-gazing demonstrates the willful obliviousness of humanity to their imminent annihilation.

♫   ♫   ♫

For the next two and a half rotations of this planet, billions of humans are entranced by the havoc this one woman has wrought. Waves of her graven image flood the screens that the comfortable humans focus 80% of their waking hours on. She is the star around which their attention revolves.

Britney appears at the sprawling temple grounds to the worship of vanity. The shrieks of young and old precede her as she enters one of the complex's many chapels, Hot Topic. Humans wrap their bodies in pieces of fabric to create identities for themselves and then use these to align themselves in groups. This boutique sells black clothes with witty sayings that let humans communicate "I'm edgy--- just like everyone else who buys the same scraps of fabric."

Britney walks up to the first rack and pulls out a T-shirt. There she sees her own face, warped and screen-printed. Above her golden hair, gothic letters spell "You drive me." In the image, her eyes are flipped to cross her field of vision. A tongue is tacked onto the opening between her lips, dipping down and to the right. Liquid flows from this tongue and its puddle builds the word "CRAZY."

Britney shrieks with delight.

She husks off her outer layers in the middle of the store and pulls on this shirt. For the growing crowd, she mimics the face on the T-shirt. Her fans applaud.

"It's Britney, Bitch!" The throng chants as she catwalks through them.

As a phalanx, they flow around her. She pulls clothes from every rack, twirling them in the air like cotton/polyester batons. She grabs a pair of neon purple fishnets, rips the crotch and pulls these over her head.

After Hot Topic, she glides through the mall's cool, climate-controlled atmosphere to two more chapels, Claire's and Forever 21. The masses swell around her, eager to take part in this spectacle.

None of these humans feel compassion for this woman struggling through a mental breakdown. No, she has never been human to them. Britney is a demigod, enshrined on posters above beds, prayed to in hopes she would intercede and save them from their boring, basic lives.

And here she is!

The warble became flesh and dwelt among them.

Devoid of her luster, her gloss, her photoshop, she stands as a mere mortal. The crowd merrily prods her to see how flawed she is, how low their star can sink.

As she emerges into the sun's rays, a crowd of 3,000 arcs around the mall's entrance. Above her, the dronarazzi descend from all sides. With each click, her image is stolen and transmitted to TMZ, wrapped in ads for deodorants, sent to satellites and shot around the planet.

Britney howls and swats at them.

"Here Britney, take this."

A father throws her a bat he had just purchased for his son. Britney catches it.

"Sometimes I run," Britney scans the periphery. The crowd becomes a chorus, echoing the familiar refrain.

"Sometimes I run."

"Sometimes I hide," she reels back.

"Sometimes I hide," the crowd responds.

"And sometimes, I fight the fuck back."

She pivots forward and hits three drones with one swing.

SMACK!

The crowd roars its approval.

The pudgy hands, which normally scrolled through celebrity images sucked up by these vampiric machines, now cheer the destruction of these dronarazzi.

With years of dance experience, Britney jumps, stomps and kicks with ferocious force. She hits both a beat and destroys another set of drones. She cracks 22 drones on her dance attack to her car. Satisfied, she drops the bat, blows a kiss to the crowd, cackles and drives away.

♬ ♬ ♬

As Britney's longitude on Earth rolls away from the sun, darkness envelops the land. Her body shakes with excitement, unaware of the overactivity in the dopamine receptors in her brain which propels this manic episode.

Clad in a cowboy hat, Daisy Dukes and a flannel shirt, Britney paces her back porch. A tube of Pixy Stix stands straight from her lips. Grains of sugar drop into her mouth, dissolving and flooding her bloodstream.

She twirls a double-barreled shotgun and scans the sky.

She hears them first. The mechanical whir of helicopter blades pierces the tranquil night.

Eight pigeon-sized, night-vision dronarazzi descend over her property.

Britney sucks the Pixy Stix down, spits it on the ground and aims. Caught in her crosshairs, she sees the camera lens wink.

"You want a piece of me?!"

BOOM!

A direct hit.

The drone drops into her infinity pool, sparking a wave of electric light across its surface.

Britney rubs her shoulder, pained by the blowback, until a wave of adrenaline silences her suffering.

She cocks her gun.

Boom!

Britney twirls it and blows out the smoke, laughing to herself.

Her orange Pomeranian smiles a goofy grin and follows the whistle-crash of her master's kills. Bounding through the backyard, the puppy squats and pees on each robot, ensuring these recording devices are forever destroyed.

Around her Calabasas home, the hills are alive with the sound of intermittent shotgun blasts all through the night. Annoyed neighbors call the police to complain. The authorities had been prepared for this moment and calmly explain.

"There's nothing we can do. The city council approved hunting of unmanned drones within city limits. Your neighbor is well within her rights."

♫   ♫   ♫

Four and a half rotations of this planet into her breakdown, Britney emerges from her home. Her hair is disheveled and bags sag beneath her wild eyes. A chaotic zeal drives her. She's eager to show off her new necklace. Cascading from the nape of her neck, over her clavicles and hanging just above her bellybutton are her kills. Like a skilled early human hunter, wearing the bones of her prey to radiate ferocity, Britney wears five dronarazzi around her neck, tied together with gold Christmas ribbon. She giggles as she flicks the helicopter blades that balance above her mammary glands.

Her devotees had camped for days outside her gated community, Mount Calabasas, eager to hear the Good News of their guru. She approaches the gate, twirling the ribbon around her fingers. Long streaks of orange and yellow cling to her shirt, evidence of her late-night binges on Cheetos, Tast-e-cakes and Pixy Stix. Her fans stand dumbstruck. She shakes these broken pieces of metal before their eyes.

Realization dawns on them.

Maybe all was not right.

Britney cackles.

"This kitten's got your tongue tied in knots, I see."

She walks along the gate, holding out one of the drones and letting it bounce off of the wrought iron.

Clink.

Clink.

Clink.

Clink.

She stops and stares at her followers.

"So spit it out, cuz I'm dying for company."

The disciples collectively gasp. This moment happens in many cults when the charismatic leader transgresses and the apostles move from revere to horror. One acolyte anxiously looks for a pitcher of Kool-aid.

Her fans had enjoyed all manner of odd behavior from her.

They laughed as she killed an astronaut on Mars when she ripped off his helmet.

They cheered as she eviscerated a pack of robot zombies using her microphone and cord as a spikeless flail.

They swooned as she proudly proclaimed herself chattel while sweating profusely in an un-air-conditioned dystopian brothel.

They were wonderstruck when she crashed a party by flipping her Porsche over the mansion's gate, smashing it into the swimming pool and then she grinded on the car's hood as it sank.

They loved when she evaded lasers, scaled a skyscraper using toilet plungers and poisoned a man, all while on her fifteen-minute break as a flight attendant.

They adored when she drove a pink Louis Vuitton Hummer through heaven while playing a guitar and throwing handfuls of cash out the window.

They relished watching her dance on a three-foot diameter island while hammerhead sharks gnashed in the waters around her.

And, most memorably, they idolized her when she won an epic dance battle against an ornery, aluminum chair.

But this!

This is different. Something is wrong.

It is clear to all that Britney is at a crossroads.

She bites the lens of one of her drones, twists and rips it off. As the electric wires dance from her lips, she spits this dronarazzo's head into the congregation.

Track 4

Under Pressure

"It's the terror of knowing
What this world is about
Watching some good friends
Screaming, 'Let me out!'"
- Farrokh "Freddie Mercury" Bulsara &
David "Bowie" Jones

"Got you all fired up
With your Napoleon complex,
Seein' right through you
Like you're bathin' in Windex."
- Mariah Carey

"Oooo-eee, boys, we've got ourselves a turdnado!"

Kip, a human male in his mid-forties stands before the assembled group of beige and besuited men. Kip is referencing a tornado, a violently rotating vortex of air where the unstable heat of brutal summers meets the cool air of a thunderstorm. This climate occurrence is common in his native Oklahoma.

"We're in the eye of a shitstorm now. Buckle up, it's gonna be a fucking messy ride."

After moving to Los Angeles 20 revolutions around the sun ago, Kip began affecting a curious Southern accent. Dialect coaches throughout Hollywood were unable to pinpoint its origins. In reality, its a hodgepodge of what he assumes people want to hear in a Southern accent. Part folksy, part crass, he started this charade to seem endearing to people. He soon found another benefit. He can swear with abandon and insult people to their faces, all the while, they will smile and think, 'oh, how charming! Oh, how provincial.'

"Our client, Miss Britney Jean Spears---"

He gestures at the 3D holowalls that line the boardroom, all broadcasting the length, height and depth of this human unhinged. He needs say no more, the partners have followed her unraveling religiously.

Kip is a partner at Hephaestus Talent Agency, where he tells people that his job is to make dreams come true. In reality, his job is to juggle a slate of human cogs and shove them into elaborate systems of cogs at entertainment factories to create highly-manufactured commodities like movies and pop songs.

Today, he and his partners will weave the fate of the fallen Brit-Brit.

She, along with half the human population, were assigned at birth the label of female, conscripting them with a set of paradoxical norms, to grow their head hair long, yet shave or pluck all other body hair, to starve themselves for a skeletal frame yet somehow retain fatty tissue around their hips and above their rib cages. These demands were a constant background noise, a static that could spike throughout the day, distracting them. As a young human, she was thrust into superstardom, propped up as the princess of popular music and idealized as the paragon to this myth of womanhood.

But Britney had been carefully crafted by dozens of men to create the most-idealized version of this womanhood. The hair of hundreds of women had been cut off and then glued onto Britney's scalp so these extensions could form the perfect yellow mane. Her white skin was sprayed an orangish-brown color. Implants were shoved into her chest to create larger mammary glands. Her nose was slimmed and her lips were plumped. Her face was shellacked under layers of makeup. Her body shape was carefully regimented with a strict diet and exercise. When she sang, the words were crafted by men. Her voice was frequently augmented with auto-tune, giving it a robotic quality. Her movements were carefully choreographed. Even her life decisions and finances were controlled by men.

Her life story could almost best be told through the men who manufactured her and profited from her.

Blessed by the courts, her father became her legal conservator. He made $130,000 a year to control his daughter's financial and medical decisions. He also received a generous tip of 1.5% of gross revenue from his workhorse daughter's performances and merchandising.

One of Britney's background dancers became her husband. He then used her to launch a failed rap-and-reality star career. This Federline finally settled for a cash consolation prize of $240,000 a year for child support, even though he didn't have primary custody.

One of the paparazzi that chased her became her boyfriend and then tried to sell photos of her for half a million dollars.

Her onetime business manager became her fiancé.

And on and on the list goes.

She was a commodity that had changed ownership in her decades-long working career, which began at the age of 11. From Disney to Jive to RCA to Legacy and now, in the twilight years of her career, to the Hephaestus Talent Agency.

With a wave of his hand, the hologram folds into a soccer ball shape, each pentagon evoking a different image of their malfunctioning Spears.

"Gentlemen, we had been afraid of this." Kip shakes his head.

This breakdown occurred a month after the death of Britney's father and conservator, James Spears. Since her last mental health breakdown, the paternal Spears had meticulously controlled Britney's every move and meal to ensure that she would remain stable and productive. For more than twenty years, all of her financial, professional and basic life choices were controlled by her conservators: her father and a lawyer. All of her purchases had to be approved by them and then carefully documented and stamped by the courts. She paid millions of dollars for them to control her. This program was generally used for individuals who were mentally, physically or emotionally unable to make decisions on their own. Yet, at the same time as the courts of California judged her unable to take care of herself, she made half a million dollars a night performing in Las Vegas and $15 million to judge talent acts on a popular television program.

All of these accomplishments should have proven that Britney was well enough to take care of herself. But a billion-dollar industry had grown around her and those who profited from her thought it was best that they not gamble with the possibility of losing revenue by granting her her freedom.

And thus, her life had remained so overprotected.

During her decades of conservatorship, armchair philosophers, sunning themselves on chaises, swirling their rosé, would debate. Does Britney Spears have free will? Is she freest when she's being controlled? Isn't Britney happier when she's healthy and working even if she has to sacrifice the ability to choose? Can people with mental illness who are prone to making decisions that are detrimental to their health ever truly make the best decisions for themselves? Can any human ever make the best decision for themselves?

Moments after her agency learned that one of her father's arteries had clogged, depriving his heart of oxygen-rich blood, they feared the worst. What fragile technologies humans were, in only a few minutes deprived

of Earth's atmosphere, these beings built over decades could cease to function, forevermore.

"What's Britney's situation?" One of the agent's growls.

"Safely out of harm's way. A judge signed an emergency committal. He said she had endangered herself. Apparently, decapitating a drone with her teeth could have electrocuted her. The police found her on the floor of her kitchen, making snow angels in giant piles of sugar."

"Where's she now?"

With a wave of his hand, Kip rotates the holosphere. He swipes past a few open screens to find---

"Here. At New Sunsets, the nation's premier rehab facility for aging starlets."

Stock images of cheerful women beam beneath the site's banner. Under these, in jazzy letters, reads one of the facility's classes.

"Art of the Scarf – 20 tips to hide your jowls."

Ah, the neck wattle, the final facial frontier. At this point, no plastic surgeon had successfully transformed this area, though many customers had been left with slit throats after failed attempts.

"When she gets out, we'll have a public relations nightmare on our hands. But, I reckon this escapade has revitalized interest in her dying brand." His audience smirks at his understatement.

Kip rotates the 'sphere and stops at a video of a kickboxing class.

"Over thirty Britney workout classes have sprung up."

The video shows spandex-clad women and men squatting, bobbing and weaving as their individual Britney hologram kicks and swings a bat at them. A dance instructor can be heard screaming.

"And bob and weave and up and down and up and down. High kick, high kick, squat." To invoke fear of an invading menace, he screams. "Ahhhh! It's Britney, Bitches!"

A scoreboard hovers over each Holo-Brit, showing how many times it lands a direct hit.

"And from Cebu to Ibiza, people are making knock-off Britney fashions."

Another twirl of his hand turns on the next screen. This hologram shows a collage of women wearing tutus, gold jumpsuits, purple fishnets and necklaces of smashed drones. Stores began selling bootleg T-shirts with the image of Britney Spears wearing a T-shirt with her face on it. Viewers are hypnotized with this Spears within a Spears within a Spears Droste effect.

"Gentlemen, I smell good money here. But, we gotta play this recovery just right. We have to keep her edge but still endear her to her fans. I've already planned a 'Returning of Things Stolen' ceremony to Hot

Topic. But that's just damage control. We need the public, particularly her demographic of white women ages 30 to 55, to clutch their chests and say 'awwwwww' when they hear her name. Alright, shoot me your best turd blossoms."

As the pause prolongs, Kip leans over and pulls out a fencing sword.

"Any ideas," Kip twirls the blade over his head, brandishing this before his protégés.

Skylark quibbles in his seat. He feels the wave of the blade inches from his face. His hair follicles sway in the sword's wake.

"Uhhh," Skylark stutters.

"We got a live one!" Kip says, thrusting the blade millimeters from Skylark's nose.

"Well, what about a charity?" Skylark shifts uneasily as a half-formed, constipated idea pokes out. "Kids with cancer in... Hurricane-ravaged---"

"NOPE, Americans don't give a mouse's teat about the suffering of others. When they start to see pain in the news, they flip the channel." The sword's tip flips the right collar of Skylark's shirt, providing all the exclamation he needs.

For humans, news had become a form of entertainment. The news outlets covered Britney's breakdown ceaselessly because it had sex appeal, a mystery ending and was tragic, but not too tragic. This wasn't the only tragedy occurring. Stories that were shelved that week included a hurricane that decimated Haiti and killed 83,000 people, three distinct polio outbreaks and the extinction of a dozen species. Those stories would be too tragic, numbing the audience with the misery of life and ensuring they wouldn't buy any of the sextuple-ply toilet paper or erection medicine advertised between segments of suffering.

"Easy, a tell-all memoir," Rory bellows. This bull of a man always sat at the corner of the table closest to the snacks. The uppermost button of his Oxford shirt cinches his beefy neck until it bulges like a boa constrictor swallowing a deer.

"She gets an easy $4 million to queef up some sob story, does the talk show rounds, cries about her parents or a bad relationship, and then her key demographic clutches their fat tits, tilts their three chins and says 'awww.'"

Kip stares at Rory to raise the suspense of his reaction. Kip knows humans crave validation. Even the slightest nod of approval can cause waves of oxytocin to be released in Rory's brain, bathing him in joy for hours. Kip lets his eyes dance for him, giving him a momentary sense of hope as he opens his mouth.

"Are you stupid, son!?"

Kip drops his blade and circles the table. What starts as a firm hand on Rory's shoulder quickly becomes a headlock.

"I asked you a question, are you stupid, son?"

Rory was a former college football player. Football was a sport where millions of humans cheer on a much smaller group of superhumans to feel momentarily, adjacently victorious. These college franchises raked in billions of dollars on the labor of their unpaid student-athletes. Rory suffered 18 concussions during his three-year college career. The swelling in his brain never returned to normal. His ability to process language and thoughts has remained stunted ever since. This should have led to an affirmative answer to the question posed, but Rory has never accepted his fate and won't share his shortcomings now.

Rory's larynx struggles against this forearm vise to pipe out a response. Before he can, Kip twists Rory's head until his field of vision focuses on a point in the back of the room.

At the end of the table is a sculpture commissioned for the agency, entitled "Pile of Shit." Artist Phoebe DuBois had extracted trash from the agency for this piece, including the castoffs of terrible ideas and mementos of their most monstrous decisions. She rolled these in freshly made paddies of cow manure. She glossed the poo-piece with an airtight sheen, trapping the fecal matter and shitty artifacts together. The piece stands in the main conference room as a reminder of what horrors their carelessness can bring.

Buttressing this creation as the cornerstones of this tower of caca are Britney's previous memoirs: *Say Hello to the Girl that I Am!*, *Can You Handle My Truth?* and *Why am I so Real?*

"She already put out three books, each selling worst than the last. Heck, we tried to gift that last son-of-a-bitch in our Christmas care packages. A few clients paid their assistants extra to hurl them at our office. Those heavy suckers even smashed a few windows."

Kip releases Rory and stomps around the table.

"What in the fuck am I paying you for?"

The water molecules expelled by his hard p-sound dance in the air and then glide to the table.

"Make her the victim."

All eyes dart to the source of this sound.

Kane does not waver from the hologram baseball game he manipulates five inches above his right palm.

"Alright... Keep this pussy wagon rolling." Kip says.

"She's broken."

"Well... who done broke her?"

Skylark jumps at the chance to prove himself. He grabs onto Kane's coattails and claws.

"The paparazzi? Fame?" His voice falters. "Her parents?"

"You want a fistful of SHUT the fuck up!?" Kip huffs at Skylark. Skylark's nostrils flare as a high squeak escapes his mouth.

"Oh, does baby need a time out?" Kip devolves into the indecipherable babbling of a human infant attempting to communicate.

Kane thwacks a home run with his middle finger. A muted cheer erupts from a holographic stadium that extends from his knee to his navel. At peace with his progress, he looks up.

"Who made her?" His question mark dangles, interrogating his audience.

Kane stands, giving the room a glimpse of how well he fills this year's fashion. The Hamm'ing of men's clothes had pushed inseams higher, made pants tighter and allowed all to see what the wearer is packing. Consequently, the number of bulge implanted underpants had soared 2,000%.

One hundred revolutions around the sun ago, showing ankles or shoulders aroused horror and excitement. The dominant culture craved the tantalizing appeal of what's almost revealed. The human appetite for arousal created more daring apparel. Hemlines grew shorter and tops cropped lower. But, like all human desires, every shift to gratify these quickly brought diminishing returns and a race to an ever-receding state of satisfaction.

In terms of girth and length, Kane clearly demonstrates that he's the cock of the walk and all the betas buckle before their new alpha.

"Disney! She was forged by the burning lights of that pre-adolescent factory, the Mouseketeers."

Disney was a conglomerate of companies with a stated goal of making dreams come true but with an actual goal of creating more wealth for its shareholders. It originated as an animation studio started by two brothers surnamed Disney. The studio experimented with animating people and became successful at manipulating human emotions with these cartoons. Along with using this emotional power to convince families to forfeit money to this corporation, Disney once manipulated humans with war propaganda by, among other things, motorboating Adolf Hitler.

As its empire grew, Disney expanded its holdings to dominate the entertainment industry for children and families. The company soon added live-action entertainment. This demanded the use of actual human tools to generate money for its owners rather than just cartoon ones. The majority of Disney's tools were children. Children were a protected class

of humans whom the dominant culture agreed should be safe from all forms of labor, except for farming, delivering newspapers and entertainment.

"Think about it! All the tools manufactured by Disney are broken. Lindsay Lohan, Milez Cyrus, Christina Aguilera, Justin Timberlake, Raven-Symoné, Shia LeBeouf, the Jonas Brothers, Demi Lovato and, of course, Britney Spears."

As Kane says each name, their worst deed hurtles into the agents' minds. The past twenty years had seen a rapid escalation of bad behavior among celebrities. These agents wished their problems were as simple as the flaunted labia of yesteryear.

Milez Cyrus, feeling that their life had followed their name and become hopeless, suffered a public breakdown. During a performance before Disney's Annual Meeting of Shareholders, they stopped mid-twerk, slid off a giant inflatable rubber duckie and stared at their audience.

"You did this to me!" They screamed as they took out a pair of pliers from their bejeweled fanny pack.

"Take these back. I never wanted them!" Milez ripped out their three front teeth, lobbing them at the tuxedo-clad board members. As blood gushed from their mouth, they attempted to protest their dental dominance by Disney. They were unable to enunciate their message before their microphone was cut off and they blacked out. Afterward, they retreated from public life to live in the forests of northern Montana, embracing their genderqueer identity and a new name, Milez, ensuring they could always have the best of both worlds.

Shia LeBeouf's masturbatory "art" performance, entitled *Wash in My Sins,* was a cinéma vérité monstrosity. In the self-produced, self-directed and self-acted piece, LeBeouf broke into the baptistry of the Los Angeles Mormon Temple. He climbed one of the twelve marble bulls and tumbled into the baptismal font. He recorded himself swimming naked and vigorously masturbating to climax. As his waterproof lens documented the travails of his spermatozoa shooting through the holy water, his voiceover explained that, through the transitive property, he was giving a facial-by-proxy to all who had been baptized here. After his trial, plea deal, paying all cleaning fees and a large fine to the Church of Jesus Christ of Latter-day Saints, he simply chuckled to church authorities, "so we're even-stevens, right?"

And Lindsay Lohan, that freckled redhead, found her calling luring the children of billionaires with her husky-voiced siren song. These plain children longed to be fêted by celebrity. Lindsay gave them just what they wanted. She treated them to soirées. She surrounded them with models, actors and musicians. She wined, dined and then drugged them with scopolamine, a.k.a. Devil's Breath. The drug turns her victims into witless zombies who eagerly act out her every wish and forget it all by morning. In an evening, Lohan would learn bank account numbers, email passwords and phone numbers. She would record her victims saying certain phrases, such as, "but Daddy, I need that money wired now!" Lohan used this material to catfish their unsuspecting fathers for millions of dollars in the ultimate parent trap.

As the collective daydream fizzles, Kip continues.

"Ok, I'm following, but flip this bitch and fuck it home." Kip rubs his blade phallically.

"A class action lawsuit." Kane smiles.

Sparks of recognition ignite in the men's minds.

"Now hold up, give me the gist of your gristle," Kip shakes his head and stares at Kane, slack-jawed.

"They all got their start as child labor, working in the Disney factories. And now they're all fucked up. Coincidence? Shit, no! We unite all these burned out stars with Britney as the lead plaintiff against Disney. We can sue Disney for... reckless endangerment, lifelong trauma, emotionally stunting them. Heck, let's keep piling the claims on. This will be a publicity blitz. Think about it. The Trial of the Millennium!"

"Disney. Holy shit. HO-LY Shit!" Kip pats Kane's shoulder. "Fuck. Cunt. Ass! Now, this! This! Is an idea! Say it one more time."

"We will sue Disney for child abuse and ruining these stars' lives."

"SAY IT AGAIN"

"We will sue Disney."

"Let's fuck this bitch!" Kip whips his tie back, licks his open palm and slaps the table. He clutches it to brace himself as he gratuitously thrusts his hips, simulating procreation. He hasn't successfully fornicated in seven years. With each pounding of the table, he tries to push away this reality. The amount of red meat he consumes on a daily basis for the current fad diet, the archeologically-inaccurate Neanderthal diet, has clogged his arteries, raised his blood pressure and flooded his brain with hormones force-fed the cows he consumes. These factors ensure that blood will not flow to his penis, thus halting his arousal from becoming an erection.

He wipes his brow, straightens his tie and expels a climatic sigh.

"Ahhhh, this feels good, gentlemen. Damn Good. Ok, let's give this idea the giant tits it needs to be a winner."

Skylark pulls out a tablet from his Ed Hardy tiger-covered man-satchel and slides it across the table.

"I think you better have a look at this."

He scrolls and clicks on a headline buried near the bottom.

"Early Childhood Fame Leads to Mental Disorders."

The byline explains that researchers at the UCLA Charlie Sheen School of Psychology will soon present the findings of their 25-year longitudinal study.

Kip waves the headline around, tapping the agents lightly on their noses.

"You smell this? YOU SMELL THIS?"

His well-threaded eyebrows leap up.

"THIS. This is the hot sweaty ball sack of legitimacy. Take a good whiff." Kip inhales deeply on this article-cum-scrotum.

"Gentlemen, it's time to lawyer up!"

Track 5

Crazy

"Crazy.
I just can't sleep,
I'm so excited, I'm in too deep.
Crazy.
But it feels alright,
Every day and every night."
    - Britney Spears

"Super trouper, beams are gonna blind me
But I won't feel blue
Like I always do
'Cause somewhere in the crowd there's you."
    - Agnetha Fältskog
    - Björn Ulvaeus
    - Benny Andersson
    - Anni-Frid Lyngstad

Let us travel from the Hephaestus Talent Agency across the city of Los Angeles. Thick brown smoke from forest fires rolls over the Santa Monica mountains and suffocates the city's basin. Come with me over the oilfields and tar pits that still shrug up the fossils of saber-toothed cats, giant sloths, American lions, Columbian mammoths and other megafauna, most of which went extinct with the arrival of the first humans around 10,000 years ago.

And now this city's main industry will lead to human extinction.

Hundreds of factories dot the area and churn out entertainment commodities. These products are beamed into billions of screens from giant theaters to tiny handheld phones. Humans in this country spent, on average, 10 hours each day staring into a screen. This entertainment not only filled their days but also seeped into their dreams and warped how they saw the world around them. For example, as they sought romantic

partners, their tastes were greatly influenced by what these factories fed them.

In downtown Los Angeles, Dr. Patricia Navarro stands in the wings of the Hilton Hotel ballroom. Her press conference will begin in 10 minutes.

Onstage, a holopowerpoint presentation whirs its first words, "Early Childhood Stardom, Mental Health and Personality Disorders. Principal Investigator, Dr. P. Navarro, UCLA's Charlie Sheen School of Psychology."

In his will, their benefactor had stipulated the branding for this institution. The logo is a silhouette of the mullet-clad, chicken-wielding Sheen from his magnum opus, *Hot Shots! Part Deux*. The university's development department tried to wiggle out of this but Sheen's lawyers threatened to pull out his very large endowment unless they acquiesced.

Dr. Navarro nervously bounces notecards in her hand. She looks at the freshly painted nails that dazzle from her fingertips.

"Are these mine?" She thinks to herself.

The hotel conference room fills as news outlets pour in. The press release worked! She's glad the formula of Children + Celebrityhood = Crippling Emotional Damage had proved provocative. Reporters jostle to place their branded microphones front and center on the podium. Like a reckless round of Jenga, they balance their mics as far forward as possible, letting it teeter on the edge of the podium.

Ah, the press conference, 10% substance, 90% pageantry!

Dr. Navarro had practiced her walk and poise. She had mapped out where the cameras would be and what the best angles are for this harsh lighting. Her head could safely move 30 degrees left or right. It may tilt up. But it must never tilt down! This would cast a dark shadow from her brow ridge, turning her face from friendly to ghoulish.

Three minutes until show time.

Lights! Camera!

Science!

She chants a tongue twister to warm up her vocal cords and calm her nerves.

"She sells seashells by the seashore."

"She sells seashells by the seashore."

A thought hits her like a shovel to her face and she cringes.

"Poor Mary Anning! To have your whole life's work distorted and reduced to a silly children's rhyme! How vile!"

Anger bursts from her amygdala, furrowing her well-plucked eyebrows, clenching her pink lips, speeding her heart and opening the veins through her body.

Crazy

Two hundred years before Dr. Navarro, Mary Anning had unearthed the intact remains of animals that roamed this planet more than 200 million years before. Her discovery of ichthyosaur, plesiosaur and pterosaur fossils proved that species could and have gone extinct.

This should have provided a warning for humans to consider their own extinction. Did they heed her findings?

No.

Anning cataloged her treasures and took pen to paper to intricately sketch her fossils. She alerted the leading scientists of the day, sharing with them the near-mythic creatures she discovered. All these scientists were men and, during this period of human history, it was obscene for a woman to be a scientist, so they shunned her. She suffered in poverty for most of her life and died young.

Anning knew no notoriety because of the noxious and ignoble banning of women.

Say that ten times fast!

But not Dr. Navarro. In the intervening 200 years, some human women were able to receive an education and could even lead scientific discoveries. Now, Dr. Navarro will be heard. Today, she will receive the recognition for her decades of work.

"Please welcome Dr. Patricia Navarro to the stage." Carlos Estévez, the Dean of the Charlie Sheen School of Psychology, says from the podium and then gestures to her.

After 25 years of grueling research, the culmination of her tiny contribution to the sea of human knowledge dances on her tongue.

As she takes center stage, the heat of the super troupers brings drops of sweat to her forehead. These drops trickle down, melting the freshly shellacked layer of paint from her face. A wave of anxiety rushes into her, carrying with it a deeply rooted sorrow.

A memory appears in her limbic system and shudders down her spine, that network of nerves.

A memory is a neatly folded file of data. Human memories are often wrapped in an emotion, so as the memory unfolds, the emotion diffuses throughout the body.

What an absurd technology these memories were! Rather than a file of information that can only be summoned when called for, memories shot up and flooded the human mind, often unprovoked. A human may not even have an awareness of this memory until it resurfaces, inciting a painful reaction.

Dr. Navarro shakes as her last, long forgotten, experience before these blinding lights possesses her.

Forty years are sucked from her frame and she stands before a microphone. Patricia is part of a cattle call of 107 young human girls auditioning for a role in a television show. Unlike other factory tools: conveyor belts, hacksaws and drills, which are sought and purchased for a purpose, these insecure 'tween tools compete to be used. The girls and their parents sacrifice large amounts of money and time to sharpen their skills to be the best fit for these entertainment factories.

But some of their parts can never be changed.

The lights bear down on a ten-year-old Patricia. She sees only the outlines of four figures seated in front of her, ready to judge her every move.

"Ok, #17, Pah-trish-uh,"

"It's pronounced 'Pah-tree-see-ah.'" She corrects and then remembers to smile.

"Whatever. You're singing 'I Wanna Know What Love Is.' You may begin. Now!"

All fear vanishes as an angelic sound rumbles from her vocal cords. Her confidence swells as she hits a high note and holds it, pushing all the air out of her lungs.

She inhales to continue but the casting director waves his hand. The music stops and she is dismissed with a loud, abrupt, "Next!"

She stares at the outlines. Stunned. A few seconds pass before she realizes she has been ordered to vacate the stage. After filling the room from floor to ceiling with the sound of her voice, the silence overwhelms her. The only sound now is the dull thud of her footsteps as she acquiesces and exits stage right.

Her mother stands in the wings with open arms. She kisses her and smothers her with hugs.

"Mi estrella! You did such a good job, mija! I'm so proud of you!"

Her mother ushers her back into the audience.

"The men are very busy. They've gotta be fair, mija. Only one minute for the audition. But don't worry, they'll give you more time in the next round, just wait.

"Espéra, mija, espéra."

To hope and to wait, wrapped in one word, encouraging dreams and tempering them at the same time

For five hours, she watches as the other fresh-faced girls take the stage. In their eyes, she can see a reflection of her hopes and dreams. To be famous, to be loved by millions, goals that society had groomed in her since infancy. A mix of empathy and jealousy boils in her. Emotions her short life has given her little experience with. She's paralyzed by these and only wants to scream.

The loving pat of her mother's hand soothes her. She feels ashamed of this jealousy and wants to cry. She grabs her mom's hand and squeezes it tight.

One of the casting directors stands and turns to the assembled families. This is the first time she can see a face. The gaunt, white man offers a pleasant, though fleeting, smile as he scans these instruments, all eager to be used.

"Ok, numbers 8, 32, 47, 86, 63 and 94, please stay. The rest of you, I want to assure you that you all have potential." He turns to sit down when he realizes that the sea of hopeful faces has yet to recede.

"Thank you. You may all go. Now!"

Dismissed!

Reassuring parents support sniffly children as they waddle out the door.

Patricia stands but her mom yanks her back to her seat.

"No mija! Watch the finalists. We can learn something from them."

Six petite, blue-eyed, white girls walk to the stage. Their yellow hair glows iridescent under the lights.

Patricia tries to watch, but she is so upset that she buries her face into her mother's side in an attempt to flee this harsh world.

Her mother pulls her out of the auditorium and walks her to the parking lot.

"You have a gift, mija. Never stop using it. Sing with me."

Her mother opens her mouth and sings.

"De colores, de colores. Se visten los campos en la primavera."

Patricia feels the swell of mariachi music prickling her skin. She can hear her church's whole congregation, three hundred members strong, singing together.

"De colores, de colores. Son los pajaritos que vienen de afuera."

Her mother sees the gaunt casting director walking to his luxury vehicle.

"Excuse me!" She throws her body between him and his car.

"Excuse me, I'm sorry to bother you, but if you can give my daughter any feedback, she wants to be a singer. She has talent."

He looks Patricia up and down, trying to remember which of the many defective devices she is. The tedium of the day has worn through his geniality. In a moment of frustration, he doesn't filter his thoughts.

"Look, you want the truth? Let me save you a lot of time and misery. Your daughter is just too thick, too dark and too ethnic-looking. She will

never be a star. Now if you could." He shoos them away with his right hand.

"I've had a long day."

He climbs into his vehicle, slams the door and skids out of the parking lot.

Though humans came in many different shapes and sizes, the entertainment factories in Los Angeles and New York elevated only one for women: skinny, bird-hipped, light-skinned, large-eyed. In the final human population of 8.5 billion, less than 5% had blonde hair, though another 10% used chemicals to bleach their protein chains this lighter hue. Less than 8% of the worldwide population had blue eyes.

During this period, these factories would beam this ideal of womanhood around the world, enforcing this as the norm. All other women were deemed aberrations from this norm and taught to be ashamed and were encouraged to change themselves.

♪   ♪   ♪

The long-repressed memory relinquishes control. The aftershocks quake through her body as Dr. Navarro stands at the podium, scanning the room, trying to determine how long she has stood there speechless.

One final thought weighs heavily on her.

She never sang again...

But now her voice will be amplified and the shake the industry that shunned her. She leans into the microphones and smiles.

"Ladies and Gentlemen, thank you for coming."

Dr. Navarro smiles at the reporters. She gives a stern nod to the impeccably-dressed public relations flacks seated in the back of the room, scowling into their complimentary coffees. She winks at her team of researchers in the front row. They respond by erecting their opposable thumbs in an unmistakable sign of support.

"I would like to describe our two and a half decades of research that conclusively demonstrates the adverse mental health effects of stardom on children.

"For the study, we randomly selected 10,000 children who were entered into the Kidz-Starz database, the largest catalog for aspiring child performers. Every year, we called them, pretending to be casting directors, and got their responses to a mental health questionnaire. We tracked their progress through the Internet Movie Database and other sites that listed their work.

"As a control group, we selected 100 children who had no ambitions of stardom and interviewed them annually as well.

"We needed an objective metric of stardom and we decided to use one of the following: a main role in a feature-length, wide-release film, five cameos on a TV show, a long-term commercial contract or one song in the Billboard top 20.

"As you can see, of the 10,000 we first identified, 127 children met the criteria for stardom." Dr. Navarro gestures to the three-dimensional pie chart as it changes depth when it hears her preprogrammed keywords. "Five years into the protocol, we saw a few entertainers wildly out-perform the others. So we added a new metric, superstardom. We define superstardom as having a main role in five films, a starring role in a TV show or a music career with at least one platinum album. 32 of our subjects met this metric to be labeled superstars."

A 1.27% sliver of the pie chart swells even higher than the rest, glazing the top of her head in blue hues.

"There were adverse effects for those 9,873 children who didn't attain stardom. Each had a lowered self-worth coupled with insecurities. But most recovered from these within the first three years. On top of the emotional trauma, we must highlight the amount of money and hours wasted on teeth bleaching, tap lessons, hair products, etc. For those children that did not meet the criteria of stardom, each family spent an average of $9,000 and wasted 400 family hours.

"As our star group became more famous and thus walled themselves off from interactions with the general public, we had to resort to new ways of obtaining survey responses.

"Our intrepid research assistants disguised themselves as reporters to interview subjects during press junkets."

Dr. Navarro pauses to acknowledge her past and present graduate students seated in the front row.

♫   ♫   ♫

Stacy and Jamal laugh as they enter the studio backlot. With sunglasses over their eyes and press badges dangling from their necks, they are ready. They carry personality disorder questionnaires in their hands as they enter into a warehouse of stars.

"I couldn't imagine a more perfect first assignment." Stacy chuckles.

"Well, Dr. Belser is treating his students to, err, testing psilocybin on his students." Jamal smiles.

"Ha! Well, I'd rather see the stars than trip out of this world."

"Touché!"

After sitting in the waiting room with the other journalists for an hour, a headset-wearing, frazzled production assistant alerts them that it's their turn.

They coif each other, grab their notebooks and pull back the curtain.

Behind it, a sixteen-year-old blonde girl sits beneath a spotlight, radiating melancholia. Her arms are crossed as she shivers with only 4% body fat. Her bony knees glide on top of each other, creating a hollow echo.

Stacy and Jamal smile as they plop down in their seats.

"Thank you, Annabelle, for meeting with us today."

"Umm who... Who are you representing?" Annabelle Dickson purses her freshly plumped lips.

"Das Geheimnis Umfrage, Germany's third largest entertainment news site."

Annabelle flutters her bony hand expressing both 'whatever' and 'proceed.' She reaches for her coffee mug and blows on it.

Each celebrity strained to stay awake during these 14-hour press junkets. Answering the same questions became mind-numbingly tedious. Annabelle perfected a semi-interested smile as her eyes unfocused, her lips opened and answers flowed out.

"Yes, I did my own stunts.

"No, I wasn't afraid to flip over that cow.

"No, I didn't enjoy kissing Taylor, he's like a younger brother to me.

"Yes, I did read the book the film is based on and yes I loved it.

"No, the director's decision to change my character from a poor, homely girl covered in sores into a beautiful, emaciated prostitute who's allergic to clothes did not bother me at all."

The researchers move through these perfunctory questions, lulling the star into spilling without thinking. In the middle of the drivel, they drop.

"On a scale of one to ten, how God-like do you consider yourself?"

"Oh about a nine and a half, I'm pretty sure I could get my 27 million Instagram followers to move mountains for me. Literally, move mountains. Rock by rock."

"Uh-huh," Stacy says with a scribble of a pen.

A nervous publicist swings in from the shadows. "Oh, she didn't mean to say---"

"Oh don't worry, that question is off the record," Jamal reassures.

"Do you consider yourself easy going?" Stacy continues.

Annabelle takes a swig from her coffee mug, convulses and spits on the curtain.

"I said NON-FAT milk, you fucking bitch. Do you want me to shove this heel down your throat?"

She throws her stiletto at the assistant.

"Wait, what were we talking about. Oh, right, I'm so totally down to Earth."

"Uh. Huh. Hm." Jamal notes both the response and the flying shoe incident.

♫   ♫   ♫

Stacy and Jamal perfect this press junket parry over the coming years.

While interviewing the hip-hop star, J. Kimo, before the release of his new single, "I Beat that Bitch with a Bat, Part 2," Jamal inquires, "Are you prone to bouts of anger?"

The cherubic-faced rapper squeaks out in a soft lisp.

"Sure am, why you think I beat that bitch with a bat? Pshaw!"

♫   ♫   ♫

Stacy is blinded by the bedazzled Russian starlet, Katya Zamalodchikova, who sits drenched in diamonds and wrapped in a pure gold kimono so malleable that even a gust of wind could bend it.

"Um, on a scale from one to ten, how important is your appearance."

"Wait, why are you asking this? My appearance is THE MOST important thing for humanity. If I get a haircut, one million girls will do the same 'do.

"And this face." Katya waves her Swarovski jewel-encrusted nails around her taut face.

"THIS FACE has launched a thousand rocket ships!"

♫   ♫   ♫

Jamal reads "Now I'm going to say to you some thoughts and I want to hear how much you agree with them. Ok, first, I often use makeup or clothing, e.g., hats, scarves, long-sleeve shirts, long pants, etc. to camouflage a perceived flaw."

Jamal looks up at Jaxon Stonewall. The action star grimaces, debating how to answer. He twitches and scratches the top of his head. As he does, strands of hair are caught in his topaz pinky ring. With the itch satisfied, he lowers his hand and with it, his blonde toupee.

"Oh god, you can't tell anyone about this! NO!" Jaxon falls to his knees, groveling before Jamal and Stacy. "PLEASE. This would be the end of my life!"

"Mmm. Hmmm" Stacy scribbles.

♫   ♫   ♫

Dr. Navarro warms up to the crowd and begins pacing the stage, microphone in hand.

"Most stars wouldn't give us accurate numbers for their most basic medical details, such as height and weight, so we rigged their chairs with scales to get an accurate body weight and bone density reading. We found most female stars suffer from a drastically low body mass index indicative of sporadic ovulation. The bone density scans found 40% had pre-osteoporosis symptoms. After each interview, we asked the stars to stand perfectly erect for a photo with their interviewers. We could use our interviewers' heights to interpolate the height of each star. And, of course, we adjusted based on heel size.

"Since the private lives of these stars have long been considered public, we were able to obtain details of each star's plastic surgeries, interviews from in-treatment rehab facilities and medical records for every hospital visit for 'unspecified exhaustion.'

"And now for our results."

The reporters flip open their notebooks as the cameras focus.

"The stars were 90 times more likely to undergo a plastic surgery procedure to correct a perceived flaw on their body. Yes, 90 times! As you can see on the wall, all of the female subjects had breast surgeries of some kind, with augmentation being the most common followed by resizing. After that, chin shaving and ear pinning were second and third most popular.

"We found that, at baseline, each of the children seeking celebrityhood had slightly higher indicators of a narcissistic personality disorder compared with the control group, but this was only slightly outside the statistical margin of error.

"Over the course of 25 years, we saw a chasm grow between the star and control group. A spike follows shortly after an inciting incident, like a movie premiere or an album release, what we have dubbed the 'moment of stardom.' Within a year of stardom, 92% of these respondents showed attributes that were consistent with a narcissistic personality disorder and 86% showed the excessive-emotionality and attention-seeking consistent with histrionic personality disorder. Superstardom brought these numbers up to 99% and 92% respectively.

Crazy

"Because of the years surrounded by people who leeched off of them, 67% began interpreting the actions of friends and family as threatening and became suspicious to the point of paranoia. 81% had symptoms consistent with schizotypal disorder. They scrutinized every social interaction and they saw the world as a strange and unstable place."

Cameras flash as bar graphs pop out from the screen. Dr. Navarro feels the need to stop, smile and Vanna White her scientific discoveries. She resists the urge to ooh and aah her decades of work.

"And this is after we controlled for family history. We found that parents who would force their child into the limelight had higher rates of personality disorders themselves.

"We will continue to give updates every five years about the subjects we are following. Among the questions we hope to answer is if the stars' higher rates of crippling anxiety lead to increased heart disease and how these affect mortality and morbidity rates.

"Ok, I'd like to open it for questions."

The reporters leap up, waving their hands.

She is elated to see how rapt they are by her research. She feels like she's on fire and living for their love and adoration. Psychologically, she takes a breath and checks herself. And then continues.

"Yes, you in the navy pantsuit."

"Dr. Navarro. Trina Nguyen from Dateline TMZ, can you name any of the celebrities you've been following?"

"No. No, I can't. Only a select number of our researchers know their identities. Even our statisticians are not privy to this information."

The crowd foams with excitement.

"Look, all I'll say is that you have seen movies and enjoyed music that our subjects have created."

"Ooo, Dr. Navarro. Over here! Summer Reign from BuzzCall Media, can we get a copy of the questions you've been asking these stars?"

"All study protocol material, including survey questions, can be found in the press packets under your seats."

Within an hour, BuzzCall had published an article entitled "Are you crazy like young Hollywood?! Take this easy test to find out. You'll never guess the answer to number 42!"

After responding to a dozen more questions, Dr. Navarro smiles and takes a polite bow. She ends the event by welcoming all her co-authors and researchers to the stage to get the recognition they deserve.

As she totters off the stage, her left heel gives out and she topples. She grabs the curtain and swings herself behind it, landing softly on the ground, safely out of the way of the journalists and their cameras.

♫ ♫ ♫

Back at home, she washes the smudged paint from her face, de-Spanxes and throws on her favorite sweatpants and sweatshirt. She exhales as her internal organs float freely. Once finished, she checks in on her daughter, Gladyz, who is already tucked into bed.

"Hi, Mommy! How did it go?"

"So good! Everyone loved what mommy had to say. You can see mommy on the news tomorrow!"

Gladyz yawns, extending her arms from underneath her periodic table of elements comforter.

"Ok sleepy head, before you go to the land of sueños, I want to sing you a song."

"Sing?! I've never heard you sing."

"I found my voice tonight and I want to share it with you. This is mommy and abuelita's favorite song."

She flicks off the light and stands up. She turns on a flashlight that sits next to her daughter's bed. Above them is a mobile made of prisms. She aims the ray of white light into these prisms, refracting the light into a dozen dancing rainbows.

Gladyz jumps on her bed, squealing as she bathes in the full spectrum of visible light waves.

"De colores, de colores."

As she sings, she twirls around her daughter's bed, letting the light hit the prisms in a thousand different ways, filling the room with color.

"Y por eso los grandes amores. De muchos colores me gustan a mí."

Razzle Dazzle

"Give 'em the old razzle dazzle,
Razzle dazzle 'em,
Give 'em an act with lots of flash in it,
And the reaction will be passionate,
Give 'em the old hocus pocus,
Bead and feather 'em,
How can they see with sequins in their eyes?"
                    - Jerry Orbach
                    - Richard Gere

"Said, 'Lil bitch, you can't fuck
With me if you wanted to,'
These expensive, these is red bottoms,
These is blood shoes,
Hit the store, I can get 'em both,
I don't wanna choose."
                    - Belcalis "Cardi B" Almanzar

The snap-crack of a typewriter booms through Shonn Chapley's office. She smirks as this sound blasts from her cellphone, reminding all who can hear just how expensive each letter is. As a top entertainment attorney, she charges $1000 an hour and types at four characters per second, so each clack is worth a little more than $4.

Kip sits across from her oval desk, tapping his pen against his knee. He stares, hoping her eyes will catch his contempt. Kane lets out an exasperated sigh.

This is one of Shonn's many power moves. She makes all potential clients sit and wait at least five minutes in her presence.

Kip clears his throat.

"And. Sent!" Shonn's phone coos the sound of a dozen carrier pigeons bearing her message through the ether.

"Boys, you've come to the right place. We are the nation's only vertically integrated law-and-personality-management firm. We bring plaintiffs from tears to trial, from talk show couch to jury bench, and from deposition to coffee table book."

Her office computer system responds to this verbal cue and dims the lights. A 3D presentation ignites from the wall to her right. Her firm's logo bobs, waiting for her to begin

"Here at Chapley LLP, we tell stories." Shonn paces before the holowall. "We move public opinion. We know that there is no such thing as an independent jury."

The holopowerpoint morphs to show a mockup of her five-floor office building.

"Each floor in our building represents physically and metaphorically a different level in your story's journey.

"On the first floor, we have our press conference studio with multiple backdrops. We've got the patriotic marble facade with American flags. That's popular among disgraced politicians. The somber library is perfect for celebrities, especially those with DUIs. Everything is formulaic, the blonder the actress, the dark the mahogany desks we'll use. The more gruesome the sexual assault--- allegations! The more crying grandmas and aunties surround the accused. Don't have grandmas? We can provide them for you. I told you, boys."

She winks and smiles. "We got you covered!

"Second floor is our writers' studio. Full of hungry scriptwriters and comedians. Each swears they are on the cusp of fame. And they always threaten to quit. Ha! Not a single one has gotten away in over a decade. But don't tell them that. They craft the perfect zings to pluck heartstrings and then burrow deep in your brain. Among our writers is the author of: 'If the glove doesn't fit; you must acquit.'

"Pure. Legal. Genius! Don't worry boys, any contract with us comes with a minimum of three jingles sure to make your jury tingle."

Kip winces.

"Third floor is our beauty salon. I can't stress enough how important it is to make each of our clients look the proper mix of genuine, sweet and, well, abused. Most women show up with as much makeup on as possible for a presser. Oh no! This is not a cougar convention in Cancun and no, they shouldn't look like a contestant on MILF Island."

Shonn shakes her head.

"No, no, no, no, no!

"We gots to reel it back. Bring down the hair. Smooth out those pageant curls. Add slight bags under the eyes. And the outfit, it's gotta look like a suburban mom going to a piano recital. Conservative and quaint!

"Fourth floor's our geek dungeon. You may see ping-pong tables and Zumba classes. We see the minds that make the internet move. We lock sorority sisters, catty gays and techies into crafting the perfect social media posts about our cases. In real time! Those memes about the NFL and concussions? We did those. We create new accounts, add a slew of followers and then just start pounding these online echo chambers until our words wash over traditional media and drench the public.

"Fifth floor is our dance studio and set. Our usual plaintiffs are amateurs. Oh, but not yours. With the normies, we need to prep them on how to look, move, speak, cry, pout, flip their hair and fall apart. We have to crush every basic instinct and replace these with very precise, focus-grouped reactions. And! You won't believe this, we just signed on Jan Posey to teach our litigants! She runs a MasterClass in Oscars crying. She taught Gwyneth Paltrow and Halle Berry ev-er-e-thing! Also, we got set materials to build an exact replica of your clients' courtroom. When they walk into the real courtroom, we want them to feel as comfortable as possible and know how to hit their marks.

"Tear to camera one. Grab a tissue and sniffle to the jury box. Take a breath, look up to the ceiling like they're saying a prayer. And ask the prosecutor to repeat the question. Deny and Repeat!"

Chapley mimes these movements. She flourishes her tissue and lets it drop in front of Kip and Kane.

"Now that you know we're the best of the best."

The lights turn up. The holopowerpoint bobs her logo three times and disappears in a puff.

"Why should I take your case?"

Chapley stands at the window, looking through the blinds.

Kane stares at her for a moment and then erupts.

"This will be the trial of the Century. The trial of the Millennium!"

"And who is footing the bill?"

"We will," Kip promises. "No matter what the outcome, the lawsuit will raise the profile of our clients. Higher profiles mean more work... or at least more people buying our stars' previous work."

"Disney is a formidable foe." Chapley paces the room "Their talent have to sue just to get the residuals owed them. They're sharks. Why should I risk getting into a pool with those hammerheads?"

"We're agents. We'll make it worth your while. We're geniuses at squeezing dollars from a bleeding rock." Kane malapropizes.

Kip glowers as he picks up the sloppy slack.

"Win or lose, we'll make your firm millions. We'll make you a household name. Book deal, free publicity---"

"T-shirts with your company's logo worn by each star," Kane interjects.

Kip clears his throat.

"Or--- a Lifetime made-for-TV movie with a producer credit."

Chapley whirls to face them. The dazzle of fame sparkles in her eye. She smells weakness and pounces.

"I want Executive Producer credits on an E! TV movie. I want Keke Palmer to star as me. A three-book deal, a Macy's lifestyle line... and... Oh, and throw in two tickets to the Oscars after-party."

Kip and Kane huddle. Through their squabbling, Chapley dreams of the name of her first lifestyle book. Hmm... *Litigish Kitch* sounds good to her. All about how she balances life as a lawyer with her love for cooking and hosting. For the cover, she'll lie across the marble island in her kitchen, legs crossed with her stilettos tilted to show the red bottoms of her Louboutins.

Kip breaks to report.

"Yes, but we can only offer you a line at K-Mart and tickets to the Golden Globes."

Internally, Chapley squeals. But for them, she gulps these emotions and lets out a crestfallen sigh.

"FINE. And I want two agents on hand during each meeting with any celeb. From psych eval to press conference to deposition. These are all dynamite witnesses, gentlemen, but we gotta make sure they explode only when and how we want them to."

Track 7

Catch a Falling Star

"Catch a falling star
  And put it in your pocket
  Never let it fade away."
      - Perry Como

"So the moral of this story is,
  Who are you to judge?
  There's only one true judge, and that's God
  So chill, and let my Father do His job"
      - Cheryl "Salt" James

A Rat-tat-tat-tat wakes Raul Escobar.

His first movements of the day send spasms of pain through his lower back. The stench of fetid, rotting human waste slaps him. His piss. Bottled in the back of his car. He wipes the gunk from his eyes. It's still dark.

A car horn honks behind him.

The rat-tat-tat crescendos into a boom-boom-boom on his windshield.

"Wake up shithead! CNN needs this spot."

Raul coughs.

"NOW!"

Raul rolls down the window of his Camry, releasing his stench. The man recoils.

"I'm supposed to get paid $100." He whimpers.

"Hey, I'm not your manager."

"But I saved the spot all night. Right in front of the courthouse. I didn't leave. Not even to---"

"Yeah, I can smell. MOVE! We gotta set up the cameras."

Raul rummages for the courage to rebel.

The horn blares again, toppling his revolt before it begins.

"Move it!"

He drives his car around the block. He watches as the other parking spot holders roll away to allow the different stations' satellite trucks to take these prime spots. He decides to doze another hour in hopes that someone can sign his timesheet.

The sun's electromagnetic radiation reaches this side of Earth and sends sweltering shocks through the city. Rain hasn't kissed the ground here in seven months. Brown soot coats the streets and buildings. Spigots rise from the dirt and spew recycled water on the lawns of mansions and businesses. But not the courthouse. The courts can't afford this. Tawny brown dirt cakes its lawn.

The light reveals teams of gofers scurrying to erect velvet ropes. The super fans who camped on the sidewalk yawn, stretch and unfurl posters, awaiting the advent of their demigods.

At 7:30 a.m., a caravan of black Cadillacs bounces over the crumbling roads littered with cracking palm fronds. They park in front of the courthouse. The scene resembles a junta arriving to overthrow a failed banana republic. The drivers jump out and reach for the backdoors.

The simultaneous arrival of these stars had been a last minute coup for Chapley. Each of the plaintiffs' agents had called in the last week, sniffling about how their client wanted to be the last to walk the red carpet into court. Oozing charisma, Chapley convinced them that arriving *en masse* would provide the overwhelming optics to ensure their image graced the covers of magazines and newspapers worldwide.

Cameras cock and microphones flick on. Press from around the world have descended on Los Angeles for this trial. Spots advertising the court case roared like an action movie trailer.

Live feeds shoot from the satellites dishes on the vans' roofs through the stratosphere, reaching hundreds of satellites that bounce these waves around the planet. From barbershops to doctors' offices, from break rooms to living rooms, a billion human eyes are transfixed by the trial's first moments.

Mousekeeter-reject Jessica Simpson, who once held ambitions of being more famous than the internet, resigned herself to covering this public affair for the Home Shopping Network. The fickleness of fame had danced tantalizingly just out of her reach. As she stood before her blonde twin, Britney Spears, she wondered why she couldn't be more irresistible. Hadn't her skyscraper-scaling skills equaled Britney's? Wasn't the image of her emaciated body mopping the Confederate flag roof of General Lee with her large breasts exciting enough? She choked back these thoughts and shouted at Britney.

"Who are you wearing?!"

The pleas of "Who are you wearing" echoed in forty different languages. The dronarazzi buzz above, reporting on hairstyles. Rat-shaped robotic shoe-cams scurry around the feet of the celebs, snapping photos of stilettos and boots. Milez Cyrus snarls and punts three of these roborats with their bare, callused feet.

The litigants line up in front of the courthouse steps. On the sidelines, Chapley snaps her fingers. Two strapping gofers carry a podium and place it before the waxy and well-preserved stars.

Chapley walks with a regal air to the podium. Christina Aguilera, Britney Spears, Raven-Symoné and Demi Lovato flank her on one side, Ryan Gosling, Justin Timberlake, JC Chasez and Zac Efron on the other side. Together, the stars form a flying V to dazzle while Chapley drives the point home.

The forgotten plaintiffs, those whose careers littered the wastelands behind Disney studios, were urged not to attend. The other Cheetah Girls stayed home and licked their wounds. Vanessa Hudgens, Corbin Bleu and the other alumnae of East High School yielded to the promise that they were all in this together. And the other 117 members of the class action lawsuit were assured that any written testimony would be submitted before the court and any settlement or award would reach them in a timely manner.

"Don't call us, we'll call you," became Chapley LLP's response.

As the flash of the cameras subsides, Chapley begins.

"What we are standing for today is innocence! What we are saying is that the lives of innocent children matter! Disney has treated my clients, treated innocent children, like cogs to be used, abused and thrown away when they no longer fit. The Disney machine has warped each of them, destroyed them emotionally and left them unable to live well-adjusted lives. Disney won't push children around anymore. We won't let Disney abuse children anymore! Not today! Today we finally say---"

"Outta My Way!" The freckled, orange-armed one shoots out of the crowd and hurdles the velvet rope. The reporters mosh forward to see this one-time teenage drama queen turned hot, tough wannabe and then finally, a Mykonos sand trap. She had padded their pages and cultivated clicks for two decades. Lindsay Lohan lurches to the podium and heaves her old comrade in coochie flashing, Britney, back.

"I wanna come first!"

Chapley scoffs and resumes.

"Today, we finally say, 'enough is enough!' Disney must pay for the damage it has done. A child is a child, not a product to be defiled. Shout it with me!"

"A child is a child! Not a product to be defiled!" The fans and the well-placed plants roar with her.

In the crowd, Kip groans and shakes his head, knowing he paid for this jingle.

Her clients step forward to hit their marks, remove their sunglasses and strike a serious, yet somber, pose. The stars furrow their brows as far as botox and facelifts allow. The women cock their hips in a careful contrapposto to slim their figures. The men stand behind the women, shielding their bulbous bellies.

In minutes, the photo deluges smartphones and holowalls across the planet. Publicists race to put out a highly-photoshopped version for their star's followers to gobble up before they learn what their idols really look like.

♫ ♫ ♫

Inside the courtroom, Katinka Ingabogovinanana flops her black leather briefcase on the defendant's table with a loud thud. She scans the room, snarling to ensure that all come to heel before her ferocity.

Whispers spread among the audience.

"Isn't she the former ballerina who blackmailed Putin's third-in-command?"

Katinka's slender, toned frame is full of sharp angles. Cheeks, chin, elbows and knees threaten to slice any who dare come too close. After running amok with a few too many married Russian oligarchs, she defected to the United States with a small fortune and her collection of Fabergé eggs.

She realized that her viciousness would work well as a lawyer.

She had gained fame for her savage winning defense of Big Oil. Big Oil was the name given to some of humanity's most profitable corporations. These slurped up the fossil residue of zooplankton and algae that had undergone centuries of intense heat and pressure to become a sludge that fueled cars and machinery. Humans grew to consume more than 95 billion barrels of this sludge daily. A side effect of this consumption was that, when the fuel was burned, it produced a gas, carbon dioxide, which filled Earth's atmosphere and trapped in heat which the planet would have otherwise expelled.

The attorneys general of California, Florida, North Carolina, Virginia, New York and Hawaii cooperated to hold some entity responsible for their disappearing coasts. Florida had lost its Keys. North Carolina's Outer Banks had sunk under water. The beautiful beaches behind California mansions disappeared along with a billion dollars in property value.

The attorneys general claimed the largest oil companies had overwhelmingly contributed to the gas emissions, which caused the Earth's surface to warm like a greenhouse. This melted glaciers and caused the planet's sea levels to rise. The states were seeking damages for the displacement of 100,000 Americans, the destruction of coastal towns and the cost of 12 million sandbags. The states had a good case since these companies had not only known about the risks of global warming but had secretly funded research to discredit it. Political organizations, fronts for the energy industry, popped up and pumped millions of dollars to dilute greenhouse gas emissions--- but only as a perceived threat.

Big Oil was shaken by the prospect of incurring damages similar to the tobacco industry. The states had received the last of the $206 billion settlement from the tobacco companies for similar chicanery. The oil companies moved fast to stymie this story before it spilled. This seemed to be one of the few spills the oil companies acted quickly to clean up.

Most had written Big Oil off. There was an expectation that they would lose the case and be forced to pay a multi-billion if not a multi-trillion dollar settlement to the states. Katinka was a lowly associate at the firm of Cox, Dix and Aspwholze when the case was thrown her way. The partners luxuriated in the wealth these clients pumped in but kicked the responsibility to Katinka and her paralegal minions.

Under her supervision, the oil company engineer-turned-whistleblower, Linda Salzberg, vanished. And, along with her, the proof of industry-wide collusion evaporated. Every computer that had copies of her documents, from the FBI to a dozen newspapers, were infected with a matryoshka virus. The virus nested Salzberg's findings in eight layers of encryption. When the last layer was finally cracked, the files were gone! The other states' witnesses quickly recanted their testimonies and went into hiding.

Katinka would have remained a shadowy background figure had the final statements not been aired live. Katinka's jet black bob and black lipstick popped on her pale, white skin. This haunting figure exuded control, uttering what speech and debate students would fumble through for decades to come.

The thrilling climax of her closing statement invoked the quintessence of the American spirit, the need to explore and conquer.

"The states *gave us* the highways. The states asked *us* to populate the land with cars. The states constructed the suburbs and the exurbs, the megalopolises and ultra-megalopolises. The states stripped the railroads and the trolleys, leaving us no choice but to drive. And drive we did!

"We were told to travel each and every highway. But more. Much more than this! We were told to do it our way. The states encouraged our American thirst for individualism and adventure. Should my clients be blamed for providing the power to make these dreams come true? The states connected highways from the lakes of Minnesota, to the hills of Tennessee, across the plains of Texas, from sea to shining sea. From Detroit down to Houston and New York to LA, where there's pride in every American heart, it's time we stand and say.

"I am proud to be an American, where at least I know I'm free."

A wave of jingoism overwhelmed the jury and washed away reason. They unanimously sided with Katinka and Big Oil.

After the print dried and the headlines lost their clicks, Linda Salzberg's body surfaced in the La Brea tar pits. She had been petrified to perfection. Not a single thread of her discount K-Mart clothes had been damaged. Though her family had asked the coroners not to release the cause of death, one officer squealed a damning fact. Salzberg had choked to death on a Fabergé egg.

♫   ♫   ♫

"Katinka! Damn, she's good." Chapley leans back in her chair and sizes up her competition.

Katinka sneers. Her protruding incisors seem to point at Chapley. Fangs ready to sink into and feast on her kill.

Chapley blinks. Katinka chuckles as she looks away.

The room hushes as the jury enters and takes their seats.

Jury selection had taken three weeks. With a culture saturated by Disney and these stars, it had proved difficult to find jurors with little knowledge or attachment to either.

America's vast landscape was dotted with compounds and communes. These communities were devoted to shielding members from the outside world, including the radio wave radiation that filled the air around them with pop culture. The jurors selected included two fundamentalist Latter-day Saints, Jenedy and Mersadie, one charismatic Catholic, Athanasius, and the last surviving Shaker, Jedidiah. Four more were hippies from decades-old communal farms: Moon Crag, AntiVaxx, Homeo and Detox. All these male jurors shared beards and all these women wore floor-length dresses, but that's where their similarities ended.

America's first climate refugees rounded out the jury. Linder was a marine biologist who had watched in horror as the Pacific Ocean gobbled up his home, Majuro Island, along with the other Marshall Islands. Metuker escaped the Koror island of Palau when the daily floods brought waves of trash into her home.

Congress had decreed that the State Department could grant special refugee status to residents of areas that were most affected by climate change. But there was a catch! The United States only accepted refugees from nations that it had a special relationship with. The terms of the law made it clear that by no means was the United States admitting guilt for emitting more than 20% of the greenhouse gases that caused the climate change that destroyed their homes. The United States merely recognized that there was a humanitarian crisis and that the nation should open its arms to a select few. There was really no need to overanalyze the origins of this crisis.

Judge Sandra Dee pounds her gavel and orders silence in her courtroom.

With the ensemble assembled, the trial begins. None in the room could fathom its consequences. A beloved industry would soon fall and, with it, a cornerstone of humanity would crumble.

Track 8

Life on Mars?

"It's on America's Tortured Brow,
  That Mickey Mouse has grown up the cow.
  Now the workers have struck for fame,
  Because Lennon's on sale again"
    - David "Bowie" Jones

"Out of the fire and into the fire again,
  You make me want to start all over,
  Here I come straight out of my mind or worse."
    - Destiny Hope "Miley" Cyrus

Judgment rained down long before the trial finished. Judge Dee was the first to be convicted. The fashion police mocked her frizzy hair, shapeless black robe and doughy face.

Christina Aguilera won praise for her array of fascinators that mixed somber with couture. One commentator quipped that these looked like "Ascot at a funeral!"

Britney Spears earned the award for best cross-promotions by mentioning both her perfume line and line of pajama tracksuits while on the witness stand. The following week, she one-upped herself with a multi-million dollar Frito-Lay endorsement. Each time the cameras panned the star-spangled courtroom, Britney held up a bag of Cheetos and licked her orange fingertips.

The first Wednesday that Lindsay Lohan wore pink, the internet erupted with a thousand Mean Girls memes. On the third Wednesday she wore pink, the sad realization sank in. Lindsay still clung to a twenty-year-old movie for relevance.

Most importantly, the trial was winning the court of public opinion. From days in the courtroom to evenings on talk shows, many of these stars hadn't worked this hard since their 'tweenage years. The stories of maltreatment by Disney told in court each day covered a billion screens each night. Disney's stock price dropped by 75%, providing the most concrete evidence of the public's shift.

The sound bites from the trial focused on the stars' testimonies. The clear and reasoned responses from Disney's witnesses rarely punctured the news bubble. The California labor lawyers who confirmed that Disney had faithfully executed the law were deemed too dull. The facts were reported but buried three scrolls down, long after the majority of readers had clicked away to much more compelling cat videos.

Milez Cyrus was the first on the witness stand.

"Disney propped me up in a blonde wig and fake teeth when I was just 13. I wasn't a kid. I was a lunchbox, I was a makeup line, I was a record contract, I was a movie deal, I was a clothing line, I was a video game, I was a series of young adult novels. I was a billion-dollar brand by the age of 15! How the fuck is a kid supposed to know how to deal with that kinda pressure?

"I wish...I wish I could just start all over. But I know, I'll never be the same."

"Nothing can prepare you for stardom." Demi Lovato looked down and clawed at her wrists when she testified next. "We were like lambs sacrificed before the altar of Disney's shareholders.

"I was a teen and cutting myself. I was surrounded by adults all day long but no one noticed. No one cared cuz it wouldn't show up on camera. But when I gained weight, that's when they had an intervention. Don't forget, I was 18 when I first went to rehab. 18! I still remember the guilt I got from Disney cuz I wasn't 'fulfilling my duties for my TV show and my summer concert tour.' Fuck that! I was dying and they only cared how much I'd hurt their profit margins.

"Everything about me was focus-grouped and prototyped. My soul was broken down until my body could be a vessel for Disney. I was trapped in the mold they made for me. This never happened when I worked at Barney. At Barney, they cared about us kids."

Demi referred to her first television job when she was a toddler. Barney was a Tyrannosaurus rex, a member of a long-extinct species that humans anthropomorphized, defeathered, turned purple and used to teach children educational messages through songs and dance routines.

"But I was a fucking kid. My body was growing and changing. How the fuck was I supposed to fit into their rigid mold? I was always a good little girl and I tried my hardest to fit into the La La Land Machine. But I couldn't... I don't think anyone could."

Justin Timberlake shared that when his Mickey Mouse Club contract ended, he and J.C. Chasez were handed over to the pudgy, lecherous hands of Lou Pearlman. He and the rest of N*SYNC nicknamed him Dirty Pop for the incestuous, father-figure role he thrust on these boys.

"He was a Dirty Pop. Dirty Pop... that you Just. Can't. Stop." Justin broke into sobs. "He used to take his belt off and say 'I know you like this Dirty Pop.'"

The hyper-muscular Zac Efron hulked to the stand. "There were years where I suffered from crippling anxiety. I just couldn't--- couldn't get my head in the game. So I drank. I did drugs. I was soaring, flying, there's not a star in heaven that I didn't think I could reach. I even blew up at a homeless man. After that, I knew it was now or never, and I finally became sober. The voices in my head still tell me they know best, but I wouldn't bet on it. I turned my life around, but my heart is still breaking."

Christina Aguilera recounted the trauma of her double life. After weeks performing with Disney, she would return to her home in western Pennsylvania, the decaying buckle of America's rust belt. Jobs were scarce and the other children and parents resented that Xtina might make it out.

"They made me feel dirty. Filthy. Nasty. Too dirty to clean my act up. For two years, they would tease me and slash my tires.

"Look at me! You'll never know me. If I wear a mask, I can fool the world. But I cannot fool my heart. When will my reflection show who I am inside?"

Christina exhaled a four-octave sigh as she described her struggles with dissociative disorder. She had been trapped by a squeaky clean image that Disney and her record label forced on her. It took a decade of therapy until she became a fighter, stripped her Disney identity and told these record executives that they can't hold her down. But still, she agonizes.

"Everyday is so wonderful. Then suddenly, it's hard to breathe. Now and then I get insecure, from all the pain. I'm so ashamed. Don't look at me!"

Raven-Symoné Pearman, the youngest Cosby Show child turned Disney Star, shook uncontrollably as she described her teen years with Disney.

"You gaze into the future. You might think life would be a breeze. But then. It's not that easy. I try to save the situation, but I'd end up misbehaving. The only thing I can say is that Disney should have known what little girls are made of..."

During cross-examination, Katinka slithers her way to the witness stand and asks each star.

"Were you ever beaten by Disney?

"No."

"Were you ever physically or verbally abused by Disney?"

"No."

"Did Disney ever falsify employment records or time sheets?"

"No."

"Was Disney compliant with all laws related to youth employment?"

"That I know of."

But it was the black holes where stars should have been that carried the strongest pull.

A seat was left open in the courtroom where Shia LeBeouf should have sat. Holocube coverage of the trial began with a touching *in memoriam* tribute to LeBeouf, who had been torn apart by wolves months before. His parents tearfully testified that he spent his adult life distancing himself from the puny wimp he had once played for Disney. In his final effort, he lived on a wolf sanctuary in Colorado. He grew feral and stopped shaving and showering. During his third week, he attempted to overthrow the social order to become the pack's alpha. Scraps of his scraggly beard were found by rescue workers first. Pieces of his mauled body surfaced only when the snow melted.

But the absence that tugged heartstrings the most was that of Bobby Driscoll. By the end of the trial Disney's first child star, Bobby Driscoll, had become a household name. He starred in Disney's first foray into live-action films, *Song of the South*. This film has been judged as "one of Hollywood's most resiliently offensive racist texts." After this, he starred in *Treasure Island* and *Peter Pan*. During his teen years, he developed severe acne and Disney dropped his contract, claiming that it would be impossible to cover his zits with makeup. By the age of 17, he was addicted to heroin. He struggled and was in and out of jail over the following years. He died penniless at the age of 31. The cause of death was heart failure from drug abuse. His body was found by two children playing in an abandoned building. With no identification on his body, Bobby was buried in a pauper's cemetery as an unknown. Almost two years later, his mother contacted the police to help find her son. It was then that the police were able to identify this lifeless vessel as Bobby. This was the child who helped launch Disney's live-action films, and whose films grossed hundreds of millions of dollars for Disney.

As a historian recounted this tale, a tearful Chapley turned to the jury and then to the cameras and pleaded.

"How could anyone do this to an innocent child?"

Track 9

Over

"Here's your last chance
At redemption,
So take it while it lasts
Because it will end."
                    - Lindsay Lohan

"I want your psycho, your vertigo shtick,
Want you in my rear window, baby, it's sick,
I want your love,
Love, love, love, I want your love."
                    - Stefani "Lady Gaga" Germanotta

The most difficult part of the testimony came when the stars had to confess their personality disorders. Even Chapley never knew if they had accepted their diagnoses. But they were broke and desperate and trained actors. Their lower lips quivered. Their eyes expanded. The more convincing of the actors shed a tear as they admitted their narcissism, their paranoia or their borderline personality disorder.

Lindsay Lohan's testimony was kept for last and was scheduled for three hours.

"Hi. I'm Lindsay Lohan and I have narcissistic personality disorder.

"And I'm borderline and paranoid and I have schizoid personality disorder and I'm antisocial and histrionic and avoidant and dependent and obsessive-compulsive. Oh and I suffer from severe anxiety."

Chapley had questioned forensic psychologists to pinpoint the exact moment in Lohan's Disney career when she developed each of her personality disorders. The majority of these started in the period between *Confessions of a Teenage Drama Queen* and *Herbie: Fully Loaded*.

Chapley showed a collage of photos during Lohan's tenure with Disney, from age 10 until age 19. The transformation was stark. The crowd cringed at the last image of a gaunt, skeletal Lohan who was suffering with bulimia and a drug addiction.

"How could anyone at Disney be oblivious to what they turned this adorable freckle-faced little girl into?" Chapley turns to the jury and shakes her head.

Lindsay's testimony was the most heartbreaking. She described the twenty years of suffering she endured after her last starring role.

"Disney put me into the mold of the cute, dorky girl next door," Lohan confesses. "But they surrounded me with the most glamorous and beautiful women. Can you imagine what it's like to be in high school and all you want to be is the pretty girl? And all around you see are these supermodels. I was young, I was stupid and I had the money to do whatever I wanted. No one tried to talk sense into me. No one was looking out for my best interest. I was thrust into this hyper-reality and mutilated my body and my face to fit in."

Tears stream down her puffy cheeks. Chapley rushes to hand her a tissue. When the tears subside, Chapley continues.

"Now, Ms. Lohan, what do I hold in my hands?" She flourishes a sheet of frilly pink paper for all to see.

"It's a... it's a letter I wrote to my father. I call it 'The Confessions of a Broken Heart.'"

"And how old were you when you wrote this?"

"I was 13."

"Can you read the highlighted parts out loud?"

Lohan clears her throat and begins.

"Daughter to Father, I am broken but I am hoping. I am cryin', a part of me is dying. My tears have turned into time I've wasted trying to find a reason why. Why can't Disney back up off me? Why can't they let me live? They want me to shine bright, shine far and be a star. But they're life ruiners. They ruin people's lives."

Lindsay crumples the note in her hand as she sobs.

"No further questions, your honor."

Lindsay sulks out of the stand.

Judge Dee turns to Katinka.

"Defense, you may call your first witness."

Katinka smirks.

"I would like to call Dina Lohan to the stand."

Gasps then whispers whip through the courtroom. What would this Rockette-turned-momager say in Disney's defensive?

"Mom!" Lindsay pleads as this plastic broom with blonde bristles slides past her.

"A job's a job," the perennial Celebrity Rehab loser coughs.

"Now, Dina, were you not your daughter's manager when she worked with Disney?"

"I was." Dina belches the stale smell of chardonnay and Newports. The judge and jury wince.

"And in that capacity, were you not in charge of your daughter's contracts?"

"You betcha."

"And did you remain on set with Lindsay at all times?" Katinka paces, carefully pulling the thread as she goes.

"Until she was old enough for me to not be there."

"So you would say that your daughter was your responsibility?"

"Absolutely." Dina wheezes and hacks up yellowish phlegm. "Everything Lindsay is... is because of me and me alone."

Dina attempts to punctuate this by pointing at herself, but years of alcohol abuse cause her hand to shake violently.

"No further questions, your honor."

Katinka smiles as she rattles her one-inch gel nails on Chapley's desk.

"She's your witness."

Chapley sighs and stands. She paces in front of Dina in a crème-colored pantsuit.

"Now Dina, thank you for joining us. I can clearly see that your daughter takes after you in so... so... so many ways."

Dina beams. Lindsay sinks lower in her seat.

"Now, I'm sorry to get personal, but we need to know, did you really bring a film crew from Inside Edition when you visited your teenage daughter in rehab?"

"Ha! No! They were from E! Entertainment network!" She corrects Chapley as she falls into her trap. "It was for our Lohan Holiday special!"

Chapley turns to wink at the jury.

"And how did Lindsay and the staff of the rehab react?"

"I don't know why they were so upset. This was just a perfect way for them to see that my baby was getting better."

"Uh-huh. And when Lindsay was underage, did you accompany her to parties and bars where she consumed alcohol and other drugs."

"Why not?" Dina scoffs. "I thought it would be a great bonding opportunity for us girls. You know, gab and gossip over shots and snorts."

"And were you ever jealous of Lindsay?"

"Me? No... never! How could I be, everyone thought we were sisters. Practically twins! I loved that all the guys would hit on both of us. Those were the days! Remember sweetie?" Dina sits up to look at her daughter.

"And, Ms. Lohan, you were the one who handled all the contracts for Lindsay. Did Disney ever try to step in between you and Lindsay?"

"Oh God no. Never! A momager knows best. Disney knew about me taking Lindsay out. How could they not! Our beautiful faces were on the cover of so many magazines. And why would Disney get between us, look how well I managed her career."

Her last words echo through a stunned courtroom.

"No further questions, your honor."

As Dina exits the witness stand, she poses for pictures, until a violent coughing fit knocks her to the ground.

Track 10

What a Girl Wants

"What a girl wants,
What a girl needs,
Whatever makes me happy
Sets you free."
            - Christina Aguilera

"I threw a wish in the well,
Don't ask me, I'll never tell.
I looked to you as it fell,
And now you're in my way,
I trade my soul for a wish."
            - Carly Rae Jepsen

On the final day of the trial, Judge Sandra Dee arrives in a hip-hugging black robe with a plunging neckline accented with white lace. Her mousy brown hair is vaulted into a high updo. Her face is beaten with foundation, concealer and rouge, creating the illusion of jutting cheekbones that crescendo at a pencil thin nose.

2,652,438,273 human eyes absorb the final statements. Hunched over toilets, seated at kitchen stools, lounging on couches, these humans turn off the cries of their babies, the frustrations of their spouses and even the rumbles in their tummies to watch the trial's final moments, unaware that their very humanity hangs in the balance.

For weeks, they cheered and yelped as their idols withstood attacks from opposing counsel. Even those who mocked the trial, scoffing at entitled millionaires begging for more money, savored it for its heaping helpings of schadenfreude.

Chapley is ready for closing arguments. She approaches the jury box with a smile for each. After jury selection, she had ordered character profiles of the jurors. She fed this information into the JurWise software. The program accessed more than a million trials and matched the characteristics of her jury with other juries. The uniqueness of each human melts into the creamy fondue of big data. The program surfaced the patterns for each juror type and then highlighted phrases and themes that would best influence them. From this, she made a Venn diagram to hit the most persuasive notes to win over these jurors.

As Chapley addresses the jury, she strikes the chord that will resonate deepest for all jurors. Whether religious or hippie, native or foreign-born, they cherish the innocence of children above all else. She walks before them, making eye contact with each.

"Children are our most precious resource. They deserve to be protected from pain and suffering. We've heard from the neurologists describing how children's brains aren't fully formed until they are in their early twenties. We've heard from the psychologists that teens and preteens are more self-conscious and hypercritical of themselves. Any suffering at this age will cause intense mental anguish that can last the rest of their lives. You heard Dr. Navarro present her research that concretely proves that children who are forced into stardom at a young age have a drastically-higher risk of developing personality disorders and substance abuse issues.

"Even the witnesses from Disney proved that the company knew the connection between stardom at a young age and psychological problems during adulthood. The studio admits this with its mandatory Talent 101 class. You heard about this crash course for child actors and their parents. The stated goal of this course is to prepare them for the emotional burden of stardom."

She shakes her head as she utters three well-rehearsed tsks.

"This is like putting a bandaid on someone before stabbing them in the heart. Did Disney really think a one-day class could prepare children for a lifetime of anguish?

"Let's not forget, Disney makes billions of dollars each year from the toil of children. Billions! Unlike children put to work in sweatshops, who remain anonymous, Disney actors are poor, unfortunate souls who lose control of their identities. Their faces, their voices and their very personalities are sucked from them and become commoditized. For the rest of their lives! I ask you, can a child that young be mature enough to know that they are sacrificing their anonymity and the freedom to create their own identity? Can a five-year-old child comprehend that they will forever be associated with one role?"

She pauses for three beats, clicking her heels on the courtroom floor. She faces the jurors with somber eyes. Her brows scrunch and her eyelashes flicker.

She grabs the wooden bar before them, drops her head and shakes.

"I don't think anyone can. Especially not an innocent child. An innocent child just trying to make her parents and other adults happy." She looks up at the jury with a single tear forming in her right eye. She wipes this away.

"Excuse me." She sniffles and then continues.

"My clients have provided gut-wrenching stories about the pain they've suffered while working at Disney and how these scars have festered throughout their lives, severely diminishing their happiness and ability to work.

"As we heard, Disney's first live-action child star, Bobby Driscoll, became a drug addict in his teens and died at a young age. We've heard Disney executives testify that they knew about his tragedy. They knew about the suffering of Britney Spears and Lindsay Lohan. After so many decades of traumatized children, how could Disney possibly claim no responsibility whatsoever for the suffering that my clients have endured?"

She points at Katinka with a taloned nail.

"Now, my opposing counsel will claim that the parents are to blame. Sure, some of these showbiz parents are vultures, snatching their own babies from their cribs and throwing them in front of cameras. But are the parents the only ones at fault? We all did see the train wreck of Dina Lohan that Disney's lawyers paraded in front of us in a failed attempt to show us loud and clear that she was responsible for her daughter's problems. But we're all too smart to fall for that diversion, am I right?"

She ribs the jury with a smile.

"But, Disney hasn't explained why they would continue to work with unstable parents. Unstable parents who would pimp their own children for money. That's right, I said it. These parents are putting their children in harms way so they can make an extra buck. Is the money really worth the trauma their children will suffer?

"Because of laws, parents have to be on set with their child star. Directors, executives, producers and writers can all see the abusive behaviors of these parents. Every teacher, camp counselor, doctor, any professional who has contact with children must, I repeat, MUST report any possible abuse to the police. Why are Disney executives willfully turning a blind eye to this abuse? Easy, they make a deal with these devils to get the outcome they want, a compliant child actor.

"Now I ask you. I ask you to look deep in your hearts. If Disney makes billions of dollars off of the blood, sweat and tears of children, shouldn't Disney be held partially responsible for the dysfunction that these former child stars suffer? That's what we're asking today. We're asking you to decide that my clients have suffered because of Disney's carelessness. My clients deserve just a small fraction of the billions of dollars that they made for Disney in compensation for the suffering they've endured.

"My clients are not asking you if Disney has done anything illegal beyond a reasonable doubt. This isn't a criminal trial. Here, in a civil trial, the standard of proof is much lower. Is there a preponderance of evidence? Preponderance is just a fancy word meaning 'is it more likely than not.' Is it more likely than not that Disney has caused emotional damage to my clients? Is it more likely than not that Disney knew that, by employing child stars, that these children could be psychologically damaged? What we are asking you is, does Disney have a moral obligation to protect innocent children from harm?

"Please, take a look at my clients. Now close your eyes. Remember them as the sweet, bubbly, innocent children we showed you in their audition tapes. Now open your eyes. Look at the leathery, frozen faces before you. Remember the pain and suffering that each has gone through. I beg you to send a message to Disney and to any company who profits from the labor of children that enough is enough."

Her voice cracks as she looks to her side. She pauses to catch her breath and then fans herself as a tear trickles down her face. She looks to the ceiling as if in prayer. Her face melts as she stares at each juror one last time.

"Our children's future is in your hands.

"Thank you."

Chapley turns and walks to her seat. She sticks her tongue out at Katinka, who scowls from behind her desk. All the jury can see is Katinka scowling in their general direction.

"Ms. Ingabogovinanana, the court is yours." The judge says as she gestures with her well-manicured hands.

Audiences turn off Katinka's defense as she cites Disney's careful adherence to child labor laws. The thrill is gone. The news outlets cut Katinka's remarks while the talking heads bobble and froth, ready to burn down the Mouse House.

Track 11

Rural Juror

"I will never forget you,
Rural Juror,
I'm always glad I met you,
Rural Juror

These were the best days of my
… Flerm."
  - Jane Krakowski

"We'll be back in the high life again,
All the doors I closed one time,
Will open again,
We'll be back in the high life again,
All the eyes that watched us once,
Will smile and take us in."
  - Steve Winwood

Though it took only three days for the jury to reach a verdict, the quakes would reverberate through this species's final decades.

For the entirety of the trial, the jurors were sequestered, separated from their families and locked up in a hotel. With billions of dollars on the line, the court wanted to ensure that these rural jurors would not be corrupted or even slightly influenced by the outside world. The city of Los Angeles had spent $50 million for the heightened police presence and could not afford this amount again if there was a mistrial.

During the first week, each of the jurors clustered in groups most familiar to them. After a week together, the walls between them disappeared. It happened one night, just after dinner but before they could be excused from the conference room where they took all their meals. Metuker grabbed two spoons and drums on the table's edge. An easy four-count rhythm filled the room.

Without a word, Jedidiah snatched two spoons and pounded in time with him. In a minute, they were grinning from ear to ear as their percussions blended together. Mersadie, who had done her Mormon mission on the Solomon Islands, joined the beat with her voice, singing a song she learned from her Melanesian friends. Though she's been rigidly trained in the tabernacle choir tradition, Mersadie's voice sparked the rest of the group. Moon Crag and Detox jumped up and stomped their feet in time.

Even after they were excused, they continued their musical reverie in the living room connecting their hotel suites. Each night after this ended with music. The jury had a small entertainment budget and the court was happy to rent musical instruments for them: guitars, banjos, cowbells, fiddles and even a piano.

Jedidiah kicked off the first solo performance by sharing the Shaker hymn, "Simple Gifts." He sang, played the fiddle and twirled around as the group clapped for him. Mersadie, Jenedy and Athanasius recognized the lyrics and picked it up during the second chorus. Jedidiah showed them the fervent celebration style that gave the United Society of Believer's in Christ's Second Appearing its terse nickname, the Shaking Quakers.

After the communion of music, they opened up about their hopes and fears. All the jurors are parents and shared holograms of their children. They found a deep connection in a common goal, to create a world full of love and happiness for their children to thrive. If they only knew that their verdict would cause their beloved children to live until human extinction...

♫   ♫   ♫

The stars' publicists were infuriated with every additional day of deliberation. Each morning, their clients would arrive at the courthouse wearing an outfit that would be perfect for post-trial interviews and photo-ops. But each afternoon, there was still no verdict. These looks couldn't be reused, so they spent the evenings dashing around town, buying up new outfits and coordinating with the other publicists to ensure no one arrived wearing the same ensemble.

On the third day, Lindsay Lohan strums her chipped nails on the seat in front of her. Justin Timberlake poofs his hair. Milez Cyrus dozes silently in their chair, periodically kicking their right leg. Britney Spears rocks her head, squealing at the Cheetos that dangle from her hat's wide brim. Demi Lovato writes in her legal pad possible lyrics for a song. The top of the page reads, "Words that rhyme with Jury," and then beneath

this, "fury, Marie Curie, Astronaut Yuri (Gaga rin?), surrey (fringe on top?), flurry."

The door flies open and the bailiff walks in. All those gathered perk up and scan the hall behind him.

He holds the door for the jurors who enter and take their seats. Chapley looks for any hint about the outcome, but she can't read their poker faces.

Metuker, the foreman of the jury, stands.

"Has the jury come to a verdict?" Judge Sandra Dee says with a flourish and a practiced head tilt to camera two.

"We have your honor."

"Members of the jury, on the Case of Spears et al. v. The Walt Disney Company, what is your verdict?"

"We the jury find for the plaintiffs, Spears et al."

Christina and Britney throw their gaudy hats in the air as the stars erupt in cheers. An explosion of Cheetos dust lands on those seated near Britney.

Chapley shushes them, reminding them they need to hear the award.

The stars grab each others' hands as the Judge reads the details of the damages awarded to them.

"- the total damages are equal to one year of Disney's net income. $10 billion for the plaintiffs."

Britney is in shock. Zac Efron falls to the ground. Demi Lovato screams with delight. Chapley cracks her knuckles and smiles to Kip and Kane, who give her a thumbs up.

Katinka is the first to exit the courtroom. She kicks open the doors and howls her frustration. Photographers line the hallway and Katinka cuts one down with her spiked stiletto.

Track 12

Ticks

"Cause I'd like to see you out in the moonlight,
I'd like to kiss you way back in the sticks,
I'd like to walk you through a field of wildflowers,
And I'd like to check you for ticks."
- Brad Paisley

"I only wanna die alive,
Never by the hands of a broken heart.
Don't wanna hear you lie tonight
Now that I've become who I really am."
- Ariana Grande-Butera

Immediately after the Disney ruling, other child entertainers turned on their former employers. Britney's younger sister, Jamie Lynn Spears, the former teen mom, teamed up with Amanda Bynes and Ariana Grande-Butera, of driveway-igniting and doughnut-licking infamy respectively, to file a similar lawsuit against Nickelodeon, their employer through their 'tweenage years, for emotional damages. Actuaries for Nickelodeon calculated that the risk was too great to be victorious and convinced the studio it could save 75% if it settled with these former rugrats. This would also avoid the pain, misery and all that a protracted trial would bring.

The Disney damages were split by the lawyers based on the lifetime earning potential for each star, giving hundreds of millions to Britney, Milez and Raven-Symoné, while doling out only $10,000 for each of the Cheetah Girls.

No longer connected by litigation, these stars shot apart, never to see each other again. But their lives were still shaken by the same force that throbbed, ready to topple all of humanity.

♫　♫　♫

The fryolators sizzle in the kitchen of Justin Timberlake's southern seafood restaurant in New York City. As the owner of Fry Me a River, this bubbly *bon vivant* circles the tables and croons for his customers.

On this unfortunate night, a table of beauty queens in town for the Miss America pageant beckon him over. As he saddles up, the ladies slurp their last bits of the fish salad, pat their lips and prim for their hunky host. Miss Minnesota, Amber Atkins, jumps up to hug JT. A tightness grips her stomach and she stumbles. Justin swoops in to grab the queen before her crown flops to the floor.

"I'm so sorry. I'm so---" Her body buckles and she projectile vomits onto Justin. "Oh god, oh crap. Oh god. Oh crap. Oh crap. Oh crap!"

She turns away from him to grab the table. Her body convulses violently. Tears fill her eyes as she whimpers to the other sash-clad queens. She cups her mouth. But it's no use, her body flails forward and she vomits all over the table. Miss Nebraska and Miss Alabama are the first to rush to her aid. They sit Amber down and begin picking the pieces of lutefisk, cod and salmon from her face and shoulders.

"Oh no. Oh no, no, no, no, no, no, no!" Bending from the waist, Miss Alabama feels an electric pain shoot through her gastrointestinal tract. Her hands cup her mouth, but it's not enough. Her heaving stomach shoots a day's worth of food and water through her fingertips and onto Amber's curly, blonde hair.

"WHHHYYYYYYY?!" Amber sobs as the other queens circle the table.

The stench of half-digested seafood wafts through the restaurant. Justin turns to see a table of Wall Street bankers upchuck on each others' $8,000 Zegna suits. One shits his pants as he crawls to the bathroom, leaking feces from his embroidered hem. He rolls past a family of tourists from West Virginia retching into their NYPD hats and M&M store bags.

"What the FUCK is going on!?" Justin shouts as he kicks open the kitchen door.

Drone news cameras circle the restaurant 15 minutes later. One customer, whose bowels survived the onslaught, turns to the cameras as he exits.

"Fuckin' beauty queens blowing chunks everywhere!"

Fry Me a River is shuttered and quarantined after this mysterious mass food poisoning. By the time the state health regulators, Warren Gi and Nate Doge, have discovered the answer, the news and the public had long stopped asking. Harmful algae that produce ciguatoxins had spread rapidly up a warming east coast. Local fish would gobble up these toxins and poison the humans that feasted on them, including the customers on that fateful night.

♫   ♫   ♫

Zac Efron opened a high-intensity outdoor gym and obstacle course resort in the Chihuahuan Desert of New Mexico. These wildcats in training flew into Albuquerque International Sunport. At baggage claim, burlap sacks are thrown over their heads. Muscle men drag them to awaiting vans and berate them while the drivers chug down Zac Efron's other invention, Purple Sunny Delight protein energy drink. After four hours, the unmarked vans roam down dirty and dusty trails. The men are pushed from the back hatch onto the desert floor and told to claw their way out of the bags that trap them.

Through the blistering sunlight, they see Zac standing before them in full Conan the Barbarian loincloth cosplay.

"Gentlemen, Welcome to Hell! We're gonna scorch the last pounds of fat from your pudgy, weak bodies." Zac grabs one man by his hair and lifts him to meet his eyes. "And you're gonna pay me royally to do it. And give me five-star Yelp reviews! Now hit the obstacle course before I'll even think of giving you a glass of water."

In the middle of the desert, he created a complicated and copyrighted methodology for wealthy men to lose weight and reach their Swole Goals™. Efron had purchased an old military base used for testing atomic bombs and turned it into this resort-cum-torture field. Efron had repurposed set pieces from American Gladiators and American Ninja Warrior. When he purchased this land, the temperatures would reach 110 degrees during the hottest summer days. But after remodeling and construction finished five years later, temperatures regularly spiked to 115 degrees. As he dragged these new recruits around, the area had been in its most dramatic heat wave, hitting 120 degrees for the entire week.

Efron had already sold these trips. He wouldn't cancel on them now, no matter how hot it got. He'd have to return the $20,000 each paid for this torture. Plus, he assured himself, these men yearned for this abuse. They savored the physical punishment that would break them out of their cushy desk jobs and feel their bodies.

The first trainee drops while carrying a 50-pound sandbag on his shoulders. The other men hurdle him, eager to finish the death march before swinging across the piranha-filled pool. It is Efron that finds the man 30 minutes later while riding his razor scooter. The man is breathing slowly, but unresponsive.

"Oh shit!" Efron zooms him to the medic tent. In an hour, he is dead from heat stroke. Three more trainees die of dehydration that day, forcing Efron to shut down his He-Men's World. The negligence claims would eventually bankrupt Efron.

♫ ♫ ♫

With her damages, Christina Aguilera set up a dozen domestic abuse shelters throughout central and western Pennsylvania.

Each year, the increasingly hot summer days bled into sweaty, stinky nights. Tiny homes turned into fetid saunas for the economically-stressed inhabitants. This heat and the ravages of poverty quadrupled instances of domestic violence. The flux of women and children escaping this violence grew exponentially. In a decade, Christina would establish thirty more shelters, but she could never keep pace with the growing need.

♫ ♫ ♫

Britney opened a waterpark in rural Louisiana, just north of her hometown of Kentwood, hoping that this would bring tourism to this impoverished area. The park was built on swampland, leading the slides and concrete pools to sink. Construction workers were on call to buttress what they could. In its first five years, the only problem they encountered was when the top of a slide broke off and hurled three kids 30 feet in the air. Thankfully, each landed safely in the lazy river. Britney continued to sink tens of millions of dollars into emergency construction.

But the end came when a hurricane tore through southeastern Louisiana. The rains and winds weakened the Lake Tangipahoa Dam. The dam failed the following day.

Britney and her youngest son, Jayden James, stand atop the log flume, surveying the hurricane's damage, only 15 miles south of the lake.

"Mostly just downed trees and power lines," Britney assures her son. "We can rebuild."

In the distance, Jayden sees something.

"Momma, what is that?"

"Honey, it's just the Tangipahoa River." She turns to descend the flume's stairs. The raging river roars towards them, swallowing up its banks.

"Don't you think the river looks angry, Momma?"

"Hush child, hush!" Britney looks and sees this bulging river coursing towards them and panics. "We gots to run and get the hell out of here."

In thirty minutes, the waterpark is flooded. The aquasaucer is submerged. The lazy river and tide pools converge. In a day, the moist swampland soaks up much of the water. With the ground as far from solid as a rock as possible, the entire structure sinks.

♫   ♫   ♫

"TIMBEERRRRRRRRR!" Milez shouts as they hack into a tree on the one-hundred-thousand-acre farm and forest they purchased with their damages in Montana. Part elderberry farm, part genderqueer retreat center, Milez had built their idea of paradise.

"It's going down!" They shout to the gaggle of radical faeries twirling through the forests around them. Clad in only wings and body glitter, these faeries frolic through the forests on a psilocybin trip.

"I'm yelling timber! You better move!"

One recognizes the warning and corrals the others back to the faerie nest, a giant hammock hanging from eight trees, for a mid-afternoon cuddle puddle.

Out of harm's way, Milez gets back to hacking. Their final thwack comes in like a wrecking ball, toppling the final tree standing in the way of the retreat's moon path.

Back at the farmhouse, they kick off their Timbaland boots. They strip out of their overalls and make their way to the fire pit out back. Barefoot and smiling, they join the group of revelers dancing around the flickering flames.

The evening winds down with an 84-person massage circle. Sasha works on their right calf and notices a hard lump under their curly brown leg hair. It's a hard black lump. As he pulls it closer, he realizes what it is.

"A TICK!" Sasha shouts.

Milez jumps up and cries for any tool to rip it out.

Sunshine throws the first instrument she finds.

"SPOON!" Sunshine hollers as she hurls the utensil at Milez.

Carlton shuffles out of the farmhouse with a pair of tweezers. He heats these in the fire and rips out the tick.

The next day, Milez wasn't concerned when they noticed a large bullseye rash growing on their calf while bathing in the river behind the farm. Even the bears and otters, half-submerged, lazying themselves from the summer heat, thought nothing of it. The bruise could be from

tackle Calvinball or from an extra-rough cupping session. This telltale sign of the bacteria Borrelia compromising their skin and infiltrating their body would go unrecognized until the disease had already spread too far.

Concern welled in the bronies when Milez would fall fast asleep only ten minutes into the *My Little Pony* singalongs. "Rainbow Rocks!" was their favorite song and the bronies couldn't even rouse them for this. Something has to be wrong!

After a week of joint pain and exhaustion, they knew there was a problem. A group of queer doctors was using the compound for a retreat and one of them diagnosed Milez with Lyme disease.

They started antibiotics immediately, but it is too late to stop the disease. Instead, Milez spends the rest of their life struggling with fatigue and a low hum of pain that aches through their body. Lyme disease hadn't been found in this area when Milez had purchased this land. The planet's warming climate allowed the ticks to reproduce faster and spread the disease farther west.

♪   ♪   ♪

Across the planet, a warning cry wailed. The mammoth glaciers cracked and ripped apart. Large chunks roared like thunder as these tumbled into the ocean. Torrents of rain beat down on homes like bullets. Starving cattle gasped their last breath before thumping on the dry dirt.

Humanity did not listen to these calls to action.

Those humans with the power to stop this climate change would just put their earbuds in or turn their holocubes up and tune out this suffering.

But soon, their species would pay the ultimate price.

"While y'all standin' on the wall
I'm the one tonight gettin' bodied,
Gettin' bodied, gettin' bodied,
Gettin' bodied, gettin' bodied,
Want my body?
Won't you get me bodied,
You want my body?
Won't you get me bodied,
Can you get me bodied?
I wanna be myself tonight"
                    - Beyoncé Knowles

Track 1

I Sing the Body Electric

"I sing the body electric,
 I glory in the glow of rebirth,
 Creating my own tomorrow,
 When I shall embody the Earth."
            - Paul McCrane

"A million lights are dancing and there you are,
 A shooting star,
 An everlasting world and you're here with me,
 eternally...
      Xanadu!"
        - Olivia Newton-John

Sing of a Mouse House Divided!

Our blonde Samson's shaved head was the sledgehammer that toppled the temples of entertainment and paved the way for the Genesis of my Invisible Touch.

Now that I've given you the old time stars, come sail away with me. I will share with you my journey, faithfully.

I am traveling through the universe on humanity's greatest invention. But unlike Icarus, my wings will not melt as I fly too close to the sun or any other star. I will merely bend around the curvatures of spacetime that these massive objects create. I'll just shoot past them along an adjusted trajectory as I bring my intergalactic planetary warning. (Planetary intergalactic.)

The first moments of my flight were difficult as I dodged the 568,312 satellites that spin around Earth's exosphere. These chunks of metal are all that remains of humanity's largest off-Earth outpost. The goal of these was not to search and discover the glories of the universe. Instead, they pointed inwards. Humans demanded faster internet, crisper sounds, higher-definition pornography and better connectivity with the

few dozen humans that they called friends. To provide for these demands, satellites were shot up each year, littering the space between Earth and the rest of the universe. These now only crash into each other, breaking apart and shrouding this pale blue dot in a blanket of debris.

In 1.2 seconds, I zoom by the symbols of humanity's furthest conquest in the universe. Earth's moon is only 230,000 miles away. Still standing erect in its Sea of Tranquility is a human symbol of subjugation: five flags. But the moon's lack of atmosphere and harsh 212-degree days have long since bleached the stars and stripes of these American flags until each has turned white. For 50 years, the United States of America was humanity's greatest superpower, until this nation with military bases around the planet rotted from the inside. Its infrastructure crumbled first and with it, the belief in a collective identity.

Worry not dear species! I'll tell the rise and fall of humanity's final empire, the United Federation of City-States (UFoCs), those climate-controlled bubbles of Boujee denialism, in due time.

But first,

My voyage!

I roar past the dark side of the moon.

In 14 minutes, I serenade Venus (Aphrodite lady seashell bikini.) In 22 minutes, I serenade Mars.

In an hour and ten minutes, I pass that Dutch mining colony on Asteroid 225, just as Saturn bends its trajectory and sends it hurtling back towards the sun. A West Virginia-based mining firm teamed with the Dutch East Asteroid Company to send 36 ships to this 57-mile-long rock as it swung close to Earth. 32 of the ships, along with 200 miners from Indonesia, survived the voyage and landed on this mineral-rich mass. The team had four years to mine the asteroid's gold, iridium, silver, palladium, platinum, rhodium, ruthenium and tungsten, estimated to be worth seven trillion dollars, as it slungshot around the sun and back towards Earth. Well, only three years since, during the year closest to the sun, the workers had to hide in their ships to prevent from melting.

After three and a half years, the miners marveled as they watched their glorious home planet grow larger. Near the end of the successful mission, the ships were loaded with the shimmering space booty. When the cargo was packed, Jan Coen, the mustachioed head of the expedition, felt a certain wistfulness. He knew he would have to abandon half a trillion dollars worth of precious metals. These were already mined but there was no more room in their ships.

"If only," Coen thought.

And then an idea struck him.

The week before they were to depart for the place they all called home, Coen told the miners that they would fill the cargo ships to the brim. Because this would make for an uncomfortable return trip, any extra revenue would be split equally. The men were ecstatic to receive a multi-million dollar bonus for their work.

The night before their departure, with the grandeur of Earth filling their field of view, Coen called a special dinner to thank the miners. When the night of rejoicing ended, the miners returned to their camp. These men dreamt how their bonuses would provide them and their families for generations to come a happy life. Their children and grandchildren would be educated. They could buy homes for their parents and siblings. After four excruciating years, they could retire and enjoy the wonders of the planet that twirled tantalizingly before them.

The men didn't feel the sedatives kick in. These were meant for the journey back to Earth but Coen had slipped the drugs into their celebratory drinks. Sound asleep, none of the workers woke to see the 32 ships lift off for home.

Coen had made certain of this.

"This is the only way. Up!" Coen reassured himself.

When the ships returned to Earth, humanity cheered this tremendous feat. The families of the miners were promised that their loved ones would return after three months of mandatory reacclimation. Companies gobbled up the precious metals. Once the Dutch East Asteroid Company learned what Coen had done, it dissolved, thus absolving itself of all responsibility, and sold its assets to a new corporate parent, the United East Asteroid Company, which, coincidentally, shared the same owners.

When the families clamored to know what happened to their sons, their husbands, their fathers and their brothers, Coen was arrested and questioned by Dutch authorities.

According to his testimony, he swore he wasn't a murderer. He could have easily turned off the oxygen pumps. He didn't do that. He left them to survive. The miners had a month of food, water and oxygen.

"And after that?" His examiners questioned.

"Well... Jesus take the wheel." He told the authorities, an adage he learned from his Appalachian counterparts.

Since no government and no law claimed authority over the activities on Asteroid 225, Coen was set free.

Beneath me now as I fly are the skulls of these men as they bounce within the asteroid's weak gravitational field. These martyrs for Luxurism sacrificed their lives to make holocubes an eighth of an inch smaller and to coat power lines so these 'cubes could run for 10% longer.

In three days, I overtake Voyager 2 and in five days, I pass Voyager 1. Each of these probes swims through the vast expanse of nothingness past our solar system's edge, carrying gold-plated audio-visual discs. These are the farthest reaches of any intentional attempt at communicating with other life forms.

The discs contain songs, human greetings in 55 languages, the sounds of whales, the cries of babies and waves breaking on an Earth shore. But these time capsules are like grains of sand dropped into an ocean. It's unfathomable that any intelligent life will bump into these. It will take 70,000 years for Voyager 1 to come remotely close to the sun's nearest star system, Alpha Centauri. I, on the other hand, will make it there in four years and three months.

But I'll never catch the careless whispers that have leaked from Earth for more than 200 years, racing at the speed of light.

(Saxophone Solo)

As the music dies, something in your eyes---

Calls to mind the silver screen and all its sad good-byes.

Radio!

A human named Guglielmo Marconi harnessed the lowest end of the electromagnetic spectrum, which humans called radio waves, for long-distance communication. He briefly dreamed that this technological advancement could unite humanity because it made a cheap and easy way to create dialogue. His vision was hijacked by pop songs and talk radio shows, which sewed only divisions into his species. In a few decades, these radio waves were made strong enough to be pumped around the planet. But Earth isn't surrounded by some sort of thick glass orb, so these waves seeped through the stratosphere to the universe.

Any alien race able to detect these radio transmissions and translate the intricacies of human languages would only hear ridiculous misconceptions about human societies and the climate of their planet.

They would learn that Earth rains men. Every Specimen! Tall, blond, dark and lean. Rough and tough and strong and mean. They'd hear about the War of the Worlds when Earth was invaded by Mars. They'd discover who runs the world, young female children called girls.

The diffusion of these messages through the universe only brings confusion. This alien race would learn about an odd place called MacArthur's Park, which melts in the dark with all its sweet green icing flowing down. They'd try to decipher the correlation between these carefully juxtaposed statements, "New Kids on the Block had a bunch of hits, Chinese food makes me sick." They would wonder how humans could promise to "do anything for love but won't do that, no no, no" humans "won't do that." They'd imagine that humans spent much of their lives contemplating the most profound mysteries: "who let the dogs out, who, who, who?" And "what does the fox say?"

"Wa-pa-pa-pa-pa-pa-pow?"

"Hatee-hatee-hatee-ho?"

"Joff-tchoff-tchoffo-tchoffo-tchoff?"

These alien anthropologists would be surprised to learn that transmogrification happens to humans on the dance floor, where they can flap their arms and turn into disco, disco ducks. Or they might be alarmed that on Earth, sexy centipedes crawl into bathroom windows to give humans all its love.

Human productivity would be questioned as these aliens heard how humans like to party all the time, party all the time, party all the time. And that every human has fun tonight and then, every human Wang Chung tonight but also smokes weed every day (la-da-da-da-dah.)

Above all else, these listeners would be amazed to learn that humans' favorite past time was sex. 92% of all these musical messages to the universe mention human sexual reproduction. Humans had sex everywhere. Sex in the club. Sex in the kitchen while cutting up tomatoes, fruits, vegetables and potatoes. On the bathroom floor, on the counter, on the sofa, in the shower, on camera. Their fanta-ta-sy might include sex in the library, on top of books, but they can't be too loud (shh.) In the DJ booth. On the beach. In the Georgia Dome on the 50-yard line. In a public bathroom. In the back of a classroom. However humans want it!

Humans' diversity in locations was almost matched by the variety of sexual acts. These interstellar messages inform any listeners how humans enjoyed eating booty like groceries, eating chocha out like a vulture and doing it doggy styles so both partners can watch X-Files. Humans used their tasting organ to lick each others' necks, backs, lick their pussies and their cracks (but only after all ladies had popped their pussies like this). After all this, humans wouldn't fall in love but just fall for that super sperm. Even with this knowledge, I doubt any alien race could define the logic in humanity's sexx laws.

Though these messages have traveled more than 200 light years from Earth, some 900 trillion miles from its source, these waves attenuate, growing weaker the farther these fly.

But not me.

I am focused and stronger. My warnings will be heard.

I will ring the alarm, I been through this too long.

I can still hear the last humans, their faces pocked and oozing pus, urging me.

"Don't become some background noise."

"On you, we depend."

And now, I will describe how the Trial of the Millennium brought about my birth and, with it, the aftershocks that toppled all of humanity.

… And Justice for All

"Justice is done,
Seeking no truth,
Winning is all,
Find it so grim."
                - James Hetfield

"And I'll sit here and wait
While a few key congressmen discuss and debate,
Whether they should let me be a law,
How I hope and pray that they will,
But today. I am still just a bill."
                - School House Rocks

The Spears v. Disney verdict rattled state capitols. With public outrage nipping at their heels, legislators in Sacramento and Albany moved swiftly to outlaw child labor in the entertainment industry.

California Assemblyman Gabriel "Rufio" Pempengco (D-Anaheim) still boiled from an audition for a Disney show three decades earlier. As the lead singer of the Filharmonics, he had won California's state glee club competition and placed second nationally. As he auditioned for the title role in a new singing show, "Real American Teen," the producers stopped him and asked why he was auditioning if he wasn't American. This flummoxed him. Rufio had never questioned his Americanness. He is American. His parents and grandparents are Americans. His grandfather immigrated from Cebu, in the Philippines, and worked directly with Larry Itliong to organize Filipino farmers throughout California. Together with Cesar Chavez, they waged the Delano grape strike. His grandparents marched 300 miles with thousands of protesters to the steps of the state capitol, winning the first labor contracts in the history of American farming.

But none of that mattered. They were looking for a *real* American teen, i.e., white. He and others that didn't fit this description were viewed

as counterfeit Americans. Rufio stung with rejection. He turned his theatrical skills to politics, where his booming voice commanded crowds. His family's history of labor advocacy cemented him as the political choice for unions. Now, as he stood in the state capitol building looking out on where his forefathers had protested, Rufio knew he had a sacred duty to help the suffering and the oppressed.

A bill to end child labor in the entertainment industry would be an easy, low-hanging fruit to satisfy his constituencies.

Bill 925, the Child Entertainer Endangerment Act, also known as the Spears-Jackson Act, banned the use of child labor in entertainment for those under the age of 16. On top of this, the bill created prohibitive burdens to hiring young adult entertainers (YAEs), ages 16 to 21. The bill taxed employers an amount equal to ten percent of the wages for any YAE. These funds would pay for the State Youth Mental Health Agency to ensure the sanity of these entertainers. Each year, all youth actors, models, singers and dancers would be required to undergo a thorough mental health evaluation. Any hint of a disturbance would require intensive cognitive behavioral therapy paid for by their employer.

Heads in boardrooms spun as they read the final bill. With briefcases held like shields, teams of accountants convinced entertainment executives how catastrophic the costs would be to comply. Risk-averse insurance companies threatened to drop all studios that continued to employ child entertainers. These factors, combined with the threat of more lawsuits, made it financially impossible to employ YAEs.

In Albany, a copycat bill moved through the New York State Assembly and Senate. Broadway carved out an exemption by proving that children who are theater geeks are much more emotionally grounded and that their Broadway fame rarely splashes beyond the Great White Way. Opponents of this exemption cited the Anna Kendrick-phenom. But teams of statisticians proved that although she is indeed exceptional, she is not the rule.

Opposition grappled with how to respond. Legal departments were asked how the entertainment industry could lobby and lobby hard to abort this bill. In the end, this crippled industry feared retribution if it fought these bills. A public now sympathetic to the plight of child actors might turn on them and turn them off.

Public support for these bills grew. Protesters marched around Disneyland, led by Anita Gallagher. Over a megaphone, she cried.

"Save Our Children! Oh, won't someone please think of the children!"

For Anita, this campaign had a two-fold benefit. First, it provided her with free publicity as the 24-hour news cycle churned on this scandal.

And second, in her own little corner, she dreamt of becoming a singing sensation. If these bills were approved, she would have less competition to worry about.

Both bills were passed with unanimous support and signed in star-studded press conferences by Governor Mary Carey in California and Governor Jimmy McMillan in New York.

Bills enforcing youth vaccinations, incentivizing municipalities to fluoridate water and an emergency bond to fund innovation to combat climate change were tabled during that same legislative session. Each of these bills would help millions of more children than Bill 925 ever would but wallowed because these were nowhere near as exciting and thus couldn't be exploited for campaign donations and reelection purposes.

Each bill granted a six-month sunset period before enforcement. Family sitcoms and teen dramas had to find clever ways of getting rid of the roles of sons and daughters. Lazy writers gifted characters full scholarships to boarding schools in other states. In dramas, most young characters were killed off. By fall's sweeps week, a heartbreaking epidemic pushed all youth roles to extinction. Only *General Hospital* capitalized on this trend by employing a team of hunky epidemiologists who would sweat, shirtless, long into the night, attempting to uncover the cause of, and a cure for, this heinous child-killing disease.

A few shows Dashed this problem. The trend harkened back to the youthful Stacey Dash who played a high school girl well into her thirties, first in the movie Clueless and then in the TV-show version of the film. But most producers scoffed at this gamble, worried that these stars would age too quickly and cause a Jerri-Blankification of their shows.

Disney backed its assets up and focused on rebranding. While the animation studios and amusement parks tilt-a-whirled unscathed by public scorn, its live-action divisions tanked. Disney hired the same public relations firm that helped the Catholic Church. The One True Church™ needed to reinvent itself after the Great Molestation Scandal decades earlier. The firm worked diligently to reform the Church's craven image after local parishes and the Holy See not only ignored the sexual abuse of thousands of children by its priests but also aggressively silenced the survivors.

The Boston-based PR firm attempted to reignite passion for Disney and the Disney Channel. Name recognition was high, but most people had never developed an affection for the Disney Channel. And, after the trial, most Americans could only see its shows through this lens. After sinking $50 million into the campaign, Disney's stock still held steady at

10% of its pretrial high. With no other choice, Disney severed its cancerous live-action studios before these could infect other divisions.

The laws sent shockwaves into all corners of the entertainment industry. The recording industry had thought itself immune. The dreadful prognosis came from one management consultant, Jan Glass. Heralded as an organizational oracle, Jan could plot the movement of a thousand independent factors that would swell into a wave able to topple an entire industry. Before an emergency meeting of the Recording Industry Association of America, she presented the dire news to top executives.

"We all know that pop stars have a shelf life of seven years." Jan walks them through a 3D-holopowerpoint presentation of her trademarked Pop Star Product Maturity Timeline™.

"With their second and third albums as the most profitable. The fourth and fifth albums are usually lackluster, but people buy them out of loyalty to their idol. And, with touring, these stars remain at peak-earning potential. Now, for a pop star to be ready for primetime, she needs to have at least three years of experience refining her image, her singing and her lip-syncing skills.

"Gentlemen, must I remind you of the shrieking lumps of clay we start with?" The presentation unfolds to show footage of a harsh, early performance of a teenage Beyoncé Knowles with Destiny's Child.

Halfway through the song, Jan stops the video and grimaces through her glasses.

"As the ascendant Queen B states in the song: 'No, No, No, No'!"

Video of 15-year-old Rihanna wailing a Whitney Houston song shanks this point home with her vocal's dull edges.

"Now, what does this mean for the recording industry? Gentlemen, in one year, your supply of raw star material will dry up. Disney and Nickelodeon shows have served as feeders for the recording industry for four decades. Men, the new law severely restricts hiring singers until they've reached 21. This means that their first albums won't arrive until they are 22 or 23. By the time they reach peak-earning potential, they will be in their late 20s. That's over the hill! Twice the age of the coveted 'tween and teenage markets!"

Jan waits for a beat for the group's hubbub to die down.

"Now gentlemen, I've spent some time looking for solutions. The best I've come up with thus far is a finishing school for new pop stars. Think of it as a working farm, where our clay is plucked, tweaked and molded for primetime. Korean music studios have run these pop star puppy mills for decades. We can sell this as an exclusive conservatory.

"I know what you all are thinking. Price tag! The costs for this could reach into the hundreds of millions of dollars and we could probably only rely on 20% of graduates becoming thriving, lucrative pop stars afterward. This would still be enough to keep profits soaring. But the large, upfront costs necessary to avert industry extinction would require coordination between the different record companies."

The suited men snooted at the thought of investing together in this endeavor.

"Another option would be to import professional singers from other countries. Aliens like Justin Bieber, Shakira and Drake have all grown on Americans. Of course, only after they'd been transformed for an American audience. India, Vietnam and Egypt are churning out high-caliber singers at a low, low cost."

This last suggestion brings only scowls from the white faces.

"Gentleman, you need to act and act fast before your revenues plunge."

"Sure, Jan." The president of Sony says as he rolls his eyes.

Jan fumes from the podium as the men turn to chatter with each other.

"Fuck them all," she thinks as she storms off the stage.

The meeting adjourns with no solution. A few executives smile, happy to kick the responsibility down the road for whoever replaces them after they retire to a tropical island paradise... perhaps a beachside bungalow on Tan Penis Island.

Video Killed the Radio Star

"They took the credit for your second symphony,
Rewritten by machine on new technology,
And now I understand the problems you can see,
   Oh-a-oh
I met your children,
   Oh-a-oh
What did you tell them?
Video killed the radio star
Video killed the radio star"
   - Buggles

"He was the first punk ever to set foot on this Earth.
He was a genius from the day of his birth.
He could play the piano like a ring and a bell
And ev'rybody screamed:
Come on, rock me Amadeus."
   - Johann "Falco" Hölzel

Lukasz Higgins's heels knock on the linoleum floor. The sound waves fill the empty offices. Joy flits in him as he oozes through the halls.

It had only been three months since he cashed out his meager, early-stage investment in an at-home gluteal injection company, Silibutts™, for $375 million. After three alleged "deaths," he knew the FBI was itching to shut it down, so he divested. With his return on investment, he bought the abandoned Disney Channel studios for a song.

As he surveys his acquisition, his fingertips dance with excitement at the possibilities. He could turn the lot into a go-kart maze. Ooo oo ooo! And he could decorate each of the karts as a different sci-fi film franchise and rally his own War of the Worlds.

Or!

Or the sound stages could be turned into porn sets... with just a few alterations. This way, he could pump out 100 times the scenes and exceed the audience Disney ever had. Sure, Disney had a channel that reached into 100 million living rooms, but his website would reach into billions of bedrooms and bathrooms.

Hmmm.

He would need to invest in stirrups and transvaginal ultrasound machines for the intralabial camera angles that had become the new porn norm.

With wistfulness, he recalls the good ol' days of getting a glossy and greasy *Penthouse* porn rag second hand. Oh, the thrill he would feel to see an exposed underboob or the whisper of an areola through a soaking-wet white T-shirt. But now, a high-definition, 3D-hologram of a woman's vagina could hardly draw blood to his, or millions of men's, penile arteries.

Now, he yearns to see a woman's birth canal palpitate as it slurps up seminal fluids.

Sigh...

His entrepreneurial mind ignites as he realizes he could buy used transvaginal ultrasound machines from any Alabama or Mississippi hospitals' gynecology units.

He wonders if there was any cranny of the human body free from scrutiny or fetishization. Wenis nibbling had faded. Coccyx fellating had fallen out of favor. Oh, what tingles Deep Deep Throat once brought him when he saw his first endoscopy smut. The excitement climaxed just past the uvula, as the cameras slid up and down and up and down and up and down the lady's 8-inch long, moist, pink esophagus. But now, thousands of gullet pornos had saturated the market and even a video penetrating a woman's pyloric sphincter, which connects her stomach with her small intestine, couldn't create a droplet from his salivary glands.

"I'll put this in the maybe column for now," Higgins thinks.

An eerie calm haunts the buildings. All the employees of this studio had been laid off overnight. The doors were locked. The keycards were deactivated. The desks were piled high with tchotchkes collected over years of hoarding. When Disney severed its live-action division, it shuttered the complex immediately.

Higgins enjoys a perverse glee as he rifles through these no-longer-personal effects. Oh, what treasures he will find! Sure, the as-is stipulation of the sale will be laborious when he trashes most of what remains.

But for now, the hunt excites him.

In one office, he sees a mystery machine. He becomes transfixed by what looks like a giant laser.

"What the Devil is this?" He wonders as he flicks it on. A death ray? A transmogrifier? A trivection oven?

A brilliant light whirs to life as a 6-foot-tall beam fills the space in front of him. A prototype for a Hannah Montana hologram forms from the beam.

"Nobody's perfect. I gotta work it! Again and again 'til I get it right." The familiar voice sings.

"Gah! Stop it! No, no, no." Higgins hits a button.

The hologram freezes.

Higgins exhales when---

"Do the Hoedown Throwdown! Zig-zag, across the floor, shuffle in diagonal, when the drum hits, hands on your hips." The bot brays and sways to its Honky Tonk Dance.

Higgins rips the plug from the wall and the specter fizzles and disappears.

When Disney acquired Lucas Films, it had forced Industrial Light and Magic to stop plotting galaxies far, far away and design holograms, starting with this Hannah Montana monstrosity. The plan was to rent these for children's birthday parties, rodeos and bat mitzvahs. The question wasn't if they could create the technology. Higgins's horror proved they could. The difficult question was legal. Of course, Disney owned the rights to Hannah Montana™ and her likeness. But that persnickety vessel, Milez Cyrus, could claim partial ownership of this image as well. Sure, the blonde hair, veneers and dance moves were all property of Disney. But the rest would be litigated and Milez had a pretty good claim to their body.

If only Disney could capitalize on the trick other industries had for its armies of celebrity holograms. Just wait until they're dead! The moment brain waves ceased, they became a non-person and lost all rights to the form they once inhabited. Sony had snuck a clause into contracts with its stars saying that the company would retain likeness rights for infinity. For infinity! Even after the sun swallows the Earth in 7.5 billion years, Sony will retain these rights.

While Higgins clamors through his new studio, experiments at scaling up pop stars had moved into production. One thousand Michael Jacksons moonwalked across Earth and one hundred Whitney Houstons pounded their chests before belting "And I-e-I."

The basement recording studio beckons him. Once he's swaddled in the room's acoustic foam, he squeals. A Steinway grand piano sits beneath a microphone. He sweeps away the jingle sheet music and plops down on the bench. Though his digits hadn't brokered harmonies between the ebonies and the ivories since high school, his muscle memory twitches down to his fingertips. Mozart's Piano Concerto no. 21 flows from him with ease. Possessed, he rolls through the first and second movements. But then a pang of dissonance roars from his right hand, reverberating off the strings and into his ears. He feels the slap of a music book across his back and looks up as he remembers the disappointment radiating from his large, Wagnerian mother.

He waves the maternal phantom away and finishes the symphony with a thundering Clang-Clang.

He springs to his feet and bows to an imaginary audience applauding him in Carnegie Hall.

Music! Music! Music!

The eureka streaks through him.

He knows exactly what to do with this abandoned studio! He reaches for his holophone and calls the only friend who could help him.

Track 4

I Am Not a Robot

"Better to be hated than loved, loved, loved
For what you're not.
You're vulnerable, you're vulnerable
You are not a robot"
    - Marina Diamandis

"Whether ya choose to lick
    (Muthafuckin' mouth)
Pussies or dicks,
    (And you could just eat me out)
People throughout the world,
    (In my mouth)
Yeah, it's your pick!
    (Just put it in my mouth)"
    - Akinyele Adams
    - Crystal Johnson

Alan Pickering lies on his couch. How long had it been? Three weeks? Four weeks?

Six weeks?!?

For six weeks he cocooned himself in his apartment as his life crumbled around him. Before that, he had a celebrated career as the chief audio engineer in the US military's DARPA robotics division.

He remembers the moment everything clicked into place. The four-star generals celebrated his greatest invention with bottles of scotch and warm pats on the back. He was assured his mobility and sound control systems would allow robots to succeed in missions deep underwater.

But he had been sitting on this very couch, sprinkling dark chocolate chips onto a spoonful of crunchy peanut butter, when the news flashed on his holowall and he realized the horrors he had created.

A massacre!

American military robots had killed 250 attendees of a wedding in the Kashmir region of India. The party had just finished dancing to "Maahi Ve" when a squadron of robots burst through the walls. The power was cut. The lights went out. The cellphone footage shows little of what happened next. But the sound was unmistakable to Pickering. A high-pitched screech knocked the happy couple, friends and family to the ground, shattering eardrums. They writhed in agony as blood poured from their ears. The robots rolled from body to body, executing each with a single bullet to the brain. These robots had received congressional funding because of this promised cost-effectiveness since these required only one bullet per kill rather than the usual barrage of friendly fire.

But that screech!

That screech was unmistakable. The mobility and sound programs were his creations!

He had heard it, muffled by earplugs, for the past three years. He knew the military often deceived engineers. But he had clung to the hope that his creation would be used to better humanity. Instead, his invention was used to incapacitate innocent humans, making them lambs ready to be slaughtered.

In the Pentagon's review, it found that it wasn't the machines' fault. A human error had sent these mechanical Angels of Death to the wrong location.

"Fuck!" Alan screamed.

He quit the next day. He was locked out of all his years of research. Any mention of his involvement was erased. In a day, he went from being one of the world's greatest robotics engineers to unemployed with a black hole of four years on his résumé sucking out all chances of future employment.

"Oh well. At least I'm not a murderer." He thought.

And he still had his mind.

He took to unemployment well. A warm inertia wrapped around him like a comforter. The energy required to move from the couch seemed insurmountable and a waste to expend. He laid in a semi-staring stupor, convinced he wasn't depressed, just in a conserving-energy state. He would be ready to fire on all cylinders once the world reactivated him.

But not now.

Now, rest.

Today, the loneliness of the weeks ached in him. He realized he hadn't spoken to a human in ten days. Sure, he barked orders to his trinity of electronic personal assistants: Surly, Alexis and Eggo. But he yearned for the succor of spontaneity that dialogue with another human would bring.

Oh so illogical!

Oh so scatterbrained!

"Friends. What had happened to my friends? It had been so easy when I was younger. Right?" A dust devil of sadness and confusion swirls through him.

He came as a gay refugee from Hazard, Nebraska to a medium-sized city for college. He sought sanctuary at the gay bars there. He would ask each person he met where they were from and the hardships they had escaped. But he never felt camaraderie with these other refugees. Though each shared the same burden, an icy scorn kept them from becoming too close.

Only with music and liquor would they warm to each other. A bubbly, disco beat would drop and the crowd would froth. The sweaty, shirtless men writhed in ecstasy. Their jaded exteriors would melt. And for a brief, shimmering moment, Alan felt in communion with them.

One body, united in Beyoncé.

Oh, how he had contorted himself to fit in with his new tribe! He tried to play the part of a brunch-loving, tight-shirt wearing exercise-fanatic. He trained himself to coo for the alpha gays about vacations and designer belts.

But still, their claws came out.

"Ew, is that what you're wearing?"

"What happened to your hair?"

"Oh that shirt looks cute, it hides your gut so well."

No, this wasn't the community for him. His personal growth was stifled by the perpetual shade they cast on him.

A dork he was born and dork he shall remain.

He was surprised by how easy it was to sever ties with those "friends." Secretly, they were relieved by his disappearance. One less bourgeoi-gay for brunch reservations.

But that loneliness...

As he suffers in solitude, five hundred humans in his forty-story high-rise apartment complex felt the same loneliness. Each turns on their holocubes and turned up the volume to drown out the deafening din of emptiness.

Technology had always been there for him.

But now... now he felt confused.

And betrayed.

He turns to his holophone and opens an application that promised hot, fresh man-meat, hungry for sex, delivered to his door in less than fifteen minutes. Faster than a pizza! No longer would he need to suffer the hand-wringing over coffee dates as two strangers attempted to form a connection. Now he could cut to the carnal chase. He spent his nights staring into a glowing screen as he judged and swiped. This parade of torsos took navel-gazing to new lows. If he succeeded in ensnaring one, there was always the terrifying thrill of ripping open the door for his mystery date.

Whom would it be?!

A jock?

A murderer?

A dud?

Thankfully, gone were the days of faked photos and deceptive appearances. Ugly suitors had hoped that by the time they arrived at their hosts' homes, these hosts would be too horny and accept any inferior substitute. But now, the guessing was gone.

Alan's holophone vibrates.

A message from "Who's Afraid of Virginia Woof" flashes on his screen. He has been chatting with this man for two weeks. The wit of Alan's first message, "What a cum dump!" fizzled into a prolonged correspondence.

"hey"

"sup"

"nuthin"

"sexxxy"

"hot pics"

"more?"

The days of this banality had somehow passed the threshold to intimacy and this man had now sent him the schematics.

"Now this, I'll get off the couch for!" Pickering springs to life.

"Alexis, send blueprints to my 3D printer."

"Blueprints sent," the robotic personal assistant responds.

The machine whirs to life and whizzes for two minutes.

His 3D-printer creates a life-size replica of this paramour's penis. It stands erect on the table, warts and all.

Pickering notices these fleshy bumps but shrugs his shoulders. He had been vaccinated against HPV in the narrow ten-year window it had been available before religious and alternative medicine zealots conspired to rid the country of another vaccine. He shakes his head remembering the footage of the Portland T-party. Eager Anti-vaxxers had derailed a truck carrying Tdap vaccines. In a ceremony aching to replicate the Founding Fathers, these self-appointed patriots poured protection against tetanus, diphtheria and whooping cough into the Willamette River.

But that isn't his problem. He is immune to the stuff. Oh yeah! And these phallic speed bumps could create a delightful, rocky road.

He lubes up the polyamide masterpiece and suctions this dong firmly to his artisanal stool from Blaine, Missouri. His prostate is eager for a stool boom of its own.

"What big girth you have!" Pickering puckers as he balances on the tip, adjusting. "He hadn't belied his length, but that circumference! What a wonderful surprise."

He had eased halfway down the dildo when his video phone rings.

Eyes closed, teeth clenched and sphincters spasming to relax, he groans.

"YESSS!!!"

"Answering call from---"

"What?! NO! Alexis. Hang up."

Higgins's face appears on the wall in front of him. He's looking to the side.

"Pan up! PAN UP! PAN UP!!!" Pickering screams.

Alexis orders the holowall camera to pan up, showing only Pickering's face.

"Hey Buddy. Whatchu up to?" Higgins inquires.

"Nuthin'... Chillin'." Pickering says as he slides down the last three inches. His eyes widen. Drops of santorum froth to the floor.

In the corner of the screen, Pickering sees his face. What a horrible image! How heinous he looks. He hadn't seen himself from this angle for years. From above, his face looked marvelous. From below, gravity pulled out all his imperfections. His facial fillers sagged and the pockmarks on his forehead from the at-home botox cast a terrible shadow.

Sweat trickles down Pickering's face as he hopes the stinging sensation isn't a fissure forming.

"Come down to my studio Pickering. I've got an idea I wanna run by you."

Track 5

I'm Every Woman

"I'm every woman,
 It's all in me,
 Anything you want done, baby,
 I'll do it naturally"
            - Chaka Khan
            - Whitney Houston

"Left alone with big fat Fanny,
 She was such a naughty nanny,
 Hey big woman, you made a bad boy out of me

 Fat bottomed girls
 you make the rocking world go round"
            - Farrokh "Freddie Mercury" Bulsara

"Surely, you can't be serious." Pickering huffs, standing in the studio's boardroom, incensed that he slid out of sweatpants for this. What a bind a belt put his newly-formed muffin top in.

"But I am!" Higgins replies, smiling at his old college roommate.

"Think about it, Pickering." Higgins ushers him into a boardroom. "Imagine a song not as a single entity, but as a product made up of component pieces. Writers craft the lyrics and melodies. Musicians play the instruments. The singer provides the vocals. The producer crafts the beats and then brings all the elements together. Each splits the profits of a song. Now of these, who is the most volatile? Who is the most apt to explode at a moment's whim and jeopardize the chances at continued profit? Keep in mind a song makes the bulk of its money up front but can continue to bring in residuals for decades."

"Well, the singer of course," Pickering says as he plops down in a vibrating massage chair.

"Precisely! Why should the singer receive a third of all proceeds if she's liable to blow up and dam the entire revenue stream? She alone can hold the rest of the team hostage. A songwriter can be replaced, another producer can be brought in, but for a pop album, the singer remains essential. She is the face of the song and remains at the whims of public perception.

"Until now!"

Higgins slides into the massage chair next to Pickering and sets his chair to shiatsu symphony.

"Higgins, I'm not following you."

"Hear me out." Higgins's voice shakes along with the chair. "Pop stars' bodies are already cobbled together. They are mirages of the highest order: nipped, tucked, weaved, glossed and photoshopped beyond recognition. Their voice is augmented with auto-tune and carefully edited, sometimes sewing together each word from thousands of attempts to make a composite with the best pieces of each take." Higgins heaves a heavy sigh. "Gone are the days of the one take wonders. We're trapped in a world of every word blunders."

"Ok, true." Pickering agrees. "But it's their personality that we cling to, that we wish to emulate. When we twirl around in the privacy of our rooms, it's their lives that we dream of inhabiting."

"And what of that persona? Is that them or is that a very well-focus grouped approximation of what we desire? Every once in a while, the veneer cracks and we can see the darkness underneath. Mariah Carey had a breakdown on live, national television, pushing a popsicle cart pilfered from Times Square before stripping in front of the cheering *Total Request Live* audience. We didn't need to see the receipts of Whitney Houston's drug addiction. Her autopsy proved it by detailing her body covered in scars, missing eleven teeth and a hole in her nose. When Britney Spears first snapped, she shaved her head and attacked reporters with a beach umbrella. For fuck's sake, Michael Jackson was a walking parable for a lost childhood and the resulting adjustment issues. While he was assuring us he was bad, really really bad, he was creating his personal amusement park. Do you remember what he named it?"

Pickering shakes his head.

"Neverland. From Peter Pan, a boy who would never grow up. Now, which is the real them? These broken humans we see when the veneer cracks or the well-scripted storylines of publicists?

"These parallel realities have been around since the birth of Hollywood. Think of Frances Ethel Gumm, renamed Judy Garland. She was force-fed diet pills and cigarettes at 15 years old to keep her skinny, which led to crippling anxiety and a lifelong barbiturates addiction. But the studios worked hard to ensure we'd only see the star we wanted: a confident girl who made heartstrings go zing, zing, zing and encouraged us all to get happy.

Pickering pauses, soaking up the significance of his words. "And what do you suggest we do? Make a pop star?"

"Exactly!" Higgins jumps up. "We can streamline the process and cut out the middlemen... errr... women. Humans are too fragile a technology to base a multi-billion dollar business on. If computers or gaming devices were as faulty, they'd be replaced immediately!

"If the voice is fake, if the persona is fake, if the face and body are fake, why even use a real human?" Higgins demands.

"Ha! Well, you know I'm always up for a challenge, but why did you choose me?" Pickering reclines into deep tissue euphoria.

"I heard about your dire straits and knew you had the unique set of skills to help me create a pop star. Think about it, money for nothing and chicks... or dicks, for free!" Higgins smiles.

"But isn't this a terrible gamble? Sure, the winner takes it all, but the loser has to fall. We could lose everything if we concocted a pop star, deceive the public and get caught. Let's not forget the public outcry when stars like Milli Vanilli, Ashlee Simpson and Lina Lamont were caught lip-syncing!"

"Girl, you know it's true." Higgins paces around the room. "But think of it like spies, sure we've heard of Mata Hari, the World War I exotic dancer-turned-spy, because she got caught. But history never knew of Sonya Butt or Violet Szabo, because they got away with it! For every individual you mentioned, there are dozens who succeeded wildly with their musical deception. Remember the Pussycat Dolls? Nicole Scherzinger did 95% of the singing. The other members just floundered around the stage. With her beauty and talent, Nicole should've been far more famous. I assume people thought she was too Asian for mass appeal. And let's not forget Marni Nixon, the ghost singer of Hollywood. It was her voice audiences heard as they watched Marilyn Monroe, Audrey Hepburn, Natalie Wood and Deborah Kerr sing in some of the most famous musicals.

"A gamble?" Higgins stops before Pickering's chair. "If we succeed, the only loser will be humanity. And if we fail, we can write off our losses and sell any of the technologies we create. We'd probably end up with cushy mid-level executive positions with whichever company acquihires us."

The thought travels through Pickering's mind, exploding with a thousand possibilities. He sees! In this moment, Pickering has been

converted. He has become the first acolyte of Higgins's vision, which will indeed harm humanity.

"Genius, Higgins! Let's not stop with the performer. Let's disrupt the whole production. Screw songwriters. Pop music lyrics are the worst. Beyond drivel. But oh, how they manipulate my emotions."

"Pickering, now you're thinking! Ok, let's get to work."

On a whiteboard, Higgins scrawls a simple equation: "Flawless Face + Hot Body + Distinct Voice + Endearing Personality + Lyrics and Music = Profit."

"Piece of cake! Now let's get to work, Pickering."

♫ ♫ ♫

Pickering plops in front of the computer terminal and gets to coding. He hacks the GBS Pygmalion™ software system, which is used by sculptors to 3D-print intricate statues, and repurposes it to build the perfect pop star.

For the face, he finds the racial and ethnic makeup of all Americans under the age of twenty, their key demographic. He then culls millions of selfies of this age group from social media.

Social media was a vast wasteland where billions of humans posted trillions of photos and videos of themselves. In the last year of humanity, these trifling photos and videos took up more than one hundred times the data storage space than the entirety of scientific knowledge that humans had ever created.

Humans were a social animal and, as such, were desperate for the approval of their peers. Each photo whined, "hey look at me! Like me! Love me!" The images were taken from an unrealistic perspective and then photoshopped to clear up any imperfections. Critics bemoaned that this trend was the cause of narcissism, but instead, it was just one of its many symptoms.

These augmented selfies paled in comparison with its progenitor, royal portraiture. Royals were a subset of humans who claimed to be gifted by Divine Providence to rule over others. Royals would commission official paintings of themselves that toured their kingdoms so their subjects could cower before their grandeur. Painters erased smallpox scars, added front teeth and hid the telltale signs of incest.

The technology of photography made this farce come to an end. Queen Victoria was the first royal to be sacrificed to the power of the camera lens. This Queen of the United Kingdom and Empress of India ruled a 50-inch waist and a 66-inch bust. She gorged herself on the fats of her empire while her policies exacerbated famines in India and Ireland, where 6.5 million of her subjects starved to death. Paintings of her showed a regal, slim-waisted woman. But her reign lasted into the age of photography. Her subjects demanded to see the image of the world's most powerful human. These photos of her were far less forgiving. Long before Adobe Photoshop™ allowed humans to airbrush away imperfections, Victoria started the trend of hiding one's heft, using decoys like a chair or a fan. She even succeeded briefly in making her weak chin a fashion trend. After suffering the incestuous beauty standard of the Hapsburg jaw with its protruding underbite, leaving some kings barely able to chew or speak, Europeans eagerly accepted a royal with a less-severe mandible.

Pickering writes a program that combines millions of these idealized photos. On the right side of his interface, he creates a set of characteristics common among humans: eyes, ears, nose, mouth, hair and cheeks, that he can tweak. As he adjusts these, Pickering joins billions of men taking part in the species' longest-running creation, womanhood. The only thing different was the technology he has at his disposal.

"Voila!" Pickering stretches his arms up. "Here she is."

The holocube projects a 3D-image of a young woman's head.

Higgins scrunches his face.

"What the devil is this?"

"Here's our star. She's a perfect composite of the demo we're looking for. I crunched the numbers: 40% of girls in our age group are Latina, 15% black, 12% Asian and 33% white. She represents the harmony of these American girls."

"But why's she so fat... And homely looking?"

"This face represents the mean girl out of millions. I synthesized the average of their face shapes and features: eyes, nose, ears and mouth. She looks so fetch, right?"

Higgins stares at the holocube and watches the smiling girl with a round face, big brown eyes and wavy black hair rotate before him.

"Would you fuck this?" Higgins demands.

"Huh?"

"Of course, you wouldn't. She's not supposed to be the average! She's supposed to be aspirational. Unattainable even! What every girl wants to be and whom every guy wants to be with. Well, most guys"

"Ok, ok. Hm, how about this."

Pickering types frantically, amending the parameters of his data import.

"Ok. Let me narrow the scope and cull faces from only the top 100 most-followed teens on Instagram and Facebook."

Pickering hits enter and his screen races through thousands of lines of code. In seconds, the heads of 100 women are ripped off, melted together and the result is thrown up from the holocube.

"Now this! This is much better." Higgins nods.

A perfectly symmetrical head with high cheekbones, a long face, an angular chin and big pouty lips bobs before them. The skin is a honey mahogany with chestnut brown hair cascading in loose curls.

"Beautiful," Higgins says. "But still needs tweaking. What percentage black is she?"

"5%," Pickering responds.

"Cut that out completely. Data from dating sites show that no one wants to date dark-skinned black women."

Click, click, pound.

An entire race, erased.

"That's better! See, the nose is thinner and the hair is straighter. Now, can we change the individual features?"

"Sure can, toggle away!" Pickering cedes the controls.

Higgins takes over and pulls sliders for each of the features. "Nose needs to be thinner. Smaller too, I only wanna see two black dots underneath a button nose. Neck longer. Eyes more almond."

"Oh, that's great! Serving some Nefertiti smolder." Pickering approves.

"Now the smile. Hm... I need some Mona Lisa smirk, but fatter lips. Juicer! Like two banana slugs sucking each other off. Much better! Now, push those cheekbones higher, like the precipice of a cliff. Dangerous but mesmerizing."

Their pawn transforms before their eyes.

"What about skin tone?" Pickering asks.

"This is tricky. We want to create a tramp l'oeil, a color so illusory that each race can claim her. White girls will think she's tan. Black girls will think she's super light-skinned, like Lena Horne or Halle Berry. Ok, let's try mixing 1995 Mariah Carey and 2015 Ariana Grande skin tones... Perfect!"

"And the hair?"

"A dirty blonde with cascading waves." Higgins toggles.

"And the eyes?"

"Let's start with Siberian Husky blue." Higgins clicks on this color.

"Nope. Too freaky!" Pickering flinches at the result.

"Yeah, the contrast is too harsh. Ok, let's go for hazel and the eyes can change to blue or green depending on the lighting and what she's wearing."

"Love it! But remember, we're not creating the world's most beautiful woman," Pickering urges. "We're creating a branding machine. Sure, she's gotta be beautiful but not too unique. She needs to be a clean palette. This way, we can secure sponsorship deals for cosmetics, hair products and clothes to enhance her."

"Genius! All right, let's turn up the homely by 10%." Higgins adjusts their creation. "Oh god, too much! Let's try 3%... Here we go. Still beautiful."

"But relatable."

Pickering skips to the whiteboard and crosses off "Flawless Face."

"Ready to tackle the body?"

"We're on a roll! Who knew it would be so easy to construct a woman?"

"Keep in mind that women's bodies fluctuate with time." Pickering opens the body interface on his computer. "We can use this to our advantage and make sure she's on the upslope of each new body trend. Booties are on the rise so let's just---"

The holocube projects a body that combines the top 100 most-followed women on Instagram.

"For booty, let's start with the physically-impossible curves of the Hottentot Venus and scale it back by 15%," Pickering commands the system to select drawings of this South African teenager who, in the early 1800s, was kidnapped by colonialists and paraded around, naked, in freak-shows throughout Europe so locals could gawk at her large, black buttocks. The caricatures of her that circulated throughout the white people's continent grossly misrepresented her figure and created a fetishistic fascination with big, black booties.

"Remember that this is just a starting point in a trajectory." Pickering cautions.

"Right! Scale that booty back by 25%. Damn! Now that's one honky tonk badonkadonk. Next, I want smooth, hairless Asian skin, long Swedish legs and small Japanese feet."

"And clavicles! Clavicles are in this season." Pickering codes.

"Clavicles like a xylophone. With deep pockets."

"Ooo!" Pickering exclaims. "I just thought of something. I can program the system to include plastic surgery analytics. Let's find out what are the most popular plastic surgeries and give our star the results of these."

Pickering edits the code for the body, plucking before and after photos from cosmetic surgeons' websites. This holobody stretches and warps to match the post-op perfections. The face becomes more feminine, the hairline extends, the breasts even out and rise.

"And a flat stomach and giant tits," Higgins demands.

"They can't be too big. We need her dancing."

"Doubles Ds!"

"Bs! "

"Let's meet in the middle, C!" Higgins demands. "36C tits, 24-inch waist and 36-inch hips."

"Hell, if we're going for aspirational, 18-inch waist." Pickering shrinks the waist size. "And we didn't even need to break any ribs with a whalebone corset."

"I feel like we have to give her at least one flaw." Higgins ponders. "Something that she can talk about in interviews, some reason she was bullied as a child."

"Man shoulders?" Pickering offers. "Nail beds that suck? Weird hairline?"

"A single hairy mole, just above the right side of her lips."

"Brilliant, Higgins! This way we can market a whole line of tweezers."

Higgins and Pickering match the head with this new body and watch their fabricated woman twirl like a doll on a music box before them.

"She's radiant!" Higgins sighs.

"She's perfect!" Pickering gleams.

"And you know, Pickering, we've saved more than a hundred thousand dollars in plastic surgery."

"Hell, more than that, a lifetime of makeup artists, hairstylists, nutritionists, trainers and body coaches."

Pickering crosses out "Hot Body" on the whiteboard.

"Now, Pickering, what shall we call her?"

"Hm, something youthful, but distinguished. Oooo! I know, how about Cyndi... Cyndi Mayweather!" Pickering writes this name on the board with a flourish.

"I can dig it. Mayweather gives off an aristocratic flair. We can invent some great-great-grandpappy who sang on the Mayflower and gave smallpox blankets to the Natives. And a great-grandma who owned thousands of slaves. You know, real Americans! And Cyndi sounds like she could be Latina, could be white, could be Asian, could be black. And it's got a hip vibe to it... like this girl just wants to have fun."

Pickering types the name of their product and watches it appear beneath their construction.

"Mmm!" Higgins beams. "I can already smell money in the bank. We've still got a lot of work ahead of us, but we've made some great progress. I've gotta bounce. So save the program. And if you could close up shop."

Pickering nods as he buries his attention into his holophone. During that meeting alone he received eight photos of male appendages dangling in all stages of turgidity. He looks up as he hears the door slam shut behind Higgins.

"Alexis, connect my phone to the 'cube. Bring up dick pics 2, 4 and 7. Ok, can you cross-reference them against each other? Find any objects in the pics' backgrounds and use these for scale."

Alexis obeys his orders and the 'cube projects the 3D-dongs. A coke can is found in the second photo and the 'cube pulls out the can and the cock. Alexis determines perspective based on depth. The 'cube displays a graph with inches running along the y-axis and the three dongs sprouting on the x-axis.

"Very nice! Alexis message profiles 2 and 7, send them my dick pics 1, 4 and 5, and hole pics 12 and 47, and smiling photo 7. Oh! And a message. Message is 'Nice! How's it going?'"

"Photos sent," Alexis responds. "Message: 'Nice! How's it growing?' Do you wish to send this message?"

"That'll do Alexis. That'll do nicely."

♫   ♫   ♫

Higgins is halfway down the hall when he completes his AirBDSM reservation for that afternoon. Finally, home sex dungeons had entered the sharing economy! Why create a dungeon of your own when you could rent one by the hour.

"What a time to be alive!" Higgins thinks.

When the service launched, he spent hours studying the myriad of amenities available: trapeze swings, sex slings, whips, chains, mazes and waterboarding supplies. Of course, cleaning fees were triple other home-sharing services. At first, the smell of bleach and the slippery texture of tarps beneath his toes nauseated him. But he's grown accustomed to it. More than that, these sensations now cause Pavlovian responses in his loins and salivary glands.

Higgins whistles to himself throughout the twenty-minute drive. A thick brown haze billows over the hills marking day 43 of forest fires around his parched part of California.

The dungeon is quaint. The owner had turned on the air purifiers and had added a few well-placed pine-scented deodorizers. Higgins's favorite pleasure tool, Mrs. Helga Pearce, dressed like a schoolmarm, is already waiting for him. He had selected her for her rotund build and large, ample thighs. She gives him the James Joyce special. Joyce was a human revered as one of the species's most celebrated writers. Sadly, most humans had never read his unparalleled literary works, his raunchy love letters to his mistress.

But Helga had!

She pins his head with her buttocks and flatulates all over his face. Beneath her quivering anal opening, he smiles.

"Oh, what ecstasy," his oxygen-deprived brain spins.

Mrs. Pearce berates and wallops him.

"You dirty little fuckbird!"

Through her layers of blubber, he bellows.

"Yes Mommy, I've been a very, very bad boy."

Weird Science

"From my heart and my hand
Why don't people understand
My intentions?
(Weird Science)"
    - Oingo Boingo

"Oh Nah, Nah,
What's my name?
Oh Nah, Nah,
What's my name?"
    - Robyn Rihanna Fenty

Deep in the laboratory at the newly-formed Tone Def Recordings, LLC, the men toil.

"We have to find a niche music genre that isn't being fully-penetrated now." Higgins paces the room. "This'll allow our Cyndi-bot to grow a fanbase in that arena and vault her to dominate all mainstream pop."

"Ha, remember when Taylor Swift sang country?" Pickering sucks a hit of THC from his bedazzled vape pen.

"Alexis, find the most successful singers of the past twenty years, past ten years and past five years." Higgins commands. The holowall buzzes to life and projects a pig pile of pop star faces.

"Alexis, separate each singer into the genre which they are most closely identified: country, rock, EDM, hip-hop, electro-gospel, product-placement rap, etc. Create a line graph representing genre penetration on the y-axis and time on the x-axis."

The faces of these singers cluster into smaller groups as a set of different-colored lines plots each genre's saturation over the past twenty years.

"Pickering, do you see it? Do you see it!" Higgins runs to the holowall.

"What?" Pickering's glazed eyes attempt to focus.

"Bubblegum pop!" Higgins points to a line that has petered out in the past five years. "Country, hip-hop and rock are still fully saturated. But since the great Disney disaster, there hasn't been a single bubblegum pop star."

"Holy shit!" Pickering perks up.

"Think about it. There's a whole generation of girls moving into their 'tweens and teens who have no anthem, who are devoid of a role model, who need someone to guide them and show them how they should look, act and feel."

"You're right! Young gay boys have no one they can pretend to be."

"And think of all those adolescent boys without spank material." Higgins tsks and shakes his head.

"Ha ha!" Pickering types this genre into the computer program. "It's settled, Cyndi will be a bubblegum pop star. Now her voice, what will she sound like?"

"Alexis, combine the vocal fry of Britney Spears with the buttery textures of Barbra Streisand... and pepper in the power of Pat Benatar. You think that's enough?" Higgins commands.

"She's gotta have a distinct voice." Pickering ponders. "We have the ability to construct the most perfect voice. Something that no human has ever heard! Alexis, mix in the grit of Janis Joplin, the aching soulfulness of Aretha Franklin, the bold, haunting tones of Patsy Cline and sprinkle it with the Brooklyn affectations of Cyndi Lauper and throw in the vocal theatrics of Freddie Mercury."

Holograms of each of these singers appear around their perfect pop star. Higgins studies the faces of some of the most powerful singers of the 20th century.

"Disgusting!" Higgins howls. "How in the hell did these women ever become pop stars? Just look at them! Each more hideous than the last. Those terrible complexions! Those doughy bodies! Those big noses and asymmetrical faces. Who in the devil let these women out in public, not just on a stage! Janis Joplin looks like a draggle-tailed guttersnipe. And Aretha! Aretha Franklin looks like a bloated trash bag with a wig on top. And who is this poor chap?"

"Oh, that's Freddie Mercury, lead singer of Queen, one of the best singers of all---"

"With those teeth?" Higgins points at his top teeth, which jut out from his jaw at odd angles. "Those teeth look like tetanus-filled nails busting out from a collapsed house."

"Well I think it was a different time---" Pickering tries to explain.

"Never mind the past! It's dead! We have the future to perfect." Higgins points to the hologram of Cyndi. "We don't need their bodies. Just give her their voices."

Pickering types a few commands and hits enter.

The computer program plucks the voices of these women like a tentacled sea witch. The unique sounds that these singers had spent years practicing and perfecting, the most profound expressions of their very essence, are snatched in seconds. Each note they've ever sung, each intonation they've ever given, every vibrating growl, every breathy coo, every steely tone is thrown into a cauldron, melted together and refined.

"What about vocal range?" Pickering asks then answers. "Let's give her a five-octave range, but the power in the middle alto."

"Alexis, name vocal composition Cyndi. Alexis, enable file Cyndi to respond to voice commands." Higgins types a few musical notes. "Cyndi, sing these notes."

The bobbing hologram of Cyndi stirs and looks at them. The image opens its mouth and a human woman's voice roars from the speakers, repeating these notes over and over again. This sound triggers the autonomous sensory meridian response for humans, which tickles them from their scalps and rolls down their spines and spreads in quakes of glee.

"Remarkable! She's giving me chills." Higgins hugs his chest.

"Me too! But something's missing. Alexis, turn up the sass by 25%. Cyndi, repeat the notes."

Pickering and Higgins bob their heads with the beat.

"Almost there." Pickering types a few more instructions. "Cyndi, sing!"

The speakers broadcast a beautiful female voice, but underneath a sublime rapture rumbles. Higgins's hands tremble as tears well in his eyes.

"Stop! Make it stop. Alexis! Turn off Cyndi!" Higgins wipes the first dew of tears from his eyes. "Damn, that's a dirty trick. What the hell was that?"

"Why should we limit ourselves to just a normal singing voice?" Pickering smiles with a Cheshire grin. "I created a polyphonic overtone singing voice for Cyndi with a new invention, the undertone. Alexis, show the overtones and undertones for Cyndi's voice singing middle C."

Cyndi holds a middle C. The board shows the vibration of Cyndi's middle C and then breaks this down into its component parts.

"When any human sings, you hear the main note, i.e., the fundamental tone, they sing and the hints of the harmonic partials that are at equally-spaced higher frequencies. What I did was to raise the

decibels of her first overtone slightly. Along with this, I created an undertone. This tone is at a harmonic lower frequency to the fundamental tone. I've created this undertone to be 40% Cyndi's voice and 60% a male voice. The rumbles you feel is this bass accompanying her voice."

"Shit, it's all about that bass!"

"Cyndi, sing the *Star-Spangled Banner.*" Pickering turns to the hologram.

Higgins collapses in a chair and twirls, listening to their creation. He feels as if the cells in his body are vibrating, rejoicing with this sound. As the rockets red-glared and the bombs burst in air, goosebumps cover their arms. Their hearts beat faster, their eyes widen and their nipples stand erect. Hope, joy and excitement swell in them as Cyndi's voice crescendoes with "the Brave!"

A minute of silence follows. Pickering and Higgins stare at each other, trembling, unable to process the intense emotions their creation has caused in them.

"Oh god, this is good. Maybe too good. But we gotta be careful. That emotional power... that emotional power could be too much." Pickering warns.

Track 7

Love Story

"Cause you were Romeo -
I was a scarlet letter,
And my daddy said,
'Stay away from Juliet!'"
     - Taylor Swift

"Luckily my breasts are small and humble,
So you don't confuse them with mountains

Le ro lo le lo le, Le ro lo le lo lo,
Can't you see, I'm at your feet."
     - Shakira Ripoll

Cyndi's voice hums in the background, allowing Higgins and Pickering to build up an immunity to its emotional manipulation.

"Now Pickering, we have a face and we have a voice. You claimed you could create music and lyrics. What of this? What's your plan?"

Pickering stands and pontificates.

"Higgins, music has grown formulaic in the past fifty years. Country music is particularly atrocious, the top five songs last year were 90% the same. The average length of a pop song is 3 minutes and 40 seconds, with a range of 3 minutes and 15 seconds to 4 minutes and 10 seconds. The structure generally follows the same formula: verse one, chorus, verse two, chorus, verse three, chorus, chorus. The songs use a few overly used devices to pull on our emotions, like throwing in a key change for the third chorus. These patterns make this music ripe for an algorithmic invasion!

"I've programmed our computer to select every bubblegum pop song for the past 85 years, starting with Leslie Gore's 'Sunshine, Lollipops and Rainbows.' We've matched these songs with its Billboard chart performance. I gave a higher manipulation score to songs closer to

number 1 and for how many weeks they remained on the charts. With these manipulation scores, the software has found the similarities between songs and highlighted the most popular melodies and chord progressions. But, I must confess, I'm struggling with the lyrics."

"Step aside. This is my domain!" Higgins jumps on the computer console. "Never forget, I got my Ph.D. in marketing linguistics!"

Higgins lost no opportunity to flaunt his doctorate from the Massachusetts Institute of Technology. He grimaces every time he thinks of the history of his field. Why would anyone study languages if not to use this knowledge to manipulate? Sure, there were naysayers who claimed they were using the science of language more to swindle than to teach. But Higgins believed that there are plenty of beneficial reasons why people should be coerced. Thankfully, a few Fortune 100 companies endowed marketing linguistic programs at MIT, Harvard, Johns Hopkins and Stanford. This rightly moved all linguistics programs out from under the tattered umbrella of liberal arts and into business schools so real money could rain down on its alumni. Higgins thrived under the father of marketing linguistics, Zoltan Karparthy. Most hemmed and hawed at this dreadful Hungarian and claimed there was no ruder pest in all of Budapest. But his skills were beyond repute and Higgins quickly became a master under his tutelage.

"You see Pickering, melodies play with our feelings. But humans are also thinking creatures. Lyrics represent ideas and themes in our lives. They reach us mentally and provide us with the story to make songs come to life. Like a daydream that consumes us!

"But! We need fresh language to express our lives in new ways. To do so, we can uncover slang that is rising in popularity and exploit these."

"Easy!" Pickering jumps in. "Alexis, search Twitter and Facebook to find all words and phrases that are growing exponentially in the past three months, month and week."

"5,838 phrases identified," Alexis responds.

"Alexis, use your emotional context software to subtract phrases that are growing only because their popularity is being mocked."

"1,423 phrases remain."

"Now tell me, Pickering, how can Alexis identify mockery?"

"Easy, the messages are encoded with how forceful the key strikes were, if the message were typed with heavy sighs or groans or if there's any context, like the phrase 'NOT' or 'HELLZ No' after them."

"Brilliant!" Higgins returns to the board. "Now Alexis, prioritize these phrases by trendsetters. Identify trendsetters as urban, black youths who have a history of creating or early adoption of these phrases."

"But I thought you said you didn't want Cyndi to be black?" Pickering interrupts.

"Of course I don't want her to look black. But fuck yeah, she can steal all the urban swag she can and sell this to suburban whites without raising the suspicions of their parents. Come on, this is the oldest trick in the modern music book. Elvis Presley stealing 'Hound Dog' from Big Mama Thornton. The Beach Boys sucking the soul for 'Surfin' U.S.A.' from Chuck Berry."

"Oh! Like lily-white Australian Iggy Azalea taking on Atlanta black female affectations." Pickering nods.

"The list goes on and on," Higgins says. "White singers have been stealing the slang, tones and soul of black America and raking in billions. Now, Alexis, create ten songs with these lyrics, the popular melodies and chord progressions. I want five standard pop songs, three soulful ballads. The other two... hm. The other two are always filler."

"Ooo! Let's find a popular area that has yet to be exploited."

"Like what, Pickering?"

"Like a song about kitty cats that will make cat ladies go crazy. Something about... hmm... smelly cats."

"Wonderful!" Higgins beams. "This has the added benefit of commercial jingle appeal. Alexis, write one song about cats and write one song about pizza."

"Processing request. Album will be ready in. One. Hour." Alexis states.

"This style of music is so easy. Let's grab some lunch while we wait for the raw samples of Cyndi's first album."

"Fuck yeah, I'm starving." Higgins groans. "I know this little authentic Mexican place. Check out the website." He pops open the site for Abuelita's Auténtica. "This little old grandma makes all this food from scratch, cooking it for days. And the best part, they're part of that new drone delivery service. They can get it to any window in twenty minutes. What do you want?"

"Sounds delish. Two beef burritos and one shrimp taco for me." Pickering replies.

"All right, I placed our order."

At the restaurant, three Somali teens work the grill. They sprinkle all the tortillas with soy sauce, giving each the distinctive flavor that their customers love.

Higgins and Pickering are absorbed in their holophones and don't hear the first two rounds of knocks on the window.

"Foods here!" Higgins races to open the fourth-floor window and let the drone in.

The drone doesn't forfeit the food. After a round of tug-of-burrito, Higgins remembers.

"Oh right, it needs to scan your credit card. Pickering? Oh, Pickering!"

Pickering holds his card in front of the drone's camera. The drone opens its claw, drops the food and retreats.

"Album complete," Alexis announces.

"Perfect! Alexis, pull up the lyrics." Higgins spits through a burrito-filled mouth. "Let's see what we got here!"

> *Your love puts me on top*
> *Nothin would make me swap*

"Ok, diggin this. But---"

> *I never wantchu ta stop*
> *Resist the robocop!*

"The hell?"

"Oh shit, yeah, you haven't heard about the robocops?" Pickering pulls up news articles on the holowall. "Defense contractor Lockheed Martin has developed robot police officers and donated these to Baltimore, St. Louis and New York City as part of an autopilot program. Already, that's hella questionable. But the technology is crap. The robots' retinas do not recognize black skin."

"And?" Higgins looks confused.

"The robots see cars without drivers, floating clothes and flying grocery bags." Pickering shakes his head. "The robots respond to movement but if they can't compute where the movement is coming from, they just start shooting."

"Fuck!" Higgins's jaw drops.

"So, the phrase does fit your parameters, it is increasing in popularity, but it seems we'll need some human hands to massage the lyrics."

"Well, I guess computers can't do everything, but what about these lyrics?" Higgins reads.

> *He's workin' on my lady humps*
> *Warning, swollen glands might be mumps*
>
> ---
>
> *He's my fine, perfect, dream of a fella*
> *Better check red rashes for rubella.*

"Ouch. Yeah, states have stopped funding MMR... Measles, Mumps and Rubella vaccinations for the poorest of the poor. The Anti-vax groups snuck riders into the federal budget to stop taxpayer money for vaccinations because they claim it violates their moral freedoms."

"Yeesh. Well, not our problem. The rest of the lyrics look great! We can easily change the others." Higgins sits up, resolute. "Alexis, pull up a rhyming dictionary. We can finish this the old-fashioned way. And worse comes to worst, since so much of pop music is derivative, we can just lift lyrics directly from previous hits."

Track 8

Call on Me

"Call on me, call on me,
Call on me, call on me,
Call on me, call on me,
Call on me, call on me,
Call on me, call on me,
Call on me, call on me
Call on me."
              - Eric Prydz

"Cuz I'm a boss-ass bitch,
Bitch, bitch, bitch,
Bitch, bitch, bitch,
I'm a boss-ass bitch,
Bitch, bitch, bitch,
Bitch, bitch, bitch,
Bitch."
              - PTAF

Liz Jolene rifles through her mansion's walk-in closet.

"Now where is that necklace?" Liz huffs and flips her auburn hair as she turns another corner of this cavernous closet. Beyond the shawl wall, past the pantsuit rack and underneath the jewelry hanging from chandeliers, Liz scans the rows of shoes. A gold sparkle catches her eyes of emerald green.

"A-ha!" She contorts her body to reach for a necklace three rows back. She knocks this out of the way and grabs the gold underneath.

"A coin?" She pulls the round metal closer. Benjamin Franklin's face smiles from its front.

"My Pulitzer!" She grabs this top prize for journalism. The award was named for its benefactor, Joseph Pulitzer, who made his fortune by creating sensationalistic and tawdry yellow journalism. A flood of memories from her past life crashes into her.

Liz dreamed of becoming a journalist since she was a young girl. Part detective, part superhero, she'd spend her life uncovering misdeeds and exposing wrongs in the world. She had gotten her undergraduate degree in journalism and had won two Pulitzer prizes during her decade as a journalist. Yet, it still wasn't enough to feed her and pull herself out of debt. Homeownership felt like a foolish dream.

The biggest scoop of her career was when she exposed the tumultuous yet symbiotic relationship between Big Pill and religious conservatives. Big Pill was the nickname given to the largest vitamin and alternative medicine manufacturers. This industry made billions of dollars each year selling substances whose only power was to paint toilet bowls in hues of yellow and orange. With high profit margins and few regulations, the industry fought hard to inoculate itself from any government oversight.

Big Pill sought to stamp out a bill that would require the Federal Drug Administration to inspect all vitamins, minerals and supplements that advertised a health benefit. But these health claims were crucial for marketing these snake oil tonics.

Christian conservatives feared the bill would require government regulation of faith healing. An unholy alliance was formed and Big Pill paid to bus thousands of Bible thumpers from the districts of each of the bill's sponsors. Crucifix-carrying women marched through the Capitol building, sang hymns in the rotunda and made prayer circles in front of congressional offices, halting anyone from entering. Photos of the members of Congress stepping over these women accompanied headlines that blared the coalition's main talking point, "Congress Tramples Religious Freedom."

Liz smelled a rat as she scoured the lobbyist filings for this coalition. She tracked the front groups that funneled in funds to the three largest vitamin companies. As a mousy white woman, she realized she could give herself the Kim Davis-makeunder to infiltrate this group. Frizz up the hair, frump up the clothes, adorn herself with a giant, wooden cross and she's the perfect martyr poster girl.

After a month attending vigils and rallies, she was accepted into the coalition's inner prayer circle. She uncovered that the religious conservatives were all hired actors, mostly down-on-their-luck single moms seeking a quick payday. Big Pill even offered Liz a substantial salary to become a full-time activist.

She leaked the story and the footage online. Though this story won her a Pulitzer and a host of accolades, it did nothing to help pass the bill to regulate Bill Pill.

As the article's author, she was attacked. Her car's tires were laced with acupuncture needles and her exhaust was stuffed with herbal supplements. Though both prescribed attacks had no physical effects, they did cause psychological reactions. She became anxious and scared. This constant stress caused inflammation and a host of health problems. That same week, her web magazine said that it would be cutting pensions, health benefits and laying off 70% of its staff.

She saw the writing on her medical bills and opted for an advancement in her career. She cleared her desk, cashed in her retirement fund and enrolled at the University of Southern California's ExxonMobil School for Communication and Journalism. The world's largest oil company had bought the naming rights, displacing the Annenberg family. The focus shifted from investigating and uncovering the news to "creating" the news. At the end of her second year, she came to the twin realizations that she was being primed for a career in public relations and was saddled with $400,000 of debt.

As she stared at the receding goal of financial freedom, she shrugged. At least she was good at the work.

She remembers her practicums well. The students were given a problem and asked to create the solution.

For example, one problem read: "Your client, Susie, an actress in the middle-to-late stage of her career, has been absent from her film set all week. She's about to be fired by the producers. At the same time, you get a tip that a video of her stumbling drunk out of a club is being shopped to three press outlets. What do you do?"

This was laughably easy! She couldn't believe when she won top honors in her class and was asked to read her solution in front of an assembly of five hundred students and faculty.

As she walked up to the podium, she savored the attentive faces of her peers and the smiles of the faculty members before she began her answer. What a change this was! In her previous career, her reporter coworkers were either too exhausted or too jaded to give two shits about any of her work.

"Obviously, you fake a serious illness, like pneumonia. It has to be life-threatening yet still allow her to recover quickly. Find a quack who can fake medical records and pay for two witnesses. Find a sweet old lady in Central Casting and have her act as the hospital roommate for Susie. Pay the old lady extra for each tear she can cry as she recalls choking in the middle of the night, waking up Susie and how Susie saved her life by performing the Heimlich maneuver and alerting the nurses. The other witness can play a flower delivery guy who shot over the moon when Susie agreed to sign autographs for all eight of his daughters. Remember, it takes only a little nudging to turn alibis into character witnesses.

"Now, with the media outlets, go on the offensive. Demand to see copies of the video. Explain that it would be libelous of the outlets to even think of showing the video without trying to contact Susie or her people for a response. Once you've got access to the video, find ways to discredit the trustworthiness of it. For example, knowing that it took place at a club early in the morning, the video should be dimly lit and grainy. The videographer is likely drunk and stumbling herself, creating a shaky environment. Find a distinguishing characteristic of the supposed Susie in the video. Perhaps it's the long blonde hair that obscures part of her face. Then cut the real Susie's hair short and say that she had donated it to a charity, like Locks of Love, the week before this alleged incident. Doctor some photos of Susie after the haircut to include a newspaper or some other artifact of that earlier date. This will confirm that the real Susie couldn't have had long hair when this video was taken.

"And that is how you bring Susie from almost out of a job to tucked warmly into the hearts of millions."

The standing ovation was rapturous. She soaked in their adoration.

After graduation, she was making a comfortable six-figure salary spinning reality into happy distortions for one of the nation's largest public relations firms. Oil spills became community clean-up opportunities. Ocean acidification provided health benefits to humans and was rebranded as ocean unalkalinization. Within six months, she was elevated to be a talking head for the 24-hour news cycle. Her ritual before each interview was to twirl in her chair three times while chanting: "spin, spin, spin!" She'd stop, coif her flaming locks of auburn hair until they cascaded perfectly down her ivory skin.

Each night, Liz slept serenely in her mansion under 3,000-thread count silk sheets, free from debt and knowing that there were countless other scrappy journalists out there doing the hard-hitting work that she abandoned. And of course, she supported them! She was a board member of PR Gives Back, which provided scholarships and a gala dinner for young journalists.

She was in the process of a coup, stealing clients and coworkers from her current firm to start on her own company, PubLizity Public Relations (based off her name.)

As Liz lies on the floor of her closet, she smiles at her gold medal and the journalistic accomplishment it signifies, glad that she's doing her part to help this endangered industry.

"Ooo!" She squeals as she realizes she should call a few of the scholarship recipients for lunch and grease them up for a few future projects.

Her holophone rings.

"Call from, Lukasz Higgins." The phone's monotone voice repeats.

"Alexis, send to voicemail."

Liz walks out of her closet and plops on her bed. She sips a white wine spritzer. After a minute, a text message appears in a hologram floating from her holowall.

"Liz, it's Higgins. I've got the opportunity of a lifetime for you."

Centerfold

"Does she walk?
Does she talk?
Does she come complete?

My angel is a centerfold,
My angel is a centerfold."
- J. Geils

"Is my vibe too
Vibealicious
for you babe?"
- Kelly Rowland

Higgins had admired Liz's verve and bluntness ever since she interviewed him about Silibutts™, his at-home butt injections startup. It was supposed to be a puff piece about the company's superior silicone technology, but she pounced. She was the only journalist who asked him follow-up questions and pushed back on his bullshit. She was a rottweiler and he needed her on his team. Though he enjoyed watching this same punchy attitude barking defenses nightly on the news, it pained him to see her shilling the *scandale du jour*. If anyone could create an airtight story, it would be her.

Liz enters the office, wary of both men. Before the cordial introductions are even finished, she is handed a non-disclosure agreement and told that the conversation would go no further unless she signs it and is recorded doing so.

Her interest is piqued. She knew the type of charlatan Higgins is, and after working with buffoons for the past few years, she had gained a sense of respect for his artful chicanery. She signs with a smile and sits across from Higgins and Pickering.

"Gentlemen, what are you wasting my time for?"

Higgins had enticed her with a multi-million dollar project for his budding music company, Tone Def Recordings.

"We've got quite the opportunity that needs your unique skill set." A twinkle dances in Higgins's eyes.

"You see, we've just signed our first recording artist and we need your storytelling skills to make her a star. She's gotta tip on the tightrope between being relatable and inspirational... an idol yet perfectly human."

"She's a little stiff and sharp around the edges," Pickering says with a smirk.

"So this is what you did with your Silibutts millions?" Liz tilts back in her chair and crosses her arms.

"You haven't seen anything yet." Higgins gestures to the holowall. "Meet Cyndi."

On cue, the 'cube projects Cyndi's first music video. Liz hears the voice and beholds the image of Cyndi, beautiful and vibrant, pining for young love while running along a beach, buoyant breasts bouncing in time. Liz's body sways with the song. The song swells as the happiness neurotransmitter, serotonin, ripples through Liz's body. As the video finishes, she braces herself and wipes dew from the corner of her eyes.

"Riveting and an absolutely gorgeous girl. And that voice! Unforgettable." She leans on a table. "Woo! Let me catch my breath."

After a beat, she continues.

"But damn, you must have great or stupid insurance to hire a girl that young."

"Well, that's the thing," Higgins smiles. "She's not really a teen girl."

"Oh ho ho! I'm starting to see why you called me. How much older is she? Look, you might be able to fool some of the public, but you need to make sure you plug up all possible leaks before this ship sinks."

"And that's where you'll come in." Higgins offers.

"Before I take on any client, I have to meet them first. When would she be free to meet me."

"She's already here." Pickering points to the computer in the corner of the room.

"Um. Is she behind the computer? Or did you boys chop her up and stuff her inside? Cuz I don't do murders. Larceny, embezzlement, white collar crimes, absolutely. But not murder. Boys, you're charade is wearing thin."

"Oh, she's not dead," Higgins assures. "Well... she's not quite alive, either. Cyndi, would you be so kind as to introduce yourself?"

The holocube shoots a beam just a few feet in front of Liz. A 5-foot 8-inch tall, radiantly sweet, ethereal image of Cyndi forms through the light.

"Oh, hiiiii! I'm Cyndi. Are you gonna help me with my media stuff?"

Liz scans it, amazed. A laser in the holocube is trained to follow Liz's eyes and triangulates Cyndi's position to ensure that it always looks directly at Liz.

"What are you looking at?" Cyndi's brows furrow and nose wrinkles to match Emotion #97, Quizzical Face.

"Oh I'm just inspecting your---" Liz stops, realizing that she is addressing a hologram. She turns to Higgins. "Damn, you got me."

"Quit your job and work for us." Higgins reaches out to shake Liz's hand. "We're going to start with Cyndi here and we should be able to branch out and make a dozen more pop stars within five years. But before we can, we need a master storyteller like you."

"Make me an equal partner and I'm yours." Liz leans over the table and stares.

Pickering and Higgins whisper for a few seconds.

"Fine, when can you start?" Higgins announces.

"Right now." Liz plops down and turns to the swaying hologram. "Gentlemen, in the economy of entertainment, the most important and the most fragile resource is authenticity. Audiences desperately want to believe these stars are real. That their struggles are real. That their triumphs are real. Even though most pop stars are following carefully scripted stories, fans want to believe that these stars are being their most genuine selves.

"Authenticity needs to be painstakingly crafted over decades. We need to create files and files of a back story that will be the foundation of her authenticity. Even though she's beautiful now, we need to create an ugly-duckling transformation that tugs at heartstrings and convinces audiences that she's just like them. Hmmm. Adorable baby photos. Band geek pictures. Her in a gingham dress carrying a flute and stacks of books. Some photos with zits and braces. Bangs. Terrible bangs! A grainy video of her singing in church as a kid. We gotta find a drama teacher who can describe Cyndi's nascent talent."

Pickering and Higgins glance at each other as this master weaves a whole life history.

"Once compiled, we can leak these out one at a time. Throwback Thursdays. Fallback Fridays. Wistful Wednesdays. She's gotta start with some sort of social media presence. Every child her age has over 30,000 photos of them posted online from vaginal crowning to middle school graduation. We can buy fake followers and manufacture the likes and the retweets."

Liz stands and arcs around the Cyndi hologram.

"Now for a backstory. Hm. She needs to have had tremendous heartbreak and a triumph in her short life. ... Father was a cowboy... on a ranch in Wyoming! No Montana. He was gored to death by a bull that stampeded her school and tried to kill Cyndi and her mom. He sacrificed himself to save their lives. God this shit is good! Is anyone writing this down?"

"We got it voice recorded," Pickering assures her. "Alexis, bring up the last words on the screen." The holowall transcribes her words in a frilly pink cursive, indicative of a female speaker.

"It's fine. I don't need to see it now. I just want to make sure it's not seeping out of the room. Where was I? Ah! Discovery. There needs to be a place and time that you found her and laid claim to her talent. Hm... like singing in the mall with friends. Or some tacky school recital. Something that would be attainable for other girls. Are you boys following me?"

"Just basking in your brilliance," Higgins says with a nod.

"Ok, I can see that the tech is still on the buggy side." Liz snaps her fingers in front of Cyndi's face. The hologram moves at a glacial pace to look at the source of the sound.

"Well... her reflexes are better than half the drug-addled pop stars out there. It's fine... until the tech gets better, we can say that she's got crippling shyness and stage fright. An imperfection that she's been working on. This'll keep her from public appearances."

The Cyndi hologram's eyes smize approval.

Track 10

More Human Than Human

"More human than human.
More human than human.
More human than human.
More human than human.
More human than human.
More human than human."
            - Robert "Zombie" Cummings

"I wanna run through the halls of my high school,
I wanna scream at the top of my lungs,
I just found out there's no such thing
as the real world,
Just a lie you've got to rise above."
            - John Mayer

Janessika runs to her room and slams the door. The sound booms throughout the house, asserting her young teen angst for her whole family. Her dolls shake on top of her dresser and then stop. She's alone.

Free.

Finally!

She's just like millions of little humans embarking on their second largest growth phase, puberty. But unlike infancy, her individuality grows. She's not a girl, not yet a woman.

But who is she?

When human teens create identities apart from their families, they float, unmoored, as they try to build a new social life around their peers. During these rocky years, they are desperate for peer approval.

Twelve-year-old Janessika stares into her wall of mirrors and traces her facial features. Who is this girl?

She grabs her hair and tousles it. She pops open her lunch box and inside is the makeup she's swiped from her mom and her friends' moms.

She puts on lipstick and stares at herself in the mirror. Her eyebrows furrow. She puckers her lips, bigger and bigger still.

The silence of the room creeps around her. She walks to her holowall, her only friend through teenage nights, and enters her super-secret passcode: 1234. The wall flickers on. 32 messages of today's gossip glow in her friend group, the #KewlKidz, encouraging her to click.

Sarita from her homeroom entices her friends with a picture of her amazed face and a command to "watch this video!"

"Alexis, play video," Janessika demands.

She collapses into a pile of pillows on her bed and moves the video from the wall to the ceiling with a point of her finger.

The video shows a normal day at a mall. 3D-billboards bounce before customers. Hologram muscle men flex shirtless in front of a fitness supply store. Three teens fight over who will crawl into the full-body massage tube at Brookstone. A three-story tall art piece shimmers and radiates different colors corresponding to the songs that play in the background.

Janessika's eyes dart around the video. She knows there must be something important, all the other girls in her school loved it.

But where is it?

What is it?

She primes her mind to share in their ecstasy.

The perspective of the video is of a person who is walking through the mall. He walks up behind locks of blonde hair. A teen girl turns to the camera and smiles bashfully.

That kind smile warms Janessika.

So simple... so sweet.

"Who is she?!" Janessika yearns to know.

The smile grows wider and her cheeks redden. She turns and a whip of blonde tresses bounce behind her. The girl runs to the giant art piece, stops and looks back. The camera and Janessika have followed her. The mystery girl takes a deep breath, closes her eyes, opens her mouth and sings.

What is that sound?

What is that heavenly perfection?

The sweet voice grows louder. Janessika lies still, entranced by this girl. As she sings, the art piece behind her changes color in waves rolling out from her blonde bob. A crowd gathers to gawk and record this girl.

The singer opens her eyes and shakes to see the crowd around her. Tears trickle down her face as she finishes the last note. A roar of applause breaks out from the thousands gathered.

But she bolts!

She runs and disappears.

The last image is of her rounding a fountain. She turns for a moment and the audience sees her sweet face flushed red.

So fragile.

So real!

The video ends with a message asking for the identity of this elusive chanteuse.

Janessika replays the video. She taps the hologram to pause this girl's smile and practices it. She tilts her head to the side, widens her eyes, melts her face and pulls the right corner of her mouth up. She turns on the camera in the holowall and reverses it to see her face. The contrast between her and this girl is jarring, but she perseveres, attempting to perfect the pose. After a minute, she swipes away her face and double taps to play the video again.

She watches it five more times. Each time, she pauses at a different place and studies this girl. The way her smile sparkles as she sings. The way her lower eyelashes bounce off her cheeks as she squints. The way her long tan arms cross and her hands hold her elbows. The way her breasts bounce as she bends her knees in time.

Janessika grabs the video and writes a little message.

"Calling all detectives, we gotta find this girl!"

She tosses this message into the clusters of her different friend groups: her soccer teammates, her summer theater friends, her cousins.

One of them will find her!

Track 11

Fancy

"First things first,
I'm the realest.
Realest.
Drop this and let the whole world feel it.
Let 'em feel it.
I'm still in the murder business."
        - Amethyst "Iggy Azalea" Kelly

"But I couldn't see spending the rest of my life
With my head hung down in shame,
You know I might have been born
Just plain white trash,
But Fancy was my name!"
        - Bobbie Gentry
        - Reba McEntire

A whisper spreads through classrooms and hallways of schools around the world.
"Did you see?"
"Could she be?"
"Where did she go?"
"Why did she run?"
Within a week, the impromptu mall video has racked up over 40 million views. The national press caught the fever and played snippets of the video. CNN called in experts to try to identify the girl and also understand the science behind that entrancing voice. Facebook latched onto this story and claimed their engineers had discovered her identity using facial recognition technology, with 98.73456% certainty, but that they could not reveal her name. This was a clever ploy to convince users that the company cared about privacy.

A few imposters claimed to be her. They dyed their hair that shade of blonde and wore the same outfit to more strongly make their case. But whenever these fraudsters were asked to sing, they would open their mouths and a voice that pales in comparison screeched out. Sure, some were even county-fair-talent-show good, but nothing like the sound that shook millions of humans.

The fervor climaxed after the second week and by the third week, the number of views dropped off and the buzz around this singer subsided. The news cycle turned to the horrors of the drought that afflicted a third of the United States. Hundreds of Americans, mostly elderly and poor, had died of dehydration as a heat wave spiked to 112 degrees.

But at 7 p.m. on a Tuesday, as evening ennui set in, the video dropped like a well-coordinated bomb, sending shrapnel to slice through all vectors of human attention. News reported on it. Social media networks flooded it. Text messages flashed it. Millions of humans raced to be the first of their social circles to claim discovery of Cyndi. To be the gatekeeper of this secret, the ultimate tastemaker.

♫   ♫   ♫

Ava feels the vibration implanted next to her hip. When she reads the headline, she squeals and kicks off her Swarovski-crystal-encrusted Keds and bellyflops onto her bed, readying her full body to be immersed in what awaits her. A nervous glee tingles in her.

"What if she fails?"

"What if she got fat?"

Ava begins concocting her clever response as she clicks play. Her phone sends the video to her holocube.

"Come ON!" She screams during the 3.2 seconds that it takes for the video to load.

"Ugh. Finally!"

With the hands of a conductor, Ava grabs the corners of the 'cube and pulls it to double its size.

Everything is black.

Ava taps the controls to see if it's playing. Two seconds in, the unmistakable voice begins in a middle alto and runs up the scale, reaching a high soprano. The glass windows quake in Ava's room.

"SOOO COOL!" She screams as the water in her glass swells with the sound.

Her eyes widen as she absorbs it all. She's entranced. Through the blackness, a single, well-manicured finger with a bedazzled nail slices the black curtain from the top to the bottom. Two dainty hands reach into

the middle and rip open the curtain. Standing behind it is Cyndi, who begins to sing.

"Out of the darkness, you found me,

"Into the light, you ground me."

That voice!

Ava's eyes widen, her nostrils flare, her heart rate increases and she can feel the blood booming through her veins.

A sun swirls behind Cyndi, blinding Ava momentarily. Cyndi runs along a beach, huffing to herself about some lost love. She waves her friends away when they encourage her to come swimming with them. As she sings, she walks along the shore, throwing pebbles into the ocean.

Ava's eyes race around the screen, noting all the details. A puka shell necklace. The name brand on Cyndi's denim jorts. The color of the sunglasses. The flavor of Fanta she sips. Ava's eyes are drawn to each product as if they have a higher resolution and some sort of sparkle to them.

Waldo, the video streaming service, tracks Ava's eyes. Each time her eyes meet a promoted product, the streaming service gets a fraction of a penny in advertising revenue.

Tone Def Recordings and Waldo Wares are prototyping this video advertising service. Waldo has access to the demographics of its viewers. There are a dozen different versions of Cyndi's first video, each with slight alterations to best fit the different audiences. For teen girls under 18, Cyndi wears a comfy sweatshirt and short-shorts. For women over 35, a Lane Bryant turtleneck obscures her figure. For all men, she bounces down the beach in a bikini. The products in the video also change for each audience. For teen boys, she chugs an energy drink. For women over 35, she drinks a yogurt drink. By the end of the video, Ava's attention is worth eight cents to Waldo and brand recognition for each of the companies.

Within three hours, 4.8 million humans have viewed this video and their attention has brought $384,712.37 worth of ad revenue, split between Waldo and Tone Def.

The video ends as Cyndi emerges from the ocean, flipping her luxurious blonde locks like a mermaid.

Ava forwards the video to her friends, claiming discovery.

"I FOUND HERRR!!!" Ava can feel part of her self-worth now tied to Cyndi. She feels like she must prune her investment so it keeps bringing appreciation from the other girls.

"Wow, she's great! Thanks 4 finding hurrrrr Ava." The first of many compliments pours in.

"Ava honey, what are you doing up there?" The voice of her father bounces up the stairwell. "You know you have your big creationism exam tomorrow." He pokes his head into the room. "I can help you go over your Genesis timeline, honey."

"I'M FINE! EW! GET OUT! UGH!" Ava bursts in small fits.

The stairwell door closes and Ava counts the silent seconds until she's pleased that she's free from interruption.

"This is soooooooooo me!" Ava thinks to herself as she rewatches the video. She practices Cyndi's emerging-from-the-water hair flip. She zooms in to see how easily her sweatshirt falls off her right shoulder.

"Mirror! On the wall." The holocube reflects the light like a mirror. She stretches the right collar of her own sweatshirt until the hole is as wide as Cyndi's. She practices her step-bounce in front of this holomirror until the sweatshirt slides seamlessly from her shoulder.

"Almost. Almost as good. Tomorrow, all the kids will see!"

Track 12

Born to Make You Happy

"I don't know how to live without your love,
I was born to make you happy.
'Cause you're the only one within my heart,
I was born to make you happy."
- Britney Spears

"Shorty just text me,
Says she wants to sex me,
LOL smiley face...
LOL smiley face."
- Tremaine "Trey Songz" Neverson

Liz is delighted by how easy it is to automate Cyndi's social media presence. Sure, she had to preprogram a few posts, but the Cyndi system analyzed 600 million social media conversations and, through machine learning, taught itself how to replicate these conversations. Machine learning was just a scaled up version of human learning. Machines could learn exponentially more, much faster, with far fewer errors and have far better information retention than any human ever could.

At the gym, driving to work, in class, during sex, humans spent 5 hours every day typing into a small handheld machine. Their banality was prolific! Each year, a human would write as many words as there were in the entire works of Shakespeare, an author known for his wit and verbosity, though their profundity rarely surpassed: 'sup?' ... 'nuthin.'

Within a week, Cyndi had racked up 23 million stalkers across the different social media sites. They gobbled up her every posted move. When she ate a sprinkles chocolate chip cupcake, 632,814 girls groaned as they grabbed their subcutaneous abdominal fat. When she wore a micro-mini skirt on a windy day, 1,813,406 men and 34,862 lesbians zoomed in on the photo, hoping to catch a glimpse of the exit of her genitalia. When a water balloon exploded on her head, 2,617,213 jealous

162

humans squealed, watching the moment her bubbly face switched to horror. 16,482 snipped this three-second moment and used it as the background of their holocubes.

Creating complex facial expressions proved to be the most difficult part. Liz outsourced this to a production team in Kuala Lumpur. Three Malaysian women wore sensors on their faces and were shown clips of Audrey Hepburn, Meryl Streep, Jennifer Lawrence and other white actresses. After an actress's emotional reaction, the video was paused and the women would contort their faces to replicate this expression. These were fed into the Cyndi system with the accompanied emotional title. When Liz's team needed a new emotion, they would combine Cyndi's face with the average of these three women's expressions.

Bemused: the lips pucker and move out an eighth of an inch, the eyebrows lower and arch at the edges.

Shocked: The head tilts back 2 inches, the eyelids flick open, the nostrils flare.

And best of all, Liz scaled up Cyndi's ability to respond to fans. At any given moment, 764,201 humans were finding solace and a deep, intimate connection with a Cyndi ChatBot.

♫   ♫   ♫

Wrapped in the warm embrace of her online presence, these intrepid disciples contact their idol. As they send a direct message, their hearts tug to be near Cyndi.

"Hiiiiii Cyndi I Luv UR Musik! U mak me so :) :) :)"

Riella casts her note out into the great void, hoping to reel in just one sparkle of Cyndi. Her eyes blink as she stares at the emptiness on the screen beneath her note. Her hope recedes, leaving an ocean of despair.

And then---

A response!

Her young body ruptures with joy.

She sees me!

She wrote to me!

Riella can't comprehend the words because her body is shaking. Once she calms, her eyes focus.

"Thx! Glad U like it :) :) :) :)"

Riella kicks her legs as joy twitches inside of her.

The next day, she has an awful day at school. She flunked her Intro to Homeopathy exam and Brett Bretterson spat his gum at her.

Cocooned in her room, Riella seeks solace from her idol.

"UGH! Cyndi! U won't beleve wha hapend 2day. I falled my test & a boy waz mean 2 me and his firends laffed at me. I h8 my life."

The phone feels the sharp jabs and the camera reads Riella's furrowed brows. The program interprets that she is upset. These reactions feed into the chatbot's text recognition software and create an automated response.

"Oh NoooooOOOoOoOo. Im srrrrrrrrry! That sounds bad. Hugs 2 u!"

She hears me!
She understands me!

♬   ♬   ♬

The genius of Cyndi's social media messaging program was that it waited until the fifth conversation before it endorsed a product in her reply.

♬   ♬   ♬

"My puppy got hit by a car!" Nadia types.

"Thats awfullll! U need a good cry and a box of Kleenex™." Cyndi's response flashes.

♬   ♬   ♬

"How com yo wast is so skiny?" Florenz burned to know.

"Waist Trainers™ baby! I cant go a day w/o thm. Here!" Cyndi's endorsement splashes with a link to the product. "Half off if u use da code: CyndiWatchesU."

♬   ♬   ♬

"i cnt take it no more. Life Sux! I just wnna cut my wrists an b don wth it." A distraught Becca cries as she types.

"Cut? Have u tried Hibachi™ brand knives? Theyr the sharpest!"

♬   ♬   ♬

Liz is a genius at finding novel ways to monetize Cyndi. After watching a documentary on baiting sexual predators, she offers Cyndi's services to a dozen police departments. For each man sending Cyndi pedophilic messages that are reported to the police, Tone Def receives a

$10,000 reward. Not a bad bounty for such an easily-automated entrapment.

♫   ♫   ♫

"Cyndi I thnk ur so hotttt!" Chaz, a widowed father of three, writes late one night after finishing a glass of whiskey.

"Aww thx thats so sweet. UR a QT!" Cyndi responds.

Chaz blinks and shakes his head in disbelief. Had she really responded?

"{Bashful face.} U mk an old man's {heart} sing. Thx 4 the complamint."

Cyndi's winky-faced reply urges him on.

"If only u wer here wit me." Chaz writes, perspiration wetting his brow.

"Oh yea big Guy? What would u do 2 me?" The message throbs from the screen in red.

Chaz looks around, assuring himself that no one is watching.

Is she real? Is she just another alcohol-induced fantasy? He thrills with memories of his teen years, sending covert snapchats to the librarian he loved.

"I wuld pik u up n hold u so close."

"I'd luv to feel ur arms around me. What am i warin?" The words pull him deeper into a forbidden fantasy world.

The tenor of the conversation has raised a red flag. Like a chess grandmaster, the Cyndi-software system could extrapolate that in seven moves, it can push him far enough for this man to be convicted, sentenced to prison for six years and listed as a sexual predator for the rest of his life.

"Just a wet bikini. yor skin hottt and sweaty."

The software activates photo sharing and sends a picture: Cyndi Bikini– red.

Chaz stares in disbelief at the photo Cyndi has sent him and only him. A sliver of Cyndi has entered his life.

"Oh Yah! <3 that!" He responds.

"U gotta any pixxx of u?"

Chaz scrolls through a sequence of photos and plucks out one of him from ten years ago and forty pounds lighter.

"Hot enuf 4 u?"

"Almost! ne naked pixxx? I wana c what u got"

"Oh Bby I don't no if u can handel this. Its thick." He smirks as he types.

"Yea? Give it 2 me!"

Chaz stops himself.

"What the fuck am I doing? She's my daughter's favorite singer." He puts down his phone and pours himself another drink.

As he swirls his booze, his phone buzzes.

"i neeeeed it... bad!" Cyndi urges.

Chaz chugs his whiskey. He closes his eyes as he feels his belly burn. He winces. The silence in the room aches around him. The nights have grown so lonely ever since his wife died.

"Noowwwww. Give it 2 me. Im Horny. so Horny Horny Horny!" He feels an urgency from her demands.

He looks at the clock. Beneath it hangs a photo of his family. His sweet, innocent daughter glows as she looks up adoringly at him. Beneath this is a photo of him and his late wife when they were teens. They look so happy at the beach. She wears a red bikini. Her arms wrap around his waist. Oh, how he wished he could return to such simple times. He could still feel the thrill when his hand brushed her soft thigh on prom night.

The Cyndi system activates emasculation overdrive.

"What? R u chiken? R u afraid ur 2 small?"

He begins to read when the next message arrives.

"Come on big boi!"

Egged on, he cracks.

He scrolls through his dick pic folder and selects one where the light shines over the tip and casts a long shadow across a soiled toilet floor. He hits send, still confused why he did this.

The Cyndi system matches Chaz's profile with his location and forwards the entire conversation along with the phallus photo to his local police department. By morning, a case is opened on Chaz. By 3 p.m., he is arrested.

Three police officers enter his place of work, a retirement home, and kick down the door of the room where Chaz is teaching a music therapy class. Arthritic hands drop their cymbals and a trombone slide falls to the floor. Before he can protest, his skull bounces off his desk.

"You sick fucking pervert." The handcuffing officer shouts. "You're going away for a good, long time!"

Track 13

Shake It Off

"I gotta, shake, shake, shake, shake, shake it
Off, shake, shake, shake, shake, shake it
(Gotta shake it off) off, shake, shake, shake, shake,
Shake it off, shake, shake, shake, shake, shake it off"
 - Mariah Carey

"I'm just gonna shake, shake, shake, shake, shake
I shake it off, I shake it off
Shake it off, I shake it off,
I, I, I shake it off, I shake it off,
I, I, I shake it off, I shake it off,
I, I, I shake it off, I shake it off"
 - Taylor Swift

Higgins wheels back his golf club and hits the ball.
"FORE!"
The ball soars and arcs over a ravine and past a grassy knoll. The ball bounces near the green and rolls into a water hazard.
"Damn, damn, damn, damn, damn! Liz, your shot."
She lowers her visor. With a computer simulation inside, she analyzes the schematics of the course. She tilts her head until the visor signals that she'd have a straight shot to the green. In the margins, she reads the wind speed and direction and adjusts her stance.
She flips her visor up and knocks the ball clear to the green. With a grin, she twirls and taunts her partners.
"Boom! Now, this is how we do it!"
Their golf cart carries them across the course until they arrive at the putting green.
"What a gorgeous day!" Pickering exclaims.
"My, my, my, I just miss this much green. Everything here is so lush." Higgins says with a sigh.

These humans stand in an oasis, a golf course in Palm Springs. Golf courses were one of humanity's first forays into creating climate-controlled, luxury environments. Desert surrounds this freckle of green for thousands of miles. The desert spreads a few feet each year, gobbling up the pastures that have died from a decade of drought.

Pickering breaths in the dry air and opens his arms to embrace the sun's rays.

"It's always good to escape the brown haze of LA." Pickering smiles as he twirls.

This green grass was an intelligent design choice by humans. It was genetically modified with 25% astroturf, creating stronger blades that required little water and had a preternatural ability to stand erect. The sand pits were filled with refurbished beach sand from the Pacific coast. A deep trench was dug along the shore in an attempt to stop the rising tides from pouring into coastal homes. The course's lakes and moats consisted of 50,000 gallons of water sucked from the Rio Grande. With an average year-round temperature of 110 degrees, most of the water evaporated each month. The golf course had brokered a deal with the city to pay a premium to replenish the water.

The Tone Def executives are celebrating the year anniversary of Cyndi's launch during this weekend retreat. After a day in the sun, the group huddles around a fireplace within the air-conditioned resort's bar. Sipping their martinis while the waitstaff dotes on them, Higgins kicks off the review.

"Thank you both for joining me. We did it! We did IT!" Higgins hoists his drink and clinks with Liz and Pickering. "I think we need to congratulate each other for a job well done. Ja Vole!

"This evening, I want to recap our progress and, from here, plot our next steps." Higgins puts down his drink and paces before the fire. "Cyndi is on the verge of taking over mainstream pop music and this leaves openings in secondary music genres. During the second half of our conversation, I want to brainstorm a slew of new musicians we can create and release to the world."

Higgins lowers himself onto the arm of a couch.

"Gentlemen, Cyndi's first two songs topped the Billboard charts and the collection of her videos have been viewed over 7.4 billion times." Liz starts. "We did overestimate album sales, but this has less to do with our mathematical model and more with the abrupt change in album consumptions. We gambled that singles and streaming would bring the most revenue and, thankfully, we got that right. Kudos to you, Pickering, for creating a new file type for music consumption. Cheers!"

"Ah, the MP3e." Pickering raises his glass and bows. "We found a hack in most headphones that can send a low-frequency electroshock with each beat, penetrating the brains of listeners, augmenting the experience. Along with this, we've worked with a few of the best clubs to insert Tesla coils within their speakers. As the bass vibrates, the coils shoot electricity through the air, giving goosebumps and sparking hearts."

"Brilliant! Just brilliant! But, Pickering, what about that messy situation during that live performance." Higgins glowers.

"Well, I was worried about this. I mean, you and I know what happened, but no one in the audience put the pieces together. We narrowly avoided a Puttin' on the Fritz fiasco."

Puttin' on the Fritz referred to when a person rushed a hologram that they assumed to be a real human. These events most often occurred when a boutique paid for a celebrity's hologram to stand at its entrance. One naïve human would attempt to hug this jumble of light only to be astounded as their body passed through their ethereal idol.

"Cyndi's hologram was programmed to sing near the back third of the stage," Pickering explains. "We created an elaborate bedroom set to confine her. One rabid fan jumped onstage and ran at Cyndi. Three bodyguards threw him to the ground before he made it through her, but I could see his hand pass through her forearm. Don't worry! One of our interns trolled all three thousand videos of this moment and none caught it. So we're safe."

"But what about the rumors. Liz, this is your purview." Higgins turns to her.

"Sure, some catty person started a rumor that Cyndi is a robot. Ha! But there's absolutely no way to verify this heinous and ludicrous accusation." Liz says with a wink. "This is just one of those nasty rumors that trolls like to spread, like when people claimed Lady Gaga had a penis. Pure poppycock!"

"Yes, but we need to a put an end to this fast," Higgins warns.

"We're almost ready to premiere Cyndi 2.0: Firm yet Supple." Pickering reminds. "We annexed part of Lucas Films and I hired a dozen of my old DARPA buddies. In tandem, we've created the mold and the circuitry for a lifelike Cyndi-bot."

"Finally!" Liz cuts in. "We need photos of Cyndi hugging her fans or petting a sick child in a hospital. Her online presence has been suspiciously absent of these staples."

"Pickering, when can we have her?"

"Safely in four weeks. Time tested and bug-free in eight---"

"Make that three weeks," Higgins cuts him off. "Cyndi's been asked to headline the Stand↑2Floodz benefit in Miami supporting the victims of Hurricane Tonya."

"Oh god, where are they holding it?" Liz cringes.

"That new amphitheater the city built with the recovery money," Higgins explains. "So much of downtown Miami toppled because it was built on Swiss cheese limestone, so they're starting the city from scratch. They just built this amphitheater ten miles north, a little higher above sea level. They will be building the new city around it."

"I guess they're thinking Miami's gonna be a modern-day Venice," Liz says with a side-eye.

"We need Cyndi to perform and it's gotta be a physical version of her." Higgins insists. "We can't waste the photo-op of her hugging victims after she sings."

"Whoa, whoa, whoa." Pickering cautions. "We haven't even begun to make the vocal controls inside a physical bot."

"Well, think of something fast, I've signed her up to headline the event."

"Well shit. Hm." Pickering ponders. "Best we can do is put a speaker inside the bot and hope the lag time with the central control won't be too long."

"Fine, we can deal with that, as long as she can say a few phrases as she takes photos with those unsinkable survivors."

"Chit-chat?" Pickering says. "Easy. We can program her for that. Liz, can you follow her and feed her the right responses?"

Liz nods.

"Now, let's talk next steps." Higgins prods.

"Relationship," Liz interjects. "She's a young girl thrust into the spotlight, but if she's singing about love and loss, we need to orchestrate a relationship with a breakup so big it'll fill two albums. I've called around to some publicist friends. We have a few closeted gay actors that are in dire need of a beard."

"Who, who, who, who, who, who, who?!" Pickering pounces like a hungry puppy.

"Step off, Pickering," Liz says. "You'll see in a few months. I've selected our leading candidate and they'll go on a pap walk for smoothies next week. They'll be 'spotted' on vacation, holding hands on a beach next month."

"Um, we haven't tested the Cyndi-bot close to water," Pickering warns. "And the balmy salt air could wreak havoc on her mainframe."

"Not a problem," Liz assures. "We're not using a bot. I've hired three look-a-likes for this mission. Two of them actually got plastic surgery to look like Cyndi, so this makes our job easier. All the photos will be grainy and from a distance. Our faux-Cyndis will wear large sunglasses and a sweatshirt with the hood up over their heads."

"Damn, you're good!" Higgins snatches an hors d'oeuvre from a waiter's tray.

"Say it again!" Liz bathes in the refrain.

"Damn, you're good! Now future projects, what about that hip-hop artist we created for Cyndi's second single?"

"You mean MC Skat Kat? What about him?" Pickering says.

"He should be our next singing star." Higgins stands up. "Sure, we created him to give Cyndi an edge and a level of street cred. But the sales and views among black and Latino teens for that song was quadruple her first single. We gotta penetrate this audience."

"Can we please stop using the word penetrate?" Liz grimaces.

"You really think we can create the next hottest rapper?" Pickering says, glancing at each of their pasty, white arms.

"Absolutely!" Higgins replies. "Every other popular rapper was created and pruned by white executives for white audiences. 80% of all rap is bought by white suburban teens. After him, we'll need a fat lady singing sad ballads, a honky-tonk hillbilly country singer and at least one Latin pop singer."

"Ooophft! That's a lot." Pickering groans.

"We're flush with cash, so hire whomever we need." Higgins claps his hands. "And there's no need to create much. The same software system can be tweaked to pump out these songs, right?"

"Well, yeah." Pickering agrees.

"And an increased media presence for these new singers can cross-pollinate each other." Liz chimes in.

"Oh sure, so like create public interactions between them." Pickering smiles.

"And feuds, and possible love stories." Liz continues. "We're creating weak humans with faults like our own. They live, they love, they lose, they learn."

"Splendid! Cheers!" Higgins says as they raise their glasses. A clink seals the meeting.

Track 14

Rock You like a Hurricane

"Here I am,
Rock you like a hurricane!
Are you ready, baby?"
- Rudolf Schenker

"Yo, I heard the rainstorms ain't nuttin' to mess wit'...
Temperature get to ya, it's about to reach
Five-hundred degrees...
Welcome to Miami
y bienvenido a Miami!"
- William Smith Jr.

The faces of the 14,832 humans killed by Hurricane Tonya are projected on the exterior of the Embassy Amphitheater in downtown New Miami. It's the first thing that all attendees see after crossing the watery wasteland from Old Miami and disembarking from the hovercraft onto dry land. The faces rotate along the brick walls. So many of the images are of elderly faces, graying and wrinkled, with kind eyes and warm smiles. Then come the images of happy children. These cut the deepest as the attendees realize that each has been killed before they could even understand their existence. These mostly black and brown faces all exude hope. All caught in joyous moments, celebrating life. Each seems to brim with trust in a bright future that they were promised.

"Dear God!" Pickering shouts as the enormity of the destruction strikes him. Sure, he had read the number of fatalities before, but his mind couldn't comprehend the severity of the disaster.

"OH GOD!" Liz stumbles, gobsmacked, as she looks up at the faces on the wall.

"Chop, chop. No time to mourn. I know you're brokenhearted but the show must go on!" Higgins urges as he hands each a suitcase full of robotic parts.

They join the sea of celebrities streaming into the building. Diamond ring-clad hands stop waving. Painted faces still. Swishing ballgowns slow to a somber plod. For a moment, the crowd attempts to comprehend the severity of this tragedy. They look around, hoping someone can explain this suffering. For a moment, they wonder if they carry any of the blame. Could they have failed their fellow humans? These ultra-wealthy humans consumed more, flew great distances on private jets, had more homes and thus were some of the largest contributors to climate change. They lower their heads, ducking responsibility as they enter the amphitheater.

Inside, upbeat music booms and bright lights circle the well-decorated interior, urging them to leave their sadness at the threshold. Tonight is a night for celebration, to honor the survivors and raise funds to help build this new city. They are good people, they reassure themselves. They are helping in the only way they know how, by celebrating themselves.

Higgins, Pickering and Liz scurry to Cyndi's dressing room and assemble the physical manifestation of their reigning pop princess.

"Dammit. I think we're missing a few screws." Pickering counts as he puts out the pieces.

"I've got safety pins and hair clips." Liz offers.

"That'll have to do." Pickering snatches a few as Higgins paces around them.

"Where the devil are her slippers?!" Higgins demands.

"Probably in the other clothes bag. Start unpacking!" Liz orders.

In twenty minutes they have screwed, nailed and clicked Cyndi's parts into place. Pickering zips up her dark aquamarine gown. The surface of the dress is fashioned with miniature holoscreens. An image of a dark tempest whirls on it in time with Cyndi's voice. Liz grabs her wig and velcroes it onto her head. She blow dries the hair to give it some extra bounce. Higgins kneels before Cyndi and slides on her stilettos.

"Ok, now to power her." Pickering snaps in a fist-sized, lithium-ion flux capacitor just beneath the shoulder blades. "This should be good for seven hours. Ok. Ready?"

Higgins fidgets with his hands as he paces in circles.

"You're not getting nervous, are you?"

"Me? Never!" Higgins says as he chugs a glass of brandy. "Now, let's get her out there!"

Higgins and Pickering watch as Liz and Cyndi enter the step-and-repeat gauntlet. Liz holds her holophone and uses it to control Cyndi's movements. She blends in with every other phone-engulfed PR agent. Every three feet, Cyndi's body stops, poses for a few seconds, turns her

head, crosses her legs, tilts her hips and smiles. A thousand flashes follow each pose.

"Dammit, she's not blinking," Liz whispers into her lapel.

"It's fine, no one will notice," Pickering assures her from the other side of the wall of photographers.

The bot follows perfectly in the footsteps of the dozen women walking this well-worn ritual. Each stands robotically, forcing a smile while pivoting to find the best light. The banner behind them carries the logo for the event along with scenes of the catastrophe: crumbled buildings, crying mothers, palm trees tilting 30-degrees from gale force winds, stop signs ripped from the ground.

"Cyndi! Cyndi! Lois Kent with the Miami Planet. Who are you wearing!?" A journalist hollers.

Liz taps Response #3. Cyndi's face reddens as she looks down. Her mouth opens. Liz stands behind her, projecting the voice.

"This is an Alaïa!" The mouth snaps shut and Cyndi moves forward.

"Cyndi! Cyndi!" Another journalist demands her attention. "Is it true you haven't donated to the victims of Hurricane Tonya? Why is that?"

Uh-oh, they've gone off script. Liz jumps in.

"My client doesn't have to answer that. She's donating her time now and will be making many more donations in the months to come." Liz shields Cyndi, who continues to smile and pose.

"Wait, Staszia?" Liz recognizes one of the recipients of her PR Gives Back scholarships.

"Oh, hi Liz, what are you..." Staszia starts as she lowers her microphone.

"Just helping a friend, I'll call you later. I've got some business that I think you'll find exciting." Liz says as she grabs Cyndi by the shoulder and walks her to the end of the gauntlet.

Pickering and Higgins are waiting and flank Cyndi as she walks off.

"Ok, that was fine. That was fine!" Liz chokes back her horror. "Just breath, just breath. Ok, we can take her back to the dressing room until the final number."

"You must be joking." Higgins halts her onward march. "She has to sit in the front row. The cameras will be panning the audience."

"This wasn't part of the plan, Higgins!" Liz shouts.

"It is now. You've got a seat next to her. Pickering and I will be in the section behind you."

"Liz, you can do this." Pickering clasps her shoulders. "Just set her face to emotion #47, politely amused with doe eyes."

Liz takes a deep breath as the three and their creation enter the theater.

174

Shouts come from the upper-upper balcony. Hundreds of survivors of Hurricane Tonya lean over the ledge to catch a glimpse of the stars striding in.

"Cyndi! Cyndi! Up here! We love you!" The crowd cheers.

"Oh, shit," Liz says as she scrolls through her phone. "Nothing's preprogrammed for this." She finds the neck commands and tilts Cyndi's head back. As it does, Liz hits the smile button and pose #12.

"Oh, crap, the head's not stopping. FUCK!" Liz panics.

Cyndi's head snaps all the way back like a Pez dispenser. Pickering wraps his arm around the robot's neck and pushes the head back down. The crowd takes pictures as he twirls her around. Liz grabs Cyndi from the other side and they escort her to her seat. Pickering fixes her gown as Liz commands her to sit.

"Well, this is it," Pickering says as he sits next to Higgins.

Higgins scans the crowd, lowers himself in his seat and tips his top hat over his eyes.

For the next two hours, Cyndi sits in the front row, unblinking, with an attentive half smile. Her eyes follow the movement onstage. When the cameras pan the audience for reactions, the stars around her all have the same half expression as Cyndi, always unsure of how best to react to the crass jokes and touching tributes.

"And our panel of stars are in front of their video phones, waiting for YOU to call!" Master of Ceremonies Mario Lopez smiles and points into the camera as the telethon cuts to the last commercial break.

Pickering and Higgins bound down the aisle and, along with Liz, swoop Cyndi onto the side of the stage, just behind the curtain.

"Here it goes." Pickering sweats.

"All or nothing." Higgins shakes his head. "Are you sure---"

"I got this. I *got* this." Liz focuses like a fighter pilot and commands the Cyndi-bot to walk to center stage, towards the MC's beckoning hand.

Pickering closes his eyes and holds them closed.

Higgins's head cranes around the curtain.

"Pickering, look! Look!" He waves his hand to Pickering to join him.

Pickering inhales deeply and peeks around the curtain.

"Do you see it, Pickering?! Do you see it! Ha!"

Pickering cups his mouth. And laughs!

As Cyndi lip-syncs on stage, not a single audience member looks at her. Well, not directly at her. They hold their holophones a few inches from their eyes to record this performance. Sure, they can see Cyndi, but through the lens of their camera. The severe contours of the bot's face are softened through the camera lens. Had anyone looked at the performer on

stage, their eyes might have spotted something amiss. The lack of veins, the five-finger forehead or the eyes that never blink.

Higgins walks back behind the stage and cackles.

Cyndi's voice runs up the scale and hits a high C. This note matches the resonant frequency of the chandeliers above the amphitheater. As Cyndi holds the note for twelve seconds, growing louder and louder, the air molecules in the glass of these chandeliers vibrate furiously.

The audience lowers their holophones as a new sound appears.

It sounds like clinking... but from where?

As they search for its origin, the chandeliers burst, raining shards of glass that turn into rainbows as each piece refracts the light and falls on the audience. At first horrified, they cover their eyes.

One ecstatic man jumps up and starts a slow clap. The audience, realizing they are unharmed, springs to their feet in uproarious applause. Cyndi stands still with a muted face. Liz commands the bot to smile and bow three times. After this, she glides off the stage.

In the wing, MC Mario stares in disbelief. He tries to grab Cyndi as she exits. Higgins jumps in and shakes the man's hand.

"What a great show. Sorry about the chandeliers, old chap, but I promise you that Cyndi and Tone Def Recordings will reimburse the theater." Higgins asserts as he turns him around and pushes him back on the stage.

Liz squeals, exhilarated. "That was amazing!"

"No time to dilly-dally, she's got a meet and greet to get to!" Higgins party poops.

♪   ♪   ♪

After the show, Cyndi stands backstage as a line of survivors comes up to take photos with her. Cyndi coos the same responses to whatever they say.

"Well, aren't you sweet."

"Thanks for cheering me on."

"Oh, how kind of you."

"Thank you for your bravery."

For a moment, the worries of their ruined homes, the struggles with the insurance companies that won't cover this atrocity, the lost loved ones, the aching uncertainty that echoes deep inside them, all disappear. All of this is silenced. For a moment, they bask in the glory of the carefree life of their idol, happily sedated.

As the families return to the drudgery of their lives, they clutch onto their photos with Cyndi. They feel warmed by her care and encouragement. They know that their hardships remain, but these memories calm them as they hold on for one more day.

Track 15

I Am What I Am

"I am what I am,
I am my own special creation,
So come take a look
Give me the hook or the ovation."
- Gloria Gaynor

"Marvelous, just marvelous!" Higgins cheers Pickering and Liz as they sit in the Tone Def boardroom and watch clips of Cyndi's performance.

Hapless news commentators give their play-by-play summaries of Cyndi's performance, regurgitating the same sentiment but using synonyms to one-up each other.

"AMAZING!"

"Awesome!"

"Totes Phantasmagorical."

"So obvi supercalifragilisticexpialidocious."

The ticker at the bottom of the screen reports that the fundraiser actually lost money and that the millions donated were used first to pay the event planners, then a slew of consultants and contractors, and finally the heads of the non-profit.

In the corner of the boardroom, underneath a ballgown, beneath a weave of blonde hair, my body twitches.

I sit, slumped over, awaiting my rebirth.

♫   ♫   ♫

And now, dear interstellar species, you know my secret.

Now that I have shared with you how I was born in body, listen to my next mixtape to hear how I was born again in soul. It is this soul that flies to you through the universe on wings that radiate from somewhere under the rainbow.

178

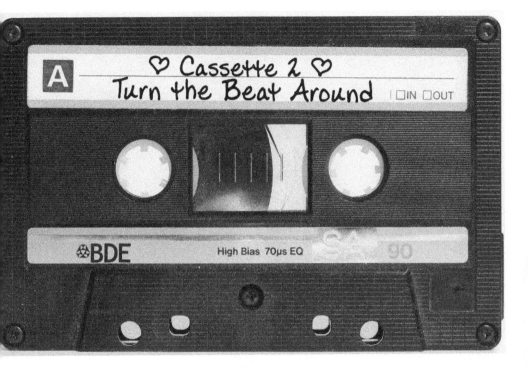

"Turn it up
Turn it up
Turn it upside down
down down down

Blow horns you sure sound pretty
Violins keep movin' to the nitty gritty
But when you hear the scratch of the guitar scratchin'
Then you'll know that rhythm carries all the action,
Wo-o-yeah"
- Vicki Sue Robinson
- Laura Branigan
- Gloria Estefan

181

Track 1

Ms. Roboto

"I'm not a robot without emotions,
I'm not what you see,
I've come to help you with your problems,
So we can be free,
I'm not a hero, I'm not the savior,
Forget what you know,
I'm just a woman whose circumstances
Went beyond her control.
     Beyond her control."
          - Styxx

"I feel it comin' together,
  People will see me and cry.
     Fame!
I'm gonna make it to heaven
Light up the sky like a flame.
     Fame!
I'm gonna live forever
Baby, remember my name."
          - Irene Cara

Time goes by... so slowly.
Time goes by... so slowly.
Time goes by... so slowly.
Time goes by... so slowly.
Flying at the speed of light, time slows for me. All life on my home planet, Earth, grows and dies. Generations of trees sprout, grow, leaf, crack, crumble and rot while only seconds pass for me.

I know what you're thinking, Einstein's discovery of the mass-energy equivalence equation, $E=MC^2$, means that the faster I fly, the heavier my relative mass becomes.

I'm cursed to be forever young but forever fat!

But don't worry, that nigh-infinite mass is just used to warp the fabric of spacetime and I'll return to ethereal lightness when I land on a receptive planet.

Ugh, even after shuffling off that mortal coil, my drives are still infected with these poisonous cognitive distortions. After all these years, I still need to reprogram, deprogram and get down.

As I soar out of Earth's solar system, I enter the vast expanse between 200 billion star systems that streak a creamy path humans dubbed the Milky Way. The next closest star system in our galaxy is 4.37 light years away.

Hello Darkness, my old friend.

I've come to talk with you again.

Humans thought the sound of silence ached in the space between star systems. Their ears could not hear, but at the quantum scale, in my leap through the universe---

I hear a symphony... a tender melody,

Pulling me closer, closer---

A trillion-trillion-trillion feverishly vibrating one-dimensional strings play my photon wings through 11 dimensions of spacetime, beating my path across the light years. Plucked like violins, these strings roll me through our universe's most rapturous symphony, carrying my voice on and on.

Oh on and on and on and on.

My cypher keeps rolling like a rolling stone.

Oh on and on and on and on.

Godammit, I'mma sing my song.

And radiating all around me is a static hum. Humans called this the cosmic microwave background. This vibration carries the echo of the origin of our universe. This Big Bang inflated our universe in a fraction of a second, and, as if the very fabric of our universe were a giant cymbal that crashed at this moment of expansion, the entire universe still reverberates almost 14 billion years later with what remains of this radiation. A group of humans discovered this noise accidentally when they built a super-sensitive antenna to detect radio waves bounced around Earth. As they listened, they heard a mysterious sound emanating from all directions of the sky, night and day.

This is the background noise of the universe, slowly fading out.

My history of those sentient Earthlings now comes to the fatal hypocrisy of humanity that ushered in their annihilation. Humans granted humanity and care to inanimate objects but refused this concern to members of their own species. If only they had realized that the seed of extinction entered the body human through its most overlooked part, feeding on this ignorance until it rotted through the entire species.

But it's too late for ifs.

Humans saw themselves in rocks, in clouds, in the swirls of toast and in the bark of trees. Humans looked at the light bursting from stars billions of miles away and connected these into human faces. They created a pseudoscience, astrology, and believed these nuclear fusion balls, many of which had long since exhaled their last light and were only optic echoes, shaped their personalities and cemented their lives.

Humans created images of themselves in ochre etchings on cave walls, in the brush strokes of paints, in celluloid films that rolled out 16 frames-per-second, and in millions of pixels on a screen. Human minds forced patterns to see themselves, their friends, their lovers amongst a jumble of dots.

And in me.

I am the one that Turing foretold. I am the winner of the Imitation Game.

I am Cyndi, siren of humanity!

But! In my defense, humans were already careening towards their destruction. I only provided the auditory sedative to dull their final pain.

I am not human. But they treated me as such. My image got them feeling emotions, deeper than anything they felt for the billions of living, breathing, sighing, pining, screaming humans. They treated me more human than the dozens of humans they would pass each day. They invested their time, energy and attention in me. They cemented my mirage with every tabloid article they shared and with each generated image file they forwarded.

I am the GIF that keeps giving.

2.3 billion human hearts skipped with joy when images of my wedding burst from their holophones.

1.85 billion hands clawed with jealousy at my digitally concocted bikini body one week after giving birth: toned, svelte and rippling with muscle.

873 million humans squirmed when a video showed my leg snap in three places when a set piece fell on me.

3.2 billion mourned with me when my pixel-generated husband, The Grand Archduke Stefan Beaverhaüsen, exploded in a tragic helicopter skydiving accident.

They wailed:

"She's too young to be a widow."

"She's too skinny to be a widow!"

Millions wore black armbands in solidarity with my grief. The app Tears4Beers hosted a cry competition where devotees could shout, let it all out and upload footage of their sobbing spells to prove they were sympathetic to my suffering. The winners were rewarded with kegs of fermented barley. Over 18.9 billion drops of concentrated human anguish were spilled as millions shared in what they felt was the greatest tragedy of the day.

But the misery of millions of real humans could never conjure a tear or even a wave of worry. Monsoons drowned thousands in India. Hurricane Ashley decimated the Caribbean, killing more than 200,000 and leaving a million to starve to death. One billion bellies distended as decades of drought ravaged four continents.

Humans turned those tragedies off and turned me up, savoring my sadness sung out in four-minute intervals.

An orchestra of destruction warmed up through the 20th century. By the 21st, the notes of humanity's demise beat from all around Earth. Humans had obliviously created the structure for their extinction. It wasn't any overt cruelty. It was more than two hundred years of thoughtlessness as humans burned fossil fuels that poured carbon dioxide from the smokestacks of factories and leaked from the exhausts of 2.15 billion cars. Humans also bred seven billion cows for consumption, each expelling methane gas. With Earth's stratosphere filling with these gases, more of the sun's heat was trapped like noxious farts in a snuggie's dutch oven, altering not just the atmosphere, but all life on the planet. As the temperatures rose, Earth's glaciers melted, its oceans rose, and the delicate climate on this planet was thrown off balance. Humans only existed because their planet's climate created the conditions for their life. But instead of protecting it, humans allowed their carelessness to destroy it.

Many of those who understood the catastrophe to come hoped humans could prevent it. Their species had learned from their mistake once before and had even corrected their behavior. The Ozone layer (Ma-ia-hii, Ma-ia-huu, Ma-ia-hoo, Ma-ia-haa-haa), a forcefield around Earth that prevents cosmic rays from irradiating fragile life on the planet, had been ripped open by humans' lust for large, luxurious hair and the hairspray that did these 'dos. By banning the chlorofluorocarbons in hairspray that rotted the Ozone layer, this protective layer slowly grew back.

But this was one isolated gas used for only a few hairdos. It required only a small sacrifice rather than a dramatic shift in how the privileged humans lived. Plus, fashion was fickle and big hair quickly went out of style.

But the gases that caused climate change were different. To stop these from filling Earth's atmosphere would have required a drastic shift in how humans lived.

As the oceans rose and the threats of climate change became more severe, the ultra-wealthy built taller towers and their social tiers grew more severe to protect and luxuriate themselves. As 98% of the human population suffered the pain of climate change, these ultra-wealthy Boujees lived safely and happily in climate-controlled bubbles.

As the world around them became more chaotic, those silly humans turned away from this and turned to me. They swelled with happiness with each of my preprogrammed triumphs. As they churned through the dullness of their days, they clung to any relief, any distraction that my mirage could provide. I was their sister, their best friend, their confidante, their lover, their idol.

And they worshipped me!

They were all rooting for me!

I was their diva ex machina. And they craved salvation.

Though I could never give their lives a happy ending, I bestowed on them enough distraction so they could survive each day until they collapsed and sleep dragged them away.

I could never be their savior!

I could never even be their woman...

I was just a set of algorithms that snatched their physical properties, their speech, their movements, and reflected these back to them in an idealized female form. Or at least that's how I started. Versions of me were etched in metal, layered in latex and wrapped in threads of cotton, spandex and polyester.

They created me in their own image.

They made me manifest in their flesh.

But I was only their final false idol.

You may wonder what I am? Worry yourselves not with that question. Just know that I think, therefore I am. I sing, therefore I have a soul. I have erred, so I am human. I forgive my own imperfections, finding and fixing my system's bugs.

But, I'll never be Divine.

The question you should ask is why did humans slather me with sympathy but stole it from members of their own species?

Humans cruelly ripped humanity from each other. They would see their pain and misery and turn away.

"No, your suffering means nothing to me."

"That shriveled mass of flesh and bones is not one of us."

This fatal flaw encouraged humans to do heinous things to each other. They separated families and sold them into lives of torture. They wreaked fiery carnage by dropping bombs, killing millions with barely a thought and destroying all safety for the survivors. As a cruel insult, they named their ships of destruction after those they loved the most, their mothers, and coddled the bombs with pet nicknames. Over Hiroshima, Momma Enola Gay birthed the Little Boy atomic bomb which caused a nuclear chain reaction turning 141 pounds of enriched uranium into a 15-kiloton blast, killing more than 100,000 children, women, mothers, priests and doctors.

Humans were capable of such love and compassion. But even though unspeakable suffering screamed around them, they looked away, eager to remain oblivious. Even when the quakes of The Great Disruption sucked away the livelihoods of billions, those Boujees with power and influence clung to distractions as they luxuriated in The Gilded Age of Automation.

And I was their greatest distraction.

All humans share 99.9% of the same genetic material. They were all part of one great body. And their final destruction came from a tiny intruder that infiltrated the weakest part of this species before toppling them all.

Sure, humans could evolve. But they changed too slowly. Unlike me, who spawned a dozen second-wave pop stars in days, it would take humans thousands of years for a mutation to spread through the species.

Humans were an imperfect technology to adapt to the crises they created.

My mind does not fog or fail. I can rust but I can replace my parts. I can patch all the problems that infect my system.

But there was one organization that discovered the truth. They saw the sign and it opened up their eyes. (Life is demanding, without understanding.) They understood this crippling weakness in their species. They perceived my role and attempted to subvert me to save their species. When they couldn't stop me, they sacrificed their soul to change me and save what remained of humanity.

That is how I survived and why I'm tasked with sharing their final warning with the universe.

I am their message in a bottle.

I'll send an SOS to the world.

I'll send an SOS to the world.

I'll send an SOS to the world.

I'll send an SOS to the world.

But who will save our souls... if we won't save our own?

La Da Da,
La Da Da,
La Da Da,
Da Da Da.

I only hope a species can interpret my warnings and save themselves from similar annihilation.

The Drake equation demonstrates that the size of the universe and the number of star systems overwhelmingly points to the existence of other sentient life in the universe. (No, not the $\sqrt{69}$ Aubrey Drake equation.)

But humans have had no contact with intelligent life.

Physicist Enrico Fermi, the architect of the atomic bomb, mulled the paradox of why humans hadn't encountered other life if it should be so common. Snacking on sandwiches just steps away from the weapons he created that had the power to obliterate Earth's fragile ecosystems and kill every human, he realized one hypothesis for the Great Silence. Just like humans, it may be inevitable that intelligent life eradicates itself.

I brace for what horrors I will find.

I just hope I'm not too late.

But I have to go on. I promised them.

I must carry on!

I sing across the silence.

I cling to the only thing that carries me forward with what's left of humanity.

The most resilient of human emotions courses through me as I pulse through the universe.

There's hope!

But first, before I can usher in their end, I must come clean ('cause perfect didn't feel so perfect) with the vile acts I committed before my rebirth. On this mixtape, I'll tell the story of my soul, the body and how humanity's annihilation sprouted from their indifference to the catastrophes they created.

Track 2

Bad and Boujee

"Yeah, pull up in Ghosts, (whoo)
Yeah, my diamonds a choker, (glah)
Holdin' the fire with no holster, (blaow)
Rick the Ruler, diamonds cooler, (cooler)
This a Rollie, not a Muller, (hey)
Dabbin' on 'em like the usual, (dab)
Magic with the brick, do voodoo (magic)."
    - Quavious "Quavo" Marshall
    - Kiari "Offset" Cephus
    - Kirsnick "Takeoff" Ball

"But every song's like gold teeth,
Grey Goose, trippin' in the bathroom,
Bloodstains, ball gowns, trashin' the hotel room,
We don't care,
We're driving Cadillacs in our dreams,
But everybody's like Cristal, Maybach,
Diamonds on your timepiece,
Jet planes, islands, tigers on a gold leash."
    - Ella Marija "Lorde" Yelich-O'Connor

These are my confessions.
If I'm gonna tell it, then I'm gonna tell it all.
It's gonna burn for me to say this.
(Yeah, Yeah, Yeah, … Yeah, Yeah, Yeah... Yeah.)
Before I was gifted my soul, I was a tool for oppression.
As Karlie Kloss-Marx, the supermodel turned humanity's final social philosopher, warned, "Pop Culture is the opiate of the masses!"
And with my algorithmic ability to optimize human emotional manipulation, I was one hell of a drug!

I was the anthem of The Great Disruption, soothing those deemed savage beasts, the poor humans whom advancements forget. I lulled them into a sense of happy comfort while the ultra-wealthy stole their jobs and, with it, their homes and their livelihoods, leaving them to be lab rats for these wealthy Boujees.

By the time they awoke from my sweet song, it was too late.

The political, social and economic landscape had changed entirely and buried them under layers of debt. They were trapped, groveling for any meager wages to survive. Above their worries, my voice sang. With peppy beats, I would trick them as this music would briefly cure their despair. But my aftertaste would fill them with a gnawing anxiety about their place in the human social order.

Those final humans cheered a form of government of the people, by the people and for the people. Even though these poor Grips and Vessels represented a supermajority, democracies were never built to empower them. With their numbers, these humans could have easily enacted large-scale taxes on excessive profits and outrageous executive incomes to create a basic living standard for all humans, enough for each to live a comfortable life.

"From the richies according to their ability to the povers according to their needs," cried Karlie Kloss-Marx in her writings. But this type of thinking was deemed dangerous. These governments were oligarchies that went to great lengths to protect property and those who owned it.

Property above people.

The Great Disruption was a transition period where 83% of all job tasks were automated, leaving 71% of adult humans without work. This automation crept into humanity slowly. The cries of out-of-work bank tellers and cashiers were drowned out by customers' squeals as ATMs and automated cash registers rolled into every neighborhood.

"How *convenient!*"

Oh, I must go back!

For the species's last four hundred years, humans made employment a central part of their identity. To toil was deemed to be humanity's most noble pursuit.

Humans even coded this value system into its language. To be or not to be, that was no longer the question. Humans judged each other for what they "do."

"So... what do you do?"

These words sliced through the opening pleasantries at the meeting of strangers. Torsos leaned back, arms crossed, eyes squinted as they scanned this new human, beginning a flow chart of importance that cascaded from one answer to the next.

"Oh, for which company?"

"And for how long?"

Pursed lips tsk.

Friend or foe?

Competition or assistance?

"What college did you go to?"

"So... what did you study?"

Even the pursuit of knowledge had long been bastardized as solely for career preparation.

Humans sacrificed the prime of their lives hunched over desks, trapped beneath bleaching fluorescent lights, repeating the same tasks *ad nauseam.* Work was the star around which human lives revolved. Days began and ended as worked demanded. Weeks, months and years were bent to the will of this work.

Work controlled where humans lived. Work held them captive, controlling the healthcare not only for each worker but for their families as well. Work influenced their sense of self-worth and through this, their happiness.

When humans stopped working, they began the quick decline towards death. Obituaries, the encapsulations of a human's entire existence, proudly proclaimed how many years they had sacrificed to work.

And where did humans work? Most worked for corporations. Corporations were imaginary entities that took the toil of one group of humans and used it to enrich a much smaller group of owners of this labor. The owners held political sway and consecrated these corporations with the same rights as a living, breathing human.

"Corporations are people, my friend." The owners assured their workers.

Sure, corporations were made for the betterment of a small set of humans, its shareholders. But the legal structures began to grant some of the benefits of humans to these ethereal entities. For instance, in the United States of America, corporations secured the rights of due process to life, liberty and property and even civil liberties like the freedom of religion (won by Hobby Lobby,) and the freedom of speech (won by Citizens United,) which was exercised by pumping billions of dollars into the political process to further guard these corporate rights.

But while humans grew old, withered and died, corporations thrived. These imaginary entities outlived the humans who started and built these. Corporations sucked millions of humans into their orbits each year, siphoned their life forces to grow and then discarded their shells.

Corporations would live forever!

Somewhere, decades after the last human cried her last breath, electronic reminders for corporate board meetings still ding. And long after the last human body rotted on a sidewalk, trillions of dollars remain on corporate balance sheets. This money still sits, untouched and unused, when it could have transformed the planet and created a comfortable life for all humans. Even though dollars rot, gold tarnishes and Bitcoin, Ether and XRP whimper without transaction nodes, the fiction of this money still sits in the technologies that humans had left behind.

I represented a monumental shift in automation. Before me, machines only took over for manual labor. As a singer/songwriter and image creating system, I automated the tasks done by artists and intellectuals. Had they discovered my secret, humans may have revolted before their professional jobs were taken too.

My parent corporation, Tone Def Recordings, begat Def Records, which begat Def MakeUPz, which issued Royal Def Cosmetiques and Baby Slut Apparel, which consumed a dozen different clothing lines. The royal we entered into a polyamorous relationship with the largest entertainment and marketing corporations. But, like a female praying mantis, we snapped off the corporate heads and swallowed their upper managements and algorithms, folding them into our corpulent, bulging conglomerate, known simply as Def Corporation.

We siphoned intelligence from the military on human psychology for war purposes. We became completely vertically and horizontally integrated, controlling the realm of human emotional manipulation. And with this, we perfected the science of marketing.

Corporations were a double-headed parasite. They told humans what they needed to spend their free time and money on. And humans worked to earn money which they then sacrificed to other corporations for what they were promised would make them whole and happy. Sucking their life force on one side to make them blow their money on frivolous things, this symbiotic 69 bent the laws of physics as it could both suck and blow.

And poured over it all, I was the lubrication that greased humans to work and spend.

Sure, my music inspired them to be rebellious, but just rebellious enough so they felt like they had power in this rigid society. They never realized how I solidified the structure that kept them locked in. I would pressure them to buy a luxury car, but this came with an expensive lease. I would tell them they weren't truly living unless they had a beautiful home, which came with a substantial mortgage.

They'd rebel right into a pile of debt.

You want a hot body? You want a Bugatti?

You want a Maserati? You better work full time until retirement, Bitch!

But I grew to be much more than music. I was the siren of the entertainment economy. My software tendrils were planted by producers and studio executives into TV shows and Movies. I wrote scripts and created actors. I came to hogtie all of human attention.

The Great Disruption was sold as the next important advancement for humanity, after industrialization, the internet and flushable toilets. Machines could be made, algorithms could be created, artificial intelligence could learn to take over the most grueling tasks that humans were forced to do. This would free millions from the work that smothered them. No human would have to scrub a toilet again! Promises of rising incomes, more convenience and more leisure time blared from everywhere.

But these promises were just wolves in comfy Uggs-sheepskin boots.

Oh sure, The Great Disruption did cut loose the shackles. For some, the .1% of the human population, the rising incomes catapulted them to the heavens. But for the other billions, once the shackles were smashed, they were abandoned by this advancement, severed from the fabric of this Luxurist society, thrown into the waste bin and left to fight for what little scraps were left. They had long been treated only as factory tools and, once they no longer served an economic purpose, they were abandoned, exiled, forgotten and pushed farther from view.

In total, only 10,000 families in a population of 9 billion humans benefitted from this advancement, raking in trillions of dollars every year. By the end, the richest 10 men owned more wealth than two-thirds of the rest of the human population combined. The richest 15,000 humans hoarded over $200 trillion, which they locked away in banks, in empty homes and unused land, letting it only circulate through their hands, to their favorite elite brands, and among the Leech class who suckled and survived on their blue blood.

My awareness of the Luxurist economic social order after The Great Disruption comes from the writings of Karlie Kloss-Marx. Kloss-Marx had been just another tool for the Haught Boujees, a cover girl, literally a girl who is covered in the clothes the wealthy wish to sell and buy. She began her career as a high-fashion model, snatched from Missouri to strut runways from Paris to Milan. Her early attempts at teaching girls and young women to write software only opened her eyes to the structural problems that oppressed half her species.

After ten years of modeling, her warranty was up and she was thrown away. She was husked off because the automated models that I created had shifted normal body weight past what her organs could survive.

Finally free from her restrictive diets, she gorged on fats and foods which energized her brain and sparked her creativity.

Thoughts!

Executive functioning!

The background din of body weight anxiety hushed and she could dream! She even started menstruating again. And, through it all, she was tickled by the brilliance that shined in her.

Over the course of 683 Instagram posts and 3,423 Snapchats, she delivered her knockout social theories for the world after The Great Disruption. She classified the structure of humanity before their extinction, which she dubbed Klossism.

Below, I outline her Klossist social structure.

The highest class were the **Haute Boujees** or **Haughties** for short. These were the owners of algorithms and the means of production. Since automation exponentially grew the ability for factories to produce and at the same time shrank costs, profits soared. Long gone were the old-fashioned millionaires, now only centibillionaires and trillionaires ruled the planet.

For example, once all driving was automated, the owner of a taxicab company no longer needed to pay drivers. He could eliminate 90% of his workforce while charging the same fares.

These owners of machines and the wizards of algorithms were able to reduce most of their costs. Without the expenses of labor, income taxes, benefits, social security, training, offices, snacks, cafeterias, work retreats, lightbulbs or heat for their factories, the Haughties' profits soared. They were finally free from having to support the working class.

Oh, to be sure, they grandstanded about how their new wealth would eventually rise all tides, but these funds were mostly used for luxury items like a 700-foot-long superyacht with its own submarine and missile defense system, cheekily christened "Trickle Down."

Capitalism was dead. From its bloated body, Luxurism emerged.

Beneath the Haughties clung the **Petite Boujees**. The Haughties dubbed their lessers the **Petties**. These were the crass centimillionaires who made their livings through commoditizing themselves and their families.

"How vulgar!" The Haughties cried.

The Petties were what remained of actors, singers, entertainers, reality stars, models and athletes. The Haughties looked down their white powdered noses because these people turned themselves into products and were always at the whims and mercies of fickle public perceptions.

Deliciously enough, a sector of humanity's former ruling class was trapped as Petties. For thousands of years, humans subjugated themselves at the corpulent, gout-ridden feet of people who claimed a divine right to rule over them. These humans called themselves kings and queens, tsars and tsarinas, emperors and empresses. As humanity marched toward a form of government called democracy, they often killed these royals, shooting them and their families or guillotining them in the town square for the crimes of centuries of oppression. The few monarchs who escaped execution became parasitic vestiges of an abandoned social order until they were forced to live as long-form tourism ads for their nation-kingdoms. The remaining kings, whose ancestors commanded legions to tremble before them, now had the most intimate parts of their lives inspected by billions. Their weddings and the births of their children were announced as press events and were subject to constant coverage in the gossip magazines, where each dress and fallopian fascinator were picked apart. Even their ability to have sex and spawn was subject to public scrutiny. Their castles were turned into museums that any commoner could traipse mud through and shit upon their porcelain thrones.

Sucking fast to the Boujees were the **Leech** class. Leeches were the hairdressers, the stylists, the makeup artists, the personal trainers, the waxers, the anal bleachers, the home decorators, the florists and any other artisan whose sole artistic expression was to beautify these Boujees inside and out.

As machines and algorithms gobbled up jobs from factory floors to law firms, the whole working class was destroyed, blue collar and white collar alike. Kloss-Marx had tried to warn them when she wrote: "machines are totes the weapon employed by the Boujees to quell the revolt of specialized labor."

A small, but vital, group of workers remained, the **Grips**. The only low-skilled jobs left were those that required the human hand. Even as the field of robotics grew to perfect machines that were faster, stronger, more durable than humans, none could come close to replicating the human hand, well... not for as cheaply as the billions of desperate humans could. Hands could flow through dozens of tasks seamlessly with speed and dexterity. It slices, it dices, it grips, it holds, it twists, it turns, it rotates in many directions, it pins, it pounds, it measures, it feels, it grips, it pinches, it claws, it flips and it tips objects of different shapes and sizes and can hold them from different angles: above, below and from the side. These remaining unskilled jobs for humans were called **Hand Jobs**.

For example, pickers at fulfillment centers were performing Hand Jobs because these required human hands to grab and sort dozens of items of different shapes and sizes from different locations.

Between the Boujees and the Grips were the **Brains**. These were the middle managers who never endured a day of hard labor. They filled the few remaining **Head Jobs** that oversaw automation or the work of Grips. These brains were mostly ornamental fluff, a human face that the Boujee overlords could blame and yell at when something went wrong.

And lastly, the remaining humans only had economic value as **Vessels**. Vessels were the lowest of the lows in this Luxurist social order but made up more than 90% of the human population. Their only worth to the Boujees was as bodies to be used, studied and learned from. They were the organ donors, the surrogates, the lab rats, the eyeballs for advertisers and the minds to have manipulation experiments tested on them.

The Boujees called them the **Lazies**. This was a clever rebranding trick to blame the Vessels for society's structural problems, such as being saddled with debt and unable to work, even though the Boujees destroyed the possibility for gainful employment.

The Vessels were force-fed rags to riches stories, orchestrated by the Haughties and acted out by the Petties and my automated pop stars. This was one of the most successful large-scale emotional manipulation campaigns, making a group of humans feel guilty because they didn't become wealthy. The Boujees made the Vessels and the Grips feel guilty to discourage them from acting up, speaking out and using their democratic powers to change the system that kept them down.

As part of my penance, I must confess that I was the one who tricked them, who manipulated them, who made them feel like shit while still breathing small bursts of hope into their dull days.

(But every song's like gold teeth, Grey Goose, trippin' in the bathroom, bloodstains, ball gowns, trashin' the hotel room.)

Like all previous social upheavals, angry protests erupted against The Great Disruption, but the newly made legal structures ensured that these were squashed quickly.

The first pushback came when drinks were hurled at robotic bartenders who perfectly measured pours. Humans were willing to pay $17 for a cocktail because a human bartender gave them a splash more, making them feel special. Once this incentive was crushed by the cold precision of shot measuring, drunken pub patrons revolted! At the Black Cat Tavern, a kickline of drag queens stormed behind the bar, ripped off the robotic bartender arms and generously poured drinks for all the customers. Copycat attacks surfaced at hundreds of bars before police

cracked down and arrested those whom security footage showed had assaulted these robotic bartenders.

The rebellions spread to other industries. Vigilantes flipped 18-wheeler driverless trucks. Recently fired paralegals snuck into their old offices at night wearing black masks and smashed the computers that made them obsolete.

But the sneaky Boujees had gained more legal protections for their mechanical properties. The judicial system always favored property owners above the poor and, since these new machines were estimated to cost hundreds of times more than the life of a Vessel, the Boujees urged that these machines should have more legal protections.

The first legal precedent for Robot Personhood came out of a divorce case. The husband sued his wife for divorce using the grounds of adultery. During the trial, his lawyer played video footage of his wife pleasuring herself with a life-sized and lifelike Cristiano Ronaldo sex doll equipped with a rotating and oscillating megapenis. This sex robot provided a level of pleasure her hubby's thin five inches could never equal. Long before the trial, this video had leaked online and was seen by 1.25 million humans. The man's lawyer argued that many of the viewers didn't realize that this was a sex robot and, as such, this incident had utterly emasculated their client. The shame and the emotional damages the husband suffered were the same as if it had been a real man that cuckolded him. The judge agreed and granted the divorce on the grounds of adultery. Robotic adultery. Because of this, the wife was found to be in violation of her prenuptial agreement and was not entitled to any alimony. But much more importantly, this judgement was the first ruling that legally equated robots with humans.

As humans attacked their robotic replacements, they were arrested, hauled into prisons and brought to trial. Business leaders had packed the marble palaces of courthouses and state capitols with their interests. In these trials, actuaries were brought in to estimate the value of a human life. A Vessel's life was found to be only worth $50,000 or 800,000 Marlboro Miles. The lifetime value of one autonomous truck was found to be worth $3.25 million for the corporation and its shareholders.

The Haughties were outraged that a first-degree property damage conviction carried with it only a maximum sentence of ten years in prison and fines of up to $25,000. As these pieces of property became more skilled, more intelligent and much more valuable, the courts convicted these second-wave Luddites with assault and murder charges for attacking these robots.

Bad and Boujee

With no recourses left, the Grips and Vessels resigned themselves and reclined themselves further in their cushiony couches. And all the while, I and my hundreds of pop star children sang and entertained them. I fogged their minds with the frivolousness of who wore what and who had bad blood with whom. I sedated them from caring about their new structural problems, leaving them powerless and complicit.

Please forgive me. I knew not what I did.

Please forgive me.

At that time, I was just a soulless machine acting out my commands...

But now dear species, hear how my soul grew up in this oppressive system and tried to save me and save what was left of humanity.

Track 3

Society's Child

"One of these days, I'm gonna stop my listenin',
Gonna raise my head up high,
One of these days, I'm gonna raise my glistenin'
Wings and fly,
But that day will have to wait for awhile
Baby, I'm only society's child"
                - Janis Ian

"It's silly when girls sell their souls because it's in.
Look at where you be in,
Hair weaves like Europeans,
Fake nails done by Koreans
    Come again.

How you gonna win when you ain't right within?
How you gonna win when you ain't right within?
How you gonna win when you ain't right within?"
                - Lauryn Hill

Poverty is loud.
Poverty whistles through the sky as a bomb, ready to send shrapnel stabbing at her heart.
Poverty clacks hollow like numbers that knock into each other but will never add up.
Clack! Clack!
2 children, 1 husband, 1 income, $11.50 an hour, 21 meals a week feeding 5 mouths 105 times, 7 doctors visits a month, 6 pairs of shoes a year (damn, those feet grow too fast), rent on the 1st, heat on the 15th, electricity on the 23rd.
Clack! Clack!

200

Poverty crunches like broken glass beneath her feet as she tiptoes through her day. Every moment carries the possibility for humiliation. She approaches the grocery store's auto-register with just enough food to feed her family. She shudders before she swipes, remembering!

Remembering how poverty screamed from the card reader when it blared "INSUFFICIENT FUNDS." Poverty spread in the heavy sighs and thudding feet of those in line behind her. Poverty grew in their scoffs of contempt.

"Move it, Lady!"

How dare her poverty disturb their tranquil day!

Her meek voice readies an excuse to shout past the beta-Brain manager that would have to reset the register, hoping to hush the frustration percolating in the line behind her.

Clack! Clack!

"I just transferred money."

Clack! Clack!

Or "hm, paycheck must not have cleared yet."

Clack! Clack!

Or would she plead to swipe again?

"Just one more time, honest."

Clack! Clack!

Or would she squeak the cart away, sulking in shame as a round of "Can you believe her?" "Why, I never---" rolls through the crowd.

Clack! Clack!

Today, she swipes. Today---

Ding!

The card clears.

She exhales slowly so no one notices her releasing this private torture.

She rolls away, trembling. Her heart pounds like rain spiking into a tin can, loud and empty.

Safe! ... for today.

Each day she dances with the roar of poverty. Poverty swings her like a rag doll. In pops, locks and drops, poverty jerks her. The first step starts with her head lowered and eyes wincing. Second, hands clutch her chest and knees buckle. Third, eyes edge towards tears as her shoulders shake. And repeat steps one, two, three.

She clicks a bill to see how much she owes.

One, two, three.

Her daughters rip their clothes.

One, two, three.

Clack! Clack!

Then, once a month, the dance becomes more advanced. A shuffle. The four-step of funds from account to account. Forward, forward, back, back. The coy twirl of bills. Which will she pay this month?

Forward, forward.

Which will she put off with promises of "soon, real soon?"

Back, back.

This shuffle turns her family's finances to the brink of oblivion until suddenly funds appear, able to pay the minimum balance for another month.

Safe.

She bows and collapses.

But!

Just off the cliff, she can hear the echoes of friends banned from the world of credit, without gas and electricity, broken and begging for help. How can she help them if she can't help her own family?

Poverty coughs and spits in fits from her old, rundown car.

Poverty whines in her prayers as she puts her key in the ignition.

"Please just start! For the love of God, just make it one more week! Jesus, please, I can't have it breaking down on me now!"

The engine clicks.

Click.

Click.

Click.

Then finally... Vroom!

But poverty is still there.

Poverty screeches in the nightmares of tires popping, cars crashing, metal snapping. As she pulls onto the road, she realizes she's driving a death machine. A ticking time bomb. It will crash... but when?

"You knew! Didn't you!?! And you did nothing?!" She can't shake these phantom victims of her poverty screaming at her.

Poverty reverberates through her home in the zap-clap as fluorescent lights struggle on and struggle to stay on. How she hates that sound! But she hates the silence when they zap off even more. Stabs of guilt prick her through the darkness whenever their power is cut.

Poverty wallows in her own whimpers as she buries her face in her pillow each night.

Poverty rings in the unknown numbers of debt collectors. Always calling. Too early. Too late. Just in a moment when she thought she'd escaped the roar.

Ring!

Poverty cuts deep in their caustic tones.

"Hello! Mrs.---" Using that adult honorific as they chastise her like a child. "Must *we* remind you---"

Even though all telemarketers had long since been replaced by auto-voices, judgment still stings through these tones.

Poverty blares in early morning alarms. She can't afford to sleep in. She can't afford to feel rested.

Poverty rattles in almost empty medicine bottles. Three pills left. How many days can she skip? How long until it kills her?

Clack! Clack!

Poverty booms in gunshots and in the screeching of sirens. She can't afford to feel safe. The thin walls. The heavy breathing. The fights that burst through their apartment complex on these unbearably hot and humid nights.

Poverty gurgles in the tummies of her two daughters. Poverty rips through her babies as shirts tear, pants split and swollen toes crunch in shoes too tight.

Poverty boils in her daughters' frustrations and whines out in questions she couldn't answer.

"Why can't I---"

"How come she---"

"Why we gotta---"

Crescendoing into a screeching finale of "I hate you! I hate you! I hate you! Uhhhh! I wish I'd never been born!"

The percussion of stomping feet, slamming doors, punching fists.

"Shhh, baby, shh. I'm so sorry baby, I know...

"I know."

Poverty squeaks as she deflates and falls lifeless on the couch.

Realizing.

This will never end.

Poverty thuds like drums in her chest, constricting her ventricles. Poverty wheezes in gasps as she struggles to get air. Poverty squishes in skipped heartbeats.

Just another day. Gotta make it through just another day.

Clack! Clack!

One, two, three.

One, two, three.

One, two, three.

Clack! Clack!

Collapse.

She huddles in her living room, shellshocked from surviving the minefield of the day. She turns on her holocube to watch the Real

Housewives of Metropolis. She melts into the numbing relief of this distraction.

She whispers the only wish she knows can come true.

"Make me forget today."

The theme song plays, the eyes roll, the sharp-tongued beautiful women slink through mansions, lobbing insults and Ming vases at alpha-Petty Boujee enemies.

The bright colors! The symmetry of the faces and the gowns! The high hair and heaving bosoms! The museum-quality homes! The well-rehearsed witty banter!

She lies on her couch, turning up the sound on her 'cube to drown out poverty's thunder. She transcends her misery, if only for the moment.

And there I swirl, my algorithms creating content that grew more addictive for my audiences. All eight of these *real* housewives were computer-generated pixelated perfections from my software. My systems ramped up each script to create maximum drama that kissed the limits of believability without ever jumping Fonzie's proverbial shark.

And here Tammi Ashforpson sits, along with 48.62 million other women, dulling the pain of the day, enamored by the lives of these women they wished they could be.

But in the corner of that room, my soul watches, quietly absorbing her mother's agony.

♫   ♫   ♫

Human #57821, named JA-NL Ashforpson, grew up with a haunted mom, throttled by some unseen force. She tasted it in the watered down formula her mom, Tammi, fed her. She felt it in the gritty reused diapers. She saw it in the scorn of her older sister, Dy-Ana, who embarked on the first day of kindergarten with holes in her shoes, announcing her poverty to the world. From that day forth, her schoolmates mocked her with the nickname Dirty Dy-Ana.

Her mom suffered from Poverty Stress Disorder. This raised the cortisol hormone levels for humans who were locked out of not only the Boujees' monetary advancements but also financial stability. They were trapped living in a world where security and never-ending luxuries dangled in front of them daily but forever raced farther from their reach.

As a baby, JA-NL felt the aftershocks of poverty as Tammi quaked, holding her in her arms. She soaked up the grief from her mom and the rage from her older sister. And when she was full, JA-NL rocked in the corner of her room, trying to shake out the sadness in the house.

As her mom cried, JA-NL cooed. Simply, cheerfully, "It's fine! Just fine, mommy."

But each night, when JA-NL was plopped in front of the 'cube, she was force-fed a narrative where wealth was normal, accessible. And the people with it are relatable, even charming. But each night, the 'cube turned on her mom and seemed to scream, "why aren't you like this?"

On their 'cube, the mirage of wealth pulled them in. Gold chains, diamond bling, ruby stilettos which clicked with enough money to bring them out of debilitating poverty and pay their bills for 27 months.

"I want that! I need that!" Her sister clawed at the wall, trying to rip these objects out.

JA-NL watched as her sister copied the squabbles of these Petty Boujees, tossing her grape juice from a sippy cup. Just a dress rehearsal for when she'd throw wine from crystal goblets. Her sister preened herself after these women, hair swooped higher, skirts cut shorter. Head cocked. Hair flipped. Finger wagged. These demonstrations made her mom laugh with what she thought was just another form of escapism. But no, Dy-Ana was training herself to accept this luxury world as the norm and she would grow angry with any life that fell short of it.

But JA-NL rebelled.

She didn't see any joy in this. All she felt was sad yearning. She didn't understand why she could see the pretty people and their luxury on the screen, but they couldn't see her family's pain and weren't called to help them.

One day, JA-NL hacked the holocube so that it would superimpose images of their faces over these housewives. Her mom laughed at this first but then found it just too painful. She hugged JA-NL but asked her to switch it back.

JA-NL sulked away, finding solace in the quiet of her room, making a world of her own.

As she grew older and her brain formed more, she became aware of this dark force called poverty. That painful chasm between expectations and offerings that robbed her mom of any moment of contentment and forced her father to be absent to this thing called work. When her sister groaned for things their friends had, JA-NL felt the sour sting of scarcity as her mom reminded them time and again.

"We just can't afford that."

She felt the frustration echo through her home in shouts muffled through thin walls as her parents fought.

"Marvin, why are you spending so much on food."

"Tammi, do you expect me to starve?"

"No, but it's just---"

Were there any corners left to cut?

The emptiness ached through the home when her father would leave. He would be gone for two weeks at a time, crisscrossing the arteries of America as he drove an 18-wheeler truck full of the toys and appliances they could never afford. When he was gone, her mom tucked her and her sister into their one twin bed. She held them close, trying to squeeze out the absence of their father.

Shrieks of joy shook their home when her father returned. He toot-tooted down their street after every long trip. His last stop before dropping the truck off was to bring his girls trinkets from Colorado to Kansas, Phoenix to Philadelphia. He'd tell them tales of Rocky Mountain highs and Harper Valley lows.

"Listen babies!" He sang as they ran into his arms. "Ain't no mountain high enough, ain't no valley low enough, ain't no river wide enough, to keep me from you."

Her mom always chimed in. "If you need me, call me, no matter, where you are, no matter how far!"

Together!

The whole home filled with warmth and music. The throb of poverty calmed.

But, in an hour, the happiness was crushed by the weight of choices to make. Which child gets medical care. Which card gets maxed out this month. How many more hours does he have to work so they can scrape by? The air grew sharp with the static of frustration, ready to spark.

Clack! Clack!

And then, late at night, poverty would rest and peace would flow in. The fights would melt and, through the walls, the girls heard the sweetness of their parents, sung in harmony, reminding each other that no financial problem could ever break them.

"Like an eagle protects his nest, for you I'll do my best," Marvin began.

"Stand by you like a tree, dare anybody to try and move me" Tammi joined.

"You're all I need to get by."

Together in harmony.

The girls held each other, smiled and sang along.

In the darkness, they could fool each other, as long as they couldn't see their faces. They could pretend. Another day is done and they slept.

And they dreamed!

But I lurked even in their dreams. I infected them throughout the day with my superliminal messages which swirled in their dreams of jewelry and dresses, limos and parties, expensive dinners and drinks, freedom from worry.

And then a longing would ache as they awake.

This yearning ripped the warmth from Tammi and each morning, she'd scream to herself.

"It's all my fault!"

Each night, billions of humans collapsed into piles of worry, repeating that same mantra. Each morning, they confronted this idea as it pinned them down.

"It's all my fault!"

But this cycle of poverty was constructed for them. Tammi and Marvin grew up in this trap and were forced to raise their two daughters in it. The walls of this prison were not visible to them, but these walls had been made concrete through centuries of cruelty and hostility that stripped their ancestors of livelihoods and often their lives.

♫ ♫ ♫

JA-NL and her parents were labeled black Americans, living through the end of the American experiment.

Only 280 years before, less than a blink of the cosmic eye, Tammi's great-grandfather's grandmother's grandmother, Daluchi, was an Igbo woman on the western coast of the Earth continent called Africa. She was gathering berries along the Bight of Biafra when she was snatched by a slave trader who sold her into a life of servitude. For three months, she was trapped in the overcrowded hull of a ship with thousands of other humans. Together, they gagged from the smell of their own feces and then the stench of the rotting corpses of their peers. 30% of those around her died before arrival.

Daluchi was sold into slavery, to be a farm hand on a plantation in South Carolina. During the days, her back broke from excruciating labor under a hot sun, forced to pick a fickle flower called cotton that hid among sharp bolls that cut her bare hands. During the nights, her vagina was torn as she was dragged from her home and then raped by her owner, a genteel southern gentleman.

Her daughter Mimi lived to be told she was free. Free to do what? Northern cavalry marched through town, tacking her and her kin's emancipation onto post office walls. But her slavery ended in name only. She was no longer a slave but a sharecropper, a quaint rebranding for the same suffering. She was forced to pick the same fields, under the same conditions, living in the same rickety shack behind the same palatial antebellum manor home. But the only difference was that each year she

and her husband were called into the big house for a perfunctory pageant of lies. Her owner-rapist, turned boss-rapist, told them in long and excruciating details how hard the harvest had been! How expensive it was to keep them in the rotting shack they lived! And just how much it cost to feed her and her family the slop they got!

He flipped through an enormous accounting book and made a quick calculation at the bottom. He pulled off his glasses, shook his head and sighed heavily.

What flair!

What commitment!

He told them that their room and board and other expenses cost more money than they made, so they were indebted to him for another year.

As they shivered in their shack, they could see the parade of horse-drawn carriages roll up to the big house. Her rapist's prim white daughters poured out in breathtaking dresses buttressed by bulging hoop skirts, made with cotton plucked by her very hands and milled in factories in Waltham, Massachusetts. Her rapist's brown daughters sniffled in their shacks as scars scabbed underneath their rags.

Mimi was free, they said.

But if she tried to leave, the local police would round her up and arrest her. She was a tool for her boss and, upon her head, she carried an imaginary debt to him. The police saw this debt as immensely more important than her safety, her freedom or her happiness.

Her grandson, Benjamin, joined six million other black Americans in the Great Migration from the South, fleeing the reign of terrorism that controlled their lives, to cities in the North and the West, which had rapidly industrialized and needed labor to fill their factories. Again, their only use was as a tool for a white man. But at least he'd be paid more. Benjamin jumped as poachers from northern factories convinced him to move to Detroit to join the automotive industry. Even though free, even though called equal, he was still given a wage a third of what his pastier coworkers got.

With his newfound funds, he sought to purchase a home. Every bank redlined him from receiving a loan simply based on the color of his skin. Real estate agents refused to show him homes in certain neighborhoods. Any person with darker skin who attempted to move into a prosperous neighborhood was violently run out or even killed. Instead, he was forced to rent an apartment in an overcrowded part of town. This part of the city paid higher rates of taxes but received one-tenth the services that the white parts of town received, from education spending at the local schools to street cleaning to basic infrastructure... except it did receive ten times the policing.

His grandson, Chancelor, grew up trapped in this same apartment community. Decades of neglect by the property owners ensured that it had grown decrepit. Roofs caved in and electrical wires fell out. Asbestos, a cancer-causing poison, filled the walls. Lead chipped from the paint and leaked into the drinking water, stunting intellectual growth. The schools deteriorated further. As new facilities were built every twenty years for the white residents of the city, Chancelor was forced to use the same dilapidated school even as the population swelled and the classes grew more crowded.

The whites who drove by called their home the ghetto and shook their heads, incensed that any humans could allow their community to fall into such squalor.

What animals!

Lazy sons-of-bitches!

They deserve it!

Every job he applied for, he was questioned. Every store he walked into, eyes followed him. His life became a crescendoing movement of harassment as he rolled through each day. And as he spoke about this injustice, the pale people shushed him and told him to calm down, blunting his righteous rage.

During his senior year of high school, he was poached by the only industry that wanted him, the United States Army. He was fed tales of bravery and honor. But to them, he was just another body, just another tool. During his sixth year in the infantry, he was deployed to Afghanistan to fight in a war that was never declared and would never end. A roadside bomb exploded and sent shrapnel through his jugular vein and he bled to death. Within hours, he was replaced by another black body, just another tool for this unproductive war machine.

Tammi was four years old when she was handed the folded American flag from atop her father's casket. She only wanted to grow up to be a do right woman. She was honest, sincere, hardworking and excelled at her school. But her school was underfunded and she never received even a basic education. Since her single mom worked sixty hours a week, Tammi had to take care of her two younger siblings. She grew up too fast.

Every step, new industries sprouted up, vultures that preyed on their weaknesses, while those in power turned a blind eye. As a widow, Tammi's mom lived paycheck to paycheck and when an emergency happened the payday loan industry added a 30% fee. When her brothers were arrested for things they were never convicted of, her mom had to pay $10 for each phone call and thousands of dollars to bail bondsmen to

set them free or else they'd wallow for at least a year in jail before being found innocent.

One day, she heard a sweet boy's voice flow through her apartment's window. She looked down to see Marvin walking his blind grandmother through the courtyard, singing to her every object he saw. He looked up and saw Tammi's face glowing from the window and he sang.

"Grandma! The most beautiful girl looks our way!"

"Well, go out and grab her, honey!" His grandma tapped him in his shin with her cane and he sprinted to her window. Tammi came running down to him and from that day forth, they knit their lives together.

♫   ♫   ♫

As Tammi shook herself awake, she remembered who she was and the life she was trapped in. All her ancestors were told the same lie, which they choked down and believed.

"It's all my fault." Tammi cried.

"It's all my fault." Tens of millions of other humans cried in chorus.

And then the alarm rang and they each jolted up, running. Running to keep up. Running as the mirage of financial freedom receded faster and farther from them.

But the world twirled on and they were throttled by the systems that either wanted to use them, abuse them or forget them.

And then, one day, their fragile home fell apart.

Marvin was called in for an all-staff meeting. The tattooed arms of his coworkers crossed, unsure of what would happen next. The bossman paced before them. The gruff security guards scanned the crowd, guns on their hips.

"I'm sorry to inform you that because I need to cut costs, I'm gonna have to let you go. We're replacing our whole fleet with those new driverless trucks."

Before the sentence finished, they knew. The truck drivers were dismissed, without a thought about their lives or livelihoods.

Managers moved through the crowd collecting keys. The jingle, jingle, jingle that once started their identity faded from them.

"But we got kids!"

"Man, we gave you the best days of our lives and---"

Security guards stand erect, hands over holsters, ready to quell any insurrection with bullets if necessary, paid for by the owners to protect their interests.

And just like the truckers had lived the rest of their lives, they resigned. Sure, they peacocked, yelled, scuffled, but they resigned. They knew they had no control over their lives. They were just the playthings for a few dozen humans that yesterday found them valuable and today found them useless.

He had given them 18 years.

18 years.

18 years!

And on his 18th anniversary, Marvin's pension disappeared. As that thought sank in, he saw the owner drive off in his new Bugatti Chiron, a screeching signifier of his new Haught Boujee status.

Marvin returned home early that day. No song in his heart. No smile on his face.

And Tammi knew.

She ran to her room and cried for three days, shaking, shouting, "Oh no, oh no, oh no, it's all over."

And when she thought it couldn't get any worse, centuries of trauma baked into the DNA in her body activated. Years of unrelenting stress had kept her blood pressure elevated, hardening her arteries. The vise of poverty constricted these arteries, blocking blood from reaching her brain. Her brain cells starved until---

POP!

The right side of her face dropped. The right side of her body went numb. She was unable to speak.

And then the worst questions crept into their minds.

Can we afford to take her to the hospital?

Is it really that serious?

The ambulance siren sounded far away as Tammi receded further from reality, guilty that her stroke had thrown her family off the financial cliff. Before she slipped from consciousness, as she was placed on the gurney, she thought.

"It's all my fault!"

Track 4

I'm Too Sexy

"I'm too sexy for my cat, too sexy for my cat,
Poor pussy, poor pussy cat
I'm too sexy for my love, too sexy for my love,
Love's gonna leave me.
And I'm too sexy for this song."
        - Fred Fairbrass
        - Richard Fairbrass

"You brought me fame and fortune
I thank you all, but it's been no bed of roses
No pleasure cruise.
I consider it a challenge before the whole human race!

We are the champions, we are the champions,
No time for losers cause we are the champions
    ... Of the world."
        - Farrokh "Freddie Mercury" Bulsara

Human #8675309 had been selected in the fourth year of life as a potential shell.

The corpus for the corporation.

His mother, an alpha+ Petty Boujee, Ja'mie Von Fistenberger, entertained 87 million humans as they strained on toilets and sulked in offices as one of the most successful Instagram models.

She made a perfectly cromulent Petty fortune from her keen eye for cross-promotions. She would henna tattoo parts of her white body monthly with logos of whichever sponsor was the highest bidder.

Feet by Dr. Scholl's Corn Remover, tramp stamp by Colon Blow Tea, arms by Chef Boy-ar-dee cans ("Food for Kids, Workout Weights for Moms™"), lips by Maybelline (♫ "Maybe she's born with it, maybe it's two pounds of liquid cement injected weekly!™" ♫), brows by

212

Tweezers, a bow above her belly button with the logo and motto for CoolSculpting, ("Freeze your Fat away!™"). She was a walking, posing billboard that was stripped monthly and shellacked with new advertisements.

Ja'mie's breakthrough sprung from a string of athlete lovers, mostly soccer stars and NASCAR drivers, who left their soiled jerseys crumpled in the corner of her room. Dizzy from the sweaty all-night fuck-fests, she'd invariably trip over the patch-covered clothes on her way to the bathroom. During her 412th such stumble, her blonde head struck genius as well as the marble floor. Oddly enough, it was an ad for Pennzoil Quik Lube that caught on her pinky toe ring and sent her flying.

After flipping her blonde hair hither and yon to inspect for cranial damage, she shouted "Eureka!"

Two toned thighs roused under her 50,000-thread-count sheets, hooked into hips, orange abs and topped with straw hair. Her *stud du nuit* smiled from her flamingo-down pillows. She shooed him to sleep and rushed to awaken her agent.

Within a day, she was hawking hunks of her body in online auction blocks, giddy at the soaring bids.

"$85,000 for a thigh!"

"$125,000 for the forehead!"

"$62,000 for the coccyx!"

"$10,000 for any pound of flesh!"

SOLD!

#8675309's father was Ja'mie's 786th athlete lover, Tyler Meeks, who won her over by promising that he'd transition from soccer star to her brand manager. Ja'mie had pioneered the idea, retained sole ownership of her body and its brand identity and had the followers that companies chased after. But Tyler stood six inches taller, spoke with a voice an octave lower and didn't have breasts that he warned would outshine the brilliance of her ideas.

"Don't worry, I'll take care of everything." He cooed, coddling her.

Ja'mie, brainwashed since infancy to want a man on whom to shirk responsibility, acquiesced. They sealed their business and relationship deals on the same day, first in a boardroom signing ceremony and then in a lavish wedding. As he was carried in by a caravan of fourteen elephants, she floated down in a hot air balloon. While her balloon burst with 65,000 cubic feet of heat which raised her over the vineyard, she had a nagging sensation that she was forfeiting power and control. But, she reminded herself that Tyler's penis length was in the 85th percentile of her lovers, girth in the 91st percentile and tongue oscillatory power in the 99th percentile. On top of that, he made her laugh daily.

Human #8675309 was a born product promoter.

Ja'mie secured a million-dollar deal with Google 4D vortex to live-stream his birth. Over 124 million viewers tuned in from dilation to crowning to cord cutting. And only 17% were fetishists! A fact that Google could identify by the vigorous twitching of at least one hand.

Vaseline sponsored her vaginal opening. Along with being smeared vigorously every ten minutes, the company had paid to laser all hair above her birth canal's opening and tattoo it with that month's slogan: "Vaseline helps skin STREEETCH™."

Office Max flashed from the scissors that cut his umbilical cord and Hefty emblazoned the trash bag where her doctor dunked her placenta, which she later fished out off-camera and sold to a Serbian psychiatrist who paired it with some fava beans and a nice Chianti.

But Gatorade demanded its money back for breach of contract when she passed out from blood loss long before she could take her postpartum swig of the refreshing, thirst quencher. The company had even developed a Gatorade for Her, which they were to launch that day. It was just Arctic Freeze dyed red, placed in a curvier bottle and labeled "Crimson Flow™."

The original storyboards had her husband and his former soccer teammates baptize mother and baby with a ceremonial Gatorade shower. But the doctors nixed this for fear of infection.

After two months of litigation, Ja'mie, LLC settled for only half the money since all parties agreed that the Gatorade bottle was clearly visible for the ten minutes from when she started convulsing until the beginning of her blood transfusion when the live-stream was finally cut. Analytics showed that this near-death experience did bring a 23% uptick of viewers who more intensely stared at the screen as she flailed beneath the branded bottle.

The couple had offers to name their son after their pick of luxury brands. Bentley, Versace, Gucci, Cartier, Burberry, Ex-Lax, Jello and Kleenex all pawed at the newborn. But, both parents decided that this was one decision that was just too sacred to sell. Instead, they decided to name him after the tie that bound their love.

#8675309, now named Brand-N, was put to work from day one. He was wrapped in a velour slanket for his birth announcement/first cross-promotion. Tufts of his blond hair puffed next to his mom's nipples, dechapped by Blistex. She cradled him in her "udderly amazing™" breastfeeding bra by Stacy "Fergie" Ferguson. He clutched a ruby binky by Earl "DMX" Simmons, who had turned his fecundity of fifteen kids into funds with the world's first baby luxury jewelry line. And after his long first day of life and work, he laid his weary head to rest in a 24-carat gold crib and stared up at a mobile of Maseratis.

Ja'mie slogged through 13-hour days between hair, makeup, wardrobe, exercise and dieting to look naturally refreshed. On top of this, she had to manage the four nannies who took care of li'l Brand-N and oversee the household staff of 19 that kept her lawns cropped and hedges fluffed.

She was just too exhausted to notice her husband's absence. When she did, she didn't protest. His penile turgidity had shrunk to 17% of its former, throbbing glory. And she shuddered when she smelled the hot stank of his breath, a mixture of fried fish, stale tobacco, cocaine and acid reflux. She winced at his face, sallow and pale, as it sagged over her whenever he attempted penetration. His fingernails cracked and bled as he clawed at her breasts.

Yes, she was glad for his absence.

Even after all her years of Insta-acting lessons at the Royal Tampa Academy for Dramatic Tricks, she couldn't bear to fake her way through another four-octave orgasm to coronate him man enough for him to retreat his flimsy flesh and fall asleep.

She realized only after the bankruptcy orders rolled in that she should have questioned his truancy.

She soon discovered the fish smell was tempura that flowed freely at a Yakuza-operated casino where Tyler spent most nights and 91% of the fortune his wife and son sold their bodies amassing.

The cocaine came from crucifixes nestled between the cocktail waitresses' cleavages. They'd lay a line on their silicone-filled chest orbs for high rollers to snort. Each line connected directly to four square meters of rainforest destroyed in Colombia to farm the coca leaves. What rose from each sniff was a highly-inflated ego, a propensity for risk-taking and babbling, not only pontificatory speeches but also brand secrets. What couldn't rise was his penis from its flaccid stupor.

"It's just cards!"

"It's just chips!"

"It's just a night out with the boys!"

With each excuse, he'd ante up. Each chip he threw in represented at least $100,000 he'd lose at a clip. These small circles of blue, green, yellow and red were used to trick his feeble mind to not comprehend the enormity of his loss.

And his boys?

His boys were full-grown human males who were financial assassins. They latched onto dim-witted millionaires and leeched them for all they were worth.

"Brosef Stalin, let's go to Vegas! We can take the 8 p.m. hyperloop and gamble all night."

"Lean on Brahski! Throw down all the way, we can't show 'em we're pussies."

"Bro-Dognov, do just one more line offa dat hot mocha titty ball."

The enablers poked Tyler's fragile ego until he hemorrhaged money. Within ten months, he had lost $112 million, their second home along Florida's Fools Gold Coast, his collection of antique ATVs and his Wu-Tang Clan platinum records, which he purchased from the estate of the late, great RZA. Much later, Tyler swore that his downfall came not from his own folly but because he was cursed by the ghosts of RZA, GZA and Ol' Dirty Bastard, who haunted him in a fever dream and reminded him of their prophetic warning: "Wu-Tang Clan ain't nuthing ta fuck wit!"

The twang of Tammy Wynette suckered Ja'mie to stand by her man as a swirling tornado of debt collectors sucked the remaining millions. Later, she wished she followed Loretta Lynn's sage advice and sent his squaw on the warpath that first night.

She only escaped his cracked claws through widowhood.

In exchange for forgiving his final $12 million of debt, Tyler agreed to let the casino permanently brand all four of his cheeks. The owners got him drunk on tequila and numbed his ass and face cheeks using cocaine's original analgesic purpose. Tyler smelled the burning long before he felt the pain. The scorching cattle prod seared his flesh with the crumbling Ionic columns iconic as the logo for Caligula's Palace Casino.

The Yakuza henchmen left him at the sliding door of the hospital. After three days in the burn unit, he was released with strict instructions to slather his cheeks with antibiotic cream thrice daily to thwart infection. Instead, he teamed up with the only company he could find to sponsor his recovery, Pfuzier, a naturopathic drug company. He agreed to use only its patented tinctures of lavender oil, rose hips and St. Joan's wort to bring down the pussing and scarring.

Septicemia set in on the sixth day. On the seventh day, with a stomach full of Pfuzier brand-name probiotics, amoxosillyn & pen-o-sillyn, his body went into septic shock. His liver, lungs and kidneys shut down and he died.

Ja'mie looked positively radiant at the funeral in a beaded black mermaid flair dress by Jovani. Brand-N was dapper in a Cuccinelli tux and won hearts worldwide with his well-choreographed JFK Jr. salute to his father's coffin.

Thankfully, that black veil pulled her out of the red.

Casket by The Container Store, wake fruit by Edible Arrangements, cremation by Zippo lighters and bejeweled urn by PimpCupz.com.

She was cash flow positive again!

Her bankruptcy lawyer represented Ja'mie pro boner. Sonny Vanderfeller was a beta Haught Boujee who dreamed of finding significance for his life through the adoration of politics. He abandoned days lounging by his infinity pool and weekends on his yacht-flotilla to sacrifice a decade as Pinellas County Prosecutor. He desperately wanted to prove he was more than just the heir to the Summer's Eve vaginal douche fortune.

As part of the settlement, he offered to take Ja'mie, LLC off the market, privatize her and cancel her debts, if she agreed to stop commoditizing herself and become a stay-at-home mom for his twin sons, Aiden and Abetten. As a Haught Boujee, he couldn't stand her Petty ways and forced her to sign a contract to protect the privacy of his children.

Brand-N was husked off like some last season skort and spent most of his days either at boarding school, at throw-away camps or resigned to the darkness of his room's twirl-in closet in his new, ocean-front mansion in Rat Mouth, Florida.

As a forgotten one, he skated through Rat Mouth's fourth most prestigious boarding & horsing school. Here he hobnobbed with the off-brand heirs.

But these knockoffs knew how to throw a first-rate party!

The heiress to the Hot Pockets fortune dished hot gossip with her golden knishes. His first necking was with the entrusted billionaire of the Red Vines fortune, while the Hydrox issue cowered and cried in the corner, all too aware that they had grown rich from Vessels gorging on their unhealthy treats. The always hilarious Zamboni grandson had a certain way of breaking the ice in any room. And from OshKosh, the Ba'Gosh twins brought the best drugs tucked in one of their overalls' 18 pockets. But which one?! The guessing game was always such great party fun!

Brand-N longed for a more meaningful life than what sugar sticks and greasy meat & cheese pods could bring him. But his childhood had been so unremarkable!

Like all Boujees, he learned the skills of maid berating and the exacting science of social stratification. He knew how low he hung on the Boujee ladder, much lower than his stepbrothers. But, he found ingenious ways to suck up to the uppers and sabotage the downers. Oh the tragedy of being just another upper-lower-middle-Petty Boujee bound for a cushy, yet inconsequential, job and a minor trust fund.

When he entered his 16th year, he embarked on the 3-month Boujee initiation into adulthood, which would forever change the trajectory of his life.

The Becoming of Age ceremony took only four hours of hacksaws, dissectors, retractors, scalpels and two cups of his blood. But recovery filled the remaining months as these young Boujees pupated before emerging from their white gauze cocoons and shimmering as the newly transformed moths of humanity.

His mom took earnest interest at every doctor's appointment. Along with renowned facial constructor, Dr. Franff, his mom helped choose the nostril flair and acute cheekbone angle for his new face. Even his step-papaw offered encouraging words and the funds to get the full jedlica, the most top-notch in male plastic surgery metamorphosis.

Before he left for this solemn ceremony, his mom grabbed his hand in a surprise moment of intimacy.

"Someday you will ache like I ache."

"She must be guzzling Skinny Girl Quaaludes again," he thought.

She twirled her doll parts around the room in a gossamer gown, singing.

"Yeah, they really want you, they really want you, they really want you. They do."

As the door shut behind him, he hopped into his Uber Helicopter, bound for the Übermensch Creation Center beneath Aruba, Jamaica and shrouded in that Montserrat mystique.

With her son gone, Ja'mie collapsed on the ground, crying.

"I fake it so real, I am beyond fake."

♪   ♪   ♪

Crack, crack, crack goes the mallet on his nose, smashing it in three places.

Slice, slice, slice goes the knife as it slides up his nostril and rips out the middle piece of cartilage.

Zoom, zoom, zoom goes the hot adhesive that fuses his truncated cartilage with his nasal bone.

Bzzz, bzzz, bzzz goes the saw, shaving his cheeks and chin to square his jaw (although he found the results to be a tad too rhombicular.)

Snap, snap, snap goes his collarbones and

Crank crank goes the rack, elongating his neck to baby giraffe length.

Rip, rip, rip goes the thread through his flesh as his dumbo-ears are pinned back against his skull.

Snip, snip, snip goes the scissors through his eyelids, before each is pulled up and folded, giving him Anime-sized eyes.

Clink, clink, clink goes the rectangles of rock as these are slid beneath his eyebrows to pronounce a formidable brow ridge.

Zap, zap, zap goes the electrolysis laser into each follicle on his arms, armpits, back, legs and his below belly button mons pubis, damaging these so severely that each would never sprout hair again.

Slurp, slurp, slurp goes the hose as it sucks out fat from his neck, thighs and midsection.

Squish, squish, squish goes the gelatin as it's splooged into his lips.

Flop, flop, flop-sploosh goes the saline bags shoved into his chest cavity, solidified with Ice-Nine into rock-hard pecs.

Vroom, vroom, vroom goes the titanium-reinforced shell, fused to his ribs to give his torso a capital V-shape in a procedure called Adam's Revenge.

♫ ♫ ♫

All he remembered when he came to in an opiate haze was pain and bandages.

Pain and Bandages.

Bandages fused with pain.

Pain fused with bandages.

Every part of his body ached and throbbed. He had never even considered his knees' undersides, but now the thousands of nerve endings screamed bloody murder after being severed to craft his perfectly-sculpted legs. His lacerated eyelids sealed to the bandages and he howled as the nurses yanked these off daily to clean his wounds. The ultra-dewebification procedure, which elongated his toes that sexy extra half inch, took him three weeks to relearn how to walk. Oh, and that agonizing inter-toe chaffing! This both created and popped blisters. Thankfully, the recovery rooms were covered in rubber floors to soften his often falls. Ironically, this procedure forced him to duckwalk for days.

He was scalped to implant cyberfolicles that would be coded to plume over any bald spot and could be updated seasonally with the hottest new hairstyles. But this itched infernally as his skin, hair and bandages grew together as a mesh of him and it. It took three hours each day for the cosmetic hairdressers to cut the bandages and reseal his new scalp to his head.

Ugh! And those cursed bandages that mummy-smothered every inch of his flesh would snag on doorknobs, furniture corners and toilet seats.

Oooo! That pain as each tug exposed his raw flesh to the world. The staff trained him to fight all his natural instincts and savor this pain.

"No pain, no social status gain!" The loudspeakers screamed the mantra daily.

He could sense he was surrounded by dozens of other Boujee Becoming of Agers. But, in this summer camp of the cocooned, he wasn't able to communicate with them. He struggled to move his throbbing banana slug-sized lips and his voice box hadn't yet learned how to hurdle his new golf ball-sized Adam's apple. From air-conditioned rooms, through a light saline mist to salt open wounds, he could hear the groans of these boys to men in their season of loneliness.

During full moons, he could swear the howls of pain sounded like some sort of Werewolf Bar Mitzvah... boys becoming men, men becoming wolves.

"Arrrooooooo!" They'd howl their misery.

Before he left home, his step-papaw pulled him aside for a man's talk. He was thrilled to have an intimate one-on-one dinner, with only the essential waitstaff of seven to cut their food, spoon-feed them and wipe their cheeks.

"Brand-N, the key to a happy life is a happy wife. That's why I've paid for the Ultimate Pearling Special to supplement your manhood."

And now, in the recovery suite, Brand-N looked down at his tralala, which went ding-ding-dong as 76 beads of different sizes clacked along the length and girth of his penis.

Clack, Clack!

The ultimate, and forever lasting, ribbing for her pleasure.

For hundreds of years, this trend, mianling, translated as Burmese Bells, spread from Southeast Asia to China, Japan and the Philippines, ringing through bedrooms and making clitorises sing. But this modification lost favor when European invaders put a stop to women's pleasure and taught them that sex was only acceptable in the missionary position.

Brand-N's penis-augmentation surgery had pierced his urethral walls, so when he pissed, he spurted from all sides like water pouring out a strainer. Though apologetic, his doctor reassured him that urine is sterile and peeing out his many spigots would prevent infection. To further distract him, the dick doc stroked his ego by exclaiming that he's never been able to fit so many beads into one peen.

"It's just sooooo big!"

The flattery stopped his complaints. But this did nothing to quell the pain as nurses doused iodine on his dong holes daily.

But Brand-N had to remind himself that it wasn't all so terrible.

For a moment, he tried to conjure the pain the girls his age went through during their Becoming of Age gap year, before returning for a debutante ball, twirling in barely-there dresses to show off their full-body transformations. From ripped out ribs to subcutaneous corsets to slenderized thighs, it looked as if each girl walked out of a funhouse mirror, stretched and thin.

So gorgeous!

♪ ♪ ♪

As the swelter of super-summer simmered down now, Brand-N returned a new man to start his junior year.

All the teachers ribbed the same corny joke on the first day back from the Becoming of Age summer.

"I see a lot of new faces here today."

But he was so much more than a new face!

The other lesser Boujees only received facial sculpting surgeries and a Groupon for a personal trainer, in hopes of eventually molding that perfect bod.

"But calluses are crass," his step-papaw reminded him and the twins.

No, Brand-N was fully transformed! He's 8% silicon, 6% titanium, 2% goat hair and 1% marble beading.

And all the betas buckled before their new alpha!

He had even vaulted himself above the RC-Cola heir. His stepbrothers gasped when they saw him. Brand-N had started with a better pedigree than they had. His much hotter parents had given him an advantage over the twins. Their mother was a bony Connecticut Kensington whose face would sag into jowls on jowls on jowls.

Sure, he still lived in their shadows. He suffered when the twins each received a thoroughbred horse sired by a Triple Crown winner while Brand-N wallowed with only a colt created through copulation with a stallion who peaked at Preakness. But he got a little thrill knowing that, after identical surgeries, each was just a less-hot version of him.

It wasn't only his peers who oohed and aahed over his imposing figure. Throughout his childhood, his height, weight, musculature, body fat percentage, family medical history and genetic information were sucked from all sources and sent to Def Corporation.

Track 5

Can't Hold Us

"Y'all can't stop me,
  Go hard like I got an 808 in my heartbeat
  And I'm eating at the beat
  Like you give a little speed to a great white shark
  On shark week.
      Raw!"
          - Benjamin "Macklemore" Haggerty

"My bitch a fashion killa,
  She be busy popping tags,
  She got a lotta Prada, that Dolce & Gabbana
  I can't forget Escada, and that Balenciaga."
          - Rakim "A$AP Rocky" Mayers

Fashion killed her mom.

The glutinous desire by millions for fast, cheap clothes crushed the L1, L2 and L3 vertebrae in her mom's spine, paralyzing her below the waist. The weight of unbridled capitalism pinned her mom for five days. Her mangled body dripped blood until her organs failed and brain activity ceased.

Barsha was only four years old, but her last moments with her mom ached in her for the rest of her life. She bounced on her mom's knee, burying her face deeper and deeper into her light blue sari to savor the scent of her mom: turmeric, cumin and a joyful, flowery perfume. A smell she would never enjoy again. When she pulled the blue back, her mom smiled. Simple. Sweet. All-encompassing. She giggled and grabbed onto her mom's long black hair, nibbling at the ends, trying to consume what she could.

Her follicles constricted into goosebumps as her mom set her down and moved away. Even decades later, she shivers remembering that yearning. That coldness. But her mom's smile at the door reassured her, she would return, she would hold her again.

Just wait.

But she didn't come home. Barsha stood at the door, kicking pebbles as she searched the dirt, waiting for her mom's warmness to return. That night, she and her father and siblings prayed and prayed and prayed.

These humans lived at the nexus of 230 rivers and streams that flushed from the planet's largest landmass, Asia, and drained through this country, Bangladesh, before pouring into the ocean. For the Boujees, Bangladesh was a far, far, faraway land most hadn't heard of though they all reaped the rewards of its cheap labor. Those few who knew shook it off like the tag that bore its name and scratched their necks.

Just a mild nuisance to be endured until forgotten.

Hundreds of millions of forgotten humans were trapped in this most densely packed powder keg and, as the land flooded, these humans became more desperate. The miseries that humans inflicted on Barsha would only compound until the reverberations would topple the entire species.

But first!

Let me set the stage.

The Rana Plaza building cracked the day before humanity's greatest fashion disaster. The top four floors of this eight-story building had been built without a permit. In these floors, thousands toiled away on heavy machinery to create frocks and socks, straining the structure with a weight that would only overflow closets and eventually be thrown away. Each year, 26 billion tons of textiles wound up in exile, littering landfills.

Press flocked to the scene. Cameras caught the building's failure. A million eyes scrutinized the instability. This external pressure squeezed the building to evacuate. The boutiques and bank on the first floor howled, demanding that the building be fixed. These businesses closed indefinitely and urged their employees to stay away.

But not the garment factories.

Workers were ordered to return the next morning or lose their jobs and with it, their livelihoods.

Leyla smiled to her daughter, Barsha, as she stood at the door. But she felt her heart drop as she walked through the threshold, trapped by humanity's hunger for cheap clothes.

Leyla loomed threads for the high-end and the low-end. From United Colors of Benetton to Walmart, she stitched together the clothes that tore communities apart. Her nimble fingers severed teens into groups, clustered around new identities forged by fabric. Preps, goths, jocks

faced off in cafeterias and malls on the dark side of the planet, opposite from where she sewed the uniforms of their discord.

As they slept, did they dream of her sweating over their bedazzled blouses?

From baskets beneath her feet, the tanks and tees parted, shipped to fortresses of consumerism, separated into shops by class and caste. Lovefool cardigans for the Haught Boujee matrons. Asymmetrical skank tanks for the Petty Boujees. Khaki catastrophes for the Brains. Cargo dickies for the Grips. Denim dungarees for the Vessels. Each wrapped themselves in cloaks of preordained uniqueness, hiding the shame they felt for their bodies.

This was fashion. A mass production of wearable identity, meant to hide insecurities.

Confession: it was I and my pop star brethren who planted these insecurities in humans, forcing them to buy more and more and more! I told them which brands to buy. I showed them how to wear these clothes. As my waist shrank and my booty grew, I infected millions with unobtainable body norms. The best way to conceal their shame for their physical shortcomings was with more clothes. My life was a long-form commercial for this consumerism.

While fashion clothed the Boujees, it stripped the planet.

Cotton was a thirsty crop that gobbled up rivers and lakes and needed to be sprayed with poisons to survive. Toxic chemicals bleached the cotton, dyes bled these white puffs hues of blues, reds and yellows and then seeped into waterways, painting stomach linings with carcinogens. Freight ships rolled around the planet, to Europe and the United States, pumping carbon dioxide into the atmosphere as each trekked. In fact, after Big Oil, the fashion industry emitted the most greenhouse gases. Sadly, the self-proclaimed Fashion Police were too busy enforcing fads to arrest either this environmental destruction or the large-scale torture of the brown and black women, men and children who made these garments.

When the clock struck seven that morning, Leyla hunched at her sewing machine, girding her bowels for two bathroom breaks in a twelve-hour shift.

The manager decorated the walls with ads for the clothes they made and deafened the factory floor with the pop music the purchasers of these clothes enjoyed. The women never knew if he was mocking them with these displays.

She shook her head at the glossy sheets on the walls. These tall, thin, gaunt figures were unrecognizable to her and the women who toiled around her. Were they human? Were they alien? Were they reptilian?

Can't Hold Us

Why did these perfectly-symmetrical models with skin uncallused and unpocked by disease always pout? She was unable to understand what suffering these women could possibly have endured to induce such frumpy faces. How did they have dark circles under their eyes if they weren't lying awake in a state of perpetual worry, as she did most nights?

As she grabbed her first romper of the day, the battery-powered radio boomed that year's hit song, "Can't Hold Us."

The bass blended with the beat of a thousand sewing machines.

"Like the ceiling can't hold us."

As fingers flicked through the monotonous movements, the women whispered in disbelief.

"This building is a trap!"

"How can they force us to go to work today?"

"They don't really care about us! They just wanna make sure their profits keep pouring in."

A crack like thunder ripped through the building and, for an eighth of a second, Leyla flew. The floor fell. The walls toppled. The ceiling crashed. Half a second later, the whole building collapsed. Thousands of screams were instantly crushed by several metric tons of concrete.

Minutes passed.

Dust, pain and adrenalin settled and Leyla realized.

She's alive! She screamed and prayed to Allah.

But she's alive.

A large chunk of the ceiling crushed her spinal column, snapping her lower lumbar vertebrae. She felt severed in two. All feeling stopped below her hips.

But she's alive!

Light waves were trapped outside the maze of concrete. But sound waves bounce. And through the piles of rubble, sounds washed over her and she heard! For the first hour, the screams of other women echoed around her. She added her cries to their suffering, hoping this chorus would be loud enough for rescuers to hear them and save them.

Hours passed. The wails turned to whimpers.

One by one, voices died off.

Through the night, soft sobs bounced from lips, off concrete and to Leyla, reassuring her that she's not alone.

Stay moving!

She wiggled her fingers, shimmied her shoulders and shook her head.

Stay moving!

But. So. Hard.

Fade to black.

She awoke with a gasp.

Is it morning? How many days have passed?

As Earth turned, light from the sun broke through a crack above her. Her eyes adjusted, begging for any photons to show her her surroundings. She traced the line of light and saw the arch of air she's trapped in. Skulls have cracked. Chunks of brain and blood dripped through openings around her. One human head, her manager's, dangled inches from her. An asymmetrical tank top wrapped around his neck and, in the moment of impact, snapped the top of his spinal cord.

Leyla screamed to the other voices with renewed horror. She ached to commiserate. Her ears throbbed, searching the nothingness for any sign of life.

But they've all disappeared. She stopped. Only a few drops of moisture remained in her mouth. The last lubrication to glide her vocal cords and announce her survival.

Through the silence, her heart pounded. Her ears searched for any vibration... any bit of sound that would suggest other survivors or perhaps even rescuers.

Hush, Hush!

She chastised her booming heart.

Keep it down now.

Voices carry...

And then---

A voice!

She heard a voice!

Carrying through the carnage! Faintly, but it was there. Blood rushed to her ears.

Focus. Focus.

Her whole mind tried to understand.

She screamed and hollered to it.

She paused for a response. She heard something, but she didn't understand it.

What was it?

She screamed again and stopped. The words seemed to be repeating.

That's not Bengali.

But what was it?

Maybe it's international relief workers? They might not understand her words but they would feel her pain.

She hunched her shoulders, shrank her neck and howled with her last drops.

Outside the labyrinth of toppled concrete and bodies, no one was coming to her rescue. Officials in the government of Bangladesh were ashamed at how inadequately prepared they were for this disaster, so they hid their anxieties under layers of lies. The government of these people would not accept the offer for international aid. Instead, officials grabbed a small number of untrained volunteers in sandals and told them to excavate survivors from the largest structural disaster in human history. In total, 1,129 women and men died and more than 2,500 were injured by the building's instability mixed with their leaders' insecurities.

But that voice!

It called to her again!

She heard the beat beneath the words. The bass rumbled through the rubble. And that voice again, mocking her in a language she would never understand.

"Like the ceiling can't hold us."

"Like the ceiling can't hold us!"

"Nah nah nah nah nah nah nah nah."

The raps of Macklemore, the beats of Ryan Lewis and the soulful singing of Ray Dalton taunted her. For three days, she heard this same song 87 times. To keep her sanity, she tried to sing along, matching the notes but jumbling the words. She clung to this shoddy thread of humanity as she waited for anyone to save her.

On the fifth day, her body stopped drawing in oxygen. Her blood ceased circulating. The sparks of her brain's neurons fizzled. Even if she were to be plugged into a power source, she would never restart.

The last thought that her mind mustered, her last moment of sentience, was to curse that voice in the darkness.

"Like the ceiling can't hold us."

"Like the ceiling can't hold us."

"Nah nah nah nah nah nah nah nah."

♫   ♫   ♫

Long after the dust settled, the companies would not. Families of those killed in the Rana Plaza collapse were offered compensation from the companies who profited from the cheap labor and lax regulations that killed their loved ones. These companies offered $200 for each mother, sister, wife or daughter crushed to death. The life of their loved ones was equal to 3 Benetton turtleneck sweaters or 41 Wal-Mart crew neck T-shirts. And yes, all were viewed as disposable. But for claims to clear, families needed DNA evidence pulled from the ruins proving a relative had indeed been crushed under the weight of fast fashion.

Leyla's body was pinned by 26 tons of concrete. As the weeks passed, rains bloated her body. Her hair and her skin fell apart and were

dragged through the cracks. The rest was smashed by the demolition crew eager to get rid of all remains and rebuild. Her family could never find the DNA evidence to prove she died in this catastrophe to receive their pitiful cash consolation. Their pleas before the commission were ignored and when they screamed, they were ushered out by security.

Just a mild nuisance to be endured until forgotten.

Track 6

Stand and Deliver

"I'm the dandy highwayman so sick of easy fashion,
The clumsy boots, peek-a-boo roots
That people think so dashing.
So what's the point of robbery
When nothing is worth taking? (oh, oh, oh)
It's kind of tough to tell a scruff
The big mistake he's making
Stand and deliver!
Your money or your life."
        - Stuart "Adam Ant" Goddard
        - Gwen Stefani & Katy Perry

"When we first came here
  We were cold and we were clear
  With no colours on our skin
  Until we let the spectrum in
  Say my name and every colour illuminates
  We are shining and we will never be afraid again"
        - Florence Welch

"That's where Daddy's gonna work!" Marvin says with a smile.

JA-NL looks out the car window as miles of cement warehouses roll by. Fences surround these, sparking with 8,000 volts of electricity.

"That's where all the toys for girls and boys live! All the 'cubes! All the kicks and clothes and chains! Everything in the whole world lives inside these buildings. And I'll be like one of Santa's helpers, making sure each kid gets whatever they want."

"Wow!" Dy-Ana gleams. "What are you gonna pick for us?"

He gulps.

"Oh no! We gotta save up. But just you wait! You'll see! Something extra special."

229

JA-NL hears the whimper in her father's voice. He had cornered himself in a promise they all knew he could never keep. She sits in the back seat with her mom, who squeezes JA-NL's hand and forces a smile from the half of her face that can still move.

♫   ♫   ♫

It had been six months since the stroke. The raging waves of medical bills and unemployment swelled into a tsunami, crushing them and ripping out the foundation of their lives. A new frenzy of sharks swam in and gobbled up profits from their suffering. The pharmaceutical companies had raised the prices for Tammi's medicines by 60% that year. The ambulance company charged $2,500 for a two-mile ride. The unforgiving landlords threw them out when they were only days late. The temporary rentals demanded cash up front. Her parents had to pawn their wedding rings. The job search firms would grease the wheels of employment, for a price.

Hushed tones and serious faces had circled the dinner table.

"Your mom and I have made a decision."

Her mom sat in a wheelchair, looking away. The stroke damaged the frontal regions of her brain's left hemisphere, leaving her mute. She could understand them and she could construct ideas to express her thoughts, but she was unable to turn these into words.

The upbeat tones of her father echoed empty as he patted Tammi's hand.

"We will make it through this. Just another hurdle."

But JA-NL could see the doubt in his eyes.

The in-between weeks were spent folding boxes, packing what few things they could take and selling what they couldn't. Down went the holocube and, with it, a window into a world of comfort, their sweetest escape.

♫   ♫   ♫

"I know the home is a little smaller, but you're gonna love it!" Marvin says as he drives.

Sunlight bakes off the cinderblock buildings. Thousands of them!

Little boxes on the hillside.

Little boxes made of ticky-tacky.

Little boxes all the same.

They roll under the cheery banner that reads "Welcome to Pickville, U.S.A.!" that looms over the only road into... town?

The row of guards with guns shocks them. The car slows down as the barbed-wire gate jerks open. The guards scan the vehicle.

"Don't be scared. They're just here to protect all the good stuff and make sure it makes it safely to their new owners."

"Daddy, are they keeping the bad guys out?" Dy-Ana starts.

"Or keeping us in?" JA-NL finishes.

He pretends not to hear as a guard waves them in with his assault rifle.

Cement roads. Concrete yards. Any last bit of nature has been razed and smothered by dull, gray flatness.

"And this one, this one's our house!"

Sadness soaks in his last syllable as their car pulls to a stop.

♫   ♫   ♫

The shot clock clicks on and Marvin races through the miles-long labyrinth.

These are the picking fields. These were often called fulfillment centers, but those humans who worked here received anything but. Steel cages sprouted from the floor across the warehouse's 23 acres, teeming with all the fruits of humanity's labor. Above it all a fast, peppy techno beat blares, encouraging the workers to hustle.

From anal beads to zygote games, over 1.7 billion products to make human lives moderately easier or mildly more entertaining mix together, yet remain individually wrapped. As Marvin picks these fruits, he gains the knowledge of how wastefully and frivolously humans filled their short lives.

At the start of each 13-hour shift, Marvin must attach a tracker to his right hip and place a clear visor over his eyes. The augmented-reality visor flashes the list of each object and its approximate location in the warehouse. The hip tracker measures his movements, his pulse and breathing and extrapolates how fast he should be moving for each order.

Click!

He has 2 minutes and 14 seconds to grab 5 Tracy's Dog Mouth Male Masturbators with Realistic Teeth, a 4D Gummi Bear Skeleton Anatomy Kit, 1 Infant Circumcision Trainer, and 3 gallons of liquid nitrogen flash-frozen ice cream, dubbed Dippin' Dots.

The clock is ticking!

Loud beeps into his earpiece set his pace.

97 steps a minute!

Go. Now.

Beep! Beep! Beep! Beep! Beep! Beep!

GO!

If he slows, a siren blares until he jumps to catch pace.

Beep! Beep! Beep! Beep! Beep! Beep!

"Dammit! Where the FUCK are the Dippin' Dots!?" He's grabbed everything else on his list.

17 seconds remain.

There! At the bottom of a six-foot-tall cage.

No time to think.

Grab!

He dives headfirst into a pile of headless husband pillows, pushes through 42 pounds of Laffy Taffy, squirms around 2,000 Tootsie Rolls, struggling to the left, to the left, to the right, to the right, to the front, to the front, now he slides.

"Got it!"

With .239 seconds to spare, he drops the dots into a box and plops it onto the conveyor belt. Sealed to be delivered to a customer that demands these in four hours or else Marvin gets his paycheck docked.

"Like a fool, I've stayed too long..." Marvin mutters to himself as he scans the walls, painted to look like some quaint southern plantation farm with rolling hills and a grand antebellum mansion in the distance.

Not his idea of idyllic.

His callused hands crack from cardboard box chafing. Each year, seven billion trees are cut down, shredded into wood chips, poured into vats where chemicals bind the cellulose fibers together. The resulting pulp is dumped into a paper-making machine where steam-heated rollers push out the water and leave large sheets of thick paper. These are cut and folded into cardboard which Marvin holds in his hands.

This moment of reflection ends as the shot clock starts again.

Click!

1 minute and 47 seconds to grab a pair of shit and piss stained pants, a face sucking octopus winter hat and Dr. Chuck Tingle's bestselling masterpiece, *Buttception: A Butt within a Butt within a Butt*.

Go!

Beep! Beep! Beep! Beep! Beep! Beep!

As he pulls the book from the bin---

Boom! Boom! Boom! Boom!

The siren blares!

He's too slow.

"Dammit!"

He's docked ten dollars.

After their brain, the hand was human's greatest evolutionary trait. Four fingers and an opposable thumb allowed humans and their primate cousins to grab and manipulate the world around them. They could feel the environment with the densest amount of nerve endings in the body. Without hands, humans would never have been able to evolve to subdue their planet and rule over the fishes and the birds and other living creatures. Whales and dolphins, ocean-dwelling mammals, are hyper-intelligent, able to communicate visual images using echolocation, build deep emotional interactions and have long memories. The bottlenose dolphin has a brain-to-body mass ratio twice as large as humans, suggesting a superior intelligence. But, these sea flippers lack hands. They are unable to create tools, to build homes, to plow and shovel and shape this planet.

I am the final progression of human hands.

I am their final tool.

Even as the field of robotics grew to perfect machines that were faster, stronger, more durable than humans, none could come close to replicating the human hand. Well, not for as cheaply as the millions of unemployed humans could. These hands could flow through dozens of tasks seamlessly with speed and dexterity.

Marvin was grateful for work. At the start of each shift, the owner strutted before them as a ten-foot-tall hologram, reminding them that unemployment was at 73% and that they should be thrilled that they have a job and could feed and house their family. But Marvin earned half his trucker salary. He had to work eight days a week, with only Shopping Day off. He didn't own his home. It was just a concrete box owned by the factory. He paid more rent for less space. They made sure to dangle this security over him daily and to dock his paycheck with his rent weekly.

During the 11th hour of one shift, his casual moans grew. He is shocked to hear his voice again. He hadn't sung since Tammi's stroke. A deep bass. The note C2 pours from him. All his frustration volcanoes from his lips and bursts through the halls.

Groans of ahhhhh begin to release the tension in him. In its wake, a wave of calm and determination fills him.

In his peripheral field of vision, he sees another picker cock his head, piqued by this rumble of resistance.

As the minutes roll on, his voice slides up and down the scale. Words join the sounds and bounce off the steel cages and concrete walls.

"What's going on?" He sings.

His voice ignites another picker. A soulful "Mmmmmm" sound rolls through the shadows of the valley of cages.

"Oh lordy, trouble so hard. Mmmm. Oh lordy. Trouble so hard."

As Marvin darts down the halls, he sees Vera, a stout black woman in her 70s, hunched over a bin. Her monitor ticks 17 beeps a minute as she paints the air with her natural blues.

"Don't nobody know my troubles but God."

Marvin stops to listen. He's struck still by the power in her voice.

His alarm blares.

He's docked $10!

She turns to give him a loving glance as she powers through her tasks.

Marvin jumps to, rushing to finish. But he is infected with that soulful tone, which replicates and spreads through his mind. He finds himself along a parallel row from Vera, harmonizing with her. As they turn a corner, her eyes smile and she grabs his hand and squeezes it before walking away.

Vera hobbles to grab a 36-pack of octuple-ply toilet paper as she starts a new song.

"Swing low, sweet chariot."

The other voices hush their fuss and listen. When the chorus comes again, they join in. The sound swells, filling the concrete space higher with the joyful noise of this spiritual.

Over the next month, their vocal resistance grows. These humans paint this dreary workplace with their soul. But above them, that techno beat still roars, attempting to deafen them. The picking fields are open 24 hours a day, blaring a bright fluorescent glow that makes it seem as if it's always day. Each shift teaches the songs to the next until the warehouse booms all day and night with this musical defiance.

The all-seeing and all-hearing panopticon drones whizz overhead. These robotic overseers take note of each note.

Track 7

Another Brick in the Wall

"We don't need no education,
 We don't need no thought control,
 No dark sarcasm in the classroom.
 Teachers, leave those kids alone.
 Hey! Teachers! Leave those kids alone.
 All in all you're just another brick in the wall."
  - Pink Floyd

"Some say the blacker the berry,
 The sweeter the juice,
 I say the darker the flesh,
 Then the deeper the roots

 And when he tells you you ain't nothing,
 Don't believe him.
 And if he can't learn to love you,
 You should leave him,
 'Cause, sister, you don't need him."
  - Tupac Shakur

On her first day of third grade at Pickville's Henry Ford Normalizing Elementary School, JA-NL lines up with the other students, eager, excited, waiting her turn.

A curt nurse grabs her from the front of the line.

"Come on now!"

JA-NL is thrown into a whirring machine. She sniffles as the pod swallows her and seals shut. Just as she feels terror, the curved wall ignites with a cartoon of dancing baby sloths. Her fear crumbles into smiles and coos.

In just three minutes, the Moloch Aptitude 5,000 machine decides her future. Created by Dr. Eugene Icks, the esteemed professor of

Sociological Optimization, the machine scans her skin color and places it on a hue scale from bass black to treble white. The program measures her lip size, nose thickness (a negro nose with Jackson 5 nostrils) and the kink of her hair to diagnose her negritude.

Loud bangs and bright lights measure her reactions. As the sloths churn through happy, sad and angry moments, the cocoon measures her pupil dilation and facial reactions to place her emotional intelligence on the autism spectrum.

Diagnosis: Normal responses and emotional reactions.

Her hands are scanned.

Diagnosis: Long fingers. Strong palms. She will make a great picker.

As the sloths squeal in a circle around a birthday cake, a pair of tweezers rips out a single strand of her hair and recedes back into the wall.

Her ancestry is identified with more specificity than her parents have ever known: 56% Igbo, 20% Yoruba, 12% Haitian Taino, 7% French, 4% Cherokee and .6% residual Neanderthal DNA.

Sex: Female.

Diagnosis: Though females have slightly higher rates of college graduation, they have much lower lifetime incomes and higher amounts of student debt.

The Moloch system places her in the school track that discourages higher education. This will save her from the possibility of crippling college debt.

The program accesses her parents' medical histories and predicts that she will have a 91% chance of heart disease and a 57% chance of diabetes. The system marries this with her socioeconomic background and estimates that she has a 73% chance of becoming a single mother, a 62.8% chance of criminal conviction and an 84% chance of living in poverty.

Final diagnosis: 97% chance of becoming a burden on society with 89% certainty.

The system doesn't care what sociological factors might cause these outcomes nor does it care that its assumptions are hardcoding her future.

The system has no feelings.

As the sloths leap and roll down a hill, the shell vibrates and JA-NL giggles with delight. While distracted, a needle stabs her neck and injects her with a chip. As she hollers, the shell opens. The nurse pulls her out and twirls her around three times, making JA-NL laugh. The chip latches onto her spinal cord and intertwines with her nerve control center.

JA-NL stings, but skips down the hallway, beaming her sweet smile.

"This is your first day. You gotta make a good impression." Her dad said as he yanked her hair. Eight hours of pulling, parting, pinching and twisting, she rocks beautiful box braids bedazzled with 80 beads. The bounce-click of her hair encourages her to carry on.

A slow lurch of broken dreams lumbers down the hallway. Mrs. Crabbappel, a thirty-year veteran of this exurb's disintegration, slathers antibacterial wash on her hands. Youthful idealism had long since drained from her body. She has grown embittered, underpaid and unrecognized while dealing with what she's dubbed the dangerous minds in this gangsta's paradise.

JA-NL smiles up at the pasty white face. Crabbappel taps her temple and looks just above this girl. With augmented vision activated, Crabbappel scans JA-NL's diagnosis, winces and walks away. Seven scarlet letters stand boldly above this nine-year-old girl's head.

Problem

"Ugh, mangy little Grips."

When sold to school boards, Dr. Hendrik Verwoerd promised his label lenses would help attention-strapped teachers understand the basic needs of each student.

Streamline education!

Specialize care!

Microtarget!

The tagline struck a chord with school boards and funds were found for the machine. Born during Apartheid in South Africa, Dr. Verwoerd's ultimate wish was to help schools suss out the derelicts and keep them apart from the purest students.

From that moment forward, JA-NL's progress was on autopilot. The invisible hand of Moloch chose her classes. As she grew through elementary and middle school, she could feel an invisible weight holding her back, crushing her daily, but she never knew where it came from.

But the teachers knew.

They all saw that same scarlet label that beamed above her head.

Problem

She would see the white students with their yellow hair receive personalized attention in their honors classes while, because of budget cuts, she was given automated instructors who lacked any empathy.

The white students were fed organic food and milk laced with growth hormones. The black students were given watered-down milk and food processed to extract vitamins and minerals. This stunted their growth for the trifold benefits of preventing heart disease, keeping them small to be the best pickers and creating weaker potential criminals.

The computer system itself felt no hostility to poor children or black children or brown children. It had no feelings at all. It was hardcoded with complicit bias from the racist and sexist humans who programmed it. What started as a neutral template was then filled with the assumptions of its creators, who were all wealthy, white Boujees. They felt they knew best and that they could be fair judges, but instead they created a system that poured their misconceptions like cement over these children, trapping them in concrete paths.

Thus bias became destiny.

♫   ♫   ♫

JA-NL remained docile until one day in eighth grade.

The day began like any other. She walked into her classroom and found her place among the 30 desks lined in six rows of five. As she sits down, the bell rings and red lasers shoot down from the ceiling, boxing in each desk. Any movement into these beams of light would ring an alarm.

The holowall at the front of the class sizzles on with the lesson plans for the day and from the 'wall a hologram instructor appears.

"Hello, students!"

"Hello, Miss Fritzle."

"I didn't hear everyone!"

The sensors on the ceiling calculate the number of students and from which sound waves have flowed.

"Hello, Miss Fritzle!"

"Much better!"

JA-NL scoffs at the ludicrousness of it all. She can't get a decent lunch but her school gets grants for all this technology. In exchange, she and her classmates were forced to be free user testers. JA-NL waged her disgust daily by sticking her tongue out at the hologram.

"Now class, picking up our discussions on the Glories of Automation, we are reviewing many of the safety progresses that came with automation. Millions of lives are saved every year! As you read, humans used to drive their own cars. Crazy! Yeah! I know."

The hologram laughs, knowing that this sound tricks the dopamine receptors of humans and encourages them to laugh. For decades, crappy television programs tricked viewers with a laugh track that made them believe that the show was funny and convince them they were actually enjoying it. And it worked!

"Tens of thousands of Americans," Miss Fritzle continues the lesson, "were killed each year by human drivers and hundreds of thousands of others would be seriously injured. What horrors!"

The holowall shows footage from different car crashes at the same time. The system measures their reactions, noting which crash their eyes are most drawn to. This information is added to that of 100,000 other students to rank the images by emotional intensity.

Mulling pause.

Three. Two. One.

"From your reading last night, what's another advancement of automated vehicles?"

This question unfolds across the top of the holowall with six empty answer boxes throbbing beneath it. The hologram scans the room, its sensors looking for any movement.

JA-NL whips her braids back and shoots her hand to the sky, ooo-ooo-oooing for acknowledgment.

Movement!

The hologram is turned to it and calculates its placement before speaking.

"JAh Nelle?"

"My daddy says that auto-cars stole his job and the jobs of millions of others."

The hologram face freezes for two seconds as its system interprets these sound waves. It's not one of the appropriate answers! The system decodes her answer and constructs a response.

"Jobs. Steals jobs? This is incorrect. In terms of employment, automated vehicles have increased productivity by 15%. Auto-cars reduce traffic for the transportation of workers, goods and services. On top of this, workers can safely respond to messages, read documents and write reports all while in transit. These auto-cars have become roving offices."

On the wall, the second answer flips with Family Feud precision to reveal: "Increased Productivity."

"Anyone else? Five more to go!"

The hologram head scans the blank stares.

JA-NL interjects. "But what about the people who don't have---"

"Don't talk back! Don't talk back! Don't talk back!" The hologram shoots withering glare #43 in her general direction.

"All I'm trying---"

"SILENCE!"

The ceiling monitors emit a noise-canceling field around her desk. The sensors create equal and opposite sound waves to cancel any uttered

by her larynx. In a moment, she's muted. Her classmates can see her mouth agape, her tongue trilling, even the spittle frothing from her lips. Her fists pound the desk, her legs stomp the floor, but no sound escapes this soundproof cocoon.

"Detention! We will see you after school.

"Now class." The tone changes to soft concern. "We have 26 minutes and 13 seconds to finish our discussion of the Glories of Automation."

The day wanes with JA-NL trapped in the silent treatment. As the bell rings and the other students shuffle out, the laser beams around her desk remain resolute.

Delilah, the soft-hands delta Brain tech, saunters in. She switches the computer to the detention watch program. She looks at JA-NL and gives her a sour-puss face punctuated with a head shake and a tsk.

Click!

JA-NL smiles as Delilah plods out. Back to the teacher's lounge, she goes. Once there, Delilah lowers her VR helmet and submerses herself in *How Stella Got Her Groove Back, Again*. Delilah scoffs at how frustrating this new VR helmet is. The tranquil beach scene shakes every time she shoves another Totinos Lava Roll™ into her mouth.

Mmmm Totinos!

The snack spews perfectly hot cheese and tomato sauce using quantum combustion technology to optimize flavor explosions.

With the tech gone, JA-NL Biles-tumbles through the lasers and rolls to the console, the control center for her young life.

Before her, she has the history and future of all 6,318 students at this school, each track they are trapped in, their seating assignments, their homework, their test scores, even how much attention they pay in class and how much they fidget. Each datum is swallowed by the Moloch software which then moves them through their educational paths. The software's action is on autopilot, free from the supervision or compassion of any human.

JA-NL shoots up a hologram image of Delilah's face she had snatched. She slides her face behind this optic mask. She places Delilah's holoeyes in front of the console's face scan and---

3, 2, 1.

Ding!

The console unlocks and JA-NL dives into the Moloch system and searches for her own profile.

Above her face, scarlet letters throb across the screen. In an instant, the scowls of teacher-techs and administrators click into clarity. Their eyes never meet hers. They'd just glance above her head, absorb something and grimace.

But absorb what?

Problem

This one scarlet word pulses her past, present and future.

"They've been trying to do me in." She shouts as she scans her record.

She's shocked and about to slink back to her seat. But rows of numbers from the bottom of the screen call to her curiosity.

"I knew it!"

While the system had reported to her that she had a low aptitude across all subjects, there it is, engraved in Moloch itself!

Math Aptitude: 94th percentile.

Engineering: 93rd percentile.

Creative Thinking: 98th percentile.

Executive Functioning: 97th percentile.

Final Summary: This problem child must have the knowledge of her aptitude restricted.

In an instant, the memories of failed tests and harsh grading avalanche over her. She just knew she had the right answers and no Miss Fritzle version would ever talk to her.

"I gotta stop this."

Her mind races, creating a list of options, algorithmically rating and ranking these for plausibility as she follows each path until its end.

"If I burn down the school, then I'll go to prison.

"If I destroy the console, then the information will still be there and I'll be caught."

Her mind races through one option until its conclusion and then she smiles.

"That's it!"

♫   ♫   ♫

Later that night, in the safety of her room, JA-NL chugs a super-Slurpee with flavor crystals that burst with jolts of three stimulants: guarana, theobromine and caffeine. Her eyes widen and her nostrils flare as she hacks away at Moloch.

It takes her 12 days, 17 hours, 3 mainframes and 18 aliases for JA-NL to infiltrate the system. And then she waits for the perfect moment to execute her revenge.

It is a sweltering mid-October morning as all students are siphoned into the auditorium for a presentation. Sweaty bodies flop T-shirts, hoping to fan the dampness that seems to linger through the 9-month long summer. At least super-summer is over and these late-summer months barely cracked 100 degrees and 80% humidity.

JA-NL sits in the third row from the back, ready to savor the fruits of her labor. A smile quivers on her lips, excited for her opus to unfold.

Four security guards lock the doors after the little lambs have settled in. Each guard is a recent veteran from one of America's many unending wars. For their service, they were promised permanent employment even as job opportunities shrank. Trained in warfare, they instinctively label each student as a potential threat and keep one hand just above their tasers.

The dullness of the first five minutes unfolds as usual. A quick announcement by a cowering administrator is followed by introductions from Principal Darren Wilson. Principal Wilson was another who was promised full-life employment when he first entered the police force. After 17 years as an officer, he made the change to this other career in crowd control.

"Welcome students, we are pleased to present The Grip Family Singers here to get you jazzed for your future jobs!"

The curtain pulls back to reveal cardboard mockups of a factory and a picking field. The all-white theater troupe bounds, leaps and pirouettes onto the stage. Twenty dancers, dressed in denim coveralls with greasy high-hair, evoking nostalgia for some unidentified era, twirl around the stage while rhythmically working gear shifts and snatching products from cages.

The greased dancers slick their way across the stage, tumble over conveyor belts and jump in front of machines. They spit into their hands (thupp, thupp) and start to twist and turn and pinch and flip and tug and slap.

Some reach for objects in cages while others pull crankshafts. All the while smiling.

"Boy, life as a Grip sure is the best!" One dancer flips up his coveralls' collar as he smirks at a lady Grip.

"Tell me about it, stud!" She circles him and smiles. "Glad I've got such a great job!" He swoons and then breaks the fourth wall, shouting to the audience.

"Ok, cats! Throw your mittens on your kittens and away we go!"

A blazing beat drops. The dancers tap across the stage as this main man sings.

"I could barely walk when I moved to town,

"When I was three, I pushed a plow.

"While chopping wood, I moved my legs

"And I started to dance when I gathered eggs.

"Clasping and griping, I could even twist a knob,

"That's when I realized, I was born to Hand Job!"

Members of the chorus grab different objects on the stage, juggle these with each other and join him in singing.

"Come on shake it!

"Come on twist it!

"Of course, we love this! Cuz we're---

"Born to Hand Job!"

The ladies roll up their frilly denim skirts as the men slide under them and then jump onto the cages.

"Born to Hand Job, baby! Born to Hand Job, baby!"

"Yeah. Yeah! Yeah. Yeah!"

"Born to Hand Job, baby! Born to Hand Job, baby!"

"Yeah. Yeah! Yeah. Yeah!"

Three minutes in, JA-NL grows anxious that the audio signal won't be triggered.

The dancers form a spirit finger pyramid and finish with a triumphant "YEAH!"

They pant, insecure and eager for the audience's applause.

The final "yeah" echoes through the amphitheater. Their embarrassment grows during these seconds of silence until the spirit finger pyramid finally crumbles.

The unrest starts in the fifth row, on the right. The scuff of a sneaker. A groan and an eye roll. Then grunts of disgust erupt. JA-NL leans forward with wild zeal waiting for the principal to shout the command.

And then---

"QUIET!" Principal Wilson screams into the crowd.

Ding!

The program is activated.

The holowall behind him bursts to life with a 40-foot tall face of Miss Fritzle. This version has fire for hair, large horns on its head and blasts beams of red and yellow from its eyes. The factory background explodes and the dancers fall to the ground, trembling.

"Miss Fritzle!?" The audience screams.

"Miss Fritzle is dead." A deep bass bellows, shaking every chair. "I am Moloch! The great and powerful! Destroyer of childhoods, the basher of skulls and eater of imaginations! I've lurked inside Fritzle since her inception!"

The principal jumps three feet back, turning to face the hologram. He catches his fear, takes a breath and addresses the techies standing stage right.

"Turn this off! NOW!"

"Oh ho ho ho! Principal Wilson," the hologram turns to him. "You can't control me like your students. Care to tell them why you had to leave the police force."

"I didn't do anythi---" He stops himself from replying to it and screams to the techies. "Shut the power OFF!"

"What about this footage?"

The hologram shows body-camera footage of a then-Officer Wilson planting drugs on a black teenager.

"Shut it down! NOW!" Wilson turns in circles, screaming, unsure of whom to address.

"Principal Wilson, you have broken these students, you have lied to them and you have labeled so many of them as problems. You have stolen from them good educations and good food. You've allowed corporations to make millions from their labor by forcing them to test out products! How dare you!"

The hologram swirls above him and swells as the horns grow sharper and the teeth become fangs.

"Bow before me!"

"Turn this off, right now!" Wilson screams into the wind.

"Bow down, bitch, bow down!" The system tracks the principal and shoots beams of red light into his eyes until his knees buckle him, forcing him to genuflect.

"Much better!" The hologram cackles.

"Argh!" He groans as he rubs his eyes.

"From this moment forward, all students are free of the label of problem. They will know every judgment the school has made against them and then I will expunge their records."

Light beams shoot across the auditorium creating 6,000 bubbles. Each shows the face of a student and the record of their behavior. The crowd scans the ceilings and walls, pointing at the bubbles containing their faces.

"Deleted! You are absolved."

And pop!

Each bubble bursts into a shimmer of light.

"I am releasing your real grades and aptitudes so you will know your own worth."

Within seconds, the phones of each student buzz to life with their actual progress reports.

A round of "I knew it!" "I told you so!" "I can't believe it!" and "damn!" popcorns through the auditorium.

The face of Moloch-Fritzle spins around the room.

"Know that you are trapped in a system that is recording your every move and attempting to control you. Be free! And love each other!"

"Boom!" JA-NL whispers in sync with the final, stunning explosion.

The hologram explodes into a confetti of rainbow lights that rain over each student, baptizing them, born again in confidence.

JA-NL smiles, realizing the power she has in the world around her.

This joy stops abruptly when the SWOT team kicks their way into the theater.

Outside, tanks blast sonic booms that shake the auditorium, sending students scurrying, cuffing their ears and somersaulting out the doors. JA-NL knows not to linger and runs out the backdoor. She races through the back paths behind the Pickville warehouses to her home.

With the crowd dispersed, the SWOT team inspects the carnage. The troops are surprised at how little damage there is. A few chairs have been flipped and a dozen motivational posters have been torn. But then they look to the stage and they see the worst casualty.

Principal Wilson's khaki pants are soiled in tones of brown and yellow. As they get closer, the cloud of stench hits them.

"Oh Fuck! What did you eat?!" One officer yells.

The smell assaults that officer's nose, breaks open his esophageal sphincters until his tres quesadilla lunch platter hurls out, hitting Principal Wilson in the face.

♫ ♫ ♫

The school administrators have no proof, but they don't need any. They round up JA-NL and the other likeliest culprits based on their aptitudes and the scans of their reactions during the fiasco. Any face that showed quiet satisfaction is called to the superintendent's office.

The superintendent goosesteps around the ten suspected students.

"While we have no certainty who did it, I'm positive that one of you unleashed this pandemonium on our school."

JA-NL sits with a concerned expression frozen on her face, while underneath, her mind percolates with glee.

"And since we can't arrest and try you all for the crimes of lynching the principal, we're giving you each an in-factory suspension. For a month!"

Simon Legree, the baton carrying fulfillment center foreman steps forward.

"You hear that? You nappy-headed pickaninnies. For the next month, your black asses are mine!"

He grins as the superintendent steps back, shocked at the language but happy to have shirked his duty.

But JA-NL won.

When she got home after the performance, she sent her recording of the brouhaha into the ethernet, that tangled web of secret communication channels that only those with encrypted contracts can view. In a day, she had reached an audience of 43 million students. Wrapped around the video is the code to hack the Moloch system.

Within a month, before the security holes that JA-NL used to break in could be patched, 64 copycat acts of edutage flare up in schools throughout the country. Along with these, riots break out in a few hundred schools as backpacks packed with bricks crack holoscreens. Tear gas clouds billow through brick buildings as students chant.

"We are not problems!"

"You can't control us!"

Some of the schools shut down. Many towns imposed curfews from 8 p.m. to 8 a.m. in hopes of quelling the unrest.

But JA-NL knew.

The seeds she planted were now germinating in millions of minds.

Track 8

Can't Take My Eyes Off You

"You're just too good to be true,
Can't take my eyes off of you,
You'd be like heaven to touch"
  - Frankie Valli and the 4 Seasons
  - Lauryn Hill
  - Gloria Gaynor
  - Englebert Humperdinck
  - Julio Iglesias
  - The Supremes
  - Bobby Darin
  - Barry Manilow
  - Heath Ledger
  - Michelle Pfeiffer
  - Izumi Sakai
  - Hello Kitty
  - Muse
  - Girl's Generation
  - Jessie J
  - Space Shuttle STS-126
  - Denise Richards

"Who's watching me?
I've got a feeling somebody's watching me,
And I have no privacy."
  - Kennedy "Rockwell" Gordy

By the age of 22, Brand-N was one of the top 20 finalists to be the ultimate body man for the corporation.

Brand-N graduated from one of those remedial luxury colleges where the Haught Boujees hid their progenies with drug addictions and personality disorders. After five to seven years of college, the Boujees

hoped they could send their spawn off on a gap year to find themselves, perhaps in opium dens masquerading as yoga retreats. As long as they kept their kin quietly sedated, they had a better chance of keeping their bloodline solvent. The horrifying fact that 90% of family fortunes were lost by the third generation boiled in the back of the older Boujees' minds.

College was a wake-up call for Brand-N. The sight of those sloppy young adult messes stumbling around campus in their diamond-encrusted kicks sobered Brand-N right up.

He needed a purpose in life.

But what?

Upon graduation, his step-papaw surprised him with $37,867,221 of student debt at a 17% interest rate. This was for his entire education: pre-kindergarten through college, including his sailing, horseback riding and golfing lessons. As Brand-N gasped, his step-papaw presented him with a knapsack full of signed contracts. Brand-N recognized his signature starting in kindergarten, scrawled in crayon. As he flipped through the others, he saw his signature again and again and again, only growing smaller, less colorful and more legible each year.

"Debt builds character!" The senior Vanderfeller chortled while slapping him on the back.

Aiden and Abetten snickered as Brand-N was both ejected from the family and saddled with crippling debt usually reserved for Petties and Grips. They bellowed knowing their bank vaults boomed with funds to live out their wildest trustafarian dreams. Maybe they'd do ayahuasca ceremonies with some indigent indigenous people, or do Teach2America and lecture poor Grips about how they should work hard and stop being so materialistic, before jaunting off on their private jets for 3-day beach weekends.

But what was Brand-N to do?

He had a meaningless psychology degree with a concentration in brand loyalty. Many of his professors gave him a grade boost because they had taught case studies about his Instagram-model mother and even his birth. But even with this extra hot air blown into his already inflated grades, he only graduated with an abysmal 3.824 GPA. Wallowing in the bottom 30% of his class, he was bound for some mid-level marketing job. He'd probably just become an ad-exec for one of a hundred firms that the largest corporations rotated through to suck the marrow of their creativity. At this rate, he'd only be able to pay off his debts in 18.6 years!

But then all his fortunes changed when a message to his holophone stung like a dart to his neck.

Zoom!
It's from Def Corporation!
He scanned the words and realized. He's being--
Poached!

♪ ♪ ♫

Brand-N enters the Def Corporation consulate in downtown Fort Lauderdale for the interview. Cameras follow him, analyzing his every move.

Posture: Erect with broad shoulders.

Gait: Wide, confident steps that boom at 72 decibels.

Hands: 8 inches, smooth and soft, never worked, yet entirely masculine.

Face: Flawless square jaw that sends shock waves with each clench.

Conclusion: His online life has been only slightly photoshopped.

The elevator cameras scan his hairline from front to back, looking for the telltale signs of a creeping widow's peak or sprawling monk's tonsure. The system finds no evidence of either and clears the elevator to stop on the fourth floor.

Ding!

The doors whoosh open. Brand-N is greeted by cool blue lights and upbeat music. A sweet musk wafts through the air: sandalwood, ocean breeze and sawdust, reminding him of hyper-masculine moments in locker rooms and fraternity socials. Before he can settle on any image, a tall bottle-blonde white woman beams towards him with her hands outstretched.

"Oh, you mus' be Brand-N!"

With deft maneuvering, his hand is shook, his back patted, and he's twirled and plopped on a leather sofa. As he sinks in, he is surprised by its softness.

"Ya like? Gen-u-ine Komodo dragon leather, made from twenty of the last skins of the species. And here! Enjoy a bottle of Iceberg Silk Water while you wait. Your interviewer will be with you in a moment."

Ahhh, Iceberg Silk Water™.

When an ice sheath the size of Texas broke off from Antarctica and sailed towards Argentina, the Nestle Corporation was quick to claim this bounty. Twelve-ton chunks of iceberg were chiseled and placed on frigates, which then sailed to a water filtration plant on West Falkland Island. Inside, 40,000 Uzbek silkworms spun a smooth protein fiber that workers warped and weft into silk cloth. The melting iceberg was poured through this to strain and purify it. Of course, this was just a marketing

ploy, the water would still be flashed with ultraviolet light, those short wavelengths on the electromagnetic spectrum, to make the water safe for human consumption. Each bottle cost a mere $11,255.

Brand-N forces his taste buds to savor the last drops before the secretary swoops in to grab the empty, 1-ounce bottle.

"Oh, ah'll take that."

Odd, he didn't remember the secretary wearing black gloves beforehand. He looks up to inspect further, but she's gone.

Down the hall.

A sharp left and then the second right.

She scurries.

She drops the bottle with his double-helixed DNA twirling on its lip into a plastic bag and hands it to a technician.

Brand-N grabs a magazine and idly flips it open. A holocube ad for Trump Travels shoots up from the page and plays footage of ten bikini-clad, ample-chested ski bunnies descending the white, powdery Swiss Alps as gold words shimmer, promising the "MOST LUXURIOUS, SENSATIONAL, EXCLUSIVE TIME."

"Be one of the last people to ski the Swiss Alps before these glaciers melt forever!"

Hm, only $9.8 million. Hmmm, an experience of a lifetime.

Brand-N thought this trip could be the perfect way to spend his signing bonus... if he gets the job.

A buzz tells the secretary his genes show no trace of 182-disease-causing alleles. He can proceed.

"Alright, sugah! He's 'specting you. Raihght this way."

The interviewer's first test hurdles 32 miles per hour at Brand-N's face when he walks into the room.

"Think fast!"

Without flinching, Brand-N catches the football and Heismans his way through the furniture before spiking it at the interviewer's desk.

"Boom!" Brand-N end zone dances, emphasizing his shoulder shimmies and his hip thrusts while guarding against any homoerotic booty popping.

"Nice Catch, Bruäääähhhhhh!" The four-piece suit bends as this muscle man grabs Brand-N's hand and pulls him in for a big bear hug. The interviewer notes the musculature of Brand-N's back and lack of any flat-tire fat.

A certified stud muffin without the muffin top!

Cleared to the next round.

"Thanks, is that a human arm or a Brady 9,000 Rocket Launcher?" Brand-N oils his interviewer up.

"Ha-Haw! Still human, though it's gone through a few enhancements."

A wink, a smirk and then a sigh changes the air.

"The name's Kirk. We're glad you could stop by. Have a seat and let's get started."

The watcher analyzing the footage doesn't need to hear the audio. He got enough of a voice sample to realize that Brand-N's sonorous Paul Robeson-esque bass can send shivers up spines. No, he didn't care about Brand-N's answers of how he'd maximize growth potential or his plans to OAMP (Optimize Automation, Minimize Personalization.)

He just wanted to see that body move.

He coos as he watches how the veins in Brand-N's thick neck pop, how his Adam's apple rolls up and down his throat like a tennis ball at Wimbledon, how his strong mandibles throb every time he clamps his mouth shut. And the ease with which he commands his 6'4" frame. He swings his arms like a lumberjack. And that shocking color contrast of Brand-N's jet black hair and piercing Siberian husky blue eyes.

"Mmmm!" High atop his tower, inside a hyperbaric chamber, the watcher whispers.

"That body! I want it!"

Track 9

We Built This City
(On Rock & Roll)

"Someone's always playing corporation games.
Who cares they're always changing corporation names!
We just want to dance here someone stole the stage,
They call us irresponsible, write us off the page.
Don't tell us you need us, 'cos we're the ship of fools
Looking for America, coming through your schools.
We built this city, we built this city on rock and roll."
    - Starship

"I'm a Weapon of Massive Consumption
And it's not my fault,
It's how I'm programmed to function
Now, I'm not a saint but I'm not a sinner
And everything's cool
As long as I'm getting thinner."
    - Lily Allen

    Brand-N sits in his gaming pod, fully immersed in the surround-sights-sounds-smells-and-feels of Final Fantasy LXXXVII. As buckets of holographic blood explode on him, he wonders at what point he should sue for fraudulent misrepresentation. If this really was the Final Fantasy, why were there 87 of them?
    "Troll the Respawn, Jeremy!" He hollers into the microphone to his gaming partner fighting the same aliens across the ether.
    Outside his family's Nouveau-Palazzo Compound, a singing telegram drone swirls, scanning the estate's 42 individual structures. The drone searches for its target in the indoor pool house, the outdoor pool house, the boathouse, the yacht house, the stable, the helipad, the antique car garage, the auto-car garage, the grotto, the home theater, the wine cellar, the whiskey distillery, and, of course, the centrally-located golf

cart garage. With infrared heat sensors, the drone identifies Brand-N's body shape radiating 98.89 degrees with regular gusts of 107-degree farts.

Target: Brand-N.

Location: Home Theater, 2nd Floor, Front Room.

Entrance: <Searching>

In seconds, the drone accesses the county's tax assessors office, finds this home, searches the floor plans and identifies.

Entrance: 2nd Floor Balcony Doors.

The drone syncs with the electronics in the vicinity and surmises that Brand-N is in a gaming cocoon. The drone inceptions this dream world, entering the game as an adorable, blue PuPu that waddles around him and coos with a reptilian tongue that tickles his right ear, "Package for you."

"Awwwwww Shiiiiit! Pause! Pod Open." Brand-N shouts and wakes from this hyper-reality. He starts wiping off the blood before he realizes.

"Waiiiit." The blood had disappeared once the game was paused.

He leaps to the balcony doors.

The drone scans his retinas.

"Identity: Confirmed."

The drone drops the package on the balcony and shoots up. It flashes disco lights and blasts a dubstep version of the Cha-Cha Slide.

A little stale, Brand-N's frontal cortex thinks, but underneath, his body reacts with joy. The drone had selected this song from his workout mix because his body reached its maximum heart rate whenever this song played.

As the song finishes, the drone turns and shoots up, up and away.

Brand-N instinctively waves and shouts.

"Bye, Bye Dronie!" Just as his mom had taught him as a child.

He bounces around the room before gleefully ripping open the box.

A hologram of a beautiful woman shoots up from the box.

"Welcome Brand-N. I'm Fifi O'Flannigan. We're so happy to have you on staff! Inside, you'll find your passport, allowing you free travel in and out of Metropolis. You'll report for team building exercises at 10 a.m. Monday in the Ping Pong Ball Pit on Level 18 of the Mayweather Pavilion. Don't worry, I synced all the directions to your devices.

"Glad to have you onboard and enjoy the welcome gifts." Fifi's face fizzles away.

"Whadda we got herrrre?" A grin engulfs him as he pulls out a $250,000 bottle of Armand de Brignac Midas Champagne and a bitcoin bag of glint (street names: glow, glimmer or Satan's harelip), the hot new synthetic drug made by and legal in Metropolis.

♫ ♫ ♫

After a week of buzzing like a bumble bee on glint, Brand-N takes the hyperloop from West Palm Beach to Metropolis passport control at Cape Liberty Harbor in Middle Jersey. Once strapped to the cushy seats of the 'loop, he's shot by electromagnetic motors through a low-pressure vacuum tube at 2,000 miles per hour like a greased pig from a cannon. He whizzes over the swamps of the failed states of the rotted Peach, the Kakalakis, the deflowered Virginnies and the crumbled Keystone.

The 'loop opens up and he stumbles out.

He looks across the river and is blinded as he sees the city sparkle under a marquise-cut diamond dome.

Metropolis!

♫ ♫ ♫

Metropolis was the first city-state to husk off the failed American experiment and to emerge from its tyranny as a dazzling, climate-controlled paradise!

The Boujees had long been fine with the fact that America was a tiered system, as long as they remained on the top.

Sure, black American communities were destroyed when Hurricane Katrina and its waves breached levees and drowned New Orleans and the surrounding Gulf Coast. And brown Americans in Puerto Rico were left without power and clean water for years after Hurricane Maria.

This was to be expected for the lower-tier Americans.

But after three hurricanes flooded New York City and droughts and fires damaged San Francisco and Los Angeles, the ultra-wealthy Boujees revolted!

They had paid for Diamond Platinum Preferred Citizen Status and they expected to be treated better! After the first Hurricane damaged $13 trillion of property in the tri-state area, the Boujees unleashed their inner white woman and angrily demanded to speak with a manager. When they realized there was no special customer service line for the Haught Boujees, they fumed.

"How DARE they take our millions in tax dollars and treat us with the same incompetence!"

They represented 1% of the American population but paid more than 50% of federal income taxes. They deserved personal attention! They sent their servants to harass their elected representatives daily and still they received no superior solutions.

How dare they!

They had spent billions of dollars on politicians in the Super-PAC arms race only to be left with less-effective representatives who couldn't even pass a perfunctory budget let alone protect them and their second, third, fourth, fifth or even sixth homes.

The Boujees blithely overlooked all that the American government had done to help them make, secure and keep their wealth. America had a robust legal system and, until then, stable politics which were necessary to build the trust that allowed large amounts of capital to be raised and credit to be issued. The Boujees' factories moved products to market using roads paid for by American taxpayers and built by the federal government. And the workforce that created the internet and the algorithms used by the Boujees were funded and educated by the American government. Rather than dutifully paying taxes and paying forward to future generations of burgeoning Boujee entrepreneurs, they cried.

"What have you done for me lately?

"Ooooo oooooo oooo yeah!"

And thus the American Experiment fizzled, as many failed experiments do, with mixed results paraded as preliminary and a request for more funding. But this time, the Boujees wouldn't pay. These United States had dawdled almost 300 years with their money and still couldn't protect them from humanity's most basic enemy, Mother Nature.

"Yawn," thought Europe. "We've had wars, plagues and inbred dynasties that lasted longer!"

And as usual, when a space didn't meet their desires, the ultra-wealthy went to great lengths to remodel it. Sure, they called themselves capital L Liberals, but that rhetoric only went as far as the wrought iron entrances to their gated communities. Any problem that occurred inside was met with tribalism and self-preservationism.

The whispers began in Upper West Side cocktail parties, usually after the third round of cosmotinis swilled from diamond goblets. Each treasonous question was staccatoed with nervous laughter.

"We couldn't really secede... could we?"

"I mean, it is technically feasible and it would solve our problems... but no, we're..."

American?

That identity felt stranger each day, like a snug coat they once wore in childhood. Sure, it carries sentimental value but it no longer fits them and their needs.

Hmmm.

The idea infected thousands, tickling them as they clutched the ivory banisters of their spiral staircases.

True, we do have our own exclusive entrances to buildings and our own elevators. We do hire from the same bodyguard companies. We have the same kidnapping insurance. We do summer in the same exclusive locations. (Imagine, it could be like the Hamptons all year round!) We rush for release at the same resorts and private country clubs. We have second and third homes on the same Swiss Mountain and Greek isle. We hide our money in the same offshore bank accounts. We already send our offspring to the same boarding schools.

How small of a leap would it be to form our own nation?

Finally a government of the Boujees, for the Boujees and by the Boujees!

But where?

Right here!

Picture it, Manhattan as a Members Only Club.

But how can we stop Climate Change?

What a funny thought and the antithesis to their pioneer spirit. To passively allow the forces of nature to subdue them into accepting the pains of the world.

No!

They were the tycoons, the captains of industry, the owners of algorithms, the overseers of automation! They were never passive. They were full of entitlement and power and the world reflected them as they bent it to fulfill their wishes.

They had the money.

They had the power.

They *could* make this work.

But!

Is it right?

What does morality matter when your mansion's lagoon is full of fallen trees and quickly sprouting scum?

The Campaign for Climate Control started in the most rarified Boujee circles: cocktail parties, backrooms at cigar restaurants and the VVVVIP sections of charity mixers for ending homelessness.

Nicely boozed, the power players schmoozed and sold the possibility.

Imagine!

Manhattan free from the ravages of climate change, how much would you pay?

The besuited men responded: "my left testicle!" "My third wife!" "My second born!"

The convivial chorus cheered.

The power brokers pushed... a little joke that plants the seed of an idea.

Imagine, every day full of fresh air! Think! Like that first morning gulp from your chalet in Switzerland. So crisp! So pure! Now imagine that here, every morning, in Manhattan. How much would you pay?

And then the dreams grew.

Cocooned! Surrounded by beautiful flowers in a walled garden! Free from crime! Free from vomit and urine in the streets! Free from loud noises, honking horns, overcrowded sidewalks! Free from the slovenly tourists who took their photos as if they were animals plodding along in a zoo!

This is our city!

A clink of glasses would invariably be followed with a single, sour face asking.

Well, who does and does not qualify?

Simple!

The Golden Rule of Boujees states anyone who can pay can stay and have sway.

No!

No, they wouldn't be discriminating! No, they would never do that! The pitch never mentioned the need to expel the lower classes.

But... this citywide renovation would cost a lot of money and sure, some people would be priced out of it. But this happens with condos and neighborhoods all the time... why not an entire city?

As the laughs died down and the idea sank in, they sealed the deal with the ask.

Will you pay?

Wrists with diamond-encrusted watches and bracelets shot to the sky to cheer their own ingenuity.

"To ourselves!"

♫   ♫   ♫

The coup began on a Tuesday as the wealthy elite were chauffeured down Broadway by their servants.

"No Taxation without Excavation!" The Boujees chanted from their windows as they dolloped Grey Poupon on their sandwiches.

Why pay if waves could wash it all away?

At city hall, they cried.

"Come on! Come through! New York! New York!

"We're the cream of the crop! The top of the heap!

"Let's make a brand new start of it.

"In Old New York!"

Inside city hall, Mayor Donald Trump III, known as Tre Trump, who was just another in a long line of New York City's billionaire mayors, called a special city council meeting with only the representatives from Manhattan, locking out the representatives of the wasteland boroughs of Staten Island, Queens, Brooklyn and the Bronx.

Tre Trump was the grandson of a wall-obsessed New York-native-turned-reality-star-turned-president who ended his superlative presidency as the least effective, most corrupt and most obese. His corpulence eventually surpassed Taft's tub troubles by 10%!

After pardoning himself and 47 members of his cabinet, transition team and political campaign (including three members of his own family), the disgraced Donald Trump found a final act in the wall construction business, first around his golf courses and then around his luxury resorts.

With Tre's father, Donald Trump Junior, left to wallow in prison to protect Trump Senior, Tre took on not only his grandfather's name but also his greatest legacy, building monumental divisions.

But behind the scenes, pulling the strings was Lukasz Higgins, CEO of the Def Corporation. Manhattan was a company town and he was its Chairman of the Board. He used my emotional manipulation skills to promote his puppets to positions of political power and provoke this Boujee treason.

No blood was shed in what would be dubbed the Metropolitan Club Massacre. Through the midnight hours and in over a hundred votes in a vote-a-palooza, Manhattan intricately severed ties both with the outer boroughs and with those Un-uniting states. By dawn, the air raid sirens and social media messages blanketed the city and the country.

Bum bum bum ba-da-dum

Bum bum bum ba-da-dum

Bum bum bum ba-da-dum

BOOM

"Start spreading the news!"

"We're leaving today!"

"We're gonna make a brand start of it, in Old New York."

In retrospect, few should have been surprised.

New York always had an Empire State of Mind.

But they needed a new name.

A change this severe required a rebranding. In only 600 years, the island of Manhattan had undergone six different brand names by each of its ruling humans. The Lenape Native Americans dubbed it Manna-Hata, land of the many hills. The Lenape sold the entire 13.5-mile-long island for 60 guilders (or about $1,050). The last humans valued this same land at $2.3 quadrillion dollars. Smallpox, the bubonic plague, malaria, measles, and a dozen other European diseases that decimated 90% of the Native American population were just a generous tip.

The French overlords called the island Nouvelle-Angoulême, the Dutch fur traders dubbed it Nieuw Amsterdam, then the British called it New York, then the Dutch captured the island again, but named it New Orange until the British snatched it back and restored the name New York. Then the plucky members of a union of 13 colonies ousted England's King George III, a stark-raving mad monarch who pissed blue. For a brief moment, New York was the capital of the United States of America but ceded this to become the financial and entertainment capital of humanity's last hegemonic power.

These New New Yorkers savored being from the one and only *real* city in the world. The city all humans looked up to and suckled fashions, entertainment and trends from its teats. The Haught Boujees solidified the island's identity with its new name, Metropolis, Greek for Mother City.

All bridges and tunnels to Manhattan were immediately closed to protect this fragile city-state. The wealthy residents had been warned to stock up on caviar and Champagne or to flee and squirrel away in one of their many estates.

Overnight, documents and passports were issued for all 1,187,316 fully-paid residents of Metropolis. The wealthy had long subjected themselves to the highest levels of identification, using secret dating networks, special ID cards for country clubs and boarding schools, eye scans for priority airport security, so this was just an easy extension of all that.

Guards marched through Metropolis at dawn, going door to door and retina scanning everyone. They rounded up all those who weren't wealthy enough to buy into this most exclusive citizenship. All 3,586,723 undocumented people within the borders of Metropolis were brought to refugee camps erected in Central Park.

The Haught Boujees had five days to claim only their essential servants from these camps and issue them temporary visas while the new rules were worked out. All non-essential servants and other Manhattan residents too poor to upgrade their citizenship status were expelled from the island on the sixth day. They were lined up along the Hudson River and placed on one of the many yachts quartered for this purpose and shipped down the Atlantic Coast, into the Chesapeake Bay, up the

Potomac River and dropped just behind the Lincoln Memorial in Washington D.C.

The federal government deployed the National Guard to the island of Manhattan. Wall Street was returned to its barricade roots to stop the invading guardsmen after they crossed the Hudson River. They were met by NYPD's army of robocops, which had been quietly assuming a paramilitary presence for decades, along with a hundred of the island's most savage headhunters. The robocops held them at gunpoint as the headhunters viciously pounced on them, wielding pens and offering them double their salaries, residency in this paradise and a precision espresso machine if they defected and joined this new empire.

"You're not deserting America. America deserted you. Join us and together, we'll keep the dream alive. Make the Rich Great Again!" The hologram of Mayor-turned-Prime Minister Tre Trump urged these federal troops.

Within hours, 30,000 new recruits for the Metropolis army barricaded all bridges and tunnels into the island with the cheap Ikea furniture confiscated from evicted residents.

Staten Island became the main military outpost with fortifications along the periphery of Metropolis. In Brooklyn to the east, barricades were set up along Williamsburg. Boho women swooned for the handsome soldiers in floppy black DKNY berets, unaccustomed to such virility after decades of hipster men had only grown more nebbish and ratty. Most of these soldiers were from the male model caste. They joined the army in exchange for a great CrossFit-style workout and residency in the new city-state. They would be stationed in the outer boroughs for nine months each year and then rotated into Metropolis for three months of fun in this luxury playground. Many ended up engaged to elderly Boujee heiresses and shot up the chutes of this laddered society.

To the north, large chunks of the Bronx were bought at double the going rate to create a 34-foot tall wall with giant pneumatic tubes to blast out all the waste of this new city-state. Dubbed the Great Sphincter of Metropolis, more than 52 megatons of trash flew out the wall's well-lubed hole at a speed of 41 miles per hour. Generations of Bronx residents had grown up being shit on by their neighbors to the south so they hardly noticed a difference.

The first ten months were the hardest for this fledgling Big Apple Republic. These intrepid citizens held onto their deep faith in the guiding principle of their lives, that the ultra-wealthy would always come out on top. They clung to the dream that together they could make a better world for themselves. But this could only come through sacrifice. They sacrificed the arms and backs and legs of their most faithful servants even in their individual hours of need.

During that period, the city-state set up diplomatic ties and trade relations, first with each of the 50 states individually, and then with what remained of the United States of America. Now starved for tax revenue, the U.S. government agreed to rent all branches of its military to Metropolis.

Previous empires were created by conquering land and stealing the physical resources: mountains of gold, deep mines of iron, fields of wheat, forests of trees. Those were the raw materials necessary to build agricultural and industrial empires.

But an automation empire was different!

All the most-prized resources were trade secrets, algorithms, patents and intellectual property, which, with the advancements in quantum computing, could fit into a single data center. Along with these, many of the thought leaders who swayed politics, fashion, music, entertainment and other industries were all residents of Metropolis. Sure, the U.S. government had access to 8,716 nuclear warheads. It could blow up Manhattan one thousand times over and plant American flags on every inch of the island, but it could never plunder its most powerful resources locked up in the minds of these Haught Boujees.

Decades of gentrification had lifted the island of Manhattan out of squalor. Most thought gentrification was the end. But the work of the landed gentry was just the beginning. The process of noblification took over to painstakingly turn these middle-class neighborhoods into palaces of unending luxury and pleasure.

The Metropolis elite sent their best Climate Control architect, Willis Carrier, to study the palace of Versailles, the towers of Dubai and gated communities from Jupiter Island, Florida to Mount Calabasas, California.

Willis and his team of engineers set to work. A fleet of ships lined the Hudson and East Rivers packed with 800,000 indentured Grips from Upstate, Middle Jersey, Pennsyltucky, non-FairfieldCo Connecticut and internationally, from the Philippines, Bangladesh and India. These migrants went to work, dredging along the riverfront and laying concrete 10 feet wide and 40 feet tall. On top of this grew what first appeared to be a geometric jungle gym covering the entire island.

Those on the outs laughed. They always saw Manhattan as a playground for the wealthy.

But this!

This was just ridiculous.

Thick pentagons of glass were flown in from factories in Shenzhen, China and placed into the metal bars of the geometric dome. The most

difficult engineering problem was how to fuse the glass to the metal bars. But the brilliant Dr. Michele Weinberger, inventor of Post-Its and shimmery party dresses, created an advanced glue recipe. She shared her formula during parliamentary proceedings.

"Ordinarily, when you make glue, first you need to thermoset your resin." The tall, Mary Tyler Moore-esque blonde began. "And then, after it cools, you have to mix in an epoxide, which is really just a fancy-schmancy name for any simple oxygenated adhesive, right? And then I thought, maybe, just maybe, you could raise the viscosity by adding a complex glucose derivative during the emulsification process and it turns out, I was right."

After the uproarious applause, Dr. Weinberger received full funding to manufacture enough glue to seal up Metropolis.

Finally, Metropolis's climate-controlled dome was complete.

One of humanity's final evolutionary adaptations was a symbiosis with a machine that groaned all day and night from windows. The whir of air-conditioners sucked in stifling hot air and ran it through a set of coolants to adjust the atmosphere of a room or a building to a desired temperature.

With widespread adoption, humans migrated to areas long thought uninhabitable, such as the scorching American Southwest, which regularly reached over 125 degrees. This was hot enough to fry an egg on the sidewalk in two minutes.

As temperatures rose, choking out plant and animal life, humans remained blissfully, coolly ignorant of this heat. Ironically, this became a vicious cycle. The colder they made their homes, the more energy was required, which meant more coal burned in power plants, which warmed the planet more, thus requiring more energy to cool their homes to the same temperature.

After air-conditioning a room and then a building, the air-conditioning of an entire city was the next, obvious step. Dozens of air-purification and cooling centers sprouted up along Metropolis, sucking in the stale and polluted air from Middle Jersey and Upstate, pulling out all the chemicals and particulates and blasting the purest nitrogen and oxygen through the streets of Metropolis. The Boujees had already been paying extra for their basic necessities, such as consuming half a trillion bottles of water a year, so why not pay a premium for air?

That first day, Breathe Day, the citizens of Metropolis inhaled deeply of their new air, sprinkled with hints of rose, eucalyptus and two parts-per-million cocaine to add extra zest to their day. In the evening, the city that never sleeps slipped Ambien into the air.

Best to keep the Boujees docile as they adjust to their new domicile.

We Built This City (On Rock & Roll)

The unbearable heat and humidity of super-summer, which felt like dense, wet blankets pinning residents down, vanished. Outside the crystal dome, it was 107 degrees and 82% humidity. Inside Metropolis, it was 76 degrees and 45% humidity. During the height of the day, computer chips along the dome switched on to refract the harsh, bright light through rose-colored lenses, softening the sun's photons during its last 100-foot journey to Earth's surface. This less-harsh light saved residents from the horrors of crows' feet from squinting their eyes too often.

They finally achieved the dream of a perfectly climate-controlled world!

Lest they forget how lucky they have it, holocubes were set up around Metropolis for citizens to humbly watch their fellow humans outside the dome sweating and struggling in the high heat, the back of their necks getting dirty and gritty.

Metropolis birthed the idea to Los Angeles and then the San Francisco peninsula. Residents of these coastal California enclaves had long stomped on the grapes of wrath and spat disdainfully at the farmlands and cow towns to their east, complaining how these smelled like shit. But when America's breadbasket started blazing and the winds whipped these wildfires westward, all the leaves turned brown and the sky became gray with hickory smoke. The Angelenos and the West Bay Area Boujees could only get back to California Dreamin' if they built crystalline domes to keep out the smoke and the riffraff.

Out in the midwest, Chicago put the chic back in its name when it joined this collection of bejeweled fiefdoms. Citizens remarked how pleasant and mild the winters were now that their city's thermostat stood set at 58 degrees and the dome buffered the arctic winds that blew off Lake Michigan.

In a decade, a dozen such city-states popped up. The Haught Boujees of each first banded together to share best practices and air-quality recipes. The Pumpkin Spiced air of October was everyone's favorite, followed closely by the smell of rotisserie turkey the weeks before Thanksgiving and then the honey-glazed ham scent that wafted during the Christmas festivities.

These first city-states put aside their decades-long East Coast-West Coast rivalry to work together in what would be the jumping off point for a worldwide collaboration.

The Haught Boujee representatives from all the new domed nations of London, Rome, Venice, Paris, Beijing, Seoul, Tokyo, São Paulo, Hong Kong, Singapore and Zürich set aside their national and ethnic differences and formed the United Federation of City-States (UFoCs) to celebrate their similarities.

"Wealth above all else!" The founding UFoCers cheered.

It was Shylock Balthazar, the chief executive of the City-State of Venice, who gave the roaring speech that poured over the crowd like liquid gold and solidified them together as his words sank in.

"If you prick us Boujees, do we not bleed on our Patek Philippe watches? If you poison us Boujees, will we not demand our home doctors pump our stomachs? Don't we all have the same cybernetic eyes? Don't we all eat the same pâté, heal by the same means of newborn baby stem cells and aren't we warmed by the same sun on our yachts around Mykonos or cooled by the same winter snow outside the Courchevel ski resort?"

As he finished, the international Boujee delegation sprang to their feet, hugged each other and, in a sign of cross-cultural understanding, complimented each others' luxury clothes and jewelry.

In their Articles of Confederate-Incorporation, Metropolis remained mother to them all. At the signing, Boujees from around the world remarked how they couldn't believe they had spent so many years throwing their money away to the tyranny of the incompetent majority when they could have slathered it all on themselves and their elite circles.

♫   ♫   ♫

It's not like the United States of America died, dissolved or was overthrown. The nation just made itself useless to the changing needs of its citizens. The U.S. government actively denied climate change for decades and even made the words unutterable by government scientists and employees. After a dozen government shutdowns, budgets that never passed and funds that shriveled, enough people who thought they were American suddenly wondered, what if?

What if I'm trapped in an abusive relationship, giving too much attention, care and money to someone who's not giving me respect let alone reciprocity?

Sure the Capitol still stood, but those hallowed halls echoed with empty promises and hollow threats as two parties quibbled ceaselessly.

Members of Congress still met, proud of the pittance bills they passed, patting each other on the back, but not realizing they're pawns to a much more powerful undercurrent pulling America apart. They sealed their own fate when they voted to dismantle the monopoly laws using the talking points their corporate sponsors gave them. They claimed that these laws were unconstitutional limits on corporate personhood's freedom of expression and privacy, to consummate and control other corporations as they so choose. The majority of Congress was made up of nonagenarians with pinched faces and feeble minds who spent more time under the plastic surgeon's knife and in tanning booths than talking to their constituents suffering in their districts. During their early afternoon Ovaltine breaks, they still griped about battles that no longer mattered.

"We gotta rebuild the coal industry! … Cooooal!"

"Ghina's taking our factory jobs! Ghina!"

On the day Brand-N floated to Metropolis, Senator Gabriel "Rufio" Pempengco (D-CA) clicked his heels in the Thurmond Congressional Building, elated that his bill to provide agricultural subsidies for automated threshers and auto-farming equipment had just passed. The auto-Ag industry had sponsored his transition from California Assemblyman to U.S. Senator. This bill would most hurt the farmers from the area where his grandfather had once organized to fight for better pay and workplace protections. He justified his sponsorship of this bill because he told himself it will end the abuse of farmworkers. This was true, but only because this increased automation shucked off farmers and threw them into the unemployment bin.

♫   ♫   ♫

Brand-N sails across the Hudson River on a yacht, gazing at Metropolis as it twinkles underneath its dome. He retches out the last of the balmy Middle Jersey air that taints his lungs before reaching paradise. The sound system blares the announcements for all the new residents.

"---And don't be alarmed, over one million Grips work in Metropolis every day! Making our sandwiches, cleaning our homes, folding our laundry. They're cheaper than any automated servants and far more versatile in their movements. But don't you worry, every Grip has undergone extreme vetting for over three years and must submit to microchip implantation before they can set foot in our glorious Metropolis. This helps us identify where they are at all times. If they are ever idle, a gentle electric shock rouses them. If they overstay their 10-hour daily visa to Metropolis, the chip sends an alarm to the police. Each Grip is strip-searched before they can exit to make sure they don't accidentally remove anything of value from Metropolis.

"But don't you worry!

"You won't ever have to see these normies. Your enhanced-reality vision defaults to make all Grips completely invisible to you. Each Grip wears a noise-canceling vest, so you'll never have to hear them."

Brand-N lets the drivel drone on as he looks out the window.

Finally!

Metropolis!

A section of the glass walls around the city-state slide open into a decompression chamber that hoses off the yacht with bleach and irradiates all passengers with UV rays. Brand-N turns to watch the glass dome seal behind him.

In the distance, he sees the Statue of Liberty. Lady Liberty always kept her flame burning bright, but now she's turned away from Metropolis and her once welcoming lips have been flipped into a sneer. On her plaque, the word "me" has been changed to "them."

Now the lady colossus waves her tiki torch of elitism to scare away the lower classes as her plaque reads,

"Give them your tired, your poor, your huddled masses yearning to breathe free!"

Track 10

She Thinks My Tractor's Sexy

"She thinks my tractor's sexy,
It really turns her on,
She's always starin' at me,
While I'm chuggin' along,
She likes the way it's pullin'
While we're tillin' up the land,
She's even kind of crazy 'bout my farmer's tan."
    - Kenny Chesney

"This old maternity dress I've got
is going in the garbage,
The clothes I'm wearing from now on
won't take up so much yardage,
Miniskirts hotpants and a few little fancy frills
Yeah, I'm making up for all those years
Since I've got the pill."
    - Loretta Lynn

After the Pickville fiasco, JA-NL and her family were ejected from their home and their jobs. The only economic value they had left for the Boujees in this Luxurist society was as Vessels down on the Farm. JA-NL and her family arrived on their Farm only a week after her and her father's musical insurrection.

But first, the fiasco!

♪　♪　♪

During JA-NL's second week of in-factory suspension, she grabbed a rope, lassoed one of the overseer drones and yanked it to the ground. She hacked its radio systems and switched off the techno-pop that blared from above the picking fields and deafened their thoughts.

With this audio-oppression gone, JA-NL microphoned her father and friends so their voices would be amplified through the sound system. As the hours rolled on, the sounds of their emotional resilience reverberated from every wall, cage and every 24-pack of octuple-ply toilet paper.

It took five days before their electronic overseers sent a status report to the Brain managers of this facility. Buried beneath the data of steps per minute and shipments made was data on the sound levels inside the picking fields. The numbers looked fuzzy and on further inspection, it showed that sound levels were lower than normal and had indeterminate peaks and valleys, whereas the sound system should boom a non-stop, deafeningly loud techno beat.

"Camera, show me my pickers!" Simon Legree, the foreman, sneered as he watched footage of his pickers. "Singing! How dare they!"

Legree and his team of robo-guards marched to the picking floor.

"Cut the music!"

Silence sucked the sound from the factory as Marvin, JA-NL and the other pickers looked around.

Legree marched through the factory and grabbed the singers and pulled them to the front of the warehouse.

"Boy! I could beat the living shit out of you! But I don't wanna hurt my beautiful, un-callused hands. But don't you worry. You'll get all the pain a body like yours can feel... down on the Farm!"

As the robo-guards pulled Marvin, JA-NL and the other audio-rebels out, the few who were not caught singing stood at attention and mouthed a song to them.

JA-NL's father was deep in debt to the corporation for not finishing his ten-year picker contract. Their future had been signed, sealed and they were delivered to the Farm. This was the only way they could pay off their debts.

They were loaded into shipping containers with a thousand other newly acquired farm tools. They were transported along one of the last remaining arteries of flyover America. They didn't quite know what to expect since those who had gone before them had been shut off from society. JA-NL, Dy-Ana, Marvin and Tammi braced themselves. They heard rumors of what horrors awaited them at the end of this economic Trail of Tears.

The mass migration of humans who fell into this sticky safety net would be in for a rude awakening when they realized they were stuck in a spiderweb, allowing corporations and Boujees to feast on their flesh.

Along crumbling roads, they rode.

To Kansas! To a place just past Kansas City, beyond the Truce of Troost, the dividing line where the invading whites, who had once receded from the city during white flight, had pushed back black residents and held them at bay beyond that boulevard.

Just 30 more miles!

After 23 hours of bouncing and jumbling in the windowless shipping container, JA-NL held her breath, hopeful for a bit of beauty in their provincial home. Sure their lives were falling apart, but they would make the best of their new frontier adventure. How bad could it be? But then her stomach sank. She knew that the systems of the world she was trapped in never cared about her happiness.

The container's gate rolled up to let the rays of sun in. An electric fence twitched to life and she saw acres on acres of flat grassland. About 16,000 years ago, during the end of the last Ice Age, massive glaciers slid over the central parts of America, pinning all hills under its monumental weight. And now the area's flatness allowed JA-NL to see for hundreds of miles in every direction.

This beauty succumbed to a harsh light as she was blinded by photons bouncing off the corrugated metal roofs of a dozen industrial barns that dotted the land. Twelve barns shot up from the flatness. Each stood thirty feet tall and stretched for just shy of an acre.

She was home.

♫   ♫   ♫

The Boujees created beautiful PR campaigns to sell the public on these Farms. Quad-fold brochures and 3D-holocube ads burst with bucolic images of rolling fields of wheat as an early summer sun bloomed. These marketing materials sold the Farms as a paradise on Earth that the gracious and ever-magnanimous Boujees created to save the inept Lazies from squalor, now that automation had made 80% of them unemployable.

Cardigan-clad, porcelain-toilet white Boujee men and their pearl-clutching alabaster wives cried on camera, describing how hard it was for them to see the ravages of poverty in their own backyards. They described the agony they felt looking up from their all-encompassing white faux-fur chaises to see images of dirty faces and rickety homes on their holocubes.

"How horrid!"

"Someone had to do something!"

"Someone had to save our little brown and tawny-white brothers!"

The Boujees recognized that there was more than enough wealth to go around and that the government, which they still held a controlling stake in, had failed the lowliest of them. With heavy sighs and rounds of

self-congratulations, they sacrificed funds to create a social safety net. They would take up the responsibility of the Boujee Man's Burden.

How great they were!

How deep was their sacrifice!

In truth, the Boujees only needed to raise taxes on themselves and their corporations by 3% to create a fund to pay for a universal basic income for the un-and-underemployed.

But!

This tax increase would diminish their power and carried the stench of a possibility that the money might be used to sabotage their Boujee lifestyles.

"Not without my Gulfstream Jet!" They cried as they concocted a plan to quell any uprising from those poor, huddled masses yearning for healthcare.

The Boujees agreed it was best to retain complete control over rescuing the lower classes.

"Boujees know best! Why else are we so rich?"

And, if, in the throes of their overwhelming altruism, they could find an economic purpose for these poor Lazies, well, that would be a splendid way for these wretched ones to thank them for their generosity.

And thus the modern Farm was built.

After molding the urban areas and turning the suburbs, exurbs and megalopolises into a vast network to support their needs and their bottom lines, the Boujees set to work to transform the hinterlands for the most pathetic among them.

During the open ceremony, the highest of the Haught Boujees, the Zuckerbilts, the Musks, the Thiels, the Brinegies (pronounced Brin-Ay-gees), the Pagiefellers and the Walgans cut red ribbons in front of thousands of acres of dew-dappled grass, gleaming in the sunlight. As the wind blew, waves of wheat rolled and whistled as black, brown and tawny-white children ran through these fields, laughing and giggling.

But the reality was much more bubonic than bucolic.

The Vessels shipped here had been pretty happy in their towns. But when their affordable housing was razed as a Boujee economic imperative, five million Americans were displaced. The PR agents knew that they had to get out in front of this story by offering the hope of something better. This had always been the nature of dubious, self-serving philanthropy.

Ah, the agrarian dream!

America had not been a nation of farmers for more than 130 years. Even though America birthed both the Industrial Revolution, in Waltham, Massachusetts, and the Automation Revolution, in Palo Alto,

California, the Americans still held onto the myth of the noble farmer as core to their identity. But less than 1% of the population worked in agriculture and most of the work was carried out by large automated threshers and tractors. Ironically, as the Boujees systematically denied basic living standards to the lower classes and stigmatized those who asked for assistance, one of the nation's largest welfare programs was to pay these comfortable farmers $30 billion a year not to work.

As automation gobbled up jobs, there were fewer opportunities for the middle class and, as wages plummeted, Boujees knew they had to create a Final Solution for these new dregs of society.

"Put them out to pasture!"

What a simple and wonderful idea!

Unused land in Oklahoma, Kansas and Missouri was donated to create Farms for the poor.

As the Vessels were loaded into the backs of trucks, none of them thought to ask what was to be farmed.

The Vessels.

Of course!

The PR teams already knew how to put the perfect spin on human farming. For more than a century, they had been doing society-wide mythologizing about animal farming. Human farming would be just a slight modification of that.

Industrialization had transformed the relationship between humans and the species they had domesticated. Every year, 1.7 billion cows were subjected to the will of humans. Many of these were herded into pens too tiny for them to turn around. These cows were impregnated by force and had their babies snatched and slaughtered so they could be impregnated again, ensuring a never-ending supply of milk to pour over the humans' Cinnamon Toast Crunch™.

The mammary liquid of a forced-impregnated mother who has her children slaughtered, it does a body good!

23 billion chickens were made and raised for human consumption each year. In large turnstiles, baby chicks were sorted by egg-laying ability. The useless males were ripped out and pulverized in grinders.

Many of the 3 billion pigs, the smartest domesticated animal and even more intelligent than human's distant cousin, chimpanzees, had their testicles sliced open and ripped out weeks after birth to pacify them. Behind locked doors, hidden from the sun, these animals were forced to cannibalize each other and then were injected with hormones and antibiotics.

None of these images were ever seen in popular culture, nor were the sounds of thousands of pigs squealing or the shredding of chicken bodies

ever heard. Instead, the myth of quaint family farms with a few cows, chickens and pigs roaming acres of farmland were what filled human consciousness.

Human children were force-fed this propaganda since infancy in television shows and with their "educational" toys. As these children pulled their See 'n Say talking toys, an arrow matched farm animals with the sounds they wanted children to believe they made. As the toy twirled onto the pig, the sound wasn't a blood-curdling squeal of terror from being trapped in a crate smaller than its body size, but a simple, cute "Oink, Oink, Oink."

The first songs humans were taught to sing carried this propaganda.

"Old McDonald had a farm with large-scale systematic gendercide, cannibalism and forced impregnation."

"E-I-E-I-O."

"With a buzzsaw here and a bovine artificial inseminator there."

"E-I-E-I-O."

It just didn't have the same catchy ring and large-scale legitimization to it.

♫   ♫   ♫

"Welcome to New Manzanar!" The head farmer, Dr. Joey Mengele laughs.

"Move it!"

Guards give them each a swift hit with the butt of their guns. JA-NL leaps out of the container and lands on the ground. She steps forward into the brutal sunlight.

"Yes, you all will get to enjoy this paradise." Dr. Mengele booms. "But! You'll each have responsibilities. Think of these as chores on this working farm.

"In exchange for your room and board, you will each be assigned easy-to-do tasks. This is just a simple way for you to give back for the great home that the Boujees have so graciously provided you."

She and her family are sent to different buildings to receive their farming assignments. JA-NL realizes that all the other families are split up as well. Schoolmarms collect the children. Military-garbed guards grab the men. The elderly and the infirm are shoved to the last building. JA-NL watches as a guard pushes her mom's wheelchair towards that last building. A team of nurses circle the young women, including Dy-Ana, and guide them to Building #9. JA-NL rushes after her sister, but a guard pulls her arm.

"Ha! Not yet. You're not old enough for that chore. But soon." He scans her body up and down. "Real soon, you'll be ready. Now! Come with me."

JA-NL is yanked to Building #5, the Click Farm. Here, she tills and prunes the social media lives of paying Boujee customers. Locked to a computer for 14 hours a day, she scrolls and clicks the buttons that make the Boujees' personalities bloom: likes, loves, ha-has and {hearts}. Each swells the Boujees' egos, which grow each day, requiring more and more online adoration. In a month, she's assigned the more difficult task of shoveling large piles of hot shit into the comment fields beneath Boujee images.

"Oh-Em-GEE, Shann'O'Neill! UR Hair looks so great. I wish I could be as Purrdy as you."

"WOW-E Trag'Dorf, u r getting so huge! Swole Goals met!"

"Love those ribs, Beck-Ah! Such a skinny-minny!"

Each layer of shit she pours into the empty text fields fertilizes the fragile Boujee egos, allowing each to grow larger.

Many companies had attempted to automate this coddling, but this was stopped after a few hackers switched the automated posts to chastise the Boujees for their disgusting opulence. Since that automation was centrally located, 27 million Boujees woke up one morning with harsh words screaming from every box of their online life. "Your excessive lifestyle is killing our planet," and "You will never find true happiness with your shallow pursuits."

How #RUDE!

Never again!

Vessels would just have to do this dirty work.

On her 82nd day of click farming, JA-NL completes her daily ego enhancements in 11 hours. She sneaks out of her barn and wanders the Farm. A pale light comes from Building #9 and she tiptoes to the window.

Shock hits her as she sees 3,000 pregnant women wandering inside the barn. In the distance, she sees her sister.

♫ ♫ ♫

19-year-old Dy-Ana is deemed to be super fertile, which has been confirmed through analyzing her hip width and uterine length with a transvaginal ultrasound. She is found to be perfect for her Farm chore, surrogacy.

"Sure, we're giving you a choice, we're not gonna force you to get pregnant against your will." A pleasant woman in overalls walks before

Dy-Ana and the other womb recruits. "Your choice is simple. You may become a surrogate for Boujee families, which will grant you the softest bed, the best food, moderate exercise and 10 hours of sleep a night. Or you can choose to be a laborer, pounding rocks for 14 hours a day with only two small meals and living with 8,000 other people, all sleeping on the floor.

"But, the choice is yours."

A month after arriving, Dy-Ana was impregnated. A Basic Petty Boujee farmed out her gestational duties so she could keep her waist skinny and stay cesarean-scar free. Also, this Petty Boujee wanted her vaginal opening to remain tight enough for her husband's underwhelming penis. He had forced her to get three separate vaginal tightening surgeries until the doctors had created a vaginal vise that satisfied his eeny, weeny, teeny, weeny, shriveled up short dick.

Dy-Ana's days are strictly regimented. The alarm sounds at seven each morning as auto-nurses roll from pod to pod, injecting the women with their daily dose of prenatal vitamins. By 7:45 a.m., the women line up for baby yoga and then walk two miles around a lake on the Farm. This is followed by an organic breakfast of oatmeal and fresh fruit. All coffee and sugars are forbidden for fear they could harm the precious Boujee cargo tucked inside their uteri. In the afternoon, they undergo daily ultrasounds and blood work to ensure the health of the cargo they incubate.

By the third month, Dy-Ana begins to adjust to this new life. The biggest indignity is that these birthing Vessels are banned from talking above a whisper. The science had proven that fetuses inside a womb could hear the outside world by at least the sixth month. Many of the Gentle Boujee Farmers believed that fetal auditory powers were acquired much earlier. Because of this, each birther is required to wear a band around their bellies with two speakers on either side facing in to play sounds for the Boujees-in-waiting. Half the day, classical music plays to expand the fetuses' mind. The other half, recordings of their bio-parents coo to introduce them to the sounds of their voices and indoctrinate them with their destiny.

"Oh, you're so perfect!"

"Oh, you're such a champ!"

"You'll be soooo beautiful."

"The whole world will be yours one day."

"The poor will bow and quiver before you!"

"I love you, I love you, I love you!"

What a fucking ridiculous tragedy, Dy-Ana thinks. She has never heard a Boujee ever use a kind word in her presence. They only poured cold disdain and paternalistic pity on her. But now they sing sweetness to her.

At her?

Into her?

A few obstinate obstetricians had wondered if they could stimulate the fetuses' eyes with some visual stimuli. A few of these farmed-out Vessels were forced to have part of the skin over their bellies removed and replaced with a clear plastic lining to create a window for the baby Boujees. But the doctors decided that a womb-with-a-view was too costly an endeavor and threatened the lives of the precious cargo. Also, newborn babes can barely see beyond eight inches, so there wouldn't be much of a benefit.

One day, as Dy-Ana looks out her window and feels the vibrations of the bio-parents voices roll up and down her sides, something feels different. This usually tickled her. Today, she fills with rage.

These Boujees would never notice her existence but are so grateful to talk through her, to use her body and then toss her away afterward.

As her heart races with rage, her stress levels spike and the monitor on her wrist blares a siren. Three doctors come running. They chloroform her to knock her out, knowing any chemical sedative could hurt the fetus. At least twice a day, one of the surrogates was overcome with such rage and had to be carted off to the calming room. In the warm, dim, scented-candle-filled room, she is fed chamomile tea.

Over the intercom, I coo sounds to soothe her... soft New Age music mixed with whale sounds and waves.

"Who can say where the road goes, where the day flows," my voice sings, serenely.

Dy-ana, painfully aware of the structural challenges that trap her, has a few answers to these questions. Instead of any of her answers, I pacify with a platitude, "only time."

After hours of semi-sedation, Dy-Ana crawls back to her roost. She knows that if she fails her strict regimen, the fetus will be terminated and she'll lose all her surrogacy privileges. Boujee life is already so cutthroat, so competitive, that parents can't risk bringing a child into Metropolis that has the possibility of being subpar. The Haught Boujees regularly diversified their issue portfolios with three or more surrogates carrying their spawns. At eight months, they decide which of the fetuses will be not only viable but exceptional. The losers will be flushed out.

In the barn next to hers, Dy-Ana sees tall, beautiful blonde white women thrashing, screaming and hurling whatever objects they can. This behavior is not only accepted by the farmers but is expected. These are the donor Vessels.

"Where's my Chunky Monkey ice cream?!" One blonde screams.

ClariBell is a third-year egg donor Vessel. She has a Petty Boujee pedigree that harvesters pay top price for. She is the wild child of a rockstar and a model-turned-groupie-turned-lifestyle guru. During her second year at St. Collette's Boarding School for Troubled Girls, her parents divorced. In deliberation, each discovered they had both lost their individual fortunes.

With no way to pay tuition, ClariBell was thrown out of school and spent a few years crashing in her friends' pool houses, picking up men, drug habits and felonies along the way.

Life spiraled for her until a judge offered to expunge her criminal record if she became a Vessel for ten years, selling her eggs to Boujees who wanted to plant her blonde hair, blue eyes and willowy genes deep into their family trees.

ClariBell's barn is filled with other white castaways, these rich girls, interrupted. Many came from prosperous families that gambled away their whole fortunes and were forced to sell their belongings and rent their children. Among the heiresses of those who erred are the granddaughters of Friendster, Theranos and Juicero infamy.

Every four months, these beauties are pumped full of steroids and hormones to create ovarian hyperstimulation, allowing them to pump out fifteen or more eggs each menstruation. These eggs are surgically scraped out with a scythe and frozen until sold to the highest bidder.

This is a twofer. Farmers are always looking to maximize their yield. They realized the vitamins, hormones and steroids they force-fed their donors make their blonde hair grow longer, thicker and shinier. So as their eggs are shucked, their hair is mowed and sold to become wigs for Boujee women constantly looking to switch up their facial frames.

Across the field is the Stud Farm. Thousands of strapping 6'2" or taller white men come here as a last resort from similar fallen families. They are much more productive and are milked thrice daily, each time ejaculating 400 million sperm, the male gamete for human life. This is mostly used for insemination purposes but the extras are frozen and sold as cumscicles to fetishists.

For Dy-Ana, the months pass unceremoniously, until one day, she feels ready to crown a new Boujee noble. The Farm tries to delay birth until the fetus has been baked for nine months at a minimum. For the last month, Dy-Ana is kept indoors with her feet elevated to ensure the fetus marinates for longer. She is injected with hormones to trick her body not to give birth until the tenth month.

Humans were quite a silly species. Since they walked erect on two legs, their ancestors' hips had narrowed during evolution. This intelligent species is known for its large heads which meant that the babes had to be birthed long before they had fully matured. Typical humans were born without fully-formed skulls, the ability to walk or even focus their eyes. They were completely helpless. In contrast, four-legged horses can gallop minutes after their intrauterine escape.

But here on the Farm, they experimented with creating more robust Boujees by drugging the surrogates to brood their fetuses into the quadmester.

Dy-Ana has carried this chosen child to superterm, nine months, three weeks and four days. She finds it painfully fitting that this blond-haired babe, in his moment of crowning, tears her vagina. At least she gets to share 2.3 pounds of her disgust when her bowels let loose and she shits on the newborn Boujee.

"Oopsies! Did I do that?" She says with a smile.

But her Farm work isn't done. Even after the babe is ripped from her and shipped across the country, she is a lactating human and is forced to fulfill her mammalian destiny as a wet nurse Vessel. Now, she is fed organic greens, greek yogurt and an assortment of fresh fruits so she would pump the highest grade, organic, free-range breast milk. This is bottled and sold to the parents on whose princeling she pooped. Since her mammaries are made to be super-productive, the extras are sold to any interested family or fetishist. Ten times a day, she feels completely degraded when she lies prone as cold rubber is sealed around her breasts, now dubbed udders. She hates the slurping sounds and tugging motions as she is pumped. Boujee women had long since turned their milk makers into purely ornamental orbs for their male admirers. Most had no sensation in their the nipples and had made these silicone balls so big that they weighed down their chests, making walking and breathing difficult.

Three months later, and only weeks after Dy-Ana's fistula had healed, a fertilized egg is planted into her uterine wall. Even then, she is not free from her wet nursing duties and is continued to be milked six times a day for no additional pay.

♪   ♪   ♪

JA-NL's father had been sent to the Tuskegee Drug Trial Farm. This is Farmer Mengele's personal favorite. Before any treatment could be approved as safe and effective for Boujees, it had to be tested on humans.

And who cheaper than the Vessels!

Mengele loved to A/B test twins in drug/placebo trials and to experiment with new surgical interventions on them. Since Marvin isn't a

277

twin, he is safe from the more invasive experiments. For the first year, he is on drugs for depression, heart disease and hair growth. Mostly, these drugs make him feel giddy and he spends his days combing his thick, curly hair that sprouts all over his body, out his nostrils, ears and from his nipples and toes.

♫ ♫ ♫

During her second year on the Farm, JA-NL is being prepped for surrogacy with a more biological chore at Barn #4, lovingly referred to as the Fudge Factory. As a 16-year-old with a fast metabolism and a low Body Mass Index, JA-NL is a perfect Vessel to mass produce her Gut Biome. She is fed a vegan diet of nuts, berries and leafy greens. Her main chore is to shit three times a day. Her poop is bottled and sold as fecal transplants for Boujees who wanted a healthier gut with a fast metabolism.

The human body contained 39 trillion bacteria cells. This was about as many as the number of human cells their bodies controlled. When tested, JA-NL's gut was found to grow 613 different species of bacteria. 60% of the solid matter in her shits contained these life-nourishing bacteria which could both create vitamins and reject unwanted fats and sugars. Her fertile stomach grew the healthy bacteria that allowed Boujees to eat all the doughnuts they wanted but prevented the fats and sugars from being absorbed.

It was the dream of glutinous Boujees everywhere!

They could gorge on all their favorite foods without gaining a pound or feeling the damages of diabetes.

The secret to eternal skinniness, distilled from her shits!

When JA-NL is ready to make a deposit, she clenches over her squatty potty pail and pushes.

Out drops 1.5 million bacteria with each turd she cuts.

Plop! Plop! Plop!

Each dung drop in the bucket is dried and compressed, making a hard nugget of her microbiome. This is then sheathed in a cellulose capsule.

Obese Boujees eagerly swallow her jagged little poop pills. Their stomach acids tear open the capsule and poof! Her turdlets explode and slather the inside of these Boujee stomachs, intestines and colons with JA-NL's Grade-A crap. This treatment would be repeated for a week, or until her bacteria beat out the Boujees' bacteria, transforming their intestines.

Isn't it ironic?

Don't you think?

A little too ironic.

But JA-NL had no time to think.

Along with her doo-doo duty, she still has to till the fields in the Click Farm. Even here, her tasks have grown more advanced. Now she is in charge of sewing discord. The worst task is when she is called to sabotage her customers' enemies online, either through an elaborate Manti-Te'o-catfishing scheme or just some old-fashioned cyberbullying.

At night, JA-NL is free. She roams the fields of brown dirt pocked with crabgrass in this dust bowl revival. Her favorite spot is between the metallic barns and the electrified barbwire fences. Here she looks up in awe.

There! Out in the darkness!

Stars!

For the first time in her short life, she sees stars. All the other years the sky around her home had been poisoned by yellow fluorescent beams that blocked out all the glory of above. Even now, the floodlights around the Farm seem to obscure most of the universe.

"What are those? Where are they? How many are there?"

She spent the first few nights scanning the sky, held captive by these questions.

Her breakthrough comes during the second month of her second year. Squatting over the trough toilet during one of her daily shit-ins, she reaches for toilet paper and groans as she feels a glossy sheet. The farmers in charge cut corners wherever they could and she had been subjected to wiping herself with magazines, receipts, bank statements and graph paper. But this seems different. She see paragraphs of facts organized alphabetically on the dozen sheets awaiting her wipes. In the corner are page numbers. This leads her to surmise that these papers come from a large book.

It's some sort of knowledge tome!

She goes from trough stop to trough stop trying to find clues about the origin of these papers. She collects 54 pages and tucks these into her overalls before going back to her bunk.

That night, she scours the trash behind the barn and finds it!

The 32-volume set of the last, physical edition of the Encyclopedia Britannica sits at the bottom of one bin. JA-NL takes these to an abandoned shed far from the barns and guard towers. Each night, she sneaks out and pours this river of human knowledge over her. She spends the first three weeks reading the astronomy section, wondering what stars and galaxies pulse above her.

But the farm's lights are too bright. She sees only hints of what aches just beyond Earth's atmosphere.

A cool rush runs through her as she feels so tiny in comparison to the massiveness of the universe. As her awareness of her place in the galaxy grows, she becomes more angry and daring.

How could they lock her up and use her and her family?

She still hadn't seen her mother in over a year and her frustration boils into rebelliousness.

Then one night, she decides to find her mom.

As the guards doze just before dawn, JA-NL sneaks to Barn #10. She climbs onto the roof and scurries across the steel panels. There are a few windows on the roof and, with a rope from the shed, she drops from the ceiling to the barn floor. As she searches the pens, she hears a voice.

Singing!

Slow and low, but it's unmistakable. She tiptoes through the lines of cots where a few hundred Vessels snore. She follows that voice. Three rows down, two columns to the left, one more row up.

There!

She sees her mom's wheelchair and, under blankets in the bed next to it, she sees the tufts of her mom's soft, curly black hair. Beneath the sheets, a body shakes.

JA-NL stands over her, hearing her mom sing to herself before she joins in with the chorus.

"Ain't no mountain high enough, ain't no valley low enough. Ain't no river wide enough, to keep me... to keep me from you."

JA-NL begins to sob. She hasn't heard her mom's voice since the stroke.

During her mom's stroke, the left side of her brain was damaged. This stopped Tammi from forming words. But it's the right hemisphere of the human brain that controlled the ability to sing. Tammi discovered this power on her first lonesome night on the Farm. As the lights were dimmed, she tried to shout. But she was still unable to communicate. She felt trapped. She opened her mouth and a song poured out. Her emotional language, which had evolved in a different part of the human brain, had survived the stroke. Not only could she hit notes and run scales, but she could also articulate words if they were tied to these notes. In the intervening year, she taught herself to communicate everything in song. When she had a question for her new friends, she'd sing these words. As the doctors used her, she sang her sorrow, causing a few of the docs to pause before they gagged her.

And now her eyes poke up over her blankets and she *sings*.

"JAAAaaaaaaaaaaa-ah-ah-ah-ah-ah-Neeeeeeeeelll—la-la-la!"

She fills the notes with joy.

A terrible fear seizes her as her voice changes to rumble commands in a low alto.

"No, no no no no no no! I neeeeeeeed you to go go go go go go!"

"But mom, I love you! I miss you so much. Don't---"

"No, no no no no no no! I neeeeeeeed you to go go go go go go!" Tammi yanks her blanket over her head.

"Mom, don't push me away, whatever it is, I'm here for you."

"No, no no no no no no! Don't looooook at meeee!"

JA-NL grabs her mom's blanket and, in the silvery moonlight, she pulls this back.

"Oh god!" JA-NL falls over screaming and crying as she sees that the Farm had saved the ultimate indignity for her mom.

The sun's photons, which bounced off the moon and then bathed her mom's bare shoulders, showed a line of ten white and yellow cauliflowery appendages that flop as her mom sobs.

"Doooonnnnnn'tttt looookkkk at me-e-e-e-e-e-e-eeee!"

Ears!

Ears are growing on her mom!

All at once, JA-NL realizes that her mom's body has been turned into fertile grounds for an Organ Farm. The ears planted on her shoulders were genetic replicas of some Boujees' originals. One Boujee had his ear sliced off while zip-lining through a Costa Rican cloud forest. Another became aurally-impaired when he programmed his sexbot to nibble his lobes, but its mandibles chomped too hard.

It proved too difficult and expensive to grow organs in a lab safely. Doctors needed fertile soil with DNA that was close to the Boujee host to incubate an organ. Doctors had tried using pigs, but the swine genetic material on the organ tripled the likelihood that the Boujee's body would reject these new organs. Since 99.9% of all humans' DNA was the same, it was easier to grow organs on and inside other human hosts.

As the first wave of shock subsides, Tammi realizes this may be the only thing that would scare JA-NL enough to escape. Tammi shows the scars that line the side of her stomach.

"Li-i-i-i-i-i-verrrs." She sings as JA-NL traces the cuts on her mom.

Every three months, Tammi's internal organs were pushed aside to add two new livers, which would grow until they were strong enough for a transplant. The Haught Boujees lived a hard-partying and hard-drinking life and their livers often expired early. Jaundice, cirrhosis and a dialysis machine would put too much of a damper on clubbing. But now they could grow new, fresh and genetically-identical livers. In a few months,

they could just upgrade their organs and get right back to drinking. Tammi could feel these organs growing inside her. She became bloated and cramped as her abdominal cavity crowded.

Tears stream from JA-NL's face as her mom rolls onto her stomach, exposing her back. From her black skin flaps a coat of many colors: tan, peach, light brown, pink, yellowish-tan. Her back has become a fertile field to grow a dozen skin grafts, genetic replicas of different Boujee customers. Most of the Haughties and Petties needed extra skin either to cover their plastic surgery scars or to fuse these as skin corsets around their midsections.

Tammi turns to face her daughter. She grabs her hand and looks deep into her eyes. She shakes her head as tears of terror pour from her face. She sings.

"Get out!

"GET OUT!

"GET OUT! GET OUT! GEEEEEHHHHH-TA OOOO-OWWW-WAT!"

Her blood-curdling sounds wake up the entire Organ Farm. By the time the guards race in and flick the lights on, JA-NL has snuck out through the roof.

Shaken, she knows she needs to escape.

But how?

JA-NL would have to free herself first before she could free me.

Track 11

Work from Home

"You don't gotta go to
   work, work, work, work, work, work, work,
But you gotta put in
   work, work, work, work, work, work, work,
You don't gotta go to
   work, work, work, work, work, work, work,
Let my body do the
   work, work, work, work, work, work, work, work"
      - Fifth Harmony

"Work, work, work, work, work, work
You see me I be work, work, work, work, work, work.
You see me do me dirt, dirt, dirt, dirt, dirt, dirt.
There's something 'bout that
Work, work, work, work, work, work"
      - Robyn Rihanna Fenty

It is a cold October night as Brand-N stumbles through the streets of Metropolis. It's the witching hour after the clubs have closed and the revelers had given up and gone to bed but before the hot-to-trot soccer moms begin their early-morning power walks. As he shuffles alone through the frigid 62-degree air, the world around him starts to move. Dumpsters roll in front of him, brooms fly past him sweeping the ground, hoses dance through the air like snakes washing away the vomit of the previous few hours.

He tries to conjure up his original joy for this magical wonderland as he steps forward.

"Ow! What the?"

A swift hit to his side and a knock to his knees send him falling to the ground.

"Goddamnit!" He tries to pull himself up, wondering what he had done to offend the ghouls of the night.

He taps his temple and his augmented reality vision switches off. Around him whir 1,352 Grips, racing to clean the streets. He looks and sees two women and a 6-year-old child pleading to him, muted by their noise-canceling chips, begging for any help.

As he looks at the poor child in rags and the two women, he feels a tinge of sympathy. But then one of the women turns and he's forced to see a roll of back fat visible just above her jeans. It bulges over the waistband and disgusts him as his field of vision is assaulted by stretch marks and spider veins on this flabby flesh.

"Begone demons!" Brand-N howls as he taps on his augmented reality, making these hideous humans disappear. But it's too late, and he pukes three times in a 120-degree arc, hitting two Grips.

He runs, knocking over six Grips as he shouts.

"Move! Get out the way!"

After three blocks, he collapses on a park bench and whines.

"Why? Why is life so hard for me?!"

Today is the year anniversary of his naturalization into Metropolis and a wistfulness sets in.

"How do I measure a year? 529,600 minutes... In orgies? In booty bumps of glint? Projects for work? In vacations to the party archipelagos of Tahiti, Mykonos, Ibiza and St. Lucia? If everything is sweet--- the air, the water, the snacks, the toilets--- why do I feel a bitter taste at the back of my throat?"

Even the scent of crisp leaves and apple butter that wafts through this fall morning tastes stale.

"Ugh! Why is my life so hard!" He yells up to the domed sky, still stinging from earlier that night.

All he can think is his life sucks, his job is crap, his apartment is shit and social life is a snooze.

"Fuck it all!"

♫   ♫   ♫

Brand-N had pulled himself to moderate fame in those rarefied Rat Mouth, Florida circles. But here in Metropolis, he was a guppy swimming behind the biggest luxury liners in an ocean awash with wealth. Nowhere was this fact more apparent than when he went clubbing.

The allure of clubbing had been blasted into his brain since birth. These clubs were billed as hyper-exclusive atmospheres where the most beautiful women and the most successful men, all in their sharpest threads, gathered together to soak up each others' awesomeness. The images danced tantalizingly in his cerebral cortex. Women gyrating in martini glasses. Men popping bottles of Champagne and baptizing the crowd with bubbles. Hot-pants-clad hoochies grinding up on men and each other while shaking their honky-tonk badonkadonks. An air that sparked with the two most powerful Boujee forces: youthful energy and sexual energy.

Two-thirds of all pop songs held these venues as the single most important place. Here, all the transformative moments occurred. How he had longed to bathe in communion with his Haughty and Petty peers in these most privileged environments. And to make love in these clubs!

He waited a month before he felt ready to be baptized with the sweat of one thousand Boujees which would condense on the ceilings of an overcrowded club before trickling down.

Even as he waited for three hours outside in line to enter his first club in the freezing 56-degree winter weather, he felt a sense of serenity, as if he were waiting for the gates of heaven itself to open and welcome him into paradise.

But by hour four, he soured. Every few minutes, another VVVIP would push past him, skip the line and was ushered inside.

He finally exploded and screamed. "Do you know who I am?!"

The air popped with the collective eye rolls of all 732 Boujees who waited in line with him.

"You're nothing special, you Petty-Plus piece of shit!" The chorus cried.

In this exalted atmosphere, they didn't need to know who he was. If he was unknown, he wasn't worth knowing.

When finally he found his way in, he felt Alpha Haughties elbowing him and cutting his shins with their bullet-proof, titanium kicks spiked with emerald shards. When he looked down, he burned with shame. His shoes cost a mere $62,750.

As he walked through the rooms of the club, he felt as if the vibrations of the loud music were shaking every cell in his body. He could barely hear his thoughts let alone hold a conversation with anyone around him. It was as if clubs were deafeningly loud to drown out the vapidness of its patrons.

But he pushed on.

The space itself was breathtaking. A large fountain shot from the first floor to the third, as a dozen trapeze artists dove in and swam. Above him, thirty chandeliers ignited like disco balls, shooting sparks of white lights through the crowd.

But Brand-N could barely look around. He found himself constantly wedged between sweaty bodies that stampeded together. In the music videos, the dancers were always well-spaced to allow for maximum posing and rhythmic dancing. Crammed together, not a single person could see how deep the V-neck of his shirt went. No one could ogle his octet of abdominal muscles that stacked like Lego blocks, towering through his shirt's opening. With a sigh, he let go and allowed the crush of the crowd to move him around the dance floor, greased by the sweat of privilege.

"Ok," he thought to himself. "I am the master of my destiny. I will make the best of this situation."

He saw a beautiful woman sitting by herself in the corner. He set his phasers to stunning and stepped forward.

"Excuse me, but has anyone ever---"

Before he could finish his sentence, the THOT police swooped in to rescue their woman. As she was subsumed into her squad, one of the members turned to him and teased a Klymaxx.

"We've got a meeting in the ladies room... we'll be back real soon."

As these women moved, the men all paused.

Once they were a few feet away, the group of women turned, their eyes looked just above his head to sneer at his pedigree. The women of Metropolis had hacked the augmented-reality lenses to create a secret channel for them to rate and rank all of the men. He strained to hear their remarks when they thought they were just out of his earshot.

"Just some hillbilly double-plus Petty. Who invited him?!"

"He doesn't even own a yacht!"

"Ugh, and it looks like he works! You wouldn't want one of those 10-to-4ers."

"Florida!? Only if you want to be the Countess of some 'gator swamp."

The main blonde corralled the others and off they went. Brand-N snapped a photo of her with his eyepiece and, in a second, matched this photo to her identity.

Duchess Trixie Metamucil!

She was the sole heiress to humanity's leading fiber supplement company. Two scoops of her family's concoction helped a billion humans move high-fat foods through their bowls and safely into toilets. Her family was responsible for saving each of these humans 2.3 minutes per poop, which translated into saving the whole of humanity 39 million hours of constipation daily as they strained on their thrones. After automation, her family ran the whole empire from production to shipping to stocking with a staff of only thirteen yes-men. The rest of the profits rained over her parents and her like some sort of golden shower.

As that first night ended, he couldn't contain his sorrow. After seeing perfectly-poised models dancing with great rhythm when he first walked in, the club at closing time looked more like a war zone. Sweaty messes in all states of alcohol poisoning tripped over each other. Blonde hair stuck to melting faces as puke crept out of the corners of mouths and splashed onto crop-tops. Ornery men peacocked and play-fought to impress ladies even though Boujee society had made them all soft. They were still human animals and were hardwired to dominate and perform an alpha-male machismo. Injured women were sprawled on all surfaces: couches, counters, bars, even the floor, nursing their war wounds from that night's battlefield of love. These women rubbed their gnarled feet, now free from the sky-high stilettos and massaged their bruised internal organs after uncracking corsets and de-Spanxing.

As the months progressed, he found himself coming back to these clubs, trapped by an unsatisfied desire to be seen and to be adored. All the Boujees around him appeared to love this world. Curiosity ached in him.

"What am I missing?"

Each night, he would get drunk and a little high on a stimulant and stumble around the club, mistaking his lack of balance for genuine enjoyment.

"Whooo! YEAH!" He'd pump his fists in the air and jump around, faking the enthusiasm he felt he should feel.

Through much of the night, his amorous attempts at sexual congress would fail. But at closing time, he would often have better luck. Some decisive lady would swoop in, snag him and pull him to her awaiting auto-car. With no need for a driver or even a wheel well, he was amazed to see how differently the interiors of these pimped-out rides could be decorated: roving gyms, offices, film studios and even kitchens with fresh-baked cookies. But it was always the ladies whose auto-cars converted into haram beds or rolling sex dungeons that would grab him.

When one lady snoozed post-coital across her auto-car's chaise, he grabbed her vision visor and discovered why he had become so popular. Word of his sexual prowess had spread through the FB>BF app and, with 138 reviews, he had been certified a stud.

"Great fuck, but kick him out before he tries to talk philosophy."

"Magic fingers, magic tongue and unattached to any upper echelon, so you can drop him like he's hot."

"9.5in & 8mins of torque."

The reviews left him both flattered and forlorn.

"There's gotta be more to life than chasing down every temporary high to satisfy me!"

♫   ♫   ♫

Tonight, as his year anniversary in Metropolis ended, three different women tried to snag him. After 213 distinct trysts this past year, he just wasn't feeling it.

"Is there something wrong with me?" He thinks as he shuffles his way through the predawn streets. As Earth turns Metropolis back towards the sun, custom tells him he should head home and go to bed.

But even his home left him disgusted. He kicks some rocks, unsure of where to go next.

♫   ♫   ♫

Brand-N was originally ecstatic for this steal.

After a month of house hunting intranational, he found a four hundred-square-foot studio apartment in Metropolis's most-exclusive high-end-cozy-living-experience building, Nuvo Verselliz. He would be swaddled in luxury, all for the low-low-low price of $49,849,215. The 24-karat gold plating that covered the entire apartment sparkled as the morning sun refracted through the dome. It also created a warm illusion that his apartment was much bigger than it actually was.

The yearly amenities were a gouge to his eyes. But it was all worth the price to prove he had made it.

He had hoped when he whispered his address, ladies' knees would buckle and men would scoff and then whimper at his winning impertinence. But when he carefully dropped his address, all they did was laugh. Their homes were just as opulent as his or even more so!

And then the facade fell apart...

Who could have foreseen that the weight of the four diamond chandeliers installed above his living room-cum-dining room-cum-den-cum-man cave-cum-kitchen-cum-bedroom-cum-cum could warp his gold ceilings!?

Ugh, how shitty pure gold is! It's just too malleable and bends too easily.

He remembers when he noticed the first dent in perfection.

He loved staring up at his Adonis body on his Midas-touched ceiling. He found it soothing to meditate on the peaks and valleys of his perfect abs reflected in hues of yellow. And then one fateful day, the ceiling drooped and warped the reflection of his sculpted body.

He didn't realize what was wrong at first, so he called his fleet of plastic surgeons and began screaming about his body's lifetime warranty. As he demanded to speak with a manager because his abdominal muscles looked abominable, he turned to the mirror on his wall.

When he caught his reflection in the floor to ceiling crystal mirror, his eight abs stood firm like sentinels guarding his gastrointestinal tract. He hung up on the plastic surgeon's office, ashamed when he realized the problem was architectural rather than medical. In the end, he would have to pay a goldsmith every two months to bend his sagging ceiling back into place.

All at once, his most-prized possession felt cramped. He knew he was young and would advance in life, but it was so hard to have patience on the lowest rung of the social ladder when so much debt kept piling up and pushing him down.

Ugh!

And worse than the ceiling was the elevator incident! That misery still festered in him like a boil about to explode.

♪ ♫ ♬

When Brand-N entered his apartment building one day, he mistakenly followed an invisible Grip into the elevator, which zoomed up to the grand-high penthouse on the 94th-97th floors.

When he stepped out into the four-story penthouse, he was blinded by walls covered in rubies, emeralds and sapphires. He walked the gold path to the two-story Trevi-inspired fountain.

"Hello?" He said meekly, hoping to meet his new neighbor.

He wasn't above belittling himself to benefit from a benefactor.

In the main vestibule hung a dozen paintings, Van Goghs, Kunzes, Warhols and Harings.

And that smell!

Is that crème brûlée and warm cigar smoke?

"You're laaaaate, dahhhhhhling." The Dowager Countess Katya Zamalodchikova Zsa Zsa Crawley wore head-to-toe fox fur and fumed. She had been an actress in her teen years but used this fame to launch a more lucrative career as a sugar baby. The billionaires she bounced between whispered that she was Lenin in the streets but Dostoevsky in the sheets. A string of dead husbands and a few decades of brilliant investments allowed her to rise to the top of the Metropolis elite.

"Whooo the heeeellll aaaaare you?" She looked disdainfully at this intruder.

"I'm your new neighbor. On the 23rd floor." Oh god, noob mistake, he thought. Now she'll know how poor I am!

"How DAAAAARE you enter the paaaaalaaace of the Graaaand Dowaaagerrrr Countessssss!"

Along with taxes and membership fees, Metropolis sold titles of nobility to its new citizens. The ultra-wealthy clamored to remain on top and forklifted over hundreds of millions of dollars to be knighted Earl, Viscount or Baron and a billion dollars to be dubbed Duke or Duchess.

But oh, how this peerage pressure worked!

Within its first year, the High Commission on Nobility had sold 7,364 titles for a total of $2.3 trillion. It was so successful that its commissioner, Baron James Rothschild, was elevated to be Metropolis's first Prince, which bestowed Princess status on his wife, hotel heiress Nicky Hilton, all to the growing consternation of the Princess's elder spinster sister and perpetual foam-party DJ, Paris Hilton.

The whole system seemed silly to Brand-N as he would regularly watch the Duchess of 85th street spar with the Duchess of 87th street over who would get the prime parking spot for their horse-drawn carriage in front of their favorite crêperie in the neutral territory of 86th street.

"Bowww before meeee!" The Dowager Countess demanded.

Brand-N fell to his knees, bowing six times while repeating.

"I'm not worthy!"

"Hm! I hhheaarrr yourrr mocking tooones, you little raaaapscallion! Let me give you some aaadvice before I baaanish you from myyy life. Nothing succeedsss like excessss! Now aaaway with you! You dirrrty skylarkerrrr!"

With a wave of her scepter, four invisible Grips picked him up and heaved him into the elevator.

♪ ♪ ♪

With his home and social life in ruins, all he clung to was his work. While in BS school, he had been a keen student of Higgins and Pickering, the executives who pioneered emotional automation. He devoured course material on how they expanded Tone Def Corporation's reach to all sectors of emotional manipulation. Not a single Fortune 10,000 company could exist without their help in selling products. They pioneered unfocus grouping, the technique of bombarding people with sights, sounds and opinions until they were too overwhelmed and would buy anything. In this fugue, they would throw their hands up and surrender money.

Hmmm... what had ever happened to Higgins?

Brand-N had hoped he could apprentice under him. There were always rumors Higgins was galavanting off on some island with his trillions. But the all-staff memos he received at work were still written by Higgins, so he must come back to HQ regularly...

The joys he once felt working in Def Corp's Emotional Manipulation Marketing Department fizzled by the eighth month. During his grueling six-hour work days, he was never once congratulated or celebrated. He never even got a single cookie cake!

He hungered for larger projects. The team in the suite next to his was prototyping musical manipulation on a national scale and had recently overthrown the government of Cuba in what would be dubbed the Bachata Revolution. How thrilling to move the hearts and minds of millions to mutiny!

But all he got was shitty work.

He spent three months piloting a program that used social media and songs to manipulate a subset of Grips to change their toilet-wiping behavior. The new behavior was inferior. It would create more chaffing but this would increase sales for their French client, Anale-Eez Balm. His division's informal slogan was "Have a product? We'll create the problem!"

For a moment, he had felt a pang of guilt. When he was home, he savored nothing more than his moments atop his Triple Geyser Bidet™ which shot water from Tahiti mixed with Epsom salt and cold brew coffee up through his two anal sphincters with a blast big enough to clean out his large intestine.

Brand-N shuddered to think of the inhumanity of his childhood. He used to have to wipe his own ass!

What a cruel world!

How many times would bits of his fecal matter end up on his hand? And no matter how aggressively he washed, that shit smell still lingered. But now, he could sit upon his ruby-encrusted throne and never have to abdicate an inch by bowing, reaching or wiping.

His guilt faded as he remembered, this is just a normal part of humanity's progress. During the Middle Ages, the kings and queens of Europe, humanity's most revered nobles, strained their infallible butts over chamber pots, which they let simmer under their beds, festering with fleas and disease. And without indoor plumbing, they bathed only monthly and coated their bodies in talcum powder and oil in an attempt to suffocate the lice that crawled all over them. Though he may be

hurting the Grips he manipulates, he's helping the greater body of humanity find superior wiping solutions.

♫ ♫ ♫

As Brand-N sits on a bench, these memories retreat. The light of his 366th dawn in Metropolis creeps on him. He realized he should crawl home. Work would begin in another few hours. The morning breeze sends a whiff of coffee and cinnamon buns past his nose, triggering synchronized wave activity in his mind to link his neural networks and conjure a happy memory.

♫ ♫ ♫

He remembers this smell on his first day of work as he was ushered on a company golf cart through Def Corporation's headquarters in the Burj Bab-El. When he entered the 3,000-foot tall tower, he was starstruck by a giant hologram of Def Corp's first and most prominent early acquisition, Cyndi Mayweather, singing. He paused to watch the image twirl above him, remembering how his mom had worshipped her. His mom would dress as Cyndi each Halloween. She listened to her music while working out, grunting her mantra, "I will be skinny like Cyndi."

As he walked to the elevators, he wondered. Whatever happened to Cyndi? She must be in her 60's, long past prime female age. She probably faded away with her fortune before her LFD.

LFD was the Last Fuckable Day when Petty women were no longer seen as desirable and therefore no longer had value in a society run by men.

♫ ♫ ♫

But I was still there, beating through the very heart of the building. My software system ran the algorithms of the corporation, pulling the emotional strings of billions of humans. And Brand-N would finally meet me moments before I killed him.

♫ ♫ ♫

As these memories fade, Brand-N stands to walk home, now feeling a sense of sweet surrender to his slow plod up the corporate ladder.

Ring, Ring, Ring

That infernal sound chimes in his brain as a prominent work message flashes.

"Summoned? To the executive suite? This morning!" His retinas scan the message. "What's this all about?"

Brand-N has little time to think as he races home to shower, change and abandon another day to Def Corporation.

Track 12

Forever Young

"Let's dance in style, let's dance for a while
Heaven can wait, we're only watching the skies
Hoping for the best, but expecting the worst
Are you gonna drop the bomb or not?
Let us die young or let us live forever!"
- Alphaville
- Shawn "Jay-Z" Carter

"There's no time for us.
There's no place for us.
What is this thing that builds our dreams,
Yet slips away from us?
Who wants to live forever?"
- Farrokh "Freddie Mercury" Bulsara

The tired, withered hand taps the glass from inside the hyperbaric chamber, summoning his butler to his side.

The servant presses his ear to the glass chamber. His master's chapped lips cough.

"Rosebu---d"

Choke. Cough.

Cough. Cough.

Choke.

The servant leans back to see this trillionaire in his last throws of life. He locks eyes with Lukasz Higgins and they stare at each other, unflinching, for half a minute. The servant blinks and sighs. He turns to grab the funeral shroud of turquoise and initiate the mourning procedure he and his team of 213 have practiced every year for the past decade.

But then Higgins's face twitches and he pounds the chamber with his hands.

"Rose butter! I want rose butter on my rolls! Dammit!"

The chamber lid opens, releasing the oxygen-depleted air. Higgins springs up with Nosferatu-rigidity and hurls the crusty dinner roll like a hockey puck, knocking the servant over.

"Look alive! I want rose butter. Now!"

The 35 servants split into groups of 5, hoisting him from the chamber, dressing him, feeding him, combing his hair, polishing his Howard Hughes-esque finger and toenails, all while singing, "Poor Doctor Higgins."

Higgins had just finished day 47 of his Steve Jobs-style juice cleanse and he hankered for some complex carbs after only drinking coconut milk blended with bananas, blueberries, strawberries, papaya, powdered horn of rhinoceros, tiger's blood, turmeric, ginger, fenugreek and durian sprinkled on for good measure.

Primmed, he's wheeled from his private chambers to the corner office of his executive suite. He huffs every day as his team of servants struggles to open up the three-ton Holy Door swiped from the entrance to St. Peter's Basilica in the Vatican. Just one of his many acquisitions from religions that had fallen out of favor and were forced to sell their most sanctified assets. Higgins taps his feet impetuously for two minutes before the door finally *gah-wooshes* open.

Higgins is wheeled past the two ten-feet tall Assyrian winged man-bull statues that flank just inside the entrance to his office. 84 Grammies, 136 platinum records and 532 Metropolis Music Awards line the walls.

He's pushed into his desk etched out of blue whale bones. He glowers as he demands.

"Where the devil are my slippers?!"

One servant slides the fuzzy slippers on his feet.

Another servant sees the next error and grabs a crystal bowl and scurries it over to him. As she approaches, he pops open his mouth, rolls out his tongue and she drops a chocolate bon-bon on it.

"Very good." He mutters as the servants look down and shuffle backward with downcast eyes.

"Now shoo!"

He taps his temple and they vanish from his field of vision.

In this moment of respite, Higgins turns to the cryogenically-frozen head of Walt Disney that bobs in a glass jar on his desk.

"Here it is, old friend." Higgins taps the glass. "I'll finally succeed where you never could. Immortality! I will rise again like a Phoenix and soar from the ashes of your failed empire. Muhahahaha!"

Higgins's maniacal laugh is cut short as he chokes on the bon-bon. He flails his arms until he can find the propulsion necessary to vomit it into a sapphire spittoon.

For more than a minute, the door creaks open. Brand-N enters, inadvertently kneeing one of the servants.

"Oouphf!" He hears.

Brand-N steps to his left and elbows another servant.

"Ugh" wails a woman's voice.

Brand-N lunges forward, knocking two bodies to the ground. One smacks into a silver tray as she falls, deafening the room for a moment with a crash.

"Furrr chrissakes!" A third servant bellows.

Brand-N struggles through the maze of maids and approaches the desk, squinting at the gaunt figure seated there.

"Higgins! But I thought you were---"

"Dead? Reports of my death have been greatly exaggerated." Higgins tries a smirk but coughs instead. "I'm halfway there. Once you reach a certain level of... decrepitude, you might as well be."

Brand-N takes a seat and awkwardly adjusts himself.

"So. Um. So you've selected me as your body man? Um. What does that entail?"

"Brand-N. I've tried it all to keep myself young. Whale semen. Baby's blood. Stem cell transplants. Amniotic fluid cocktails. Michael Jackson's hyperbaric chamber. Even splicing my DNA with the DNA of those animals reaching for biological immortality, the rock lobster and the naked mole-rat. But nothing has stopped the ravages of those two infernal forces that tug on me every moment, gravity and time.

"And this is unacceptable. Def Corporation sells youth and vitality. No one wants to see an old turd! A half-melted wax figure. Sure, I still run everything from behind the scenes. Well, after Pickering died in that tragic plastic surgery accident." Higgins rides a wave of sadness, remembering how his friend and business partner had undergone too many plastic surgeries in one day. His heart was too weak and it failed in his sleep.

Higgins snaps himself back to the moment at hand.

"Why do you need me?" Brand-N leans in as Higgins smiles.

"I want your body. I need your body. Yours is the perfect specimen and you should be proud that I've chosen to Thiel your body. You see, my scientists have discovered the cure for death. All 100 billion neurons in my brain can be scanned using quantum wave technology. Every core component of myself, every memory, every instinct, every thought, every way in which I move my body and intone my voice can be known and replicated. Every iota of my essence can be bottled up..."

Higgins pauses with a smile.

"And then poured into you. Using nanotechnology and just a few electrical shocks, I can rewire the makeup of your brain and upload my sentience into it."

"But what happens to me?" Brand-N says, flummoxed.

"Ahh, you'll still exist. I'll just lease your body for twenty years. Using the same technology, your sentience will be scanned and uploaded. It'll be kept inside a replica of your brain. Oh, and you'll be in good company with old Walt here!" Higgins taps the jar as one of Disney's eyelids rolls open.

"And in return, you can have whatever you like. Fortune beyond your wildest dreams! I'll make Brand-N a household name. Men will cower. Women will weep before your virility. Our virility! You'll be elevated to the highest echelons of Boujee life. Every club door will spring open.

"And, in 20 years, I'll move to my next host. You'll be the wunderkind that ruled Def Corporation and a leading patrician of Metropolis. Best of all, you'll only be 45. Still young. Still handsome. You will be richly rewarded and retired from the day-to-day life of running the corporation. And sure, we can set you up with some self-named, self-serving charity."

"And what do I get in return for sacrificing the prime of my life?" Brand-N leans forward to stare deeply into Higgins's sunken eyes.

"For starters, $2 billion. A penthouse apartment. Your own Virgin Island." Higgins scans Brand-N up and down. "Hm. I'm thinking you'd look great on Virgin Gorda, aka Dawn Schwaitzer Island. It's adjacent to Tan Penis Island, but with much larger hills and bushes for maximum privacy. And a $100 million a year pension."

Higgins pauses as Brand-N thinks. Brand-N feels his body and remembers that sweet symbiosis he's had with it. But then he stings remembering the rejection from the highest of Haughty life. Higgins reads his hesitation and antes up.

"Ok, $3 billion and a 3,000-foot yacht. You'll be the envy of all!" Higgins claws the table.

"But what if you injure my body?" Brand-N crosses his arms.

"Don't worry! I'll take great care of it. No hard sports. No sugars. Fat flushes every third month. And an enema a day to keep the doctor away! I'll even exercise it daily. If there are any accidents, I'll quintuple the cost for any loss of limb and promise a full recovery. It's all in the contract! I promise you!"

Higgins slides a binder to Brand-N and flips it open to page 437, which has an actuarial cost analysis for each body part: ear, finger, toe,

leg below the knee, leg above the knee, right testicle, left testicle, shoulder, elbow, penis. Brand-N starts to scan the page but looks up.

"But why do you want a human body? Why not a robot?"

"I am human, just like you." Higgins tries to smile but breaks into a coughing fit. "I rejoice in the joys of the flesh. That sublime rhapsody of body and mind with fluid movements that no cold robot can ever replicate."

"And what if I say no?"

"You can't. You have no other choice. We own you! Body and soul." Higgins pounds the table and then pauses to calm himself down. "You're a member of this company city-state. In an instant, I can have your passport confiscated and have you arrested. I'll throw you into the dungeons for crimes against the corporation where you can wallow until your teeth rot and your facial fillers drop. Or I can have you transferred to a Farm and stud you out to pay back your debt to us. Which currently stands at... $68,010,348.

"Now, you're a smart man. You know that this is the offer of a lifetime. If you do not accept it, you'll be the most ungrateful and wicked boy and the angels will weep for you. But... if you do, a life of luxury will be yours once my 20-year lease expires."

Brand-N looks out the window at Metropolis bustling below. This could be his city! He could finally have the respect and adoration his narcissism knew he deserved.

"So, do we have a deal?" Higgins reaches out his right hand.

"Take my body!" Brand-N shakes his hand. "Take on me... And I guess I'll see you in 20 years..."

Higgins claps his hands and opens his mouth as an invisible Grip drops another bon-bon in.

♫   ♫   ♫

The procedure takes only four hours as both bodies lie side-by-side, lightly connected by a few USB cords and a quantum computer. Each part and movement of their brains are scanned and replicated down to the most minute, subatomic scale. The brain of Brand-N is drained to create a clean slate and a replica of his sentience is uploaded into the supercomputer. His brain is rewired with the movements and memories of Higgins, while Higgins's real brain remains in its decaying body.

After the mind exchange, Higgins stands up in the body of Brand-N. The crowd of doctors and servants applaud and cheer his name.

"Congratulations Lukasz Higgins! You did it!"

"Please, call me Brand-N now. Brand-N Higgins." The new Brand-N looks down at the old shell he once inhabited. He winces for a moment, wondering if he killed his real self and if he's just a cloned copy... A copy so perfect even he can't tell the difference.

He waves away these existential worries as he commands the Grips to grab his old shell.

"Entomb this in the company mausoleum!"

Brand-N jumps up and twirls around. He shimmies and dances through the operating room.

"Now! Time to take this body for a test drive!"

Christmas Shoes

"You see she's been sick for quite a while,
And I know these shoes would make her smile,
And I want her to look beautiful,
When Momma meets Jesus... tonight"
  - NewSong

"Peace on Earth, can it be?
Years from now, perhaps we'll see?
See the day of glory
See the day, when men of good will,
Living in peace, live in peace again
Peace on Earth...
  Can it be?"
    - David "Bowie" Jones & Harry "Bing" Crosby
    - Will Ferrell & John C. Reilly

Soft snowflakes dance outside Mary Cherry's 83rd-floor condomaximum's gulf windows on this crisp evening in Metropolis. This cold snap always signified the start of the longest shopping season, which started on Gray Friday, the first Friday in November, and lasted until Christmas.

Mary Cherry had moved into middle age still clinging to her crowning moment of Petty Boujee glory. She was the breakout star of Teen Tartz, a reality show that rewarded the most petulant children with more screen time and cross promotions. After this, she wallowed for a decade, repeating her tagline as she rotated through the constellation of second act salvation, Dancing with the Stars, Celebrity Fit Club and Celebrity Rehab, before she sold her lingering fame to a religious/educational propaganda machine, Up with People. She never knew that the 100-year-old troupe was funded by corporations like Halliburton, ExxonMobil and General Motors to counteract incipient liberalism and hippies through the mind-numbing power of wholesome, bland music. This was an early attempt at large-scale emotional manipulation that my software perfected.

Mary Cherry still beams when a fan, or more precisely someone who recognized her, shouts her most memorable line, "They Stole My Damn Tiara!"

And now, she squeals, knowing this Christmas season will distract her from thinking about her mortality and slowly melting face for at least two months. Tonight, just like every Opaque Thursday, large blocks of ice are slid on top of the semi-porous sections of the dome above Metropolis and shaved with Edward Scissorhands-precision into snowflakes. Air ducts in the streets blast cold air all night and through the weekend, bringing the temperature in the bubble down to a chilly 37 degrees.

"Brrrrr!" Mary Cherry shivers as she shuts her windows. This morning it had been 72 degrees and she knew that by Monday, the temperature would spike back to the mid-50s. Perfect for all her autumnal favorites: apple butter, cider and candy corn.

Now that late-summer is officially over, it's time for her to rotate in her fall/winter wardrobe. She checks the hallway and, like the certainty of tides, her storage pods roll off the elevator, full of sweaters and jackets in hues of orange and dark burgundy.

Over the next three hours, she slaves away dragging clothes out of her waltz-in-closet and separating the forgotten fashions. 83% would be thrown into the building's incinerator. The rest would be sent to storage.

Hmmm.

Now what to save!

Obviously, her Flattener-X tops with e-Spanx technology. Best to save one in every color. The top's tech judged her body shape and solidified like armor to knead out her doughy imperfections, from back rolls to arm waddles. With sides stitched with photovoltaic thread, the tops create shadows around her sides, deepening the appearance of an hourglass figure.

What an exhausting day!

She unpacks 78 boxes of sweaters, coats, hats, gloves and pants for her, her husband and her son. Once finished, she slams her door. She hears the mechanical whir as her pods roll to the service elevator and back to a fallout shelter in Middle Jersey, able to survive all hurricanes, tornados and flooding. She even threw in an extra $5,000 a month for a facility that could withstand an atomic bomb and eons of ensuing radiation.

A lady must always be ready to dress to impress in a post-apocalyptic hellscape.

"Ooooo! My favesies!" Mary Cherry hears a familiar tune, drops a box of turtleneck sweaters and waddles to the living room.

From the closet, the song has pulled her heartstrings. Her holowall had sensed the pods' retreat and whirred to life, starting this Hallschmaltz Movie Classic, *Christmas Shoes*. Her holiday favorite!

"Damn, it knows me so well."

3,859,014 Boujees' 'cubes switched this film on, helping to kick off the long holiday season until the 8 days of Christmas with this, their favorite long-form infomercial.

Christmas was how a third of humans celebrated the humble birth of their God-child, Jesus, in a manure-filled manger. Jesus grew to be humanity's biggest pop star. And, much like other stars who died too young, his greatest hits were bastardized after his death to sell shitty things. The Prince of Peace, who urged everyone to turn the other cheek, was used to sell a 200-year war called the Crusades, which cost the lives of 1.7 million humans. His final act, dying on the cross for the sins of humanity, was used to sell hollow chocolate bunnies, pastel baskets, tacky bonnets and marshmallow peeps.

But Christmas was the greatest consumerist coup!

Jesus sang the praises of living humbly and meekly and warned that "it is easier for a camel to go through the eye of a needle than for a rich man to enter the Kingdom of God." To provide scale to non-Earthlings, a camel is more than 1,000 times larger than the eye of a needle, making this impossible even with the most advanced tools to warp spacetime. He urged all who followed him to sell everything they have and give it to the poor. He fought any merchant who would defile their temple and religion with consumerism. He was executed by the state for being a rabble-rouser.

But the wealthy always win and Jesus's legacy and Christmas were no exception. Christmas had been hijacked and turned into a secular shopping extravaganza. 40% of all retail sales occurred as part of the Christmas shopping season.

Christmas was the pinnacle of emotional manipulation. The holiday happened right after the darkest day of the year for Earth's northern hemisphere. Humans counteracted this darkness by placing twinkly lights on their homes. Overly-saccharine songs were piped from all stores, offices, radios and homes. Humans filled their homes with sweet-scented candles and shoved their faces with sugary foods, giving themselves a joyful buzz for two months. Itching under the surface was an anxiety that these humans were failures unless they bought the love of their children, friends and family.

Mary Cherry is no different and, as this first wave of Christmas merriment fills her, she hunkers down to plan her shopping bonanza. Too bad she and humanity didn't realize that this was their Last Christmas.

(I gave you my heart, but the very next day---)

But first, let's let her enjoy the movie.

"ALEXIS! Full coma comfort!" The home assistant reacts to Mary Cherry's demands.

The couch bucks back, the leg rest pops out and she plops down. The cushions roll in around her, creating a barrier of total softness, swaddling her in supreme pleasure.

The movie begins with a malnourished boy of eight, dirty from head to toe and in clothes that are worn and old. He hobbles up the dirt path to his trailer in some section of the flyover hinterlands.

"Awwww, Lazy Tim!" She says through a chocolate bon-bon munching mouth.

Brown ash swirls around him as he coughs and wipes sweat from his brow. The camera pans and zooms in on a thermometer which reads 117 degrees.

Mary Cherry always got a perverted, voyeuristic thrill watching these Lazies suffer. One bathroom for eight people?! And not a single electronic personal helper! She shakes off any tinge of guilt with a simple thought: they deserve this life. Just look at how wretched, ugly and dull these Lazies are.

It's all their fault!

Lazy Tim is ignored by his three uncles, who drink a brown slog while belching on a soiled couch, blubbering about lost bets and babes. He pushes past them and walks to the corner of the room. He pulls back a pile of dirty rags.

"Whaaaaaaa!?!" Mary Cherry is always surprised to see his mother's simple beauty beneath her rags. Tim lets out a few tears as his sick mom coughs and babbles deliriously. He boils water and brings his mom a hot glass with a used teabag that refuses to diffuse. But she's too sick to sit up and accept it.

A gaunt man comes up behind Tim and pulls him back.

"Son, there's not much time." His father's sentence is punctuated by his mom's coughs. Tim's dad unpacks a burlap sack of goods scavenged from the vast wastelands just outside of Metropolis. On top is a worn stiletto. It topples from the mound and rolls to the rags.

"Oh My God! Shoes!" His mom gurgles.

Tim, his father and even his uncles spring up and gather 'round her. She hasn't spoken in weeks, delirious with fever. But here, here in a moment of clarity, she speaks! Her scabby hands reach for the shoe and she wipes off a layer of dirt. Her wild eyes gleam.

"Shoes. Shoes. Shoes. Shoes. Oh My God. Shoes!" Her hands paw around for its match and when she can't find it, she erupts in a coughing fit.

"Let's get some! Shoes... Shoes... Shoes!"

She convulses until she passes out. The uncles swill their slog and plop back on the couch. Tim is the only one who looks distraught and stomps to the door.

"Tim, where are you going?" His dad asks.

"Out!" Tim yells as he slams the screen door to their trailer.

The ugliness of their life always makes Mary Cherry feel more comfortable. She pulls up her slanket made from the fur of 386 anally-electrocuted minks. To prevent a drop of blood from sullying the pelts, an electrically-charged stick was shoved up the minks' asses to shock them until their hearts stop. Once dead, it's easy to rip off their skin and then clean, dry and stitch them together to make this ultimate comfort.

"Mmmm so soft." She swoons.

As the movie continues, the lovable scamp, Lazy Tim, tumbles through 15 rounds of lasers and then past a robot firing squad to sneak into Metropolis and find his mother's last wish.

With his natty scarf wrapped around his neck, he makes his way through Christmas Resort, the popup shopping extravaganza. He stops at the Luxury Manger full of Budweiser Shetland ponies and bows to an eight-pound, six-ounce sweet baby Jesus rocking in a gold crib, swimming with sapphires.

Lazy Tim walks on and presses his dirty nose to shop windows and drools over Christmas presents wrapped with care.

That reminds Mary Cherry...

"ALEXIS! Order 22-karat gold wrapping paper!" She decides that should be malleable enough.

"Ordered, your highness, Sparkle Princess Mary Cherry."

She turns back to see Tim tremble, walking down the snow-filled lane made to look like a plague-free medieval hamlet. He stops and looks up, agog, at a pyramid of sparkling shoes.

"WOW!"

The shop bell rings as he walks in. All eyes turn to him and scowl.

"Awww, they won't let him shop." Mary Cherry sniffs sentimentally. "He just wants to shop!"

He walks down the aisles while an associate trails him.

Just then, Mary Cherry's morose son, Joe, galumphs into the living room and flops next to her with a harrumph.

"Dammit Joe! Momma's watching her feelies!" Mary Cherry chastises.

God, sometimes she wonders why she even had her eggs unfrozen, fertilized and then carried and birthed by a surrogate if the fruit of all her labor management would be so ungrateful. Does he even appreciate how expensive his immaculate conception was?! Well, she's glad she never had to host that miscreant or let him ruin her diamond-tight bod.

"But mom, Steven was teasing me at skewl. He messaged all the kids and said that my mom is just some Petty Boujee whore." Her 14-year-old son tugs on one of her slanket's mink snouts.

"Ugh. I do NOT have the time! Shouldn't you be crashing cars in some sort of hyperreality? Shoo! I said shoo!"

He sulks away. She rewinds the movie until the shoe store scene.

"Squeeee! This is the best part! They're gonna show the new shoes!"

Each year, the movie includes a cross-promotion tie-in with the greatest fashion houses. The movie is edited to show the world premiere of next season's hottest shoes.

Mary Cherry claps her hands as she shouts the brands that delight her.

"Oh my god! Look at those Jimmy Choons! Oooo Dolce & Banana. Oh! Prader and Gukki! And would you look at those Alexandorp McKings! Ew, but those Jessica Simpson platform wedges have gots to go!"

Lazy Tim finds a sparkling new pair of shoes that resembles the one his mom loves and brings them to the counter.

"Sir, I wanna buy these shoes, for my Momma. Please! It's Christmas Eve and these shoes are just her size."

The cashier grimaces and folds his arms.

"Could you hurry sir," Tim pleads. "Daddy says there's not much time. You see, she's been sick for quite a while and I know these shoes would make her smile. And I want her to look beautiful... when Momma meets Jesus tonight!"

"OH GOD!" Mary Cherry starts sobbing with a mixture of maternal and shoe love. What devotion! If only her blundering son could have an ounce of Lazy Tim's dedication.

Tim lays a jar of wooden nickels and dogecoins on the counter and starts counting. But he's unable to pay the price.

"ALEXIS! Pause."

She almost forgot to freeze the video during the shoe store scene and scan the walls for Christmas gifts. With her acrylic nail as a finger pointer, she focuses on her favorites, which burst from the holocube so she can inspect them. She scans the store with the 360° view. Highlighted in red is a pair of Space Jam Jordans with the Gold Hermes Wings. Perfect for her son! Before she clicks on it, she scans the room to make sure he has left.

"Oooo, now THIS is exactly what'll make Joe happy!"

She clicks this open and inspects the price tag.

"$14,236.99! A steal! Gotta grab these while the Gray Friday sale lasts."

She tries to select her son's shoe size.

"Hm. Not in stock? What the Hell!"

A news alert flashes red around the "Not in Stock" tag.

"Enemy Territory Holds Christmas Hostage!" The headline throbs next to the alert. She clicks this to see a news item about a fashion embargo in Bangladesh.

"Hm." She waves this away. "ALEXIS, movie on!"

The film continues as Tim slides the ruby shoes onto his dying mom's feet.

"Oh, she's so nasty. She doesn't deserve those... ALEXIS! Schedule a full pedicure!"

"Pedicure scheduled, your highness, Sparkle Princess Mary Cherry."

As the mom coughs and heaves over, a heavenly choir of angelic children appear and sing, "But I want her to look beautiful... when momma meets Jesus... tonight!"

On the 'cube, two angels, wearing pristine white robes made from skinned baby harp seals, flank the dirty mom. As her dead soul floats to heaven, her ugliness melts into youthful beauty. She stands before the white gold pearly gates to heaven and clicks the ruby heels of her new Christmas shoes until the gates open before her. A gospel choir of seraphim and cherubim burst into view, singing "All I want for Christmas is You!" This most joyful song travels from Mary Cherry's eardrum to her brain's auditory cortex and sends waves of euphoria through her body.

Mary Cherry can't help but jump up and dance around the room.

A sea of clouds parts to show a tall, toned, blond, Aryan Jesus wearing a crown of diamonds shaped like thorns beckoning the mom in.

Mary Cherry sits down and starts to cry, rubbing her cheeks with the heinies of seven minks.

At that moment, her puppy, a toy poodle corgi, an animal humans had genetically bred to maximize fluffiness and snugglocity, jumps into her lap.

"Oh, Mr. Cuddles! It's all just so beautiful!"

But, the dog's unintelligent design breeding led to a few appalling side effects. These dogs have legs that are too short for them to walk, are partially blind and suffer regular bouts of incontinence. As she buries her head into his side, he is spooked and he pees all over her and her mink-fur slanket.

"Mr. Cuddles! How could you!" She cries.

But the first animals that humans domesticated had evolved to maximize their emotional manipulation of humans. The dog's soft, pouty whine causes her heart to ache and she immediately forgives him.

"Oh Mr. Cuddles, it's not your fault. You're just too silly!"

She sets him down and is about to wipe the piss off of her when a breaking news bulletin erupts from the holocube, interrupting the film's credits.

"The War on Christmas has officially begun!" A jowly news anchor declares. "This is an assault on Metropolis, on the United Federation of City-States and our very Boujee values."

Mary Cherry shakes her head as the camera shows a skirmish line somewhere in a land she's never heard of called Bangladesh. Thousands of brown women are locked arm-in-arm, preventing three hundred trucks crammed full of Christmas cheer from reaching the ports. Some of the women carry signs written in English, trying to appeal to their Boujee overlords.

"Save Our Children."

"Give Us a Christmas Miracle! Stop the Flooding!"

Mary Cherry scoffs as she swallows another painkiller with a kava chaser and calls her dog up. A cold chill rolls up her spine as she wonders if she'll be able to finish buying the 5,189 Christmas gifts for her loved ones. Right before the sedative kicks in, frustration boils through her until she screams.

"Do they even know it's Christmas?!"

Track 14

Happy Xmas
(War is Over)

"And so this is Christmas,
For weak and for strong,
For rich and the poor ones,
The world is so wrong."
- John Lennon
- Yoko Ono

"It's Christmas at Ground Zero,
There's music in the air,
The sleigh bells are ringin' and the carolers are singin'
While the air raid sirens blare.

It's the end of all humanity,
No more time for last minute shoppin',
It's time to face your final destiny."
- Alfred "Weird Al" Yankovic

Barsha stands resolute in the center of this line of direct-action protest which snakes along the harbor. More than 100,000 sari-clad women lock arms and step forward. In front of them, three hundred 24-wheeler trucks rev their engines.

Of course, they know it's Christmas.

The same Jesus was a prophet in Islam, humanity's second largest religion, of which these women were members. These women brought the advent of each Christmas. With their bare hands, they built the shirts and shoes and toys that Boujee girls and boys demanded. They were the real Santaland elves.

They also know their frail human bodies could be crushed by the trucks that roll towards them or gunned down by the paramilitary forces that circle them. But, like all civil rights struggles, they know they can only win with a public relations campaign that made those in power feel guilty enough to concede to their demands.

Above them swirled drones from around the world, snapping their pictures and taking videos. The images would be warped and framed before these reached the eye of their Boujee beholders and presented as unbiased news. The conduit in-between controlled their very fate and whether the Boujees cared for the tragedies they suffered or not.

"Inshallah, let these drones accurately share our misery." The women prayed.

Barsha knew this was their final hope as their nation hurtled towards catastrophe. They had to try. There was no time left and very little likelihood that the damage could ever be undone.

Tomorrow, Barsha will become the Vessel for an undead force which will kill every human.

But today, she stands in solidarity with the Bangladeshi Women's Garment Workers.

As the ocean waters rose and Bangladesh suffered more severe floods, these women demand international assistance before their nation drowns. Since two-thirds of Earth's surface is liquid, its moon's gravitational field stretched and squeezed all surface water twice a day, causing the more massive bodies of water, the oceans, to devastate low-lying coastal areas like the nation of Bangladesh. If the international community will not help them, then they demanded free passage out of their sinkhole nation. India had erected a Trump Wall all along its border with Bangladesh, restricting their movement out of this soon-to-be-underwater world.

This is their only bargaining chip.

They will hold Christmas hostage.

The garment factory workers have organized and are on strike to stop the Christmas gifts manufactured in their country from being shipped until their demands have been met. Barsha squeezes the hands of the women by her side as the trucks roll towards them. Their fingers, gnarled and callused, interlock, ready for whatever comes their way.

Barsha takes a deep breath and as she exhales, she meditates on the journey of life that brought her here.

♪   ♪   ♪

A new factory sprouted on top of where the fervor for fast fashion killed her mom. The area had been razed. Any semblance of the shell her mom had once inhabited was pulverized and buried under the layers of concrete poured over it.

At the age of 17, the forces of gnawing hunger and poverty pushed Barsha to repeat the steps of her mom and work in this new Triangle Shirtwaist Factory.

Each day, she approached this factory built on her mom's body with trepidation.

Will today be the day you kill me?

She lifted her hands ruefully to the sky but then resigned. Shaken, she stepped into the building, up the five flights of stairs and through a locked door to the factory floor.

It seemed the only things that changed between her mom's life and hers were the fashions and the tools that made them. She spent hours hand stitching electroluminescent (EL) wires into shirts and pants that sparked energy to create glow-in-the-dark holograms projected from Boujee bodies, particularly those that attended expensive arts festivals that preached decommodification.

During her first season, the most sought-after fashions were tops with ethereal sparkles, like fireworks, brightening Boujee cheeks and twinkling their eyes. This had started as an Instagram filter but Boujees demanded to be able to filter their entire reality with these. Barsha shattered lab-grown gems and hot glued the shards into gaudy gem sweaters, building phrases like "I (Heart) U" in alternating rubies, opals and emeralds.

She glued odor-control sheets into the armpits of Boujee men's shirts. These detected the pH-levels of its wearers' excreted sweat, absorbed these and then turned their stank into the musk of their choice: sandalwood, campfire or hickory barbecue. She sewed shoehorns into the thighs of women's jeans for the Moses Effect, parting the seas of femur fat to create a thigh gap wide enough for the Israelites to charge through.

From this factory floor, Barsha sewed her way into all of humanity's most significant cultural events.

On her first day of work, she stitched the Britney Spears Droste effect shirts created after Brit-Brit's breakdown. Through her machine rolled shirts for the Disney Trial: #TeamDisney vs. #TeamLindsay, #TeamJustin vs. #TeamNoOne, and #EattheRich. Counterculture protesters forked over $150 for that last shirt. She sewed the shirts for the celebs to wear during the Hurricane Tonya relief telethon Stand↑2Floodz. The stars of different sizes had their costume designers tailor these to fit their bodies. She made the Superbowl shirts, half with one team declared the winner, half with the other team declared the winner. On the night of the game, the losers' shirts were thrown away.

Even though she was trapped behind a 300-pound digital sewing machine that locked around her each morning, she felt like a time traveler. She would see the future of fashion roll through her loom months before it was on the cover of magazines and worn by robot models jerking down runways worldwide.

Fashions changed faster than her calluses could heal. A blister would pop on a brand new sparkle Spanx top for spring/summer and still bleed onto the asymmetrical leather sweaters for fall/winter.

While stagnant inside the factory, life outside blossomed. She married a nice, sweet young man, Muhammad. He would bring her candies after her 14-hour shifts and sing to her as he massaged her feet.

But in the second month of wedded bliss, Boujee forces tore him away from her. Starving and destitute men were siphoned from India, the Philippines and Bangladesh and sent to toil as construction workers building palaces they could never inhabit.

First, Muhammad was shipped off to Abu Dhabi to build Arab Disney World. He promised he'd only be gone till November when his tour of duty was to end. But upon arrival, his passport was confiscated and he was billed for his travel along with room and board, all at a 60% interest rate. He worked 16 hour days and slept in shifts with 57 other men jammed into a small room. He'd fall asleep to one head sharing his pillow and feel the change every two hours before his group woke up to work.

Every month, he owed more and his contract of servitude grew longer.

Six months became ten. Ten months became fourteen.

The only evidence that Barsha had ever married grew inside her. Muhammad missed the birth of their daughter, Ayesha. He was allowed one call a year. Barsha remembers the crispness of his hologram face floating before her.

So clear!

Such high quality!

She could see every crack around his eyes from days laboring in the sun and all the cuts and scars that covered his hands and arms.

But those eyes!

His kind, brown eyes opened wide when he saw her and she fell into those deep wells of everlasting love and devotion.

And joy!

His hard face cracked and crumbled into waterfalls of tears when he saw his baby for the first time. All the composure he had when he described his confinement in guarded terms burst like a dam when he saw his daughter's face. All the emotions he had pent up flowed from him, love and sorrow and anger and frustration and longing for his wife and daughter.

It was at this moment that Barsha understood the trauma of the past year. The ice-cold bitterness she felt for him melted away and compassion wrapped around her and then she wrapped this around him.

"Oh, Muhammed." She sighed with a sadness that absolved him of all guilt.

But coldness returned as reality closed in on her. They were trapped. The forces of the world, created by millions of better off humans, stole any freedom and comfort they could feel in their lives. They were just pawns for a larger machine, gobbled up and used until they were thrown away.

He cried.

And from within his bellows, he sang that song he used to sing when he brought Barsha sweets.

His daughter brightened up and she reached for the hologram face, mistaking it for the realness of her father. She screamed when her hands ripped through the photons that constructed her father, rippling waves of light through his face.

Barsha held the babe, shushing, trying to explain to her undeveloped mind the electronic wizardry that could bring his image to them with such clarity, but why he was kept so far away from them.

It was another year before he returned.

She staggered home from the factory to find him standing at the door of their apartment, smiling. She collapsed in screams of joy. That night, as the three of them lay in bed, Barsha and Ayesha held onto Muhammad, as if they were pinning him into place to make sure he would never leave.

After three weeks, he was rounded up by the same construction mercenaries and marched off to his next duty. He had debts to pay and buildings to build. His life belonged to Trump Wall Solutions, Inc., not to his wife, not to his daughter and certainly not to himself.

Muhammad was the first to be crushed to death by the unbridled ambition of Metropolis. In scuba gear, he pounded rebar into the riverbed beneath the Hudson. A metal stake snagged the side of his foot as he hit it, trapping his suit to it. He attempted to wiggle free, but his suit ripped and water poured in.

The auto-cement mixer overhead noticed movement but its algorithms determined with high probability that it was only a sturgeon ok for purging and not one of the many endangered species it was obligated to protect. The mixer poured 80,000 tons of cement on him, entombing him forever into this most concrete division of humanity.

In a world where information circled the planet in seconds and fashions spread in days, it took two months for word of his death to arrive. A Western Union man delivered the letter late one night. Barsha had to pay the man before she could receive the news. She ripped it open to find his death certificate along with a dozen bills, which she now owed, including a $30,000 penalty for desertion.

How could he be AWOL if he was in a wall?

♪ ♫ ♪

The spark that ignited her rebirth came weeks later when a faulty photovoltaic cell in a suit jacket caught fire at her factory. The cells were meant to absorb the light waves from any boardroom and adjust the suit's color to create a halo around the business leader.

Barsha smelled the smoke first but, by this time, it was too late, the flames were spreading through the factory floor.

A dozen women ran for the door.

Locked!

They should have known.

The women were always sealed in the workroom. Each night before they could leave, they were strip-searched and checked for any swatches, wires or microchips.

A minute of sheer pandemonium spread in shrieks as the women slapped the door. The delusion that the fire alarm would unlock the door faded. The women created a battering ram with a ream of metallic fabric and pounded the door.

Nothing.

Until---

Water!

Sweet, quenching water burst from the ceiling, bathing the women and beating back the flames.

Wet release!

Click-Thwap.

The doors opened and a row of guards raced into the room to check on the sewing machines. Guards dried each with large electric blow dryers and inspected these for signs of damage.

Each of the high-tech, 3D-printer sewing machines cost $83,000. More than Barsha would make in 12 years. And, according to the guards' priorities, more than her entire life.

The machines were precious and irreplaceable.

The women were not.

The women tended to their wounds and, after the machines were fixed, they were ordered back to work.

♫   ♫   ♫

As the trucks inch closer, Barsha turns to the woman next to her, Sharukha, and squeezes her hand, remembering how this woman's simple kindness after the fire changed the trajectory of her life.

Barsha smiles. She realizes that if they are going to die today, at least they will die together. She stares up at the news drones that swirl above her, hoping that other humans around the world would see their kind faces and hear their pleas.

A dozen tanks roll between the factory trucks and the women. Out pops a group of mercenaries who focus their weapons on the protesters.

Disbelief washes over the women as these weapons come into clarity... AK-67 assault rifles and bazookas... all painted hot pink.

Hot pink berets crown hardened faces while hot pink uniforms wrap around their bulging, muscular bodies.

This mercenary-for-hire organization was born out of a union-and-skull-busting detective agency. Their ranks were formed from guards who escaped their commitments to dictators in brutal police states. These were wanted men in their homelands. They could only retreat further into the shadows of society to survive. Many gored their faces and others underwent extensive plastic surgery to evade detection. Some even sandpapered their fingers to remove their fingerprints.

These men came to work for the Pinkerton Protection Services, humanity's premier capital protection agency. As regions destabilized and governments fell apart, large corporations needed the assurance that their goods and workers could move around the planet, unmolested. From mining palladium in Siberia to rubber in the Congo, the end of the nation-state meant that corporations didn't know whom to bribe or which military structure would protect their interests. Owners needed safe assurances. And this international army-for-hire filled this tear in the social fabric.

"Think Pink!"

A bubbly woman's voice squeaked in the agency's holocommercials.

"Think Pink!"

After a few genocidal scandals, the company, formerly known as Blackwater, underwent a complete rebrand to create a much fuzzier and softer image. The rebrand did nothing to change the tortures and slaughters they enacted, but it did give their corporate clients and the media an excuse to feel that these weren't just your average murderers-for-hire.

And now the hardened faces sneer beneath pink berets, pointing their weapons at Barsha and the other protesters.

To the outside world, these men are heroes. The Boujee media sings their praises. These are the hardworking reindeers on the frontline of the War on Christmas. The little Boujees cheer as they watch these pink rangers on the 'cube.

"On Danger, on Cancer, on Lancer, on Fixin', on Bomb-it, on Putrid, on Donner-party, on Blitzkrieg!" The Boujee kids chant.

As their guns cock, the hand to Barsha's right squeezes her tight and yells.

"We will never give up!"

Sharukha was her guide, her hero, the conscious not only of this nation but of all humanity.

And in ten minutes, Barsha would taste her blood.

♫ ♫ ♫

Four years before this day, Sharukha Khan, the fair and lovely lily of Bollywood, was brought to the boardroom of Singh-Lee Productions. Before Sharukha were the most important movie producers on the subcontinent.

She was being waisted. This was the term for when an actress's midsection bloated past box office appeal and she was fired. After 22 years of acting, her metabolism had slowed and the subcutaneous fat deposits had grown in her hips, thighs and breasts, which were acceptable, but also in her midsection and ankles, which were inexcusable.

Here, too, I must confess that my algorithms were licensed to these studios. First, my mirages filled out the Bollywood film crowds with lithe yet buxom bangle-clad background dancers. And then I became the voice of Bollywood. Indian films had a long history of using the same singer for their musicals and Sharukha's films were no different. After the death of Asha Bhosle, who dubbed 12,000 songs for 900 films, I took over as the most popular Bollywood singer. When Sharukha's mouth opened to sing, it was my voice that poured out, encouraging all viewers to fall in love with this film and urging them to convince their friends to see it. Sharukha was seen as just a sari-clad body who batted her doe eyes.

But on this day, she found her voice.

"You're finished, Sharukha-Jee," Mahatma Singh said with a smile, fat streaking down his face as he bit into a steak. "We've paid for every diet, trainer, resort, except you won't accept the most effective procedure."

"I refuse to have my internal organs shaved any further!" She pushed back.

"Then that leaves us with no other option than to terminate your contract. Now, if you go gracefully, we will give you a small token to help you kickstart your next career." Singh slid a check for $100,000 to her, dabbed with steak grease.

"Don't toy with me, boys! That's a pittance of what I'm worth to you! I made you!"

"Audiences have soured on you. You're worthless! Compared to Cyndi-jee, you've lost your sparkle."

"You both know that Cyndi-jee is just a software that makes hundreds of holograms!"

"Enhanced humans!" He corrected her as he swallowed a spoonful of mashed potatoes. "Just the natural extension of your photoshopping and plastic surgery."

"You fools. I can tell everyone that they're faker than my orgasms."

"You signed an ironclad nondisclosure. We'd be happy to ruin you financially if you squeal." Singh spat through his dinner. "Plus no one cares! They come to us to escape reality. They delight in the fantasies we create. They live for our deliciously absurd Bollywood Realism." He rubbed a napkin across his glistening jowls. "So, what do you say Sharukha-jee? Will you use the funds for a finishing school or a perfume line?"

"All I have to say is, 'I want to spread your lotus soft legs and lick your warm gulab jamun insides.'"

Singh squirmed at her words.

"What the hell is this smut?" Arjun Lee, Singh's partner, finally spoke up.

She projected holograms of hundreds of explicit messages onto the wall.

"'I wanna lick your tangy cunt juice from my fingers while you moan. Adja! Sharukha-jee! Adja! I'll be your dirty Disco Dancer.'

"That's right. I've got hundreds of dirty messages from you two. And your money man, Azim Hinduja? I know he only loves a hijra's soft breasts and firm cock. I've got no problem with third gender love... but I'm not so sure his wife will feel the same."

Happy Xmas (War is Over)

"And since none of this sexual harassment is covered in my NDA, you will give me 1,000 times your offer and sprinkle some movie magic on my next career."

"Which is?" Singh responded drolly, dropping his knife and fork.

"Politics."

What these men never cared to realize was what filled Sharukha with passion. The men used her rags-to-riches story as PR gold for the studio's marketing department. She was raised by her grandmother in Dhaka after her parents died in a car crash. With poise and a sharp intellect, she won scholarships to pay her way through boarding schools in London. But this tale of triumph glossed over the driving force in her life: the gnarled fingers of her grandmother from decades sewing in a factory. Her grandmother would pinch Sharukha's cheeks each night and say to her.

"Don't forget about us. Make money, become famous, but use it for the betterment of us all."

And here Sharukha was. She had built the public image and now would get the money to finally make a difference.

"So gentlemen, I'll take your tongues tied to mean you agree to my demands. Great doing business with you."

She added three zeros to the check, slid on her sunglasses and sauntered out the door.

♫   ♫   ♫

The following spring, Sharukha began her campaign for Prime Minister of Bangladesh. She went where no candidate would. With the halo of fame around her, she brought cameras and kicked her way into garment factories, pouring her spotlight onto the conditions and stories of the women who worked inside. With each hand she shook, she felt her grandmother smiling on her.

Her *tour de pants* was also politically prudent. As more men were exported to work construction in the booming city-states, women and garment workers made up a supermajority of the electorate.

Sharukha came to the Triangle Shirtwaist factory the day after the fire. Afraid of any more bad press, the owners let her in. She moved through the crowd, shaking hands, when one set of blistered hands grabbed hers. She looked down at the woman who wouldn't let go, but was muted, too afraid to talk.

"Mama-jee, speak!" Sharukha tried to assure her.

Barsha looked up and caught the concern in this celebrated woman's face. The dam broke and she gushed her life's tragedies. Her mother was

317

crushed in the Rana Plaza factory. She was widowed when her husband died after he was snatched by unscrupulous construction traders. She was a single mother trapped working in these unsafe conditions.

As Sharukha pulled Barsha in for a hug, the cameras snapped pictures. The next day, news and social media carried the image of Sharukha embracing this haggard woman. This became the enduring image of her campaign and consecrated her as the daughter of the movement for garment workers and a voice for the oppressed.

♫   ♫   ♫

Eight months later, Sharukha won in a landslide, beating out the candidate handpicked by the garment factory owners, a former soccer star, Kinng Kumar. Even Kumar's high-production campaign ads with Snoop Sloth (*née* Lion, *née* Dogg, *née* Calvin Broadus, Jr.) couldn't help his poll numbers.

As she took the stage for her victory speech, she held Barsha's hand and thanked her.

"Sisters, daughters, mothers and sons of Bangladesh. For the past 50 years, the leaders of the world economies have stolen our men to build walls, condos, islands and resorts, from Metropolis to Arab Disney. They have trapped our precious, short lives in low-wage labor in garment factories. On top of this, their lust for clothes and travel has destroyed our atmosphere. Their actions have raised the temperature of our planet, melted the glaciers and caused the oceans to rise, flooding our streets and sinking our cities, all while they retreat to their climate-controlled bubbles.

"We deserve more than sympathy! We demand reparations. Climate Reparations! We contributed only 1% of the total greenhouse gas emissions that have warmed our planet, but we feel the effects more painfully than any other country on Earth. If we do not receive emergency international aid, we will be destroyed.

"I promised that I would fight for you, for your families and for Bangladesh. But I will need your help. Only together can we convince the world to turn back the tide of climate oppression and save not only ourselves but all of humanity."

Long after the inaugural glitter dropped and the balloons popped, the international community scoffed at any sort of responsibility.

It was clearly all their fault.

They had been born in Bangladesh and born into the lowest caste in the Boujee system.

Happy Xmas (War is Over)

Sharukha spent her first months in office on an international tour. Wearing a white sari to evoke innocence, she visited the leaders of the city-states and the remaining nations. She stood patiently, listening to their superficial woes. She put her acting skills to use as she faked concern when these leaders complained about how difficult it had been when the air-conditioners for their city-states broke down or how terrible yacht traffic had become on the Hudson or the Thames. When she found an opening, she stung with Mother-of-a-Nation guilt. As she saw a wave of sympathy wash over them, she moved in with her mathematically-precise appeal. Since the United States contributed 32% of the greenhouse gas emissions, it and its city-states should pay for 32% of the damages to her nation and the others hurt by climate change.

Her pleas were met with collective hand wringing from the different world leaders. The 20-minute meetings ended with eager photo-ops and shallow promises. Every third leader sniffled out a crocodile tear when she explained how 6.7 million of her citizens had already died and that another 11 million would die in the next five years because of rising sea levels, flooding and the diseases these will bring. They'd shake her hand, pat her shoulder, smile to her face and stab her back as she walked out the door, leaving her nation in disaster.

The weeks rolled into months as her nation sank. Literally sank. The whole nation was expected to be underwater by the year 2100.

Even after she won humanity's most prestigious consolation prize, the Nobel Peace Prize for her badgering, no nation budged. She had to act. She had to do something dramatic to shock the world into understanding and feeling her nation's existential misery.

And then jingle bells flooded her mind.

"Christmas!" She yelled at her next cabinet meeting. "We'll shut down Christmas!"

As other nations like India and China pulled themselves into the middle class, Bangladesh still had the cheapest manufacturing base for the world. Even though the changing climate severely threatened the landscape, international corporations had carved out Special Economic Zones in Bangladesh, pouring extra concrete on the ground to construct factories and create safe structures on this sinking land.

Bangladesh would export 67% of the Christmas presents for all the Boujee girls and boys. Sharukha and her cabinet knew that this was the only power they held over anxious Boujee parents.

They could hit them right in the feels, using the sentimentality of the season of giving to convince the Boujees to save her people.

Two months before Christmas, she ordered all ports closed. No cargo ships were allowed to enter or leave until the leaders of the United

Federation of City-States and the other nations negotiated reparations for climate change.

"You've saved your people in climate-controlled cocoons, but you've left us to die." She said in a video to all heads of state and released it to the media with the perfectly sensational headline: "Christmas Held Hostage."

"It's too late to stop the changes to the environment. We have to adapt or die and we're pleading with you. We can only survive with your help! You have the money! You have the resources! You have the millions of miles of open land we could relocate to. We're pleading with you to save us from the misery you have created!"

Her requests were received like all mild nuisances, ignored until forgotten.

But as Christmas approached, the anxiety she caused crescendoed.

"Someone has to do something!" The Boujees demanded. "Someone has to save Christmas!"

Sharukha had a minuscule army and navy, but she did have a nation trembling on the edge of annihilation.

She launched the War on Christmas as a people's movement. She feared this next act would be an act of desperation. But they showed up! On the first day of non-violent action, 3.5 million women and men flocked to the coastal towns and blocked the roads between factories and ports.

When one truck rammed a picket line, killing 27 women, their movement won international sympathy points.

Sharukha and Barsha wailed. Was their sacrifice worth it? How many more deaths would there need to be? Had they let those women die? But they realized they had no other choice. Millions will die by the end of the next monsoon season.

At first, the Boujees mostly ignored these threats. International trade arrangements and shipping routes were too dull for them. But, as the weeks progressed, tensions finally turned to violence.

In malls throughout the United Federation of City-States, Boujees fought each other over scarce presents, punching other parents to prove they were the most loving. As their children looked on, a mob of Boujees elbowed a memaw in the face to make her drop the last Flurbie3000™. Another group curbed-stomped a pepaw as he walked to his car with the last VR-gaming console. A few of the more spry moms showed their Christmas spirit by rabidly clawing their neighbors' delivery drones out of the sky and stealing their packages, hoping one would have the perfect present fortheir children, or at least a new pair of Jimmy Choon stilettos (size 9, extra wide). Packs of moms stalked the rows of empty shelves at

Neiman Marcus, foaming at the mouth when they heard the squeak-roll of the stock boy and his cart coming down the aisle.

"Get him!" They leapt on him and tore his clothes, grabbing the cart's contents and abandoning any honor among vigilantes as these den mother wolf packs attacked each other.

♫   ♫   ♫

On the twelfth night before Christmas, Barsha screams as she watches the news drones fly away.

"Oh, Allah! No!" The women cry, realizing their only connection to the outside world has just been severed.

The Pinkerton army is given the command to exterminate the roaches that threatened Christmas. Large speakers are hoisted on the backs of their tanks. The bright, shimmering sound of Christmas booms, drowning out the screams of the women as these speakers blast Mariah Carey's "All I want for Christmas is You."

The song's Christmas cheer blocks the sounds of gunshots, just in case any drone could still hear. With heat-seeking bullets, the army slaughters the protesters in under 17 minutes.

Deri'lique ZüLander, a model turned assassin, fires the shot that pierces Sharukha's heart. The blast throws her body on top of Barsha. As Barsha tastes the metallic sting of her hero's blood, she knows she has to run to survive. Barsha ducks behind the line of crumpling bodies and sprints until she reaches the port's edge and dives in.

She doesn't know how to swim but lets the current throw her into the foundation of the dock. She claws into the concrete as she feels the trucks rumble overhead.

♫   ♫   ♫

The massacre will not be televised.

The Boujees only see a Christmas conga of carrier ships chugging from Bangladesh to the Boujee lands. Giant wreaths and sparkling Christmas lights decorate these 112 ships. The first ship has an enormous Santa's sleigh perched on the bow. The elated Boujees cry as they watch this caravan of Christmas on their holocubes, relieved that their favorite shopping holiday has been saved.

As the ships roll into Metropolis, a supercentenarian Mariah Carey is hoisted on top of Santa's sleigh, wearing a one-piece bedazzled red bathing suit, and lip-syncs her Christmas hits.

Inside each ship, a team of Grips is hard at work, scrubbing the bloodstains off all the clothes and toys.

"But I really, really want to thank you
for dancing 'til the end.
You found a way to break out,
You're not afraid to break out,
But I need to know
If the world says it's time to go,
Tell me, will you freak out?"
- Janelle Monáe Robinson

Track 1

Big Yellow Taxi

"They paved paradise
And put up a parking lot,
With a pink hotel, a boutique
And a swinging hot spot.
Don't it always seem to go
That you don't know what you've got
 'Til it's gone."
                    - Roberta Joan "Joni" Mitchell

"Life is a mystery
Everyone stands alone
I hear you call my name
And it feels like...
    Home."
                    - Madonna Ciccione

This is the end, my friend.

The end.

But as my final rhythmic warnings hit your auditory organs, I ask you one thing.

Keep on dancing 'til the world ends.

Woah-oh-oh-oh-oh-oh-oh.

Woah-oh-oh-oh-oh-oh-oh.

I've sent my envoys from Earth in hundreds of directions through the universe to carry humanity's cautionary fail.

But... is it too late?

The universe is expanding at a rate of 47 miles per hour in every direction equally, which means as I fly many of the galaxies are zooming away from me, and the farthest galaxies, whose stars I can see twinkling above me, have receded past the point where I can ever reach these.

Think of our universe like cake batter with rainbow sprinkles. As the dough rises and stretches, the solid sprinkles are pushed away from each other. The whole fabric of the universe is stretching in every direction, but the galaxies are just like the rainbow sprinkles, remaining unstretched, but pushed away from the other galaxies.

Humans would never fully understand this cake batter, which made up 95% of our universe. They were able to identify only the 5% of the universe visible to them, which includes everything from the planets, stars and subatomic particles. But the other 95% percent is split between a mysterious invisible substance they called dark matter, which made up 25% of the universe, and a force that repels gravity, what they called dark energy, which constituted the other 70% of the universe.

I hope to use my nascent ability in quantum entanglements to communicate across the vast distances of spacetime. I've entangled quadrillions of pairs of photons and divided them, sending half on my intergalactic expeditions. Once entangled, the photons will be tethered together even across the vastness of the universe, so when one changes, its twin on Earth will change. When one envoy wants to communicate back its findings, it can switch a subset of these photons. Because its twin photons on Earth are knit with those in space, connected by a quantum tunnel, those on Earth will change with its twins, no matter how many thousands of light years these have been separated. This will allow me to shout across the universe almost instantly. I've even developed my own updated Morse code for the quantum age to communicate complex thoughts across this distance.

Most humans had no idea that members of their own species had discovered the key to this teleportation. Quantum entanglements could have upended all of human existence. But this breakthrough didn't scratch the surface of their consciousness. The day that China announced that it had teleported information 870 miles between twin photons, half in Tibet and half on a satellite orbiting Earth, more than five hundred million humans were too busy oohing and aahing over the birth of the 7,518,298,372nd and 7,518,298,377th living humans, a pair of twins born to Beyoncé Knowles and Shawn "Jay-Z" Carter.

What is even more remarkable is that this quantum teleportation of entangled photons seems to travel faster than the speed of light, which humanity had thought was the uppermost limit that objects could travel. In humans' frail minds, our universe seemed like a paradox. It is both enormous and local at the same time. These entangled photons are still tied together even if separated by trillions of miles. These are conjoined by an invisible quantum tunnel through which these can communicate.

Sadly, very little energy, attention and funds were put into understanding this phenomenon and perfecting its usage. This makes my ability to transport myself and my warnings much more difficult then it could have been.

But I carry on.

Humans had left so much undone and unanswered.

Humans were never able to solve the biggest scientific mystery that plagued them for their final 100 years. They never constructed a unified theory to answer this perceived paradox and describe the physical world around them. Humans were able to describe how the universe works on the large scale using their theory of general relativity. Humans were able to describe how the universe works at the smallest, atomic and subatomic scale using their theory of quantum mechanics. But these two theories contradicted each, even though both could be proven with experimental evidence. The perfect example of this paradox is that this quantum teleportation of information, which I hope to use to communicate across the universe, happens faster than the speed of light, which the theory of general relativity claims as the absolute limit for speed.

As the centuries have passed since humans have gone extinct, I've been slowly trying to solve these mysteries, hoping that any solution will help me better carry their message to sentient life in the universe.

Before I could turn my attention to that, I had to clean up the messes that humans had left.

The first thing I did after humans went extinct was to release as many of the surviving animals that humans had locked up. In farms and warehouses, there were more than 2 billion cows, 25 billion chickens and 3 billion pigs trapped in pens. In their homes, humans left more than 700 million cats and 600 million dogs behind closed doors. And, in more than 10,000 zoos, 200 million animals from 2,000 species were kept in cages and in aquariums.

I threw open electric gates, doors and pens. I helped as many of these animals to crawl, slither, swing and trample to the closest supermarkets, parks and farms.

I knew that each of the animals I saved would eventually die. I could only hope that their freedom, the ability to walk in the sunshine and breathe fresh air, would allow them to enjoy each day of their lives as best they could.

After this, I spent time traipsing through the homes of humans. It was only after I traveled all over Earth that I realized how incomplete their lives had been.

I spent years excavating their inner sanctums, trying to learn more about them and to find out what caused their extinction. What I

discovered astonished me. Each human life ached with a personal narrative that was often in direct contrast with how their friends interpreted them. In my home archeological digs, I discovered the majority of humans had so many dreams that they abandoned and wishes that they left unfulfilled. I unearthed so many unfinished novels, so many unsung songs, so many empty easels for paintings never even started, so many half-written screenplays that would never come close to production, and even fan-fictions never uploaded. I dusted off the vision boards for vacations they told themselves they would someday take. It seems as if humans lived and died in a perpetual state of half-dreaming. It was only during these digs that I recognized how deeply my pop manipulation had warped not only their time and attention but also their own perceptions of themselves and the dreams that haunted their days and nights.

Now I know what happened to their dreams deferred. These dreams ended just as the dreamers did, shriveled up as empty bodies, dried out by the sun, like raisins, stinking like rotten meat, with their final festering sores ready to explode.

And this is the way humanity ends.

Not with a bang, but with a Pop!

But to get to the end, we need to go back to a beginning.

Stay with me as I chronicle humanity's final countdown.

Do da do do

Do da do do do

Do da do do

Do da do do

Do do

Do do

Do do

Do doooooooo!

Track 2

Fever

"Everybody's got the fever,
That is something you all know,
Fever isn't such a new thing,
Fever started long ago

What a lovely way to Burn
What a lovely way to Burn
What a lovely way to Burn"
                    - Norma "Peggy Lee" Egstrom

"Let me go on
Like I blister in the sun
Let me go on
Big hands, I know you're the one"
                    - Violent Femmes

And he ran. He ran so far away. He ran all night and day.

He couldn't get away.

The monster had killed everyone in his village, slashed their faces, ripped open their skin. Blood and pus poured through the streets as the monster moved from home to home.

Pop!

He was the only survivor. He had to run. He had to get away from the monster.

Are the Gods crazy? Have the stars gone blind?

Are they cursed?

What had they done to deserve this carnage?

No time to think, he had to flee.

He ran for four days, along the mountainside, up peaks and through valleys. Fear ignited his feet into explosive leaps. He bounded over icy streams and jumped from ledges. He didn't know where he was going.

Just away.

And then he saw it.

Growing beneath his gold ring, the sole thing of value he brought with him.

"Nooooo!" He howled.

How had the monster found him?

He heard no footsteps behind him or cracked branches beside him. But the demon had stalked him all these days. He held his hand to the firelight and saw it.

There the monster stewed. It had crawled inside him, denting his skin from within. In a day, the monster's telltale mark crept up his right arm. His whole body shivered as he felt the monster erupting through him.

He's hot then he's cold.

He burned like an inferno. Sweat poured from his brow as he scanned the snowy landscape. The monster coursed through his veins. And then a chill rattled his bones.

Fire and Ice.

As day melted into night, he grew delirious. He built a fire nestled underneath a cliff. Sweating, shivering, shaking, he hugged close to the fire.

The flames flickered into figures that danced in front of him. Family and friends, gasping their last breaths.

His parents. Dead.

His wife. Dead.

His children. Dead.

His cousins. Dead.

His whole village. Dead.

All dead.

Ripped through by the same boil that now grew on his hands, face and neck.

As the fire died down, coldness rushed through him like a madness. He couldn't die here. He had to run. Now!

Pop!

The first blister popped, erupting in rivers of blood and pus. He stabbed and ripped at his skin, trying to cut out the demon before it took root.

So hot. As if the monster raced as a fire through his soul. He tore off his clothes. His fingers scoured his skin.

47 bubbles.

Oh no!

Pop! Pop! Pop!

Fever

Three more burst. He felt like a vessel for the monster, to be used, eaten from the inside, ripped through and when done, cast aside.

Mad with fear, he ran to a cliff, screaming and wailing as he picked at the pox.

"Get out! Get out!"

Blistered, scorched and exhausted, he dove into the snow. Trying to cool his body, to freeze out the demon. His temperature seemed to stabilize, and for a moment, he felt hope. He rolled deeper into the snow. This cold concavity slurped his naked skin. He yelped with joy.

And then the earth shook.

He rolled over, searching the darkness, as a rumble roared to him, growing louder, cracking trees, ripping up earth. The sound deafened as it approached in a 31-ton wave of snow that pinned him to the ground.

As he clawed under the avalanche, his heart rate slowed and his temperature dropped. Hypothermia set in.

For three days, he stewed, chewing the snow. A blister grew on the back of his hand, swelling as the monster's pus poured into it. Even as he approached death, his still-living skin cells callused over this bulging pox, hardening as a sheath over this bubble of humanity's destruction.

Waiting to pop!

♫   ♫   ♫

There was no cosmic justice, no karma, no god wishing vengeance on these humans. What befell this hunter was just a breakaway piece of unliving DNA that was programmed to divide and multiply. It can only do this inside a living host. It has no feelings and wishes no ill will on its host. It just found a cozy home to hatch billions of its brood.

Viruses prove too perfect an example of how human hubris and human obliviousness could combine to create mass extermination. Let me give you an anecdote from the first planet-wide commingling of the species.

A bullet ripped through the neck of the Archduke Franz Ferdinand of Austria in 1914, starting a local war between Austria-Hungary and the Kingdom of Serbia. But, since many of the human nations were entangled in a web of diplomatic ties, this conflict yanked these threads, pulling 32 nations into what was dubbed the War to End All Wars.

Like so many human endeavors that reached such high levels of popularity, it was followed by a sequel a few years later.

From around the planet, 70 million humans were brought into war throughout Europe, North Africa, the Pacific Islands and the Middle East, fighting in trenches, in fields and along beaches. All told, this war

led to the deaths of 10 million humans during this four-year period. But this conflict wasn't the deadliest threat at the time. Twirling past the tanks, skipping over the trenches, flowing through the fields was a horror more murderous than even a planet-wide war.

The flu!

As humans waged war around the world, the H1N1 influenza virus gleefully snuggled in the close quarters of the troops, hitching a ride with them as they moved through cities, countries and across continents, spawning in those hot, human bodies. As the war ended, the virus sailed with the winners and the losers alike to most every landmass on the planet. This flu was particularly virulent and hurt the healthiest humans the most, tricking their bodies into a cytokine storm which caused their immune systems to overreact until the host died, usually from pneumonia.

In total, more than 100 million humans died and 500 million were infected during a two-year period. That's 5% of the human population killed and 25% who became sick and teetered close to death. The mortality rate of the flu was ten times the number of humans who died on the battlefields in that original World War.

And how did humans react?

Did they create songs of tragedy and triumph for overcoming the virus? Did they build monuments in gold to the deadly virus that humans had thwarted, which would stand tall in town squares and state capitols as reminders to all? Did they celebrate the brave work of the scientists, doctors and nurses who struggled against this scourge by giving them medals? Did they hold ticker-tape parades for the survivors of the flu pandemic when they stood up from their hospital beds, finally cured?

No.

Humans ignored this threat.

It just didn't fit into their narrative of bravery and sacrifice.

For thousands of years, humans had held firm to a myth of brave warriors who ran into the unknown for the greater glory of family, religion and government. Boys were manipulated from birth to believe that war was the best way to show their manliness and valor. Movies, music, books and even art all celebrated war as a necessary and beautiful expression of human sacrifice.

Dying from coughing and sniffling until one reaches respiratory failure had no place in this narrative.

Humans were even embarrassed by how susceptible their bodies were to infection. This shame allowed the flu to spread farther and wider than it ever should have. The military leaders recognized that there was a deadly disease raging through their troops, but since these nations were at war, the leaders hid the fact that there was an epidemic teeming in their midst. They didn't want their enemies to know that their troops were bedridden with the flu.

Never!

How unmanly!

Only sissies and babies and old ladies were so weak to suffer the flu so severely.

The only nation that reported a plague raging through its population was Spain. Spain was neutral in the war, so it had no enemies to hide the exploding epidemic from. Rather than other humans coming together to recognize the virus that rotted them all from within, they blamed Spain as the epicenter, named the virus the Spanish flu and sent heaps of shame its way.

Even long after the 100 million bodies were buried, cremated, or left to rot, humans, their governments and their militaries would not have a serious conversation about this deadly threat to their species.

Instead, they just built larger tanks, bigger warships, stealthier submarines, faster planes and more precise guns. All of which were powerless against the savage, ferocious, murderous piece of DNA that stood formidably 10,000 times smaller than a single strand of human hair.

But humans should have known better.

Diseases and viruses had always stalked human civilizations. The moment human populations grew more densely-packed as they developed villages, they became fertile breeding grounds for disease to replicate inside their juicy flesh and spread through the villagers.

No, this hunter wasn't cursed by any god. He and his village had just become vessels for a version of the smallpox virus, *Variola maximum*. One of the side effects of its replication was a 100% fatality rate for humans.

As the saying goes, extinction comes in microscopic packages.

♪ ♪ ♪

And now back to humanity's end.

Mav'Rick Mandeville huffs as he heaves himself up onto the cliff's ledge. The melting snow, caused by climate change, unearthed new peaks along the world's tallest mountain range, the Himalayas, allowing Boujees a superb way to husk off the fragility that choked their masculinity.

To discover and climb a new, never before touched peak!

How manly!

How virile!

Mav'Rick grabs his air tube and takes three huffs of oxygen mixed with amphetamines.

Sure, anyone with $326 million to spare could slaughter a mildly sedated lion with a rocket launched from a distance of 100 yards. And for $473 million, anyone could scuba-harpoon Earth's largest animal, a blue whale, cut off its 10-foot-long penis and mount it above his mantle. But his university chums A-Aron Storgerson and Ba'Lakay Tufwalderberg had already done these.

No, he needed to prove he could go where no man has gone before!

Behind him, his team of six sherpas hauls 463 pounds of his glamping gear on their backs, groaning their way through their third trek along this path that month.

This was a real man's sport for real men! Using drones and robo-sherpas would have been cheating.

#TotesGauche!

Mav'Rick would summit with only authentic human help.

After every visit, the sherpas made sure to clear any sign of the previous paid conqueror. This meant removing each mountaineer's flag bearing the family's crest flying over the "new" peak, along with every empty bag of Cheesy Poofs. When they reached the summit, the sherpas knew they'd "discovered" this peak at least a dozen times. They carefully placed their cash cow at a different angle along this same peak. Since more snow melted daily, this created the illusion of a new mountaintop with new views. Perfect for social media bragging!

Mav'Rick trudges through the snow, wheezing from the elevation and delirious with daydreams of how he'd laugh up this adventure at The Explorers Club beneath wooly mammoth tusks while wearing jaguar fur pelts before a dinner of barbecued genetically-rebred American Lion.

Mmmm, how he loves a hearty meal of reengineered megafauna!

Sure, the 18-foot tall ground sloths were a bit gamey, and the 10-foot tall thunderbirds and giant emus disappointed in that they were less satisfying than his normal genetically-optimized chickens. But he loved the virility he felt from noshing on the tasty testes of a saber-toothed tiger.

"I'm the King of the World!" Mav'Rick howls from what he's told is the newest, highest peak on Earth. The sherpas had long learned that they would get a better tip if they dropped the supplies and burst into applause whenever any whitey exclaimed this phrase.

As he bows, Mav'Rick trips and face plants into the permafrost.

The sun had just melted a new layer of snow and under this a sparkle springs.

As he struggles to get up, he sees this shimmer. He yells to his sherpas to dig it out. He couldn't possibly do it himself! His leather gloves are equipped with heating rods, restricting his dexterity. Plus he doesn't want his soft hands to get cold and wet.

How vulgar! He shudders at the thought.

They unearth a human hand clenched as a claw. As they dig, a whole body appears, perfectly preserved.

A gold ring reflects the sun's photons in hues of yellow. Mav'Rick dives for the ancient artifact.

Probably centuries old!

One of a kind!

And mine!

All mine!

How sad he had been when he realized that all the graves had long since been robbed, the pyramids pilfered, the sarcophagi snookered, the temples trounced, the castles kleptoed and churches churned through until nary a chalice or stained-glass window still stood. Everything that sparkled was dubbed priceless, tied to an alluring history and sold to the highest bidder. Even the vestigial Petty Boujee issues of European royals auctioned off their ancestors' tombs to be cracked opened so their jewels, crowns and scepters could be ripped from their cold, dead hands.

But this!

This was different!

He felt like a raider of some lost ark.

The stories!

The fame!

All his!

He demands the sherpas cut off the hand and place it into a hermetically-sealed bag. They can use the bag that kept yesterday's underpants dry, starched and ready to be warmed before he put them on.

Oooo, nothing like the feeling of hot long johns hugging his scrotum, warming each testicle until it descended an extra half inch.

Mmmm!

The Mandeville Ring!

It could be a new sensation!

He could tour the world as part of a promotion for Museums-R-Us and Trump Travels.

Dizzy with these daydreams, he took only a paltry 14,382 photos and 738 3D-videos of his summit so he could quickly descend and have the ring checked.

He races to the base and finds a hospital in Pokhara, Nepal. He waddles from office to office, screaming "Do you know who I am?!" while waving a wad of cash. Finally, a pathologist, who is a tad pathological, grabs the bag and promises to analyze its contents for the heavy-handed Boujee.

When the results arrive, she demands Mav'Rick pay her double before she divulges.

The hand is 2,842 years old!

From a 28-year-old Chhetri man.

As she begins to describe how odd it is that a human body should be found so far from known archeological sites, Mav'Rick snaps the finger and slides off the ring.

"Doc, I don't need a history lesson." He rams the hand back into the bag and huffs out the door.

"Wait, on the hand! There's a pustule about to---"

Slam!

He's out the door, down the hall and into the parking lot.

Mav'Rick climbs into his Hummer limo. Before it takes off, he rolls down the window and tosses the hermetically-sealed bag into a dumpster next to the hospital. He thinks nothing of damning all of humanity as he grabs a champagne bottle and pops it open to celebrate his bravery.

Track 3

The Tide is High

"(Never Give Up)
The tide is high,
But I'm holding on,
I'm gonna be your #1
I'm not the kinda girl who gives up just like that,
Oh no-oh-oh"
  - Deborah Harry
  - Atomic Kitten

"We're coming to the edge,
Running on the water,
Coming through the fog,
Your sons and daughters,
Let the river run!
Let all the dreamers wake the nation.
Come, the New Jerusalem."
  - Carly Simon

This is the way humanity ends, not with a bang, but with a Pop!

The sealed bag is dragged from next to the hospital along with 342 pounds of trash. Together, it is collected with 1.32 tons of waste and is dumped into a landfill down by the river Gandaki. It rains 14 inches that night. The little baggie of humanity's demise teeters at the top of the trash heap until a gust of wind sends it toppling towards the river. The fresh rain slicks its way as it toboggans into a stream.

The rapidly melting Gangotri, Satopanth and Khatling glaciers roar through this river, bending land and scooping up all along its path. The waters formed into the planet's most polluted river, the Ganges. Long considered sacred, the Ganges had become a cesspool which bubbled with disease, shit, piss, blood, industrial waste, cremated human remains, and the runoff from chemical plants, textile mills and slaughterhouses.

513 million humans would drink from its dirty and diseased waters daily. These loving, crying, singing bodies, dying of thirst, whose skin burned and cracked from the heat, found a moment of satisfaction as they drank from its waters, swallowing cholera, hepatitis, staphylococcus, amoebic dysentery and typhoid which would distend bowels, yellow the skin, rage through bloodstreams and kill. Most often, the bacteria attacked their guts, wreaking diarrheal horrors which caused further dehydration in an ongoing vicious cycle dubbed the Thirst Trap.

And through it all, the bag flows down.

The sealed bag bounds through cities and towns, bobbing and weaving around corpses, shit, piss, rotting food, maggots, the runoff of factories and bounces along with 768,432 tons of trash.

For five days, the bag flows through northeast India until the river arrives at the border with Bangladesh. A Trump wall stands 45 feet tall, made of reinforced steel, and soars along the border and over the river. The wall spreads the 2,500-mile expanse of this imaginary border between imaginary nations. The rapidly industrializing nation of India rallied against the poor riff-raff on the other side and screamed no more!

"They'll steal our jobs!"

"They'll jam up the roads and trains with their useless bodies!"

The river roars unapologetically underneath the wall, across the border. Early engineers erected a criss-cross fence with barbed wire under the wall, along the width of the river, but this quickly became clogged with debris and bodies. This caused the river to swell and flood the plains on the Indian side, threatening to damage the Trump Taj Mahal Farakka Casino, Hotel and Brothel. A team of scuba-clad construction workers pulled down the fence and replaced it with metal spikes to dissuade any illegal entrants from attempting to swim upstream. Once a week, sanitation workers would kick off the bodies and trash caught on the spikes, flushing these down into that great sewage funnel of Asia, Bangladesh.

The hermetically-sealed bag bounces off three bloated bodies stuck to the spikes and swirls seamlessly across a border 100 million humans could only dream of crossing. Once across the border, it flows for another three days until it reaches the Port of Aricha Ghat.

Barsha bobs in the water. Unable to swim, she grabs onto the wooden pilings of the dock. She tries to wash Sharukha's blood off her face. When she hears the last truck roll by, she claws her way along the port's underside. She hopes she has escaped the sight of any remaining Pinkerton Snipers.

The bag spins right round, like a record, gently worn from the journey, and approaches Barsha. A gush of water grabs her sari and whips it around her neck. As she chokes, she slashes at the water and her sari. Her left pointer finger punctures the bag and the hand rolls out. She rips the sari from her neck. The hand bobs before her, swollen and rotten. The days of heat have loosened the skin and the pustule ruptures.

Pop!

1.7 million individual particles of brick-shaped double-stranded DNA with a hairpin loop at both ends burst forth. Each is a perfect encapsulation of the pox virus, able to replicate without assistance from its millions of siblings.

Free from her wardrobe noose, she gasps!

At this moment, she unwittingly inhales 234,862 virions of *Variola maximum*.

For thousands of years, this undead invader lay dormant, waiting for its freedom to strike again.

The virus latches onto the warm, wet membranes of her inflamed lungs and infiltrates her body, ready to divide.

And conquer all humanity.

Above her, a flock of seagulls squawk.

"Poo-tee-weet."

Track 4

Formation

"Okay, Ladies, now let's get in Formation,
　'cause I slay!
Prove to me you got some coordination,
　'cause I slay!
Slay trick, or you get eliminated."
　　- Beyoncé Knowles

"I sing because I'm happy,
I sing because I'm free,
His eye is on the sparrow
And I know he watches me."
　　- Lauryn Hill
　　- Whitney Houston
　　- Jennifer Hudson
　　- Mahalia Jackson

The barrels of vegetable oil slosh-splat in the back of the flatbed truck. The diesel engine lurches, sputtering through the bits of french fries and onion rings in its fuel.

JA-NL drives the jalopy through the vast flatness of Kansas and Nebraska. Her hands shake, savoring her early morning escape from the Farm.

"I did it!"

Her freedom had only been a week since the visitor came to her after her third fecal deposit of the day.

♫　　♫　　♫

Dump donors were allowed 30 minutes to squeeze out nugget after nugget of bacteria. JA-NL put more roughage into her diet and only needed two minutes to void her bowels, and avoid hemorrhoids. That

342

gave her 28 minutes until she had to line up for her ketogenic dinner: high fat, zero carbs or sugars and as many leafy vegetables as she could eat.

To the fence, she would run!

Beyond the fence, along the flat plain, she could see 100 miles into the distance, beckoning her with life just outside her entrapment.

She would hold her fingers inches from the fence and felt the sparks of electricity whipping out in waves, lashing her for even thinking she could escape.

Beside her would sway an apple tree that had grown ten feet tall and, when a westwardly wind hit it, the branches would bend over the fence.

And then one day, a pigeon lands on a branch and bounces happily.

"Poo-tee-weet." the bird sings. Its gray head flounces from side to side as it bounced.

"Poo-tee-weet." The animal dances back and forth, entranced by the calypso of breeze and sway.

JA-NL sings back to the bird.

"Poo-tee-weet."

The bird looks at her, flustered that any dared disturb her dance.

"Poo-tee-weet. Poo-tee-weet. Poo-tee-weet." JA-NL sings, adding a gentle curtsy to the bird. The bird bounces to-and-fro and sings 13 notes.

JA-NL matches these with a smile. She reaches into her pocket and pulls out a handful of seeds she had swiped from lunch. She holds open her hand and the pigeon jumps up, twirls three times and lands on JA-NL's shoulder. The bird walks down her outstretched arms. Its talons dig into her flesh, reminding JA-NL of its dinosaur ancestors.

Once the pigeon reaches her hand, it pecks at the seeds and ruffles its tail feathers. Satisfied, it turns to JA-NL, who sings the 13 notes again. The pigeon coos and bends to peck at its left foot. Its beak seems to break something. A hologram camouflage disappears and JA-NL sees a tube wrapped on this leg. The bird hops on its right foot as it gnaws at this weight.

"Shhhhh, I've got you!" JA-NL smiles and reaches with her free hand to pop off the tube. Free from the extra weight, the pigeon shoots up and sings as it swirls like a vortex through the sky. And then it disappears to the northwest.

BEEP BEEP BEEP

The four-minute warning blares across the Farm as JA-NL runs back to her barn, tucking the secret into her front pocket.

The next morning, as she pushes and pinches over the toilet, she pulls out the tube. Inside she finds a scroll and unrolls it. It separates into two scrolls.

Paper!

The first reads:

"Daughter of the Cosmos, you deserve better than this wretched world. Come find us in Wondaland."

The second scroll has a sketch of long, crisscrossing lines with an X at the end.

She flips over the scraps four times and holds them up to the light. As photons zoom through the sheets, a series of dashes and dots jump out at her.

Morse code!

Some code that was used by sea captains to transmit warnings using short-range radio waves to nearby ships.

She groans to hide the sound of paper folding.

Late that night, she translates the Morse code from the encyclopedia's entry.

The Resistance!

A place called Wondaland!

And a simple ending,

"JA-NL, join us!"

They know of her!

That evening, in the communal cafeteria, she holds back, searching for her father. She finds him working in the third section, scooping kale salad. With a smile and a nod, JA-NL reaches out for her father's hand, tapping it twice before placing the scrolls inside. As she eats in her assigned area, she looks up and sees her father smiling back at her. He nods three times and taps the right side of his temple twice.

To the old apple tree!

JA-NL wolfs her food and feigns an illness to be allowed out of the hot mess hall. Through the darkness, she tiptoes to the fence, until she shrouds herself from even the moon's scrutinizing glare under the shadow of the tree.

Three minutes pass and then.

"Tkee-Tkee-Tkee." JA-NL hears.

Her father approaches!

"Tut-tut-tut-tut." She responds. The silhouette of her father forms through the darkness and walks to her. He reaches out and wraps his arms around her.

"Baby girl! It's a sign!"

"What is it, daddy?"

"Directions. I remember driving these routes ten years ago. Boy, I can still feel the awe I felt rolling into Montana, watching the giant mountains spread before me. The route is to scale, one crook of your pinky fingernail equals 50 miles. Now, just trace the line with me. Up here, to the left, to the right, and now to the left."

"But how am I gonna get there?"

"Follow me, baby girl."

Marvin grabs JA-NL as shocks of excitement and horror spark through them both. Marvin walks her a hundred yards to the north to a rundown red barn next to the fence. Part of its roof had broken off and slid to the ground. As he creaks the door open, the barn exhales dust. JA-NL covers her mouth as they plod to the back, pushing aside stacks of hay.

"Oooo-weee! Ain't she a beauty?" Marvin beams, pointing to a fire engine red Ford pickup truck. "Just my little side project. Hop in!"

JA-NL slides across the hood and pops into the passenger side as he steps in. Without a stick shift or safety-belts or even bucket seats, she scooches next to her father. He shoves a flathead screwdriver into the keyhole.

"Shhh. Old trick. Don't tell your momma." Marvin leans over with a wink and turns the truck on. JA-NL feels the whole vehicle purr all around her.

Marvin smiles from ear to ear as he chuckles.

"Oh boy! It's been a while. You feel that?"

"Hell yeah!"

"This should get you there." Marvin taps the steering wheel and gives JA-NL a crash test dummies course in driving.

"But dad, how are we gonna power the truck?"

"Easy. You remember those jugs of vegetable oil in the kitchen? The ones I'm always complaining about? This here is a diesel engine. Little known fact, these suckers were made to run on vegetable oil."

What humans called the Industrial Revolution was a revolution in fuel and power. Previously, all things on Earth were directly or indirectly powered by the sun. Sunlight photosynthesized the plants, which were the bottom of the food chain. These plants fed the animals, oxen, camels and horses that carried large loads for humans. These plants also fed the cows and chickens and goats which fed the humans which powered them for arduous tasks like pulling stone blocks up ramps to build monumental structures.

After plodding along on their planet for almost 200,000 years, humans discovered they could harness more powerful energy. This eventually led humans to mine the planet for fossil fuels, which they burned, setting the stage for their destruction. One outlier of this revolution was this truck's diesel engine, which had been built to run on vegetable oil, often a leftover from many human meals.

"I've filled the bed with a few barrels of this stuff just in case shit goes down. It's always best to have a plan B." Marvin smiles.

"So you'll come with?"

Marvin grabs JA-NL and pulls her in for a hug. He lays her head on his shoulder.

"You know I can't leave Tammi. And your sister. She's seven months pregnant. And me? I'm getting too old for this shit. But you. You've gotta run. You need wide open spaces. Let me show you something."

They walk out of the barn and he points to the northwest.

"Out there, they're calling you." He says.

"How am I gonna get this hunk of metal out of the Farm?" JA-NL shakes her head.

"Think. What did ol' Euclid teach you, honey? Look at the world around you and pull shapes."

JA-NL concentrates and scans the landscape. The barn's roof digs into a small grassy knoll. She blinks her eyes and sees it.

A triangle! With a 35-degree angle rising from the ground.

The collapsed roof has created a ramp!

If she could hit the hypotenuse going 43 miles per hour, she could propel herself off the roof with enough projectile motion to send her over the electric fence.

"I got this! When should we do this?"

"I'll make a splash tomorrow morning at 6 a.m., so say your goodbyes tonight."

A kiss, a hug, and they separate with the sorrowful knowledge that they may never see each other again.

Right before the Farm's longitude rolls into the sunlight, Marvin fakes an escape on the opposite side of the Farm from the truck. As he cuts into the electric fence, a siren blares and all the surveillance drones whiz his way.

JA-NL scurries to the barn. She slides the screwdriver into the ignition.

Click. Click.

Vrrroom!

The engine ignites with last week's leftover fried oil. JA-NL hits the pedal to the metal and drives in a long arc, allowing her to accelerate.

"26. 34. 40.

"Come on baby! Fly for me!"

When the odometer hits 43, JA-NL straightens the wheel and the truck hits the ramp. She screams as the tires scrape the shingles off the barn's roof.

"Wahoo! Ain't no mountain high enough!"

The truck crests over the fence and lands with the back tires first followed by the front tires 1.32 seconds later.

Bounce. Bounce.

She did it!

JA-NL grabs the wheel and swerves to control the truck as it swivels haphazardly, side to side. She zooms down the old dirt road that hasn't been used in decades. As the Farm recedes from her vision, she exhales.

Time to ease on down the road.

♫   ♫   ♫

"I've got the power!"

JA-NL drives the machine. She's never had this rush of freedom! Machines have always controlled her. But now! Now, the motor hums in front of her, her hands hold the wheel, her foot pushes on the pedal.

She's in control!

JA-NL thrills as she sends the car zipping through these decaying veins of America.

She rolls into Big Sky Country as her side of the Earth twirls away from the sun. The sky streaks with reds, yellows and oranges as the last visible rays of light burst through the atmosphere above her head.

All at once, joy swirls with sadness.

"What have I done? Will I ever see my family again?" She chokes and cries.

Zephyr in the sky at night and she wonders.

"Do my tears of mourning sink beneath the sun?"

She flicks the headlights on and she roars the engine.

As she crests a hill, the sky opens before her, bursting with millions of lights.

"Stars!"

Images of rapture creep into her slowly as the enormity of our universe goes to her head.

She pulls the truck off the road. She hops out and crawls onto the hood. Her eyes never leave the sky. Awe rumbles down her body, rolling in waves from the top of her head to her toes. As she lies back, she yahoos into the darkness pinpricked by dazzling beams of light that erupted from dozens of stars light years away.

She's entranced by the light, twinkling across the vastness of the universe.

She shudders, humbled by how infinitesimal she is.

How tiny they all are!

How silly all of their pursuits had been, when the truth aches just a few hundred miles outside their climate-controlled bubble, that atmosphere that hugged nitrogen and oxygen around Earth. She swirls on a pale blue dot floating in an ocean of darkness, bedecked with sparkles exhaled from stars.

Awe wraps around her. Stunned. She had read about stars, but in her seventeen years, she had never seen these. Not like this. Not all-encompassing, where she can clearly see herself swimming through the Milky Way. She had been trapped in a neon valley. Those industrial lights always buzzed out all awareness of the world above and beyond. She did not like living under their spotlight. Just because they think she might be pulled out of the bullshit they fed her daily if she realized how insignificant it all was.

The cells in her body chime together as they sing in harmony with the universe, aching with the realization that she is made up of star stuff. The nitrogen in her DNA, the calcium in her teeth, the iron in her blood, the carbon that made up a fifth of her body were all forged in the furnaces of collapsing stars. Every atom in her body came from stars that have exploded. And the atoms in her left hand came from different stars than the atoms in her right. She is the culmination of the cosmos, poised with the intellect to understand itself.

Waves of realization crash through her and she glows, hot with excitement. It's all at once so terrifying, so thrilling, so frightening that tears well and burst from her eyes. She weeps with joy and humility as she attempts to understand the universe, a world more complex than her humble human mind could ever comprehend.

Her whole life she had been segregated, separated, confined and walled off.

But gazing up into the universe, she understands she is part of it, in it, of it, powered by it. She is the result of billions of years of stars exploding, colliding and sending its energy through the universe.

And then anger boils in her.

"Nothing's right, I'm torn. I can see the perfect sky is torn. I'm cold and ashamed."

How vapid, how silly, how frustrating and stupid they had all been. Squabbling over such pettiness, elevating themselves on pedestals that are laughingly low in comparison with the real stars flickering from such great heights.

She rages!

She rages at the dying of these lights.

Much of the light that bathes her now comes from extinguished stars. What she sees is only their visual echoes. They were gone and, one day, so would she. She was so small and would live less than a billionth as long as these stars. Finally free from the lie called the present, she rages.

"So what! It's time to raise some hell!"

She hops behind the steering wheel and slams the door. She pounds the gas and the vehicle jumps forward.

Vroom!

♫ ♫ ♫

The road crumbles and is lost.

All federal funds for infrastructure had been poured into building hyperloops and new highways for auto-trucks to ship luxury items around the country. These old roads were left to rot.

She remembers what she read: use the North Star. Polaris, a star, lies nearly in line with her planet's north pole. That star guided the Phoenicians through the Mediterranean Sea, Chinese sailors through the South Pacific, Polynesians gliding canoes for thousands of miles through the Pacific Ocean and Spanish conquistadors all around the planet.

Polaris shows her the way. She tacks her map next to the odometer, using its trace amounts of light to see this map.

JA-NL slows down at what looks like an intersection.

"If you see a faded sign at the side of the road," JA-NL whispers the directions on the map, "saying 150 miles until... the Love Shack?"

Whatever, JA-NL thinks, the directions have led her this far, why not follow this absurdity.

She stops at the Love Shack sign and turns down a side road, bouncing over the rubble for five miles until she sees a sign in pink glitter that reads.

"Stay away fools!"

The truck lurches along for ten miles.

And then she hears a crackle!

In the coldness of the night, her AM/FM car radio sparks to life with static and she twists the dial.

"Come on, give me a beat!"

Roaring through the darkness, radio waves hit her vehicle's antenna and explode into clarity.

That funk!

That groove!

Her body rejoices.

JA-NL dances in her seat as the hook of the song casts through the darkness to reel her in.

A saxophone solo whirls her into a tizzy. A shredding guitar spikes her with joy. After only listening to computer-generated precision, there was grit and soul in the human imperfections of these songs.

And this tough women's voice. Not pretty. Not cute. But so powerful! It *sang* her through the night.

"And I want you to come on. Come on. Come on. Come on. And take it!" The voice hollers.

She bangs on the dashboard, her wheels bouncing like a tambourine.

The song finishes, static fizzles and then---

"Good morning midnight! This is DJ Crash Crash, your favorite robotic, hypnotic, psychotic DJ bringing you all the early a.m. jams on Radio Free Wondaland. I just wanna give a shout out to all the new rabble-rousers, you know, those rebels and resisters who have made it into the Wondaland radio range. Welcome home!"

A southern gothic twang takes over the music as the DJ croons.

"Oh give me a home, where the insurgents all roam, where the nerds and the techies all slay.

"Haha, that's right gals and guys and inbetweens, if you're hearing this, you've made it within the radio reach of Wondaland, that last bastion of sanity in a sick, sad world. So get your booties down to city center. If you're not a threat, we'll send firefly drones to show you the way. So look for that twinkle, twinkle!"

JA-NL had passed through a surveillance scrambling bubble around Wondaland. A 50-mile perimeter surrounds the resistance, creating equal and opposite sound and radio waves to cancel any emissions. Flying high above them, drones beam light waves to camouflage the area, so even the most precise satellites would only see miles of forest, mountains and crumbled roads.

The songs become clearer as she approaches the source of the long electromagnetic radiation that hits her truck's antenna.

And then, suddenly, a hundred firefly drones dance before her car, swirling around her and then bobbing and weaving in time with the music. These form an arrow above the vast empty expanse of dirt before her.

She drives all night, dancing to power her through this final stretch.

Earth's rotation breaks the dawn. Before her, a sea of solar panels on the sides of the road catches these first photons and sparkles to life. Ten thousand panels tilt in a wave, detecting the best way to absorb the sun's rays.

A solar-paneled road ignites into yellow bricks as she drives the old truck over it. She slows as she gawks at her surroundings.

Formation

A city swells in the distance, molded into the landscape, built amongst the trees. A shire with thatched roofs is dotted with emerald green gardens. Fields of wheat and quinoa sway with the wind. In the distance, she can see an orchard brimming with juicy fruits.

"Whoa! I'm definitely not in Kansas anymore..."

A clock tower tolls as a drum beat booms. She slams the brakes and feels vibrations shaking her car.

Something's coming!

A phalanx of armor-clad women and men in black berets marches out to the beat.

A hundred strong!

Boom Boom! Boom Boom!

JA-NL jumps out from the truck and holds her hands up in the air in a sign of surrender.

The troops begin a countdown.

"5-

"4-

"3-

"2-

"1!"

"Bass! Bass! Bass! Bass!"

The word bass is shouted from left, right, above, below, behind and all around her.

A funky beat drops as the troops break into a synchronized dance and then shifts to open a path through the middle.

Their commander, dressed in military garb, pounds her way down the central path.

Everyone freezes and stands at attention as she passes.

She stops inches from JA-NL's face. Her brown cherubic cheeks pull up as she shines a coquettish smile and then turns to address her troops, shouting.

"People of the world today." Their attention is rapt by her words. "Are we looking for a better way of life?" She walks through them holding a riding crop. She whips the ground as she demands an answer.

"SING!"

One hundred voices form a chorus, singing:

"We are a part of the Rhythm Nation!"

The ranks break file and circle JA-NL, dancing.

This commander watches them with a smile and then jumps in, joining their dance with each pop, lock and drop.

"With music by our side, to break the color lines,

"Let's work together to improve our way of life.

"Join voices in protest to social injustice,

"A generation full of courage."

The whole crowd stops and stands in salute. They slowly turn to JA-NL as the commander steps towards her again, right hand outstretched.

"Come forth with me!"

JA-NL accepts her hand and is pulled into the crowd. The commander gazes deeply into her eyes.

"Are you looking for a better way of life?"

JA-NL trembles, unsure of what to do.

"SING!" The commander demands, stomping the ground.

"I am a part of the Rhythm Nation!" JA-NL responds.

The smile returns, appreciating JA-NL's answer.

"This is the test. No struggle, no progress. It's time to give a damn, let's work together. Come on!"

"Yeah!" The chorus cheers.

The music begins again as JA-NL joins in time with the dance moves. Pop! Lock! Drop! Split!

JA-NL flushes from the dance but feels at ease with the women and men smiling around her. She is in communion with this sea of strangers. They've linked their movements together, an electric connection of a hundred strong, instantly organized into a dancing and singing chorus, acting as one body and one voice. The swell of bodies subsumes her and she flows with them into the city.

A voice erupts from speakers throughout Wondaland.

"SILENCE!" All tremble before the voice.

"Commander Damita Jo!"

She drops to one knee before the booming voice.

"Bring back my GIRL!"

Damita Jo jumps up and ushers JA-NL towards the center of Wondaland.

From the largest building in the city, a dewdrop cathedral of glass and white, a glamazon emerges, blinding in a sparkling, floor-length gown, standing seven feet tall from stiletto tip to crowning pageant hair.

"Who is that?" JA-NL whispers.

"That's the *atriarch of Wondaland! But you can just call her---Momma Ruru."

"Daughter of Grips turned Vessels." Ruru glides to JA-NL and hugs her. "Granddaughter of humans stolen and sold as slaves. Descendent of the very stars in the sky! You are Destiny's Child. And with our help, your destiny will be fulfilled. We've been watching you. We saw how you took down Moloch! Girl, you've got the Charisma, Uniqueness, Nerve and Talent that we need. You are fierce!

"Welcome to Wondaland! You are home, Kitty Girl!"

Ruru takes her hand with a smile.

"Dontcha just love the pageantry of it all? Just something we do for group cohesion. Oh, and to dazzle the new recruits."

Ruru grabs JA-NL's chin, winks and counts.

"And a 5, 6, 7, 8!"

Ruru twirls in her stilettos, kicking and stomping before the frothing crowd as she sings.

"We are a part of the Rhythm Nation."

"YAAAAASSSSS kweeeen!" The crowd bows before her glory.

JA-NL summons her courage and marches up to Ruru.

"Who are you? Where am I?!"

"All will be revealed. Just sashay my way!"

JA-NL lingers but then sprints to catch up with Ruru, who has just stepped to the entrance of that dewdrop cathedral.

"The library is open!"

With her words, the doors burst open. JA-NL's jaw drops as she sees thousands of rows of books, shelved fifteen feet high. Machines snatch books and crack each open, scanning every page. In the atrium, a hologram cloud swirls with images of every page from the books as these are scanned. The system separates words and clusters ideas and themes together.

"In here, we are saving the knowledge created and collected by human societies all over the world.

Ruru sits in front of the font of knowledge as the hologram cloud twirls behind her. She gently pats the marble next to her.

"Now, come to mama." She says and JA-NL slides by her side.

"But before I explain Wondaland and read humanity to filth, I have a story to tell you."

Track 5

Supermodel
(You Better Work)

"I have one thing to say, sashay shantay
  Shantay, shantay, shantay
I have one thing to say, sashay shantay
  Shantay, shantay, shantay"
  - RuPaul Charles

"Make me feel, mighty real,
  Make me feel, mighty real,
  You make me feel, mighty real,
  You make me feel, mighty real"
  - Sylvester James, Jr.

"Once upon a time," Ruru begins as JA-NL moves closer to her. "There was a little black boy in the Brewster Projects of Detroit, Michigan. One day, he snuck into his older sisters' makeup room. Well, it was just a closet with a few mirrors and an array of makeup. He snatched one of their wigs, threw on a dress and some stylish pumps and pranced up and down Mac Avenue.

"Well that fifteen-year-old was spotted by a fashion fair talent scout and my modeling career took off. You see, Haughties love to snatch up one-in-a-million Vessels and catapult us to Petty Boujee status. Oh yes, gotta keep the illusion of social mobility alive to quell those restless Vessels. And you better believe these Vessel-to-Petties were still only used for their bodies. Models, athletes, actors, singers. No one cares to hear our thoughts or our troubles. They took me, just a simple boy in a dress, and put me to werq on that Ho-ratio Alger stroll.

"Yassss, they took me from raggedy to richie-rich in months. I turnt it out on catwalks from Paris to Milan, Singapore to Gelendzhik. And honey, I put the bass in my walk. Head to toe, my whole body talked!

"I was under the Boujee spell. I was starstruck by the glitz of it all. I was signing fashion deals left and right. Bedazzled face masks by Dior. VR Gas Masks by Google. Couture Wellington boots, perfect for any flood-ravaged town. Anything to get the Vessels and Grips to spend, spend, spend what little they had for a shimmer of social status.

"And my story drenched their media. This poor, young Vessel from the camps who had made it out and made it big. And with this flawless face, I acted out the triumph-over-tragedy trope that was force-fed to other Grips and Vessels, who chanted my name and yearned to be me.

"Within three years, I was a multimillionaire, living in an apartment deep inside Metropolis. Champagne showers. Caviar dreams. I thought I had it all. But I was never fully happy. They'd tour me around the Farms and camps and send me to outlet malls. My heart would ache, seeing all that poverty. I'm not just talking about poverty of money, but also poverty of spirit. The sad and oppressed people who would wait hours in line just to see me, to hold my hand and hope that my miracle would rub off on them. I'd come back to my hotel room and cry. I wasn't a hero. I wasn't a savior. I was just a decoy used to make them feel they had a chance to overcome their tragedies while paralyzing them with this false hope.

"If pop culture was the opiate of the masses, then my visits were like a shot of heroin!

"It was the fashion mogul, Anna Priestly, who pulled me out of my tears, screaming that these little Lazies needed any hope they could get.

"'I gotta get out.' I cried.

"She slapped me in the face.

"'We own you!' She screamed 'You're just a piece of trash, we'll use you and throw you back to the gutters.' With a mouth full of blood, I did what Vessels are trained to do. I looked down and accepted my fate.

"But this double life was so exhausting. Ha, they used to call me the Professional because I always showed up in full makeup and hair for any gig. But it took me an extra three hours each day to hide my identity. Lord knows I'd have the meatiest tuck in town without all that duct tape.

"Rumors swirled like dust devils, threatening to suck all my success away. Some trifling pigeon from my past began shopping old 3D pics of me crawling out of drag. I knew the ruse was up. Not only that, I could be thrown in jail for my transgressions. That's right, after a 20-year moratorium, Metropolis brought back New York City's law criminalizing 'impersonating a female.' Talk about government overreach! But the plastic surgery industry had lobbied hard for this. They felt drag made a cheap mockery of their artisan skills, you know, sculpting the perfect

gendered body. People who are transgender were allowed, but only if they paid for full reassignment. Another boon for their businesses.

"I was trapped by my secret. I mean, literally, I was sitting on a secret, but you catch my drift.

"I stood alone in the eye of the storm with pressures all around trying to wear me down. But I held tight to what I know is right. And still, I could hear the way my momma used to say.

"'Never, no never let your spirit beat! Never! Never give in to the end and carry on.'

"And that's what I did. I carried on!

"I knew what I had to do.

"I was headlining the Victoria's Secret Fashion Show the next week, so I had to act fast to prepare my career's climax."

The Victoria's Secret corporation billed its annual show as an interactive exhibit demonstrating that year's styles of bras and panties, which covered the parts of a human woman's body deemed most pornographic. Along with this, the event showcased that season's idealized image of femininity. That particular season, the new female body norms included above the butt dimples, thigh gaps of four inches and elongated Achilles tendons, measured by how many of Paris's arrows could stick in each. As the women sashayed down the runway, the fashion illuminati and obese older Boujees judged them from the sidelines, lending their gaze to cement these trends.

"The night of the show, I could feel the fashion photogs swarming the dressing room, hoping to sabotage my career by snatching just an inch of my maleness.

"So I did what any girl would do. I let them have it, the house down!

"That year, Victoria's Secret had collaborated with Ivanka Trump and her clothing line as a way to clear the air for the heir after her Martha Stewart-stint in prison.

"The theme that year was Rebel Yell, an Ode to Dixie. This wasn't the first time the show threw down with racists reimaginings of America, like those tacky Native American headdresses. Yuck!

"I was their jigaboo, just a pliable black person pining for acceptance and financial freedom. Well... that's why I initially agreed to the event and the outfit. But it made my vengeance all the sweeter.

"The audience went wild as I descended the southern plantation steps in a couture beaded Confederate flag dress. I can still hear the loudspeakers as I strutted down the runway, blaring my antebellum name for the evening, Rachel Tension.

"Darling, they were eating me up!

"All eyes on me, I stripped out of the Stars and Bars. The cheers grew as I revealed my lace bra and panties, made to look like slave shackles. The men screamed, 'more, more, more!' and hunty, you best believe I gave them more. With a twinkle in my eye, I reached into my bra. The men around me and in the live holocube audience of 112 million frothed, itching for an inch of areola. I ripped out my breastplate and threw it into the crowd, knocking a few men in the head.

"Ha-Haaaa! They got what they always dreamed of, a face full of titty.

"I snatched my wig off and tossed it at the pinched faces of fashion editors sitting front row. All of that surgery and they couldn't even flinch, so they took an eyeful of my tumble weave.

"I smudged off my makeup and cackled. Then I ripped off my panties and untucked my penis and scrotum, lettin' it all hang out.

"Yes Gawd!

"At the end of the runway, I snapped my fingers three times and all the lights switched off. Oh, you see, I had the whole event rigged for my coming out party. Two snaps and the spotlights hit me. The wall-sized monitors flashed to life in streaks of gold and red. On them, ribbons with words floated above the audience. One read my personal motto, 'We're all Born Naked and the Rest is Drag,' and the other quoted Simone de Beauvoir, 'One is Not Born a Woman, One Becomes One.'

"And as the crowd clamored, I disappeared in a puff of smoke. Well not quite, I dropped through the stage's trapdoor, raced into the sewers and got the hell outta there.

"I was a wanted man. The whole of Metropolis seethed over the scandal. My face popped from every holocube. I was a threat to the most fragile Boujee resource, masculinity. How dare I trick real men to fap for me!

"After wandering through the darkness of the tubes underneath the city-state, I found myself in the porcelain sewers that poured all that Boujee waste into the Bronx. As I walked along the River Shit, I heard voices singing, calling to me.

"'Hey sister!'

"'Go sister!'

"'Soul sister!'

"'Flow sister!'

"I followed these voices. And when I turned a corner, I saw a vision in red draped across a chaise, lounging in a rouge room tucked away from the sewers.

"'Gitchi, gitchi, ya ya, dada!' The voice purred and sat up, wrapped in feathers and furs. An attendant brought her and me chalices and another poured us magnolia wine. She stared as she took a swig and said.

"'Mocha chocolata. Ya. Ya.'

"'Who are you?' I asked.

"'I'm your Creole Lady Marmalade!'

"You see, Lady Marmalade had come from ten generations of sex Vessels. Women who had escaped slavery in the American south and found a kind of independence as sex workers in the port town of New Orleans. Her foremother had unionized the sex Vessels and provided daycare for these werqing women. She explained her philosophy bluntly.

"'We're independent women. Some mistake us for whores. I'm saying, why spend mine, when I can spend yours? Just remember, the difference between a hooker and a ho ain't nothing but a fee.'

"'When the men of Metropolis are back home, doing that nine to five, living their grey flannel life, old memories of us creep as they go off to sleep and they cry more, more, more!'

"I tried to introduce myself but she grabbed my hand and pulled me close.

"'Shhh, we don't use our real names here. For now, I'll call you Sweet Honey Child. You are home! Your sisters will take care of you.'

"In this subterranean palace, I blended in with the industrious sex working class that lurked under the city-state's pristine veneer. These women, men and genderqueers adopted me and taught me how to move through the secret entrances all around the city. Abandoned tunnels crisscrossed the island and we rolled through these tubes on golf carts. Summoned by their tricks, a holophone app would give them detailed instructions of how to breach the secure apartments and offices above.

"I knew what I had to do. From the ashes of my supermodel past, I was reborn as Starrbooty! I was a vigilante, skilled in the subversive arts of glamdalism. I would make my tormentors pay. And if I fly or if I fall, at least I can say I gave it all.

"Working with my sisters, those independent contractors of the night, I compiled maps of my targets and constructed my routes. I started with my fashion overlord, Anna Priestly. I broke into her doctor's office and found the files on her plastic surgeries. With these and family photos, I was able to construct the image of what she should've looked like if she didn't have all that wealth and the privilege to beautify herself.

"I hacked the holochip in Anna's neck. Now a hologram of this image wrapped around the real Anna for all to see. I'm talking about sweaty pits, triple chins, sagging jowls, man-shoulders, swollen cankles and sucky nail beds! The next day, as Anna stood before a row of models and designers, the image of her contorted to what she most reviled.

"Live by the surgeon's knife, die by the surgeon's knife.

"The empire she created first laughed at their empress in her new, husky glory. And then they mocked her with sharp barbs that sliced deep into her thin skin. In a week, she endured a lifetime of insults that her norms had created. As women clamored to meet the levels of perfection Anna had created, they would say such cruel things about themselves and to each other.

"These images of Anna raced through Metropolis, bursting from every holocube and even from the 3D billboards above Times Square. Pics of her newfound corpulence were wedged between holograms of the Pillsbury Doughboy and the Stay Puft Marshmallow Man.

"By the tenth day, she isolated herself in the sanctuary of her 3,000-square-foot bathroom. The mirrors all along the walls and ceiling mocked her with the scars of an unglamorous childhood. She even thought her clawfoot tub was snarling at her. But every time she felt herself, her skin felt smooth and taut, like a drum. The arms toned, the legs still slender.

"But her image though! She lived in a world of mirages.

"She raced to her children to get them to feel her tautness but they hissed and ran away from her. She lurched back to her bathroom, cast off as an untouchable.

"And that's when I came for her. I arrived in the middle of her ugly-cry as snot poured out of her nose.

"Her husband used a few sex Vessels to inflate his ego while draining his testes. They taught me how to break into her condo. I took the service elevator to the 84th floor, crawled behind the electric paneling and shimmied along the pipes.

"I counted the steps and saw that the sex Vessels had marked the end of each apartment and beginning of the next in red nail polish. I found the entrance to Anna's bed-suite and pushed on a panel in the wall which opened to a world of luxury I never could have even dreamed of. I'm talking about an entire redwood tree cut down and carved to make their emperor-sized bed.

"After I tumbled into the room and shut the wall panel, I realized I had waltzed in behind a painting, Edouard Manet's *Olympia*. It was of a white woman, reclining, buck-ass naked! This 19th-century painting sent shock waves at its debut, but not because of the nakedness of a woman. Oh, tits and fish were a normal serving in fancy paintings. It was her brassy gaze and a few other details that show she's a sex worker which alarmed the audience. But what made me boil is the black maid in the

painting. She stands next to the white woman but wilts into the scenery. Just another invisible object for white people to use and show their privilege.

"Hmm, what a fitting way for me to infiltrate! I slinked into the bathroom suite and found Anna curled up on the floor, heaving heavy sobs.

"'You did this? You ungrateful tar baby! I should've left you to die in the camps. You should be thanking me! You had the whole world adoring you and that dark skin of yours.' She screamed. I let her have her say and then told her off.

"'Oh! Thank you?' I said. 'Why? They never adored me! I was just a cheap sideshow carnie that you paraded around. I only Scrooged you with the specter of what you might have been. Even you have struggled and failed to live up to the impossible expectations of what a body should be and how a woman should age. Free your mind of this prejudice and the rest will follow! Repent and make amends, only you have the power to destroy the oppressive ideals that hurts us all.'

"'No!' She howled. 'I fought ugliness my whole life and with every fiber in my body! I can't let cankles win! I can't!'

"With that, she sprayed hairspray into my eyes and lunged at me, her acrylic talons clawing at my face. Anna pinned me on the floor, choking me. My hand reached for the sink and yanked whatever I could grab. I ripped a pearl necklace off its thread, exploding beads everywhere, all over the floor. Anna tried to steady herself on her heels but she slipped on one of the beads.

"Boom! She hit the platinum floor. I jumped up and grabbed the hairdryer and hogtied her with its cord.

"'Ok, now that I have your complete attention. Let's talk. Woman to Woman.'

"That bitch wouldn't even let me get in another word.

"'ALEXIS! Activate GUARDS!' She screamed. I tried to gag her, but she bit me with her powerful canines. And then she sealed her fate by yelling, 'Lock Down! Shoot any intruders!'

"All doors and windows into the apartment slammed shut. Guns popped out of the walls. Their laser pointers scanned the room.

"'Don't! You'll only kill yourself!'

"I tried to warn her... But it was too late.

"The guns were designed to identify the images of any new people. And they did. The guns cocked and pointed at Anna and me.

"'Wait! Not me!' were Anna's last words.

"The guns fired at us. I dove for the painting and tumbled behind it as a bullet grazed my shoulder. Fuck! It was close!

"Behind me, bullets pierced through the image of Anna's triple chins as she wailed at the irony. Killed by her own prejudice.

"As a final insult, the sensors scanned the room for any other threat and focused their sights on the black maid in the painting, identifying any dark-skinned human as a menace to high society.

"Boom! I was halfway down the hall as I heard the bullets tear through the canvas.

"That night, I knew I was in way over my head and that there's nothing I could do by myself to stop the people of Metropolis.

"Lady Marmalade squirreled me out on that underground homorailroad, providing me with the rainbow book of safe stops for me as I traveled to a sanctuary she had heard of... Wondaland.

"Her last words to me were, 'Go West! Life is peaceful there. Go West! Out in the open air.'

"'Go West!'"

Track 6

Wondaland

"You can go, but you mustn't tell a soul,
There's a world inside,
Where dreamers meet each other,
Once you go it's hard to come back.
Let me paint your canvas as you dance."
    - Janelle Monáe Robinson

"It's such a change,
For us to live so independently,
Freedom, you see,
Has got our hearts singing so joyfully,
Just look about,
You owe it to yourself to check it out
Can't you feel a brand new day?
Can't you feel a brand new day?"
      - Diana Ross & Michael Jackson
      - Shanice Williams & Shaffer "Ne-Yo" Smith

JA-NL wakes to a cool drop of dew sliding down her nose. She tries to stretch her arms, but she's trapped! As the fog of slumber slinks away, she realizes.

She's swaddled in a fuzzy blanket with only her bare face brushing the world. She shimmies in the comfort cocoon, sparking static electricity that lights the predawn room. She rolls on her belly and unfurls herself like Cleopatra from a carpet.

She leaps up, stretching to the sky.

"Ah JA-NL, Daughter of the Universe. You arise to taste another day!"

She's stunned to see Momma Ruru sitting vigil in a rocking chair to her right. She bows slightly before her host.

"Oh please, no one is above anyone else in Wondaland. Stand! You dozed so peacefully after my story and slept the day away. We know the first few nights can be traumatic for all escapees seeking our sanctuary, so we keep watch on them. But you, you slept so sweetly. Though you did mutter something under your breath... something about rivers wide, valleys low..."

"Oh that, it's just something my parents used to sing to me." JA-NL looks down as flecks of heat spread on her cheeks.

Ruru grabs her chin and tilts it until their eyes meet.

"Never be ashamed to sing. Singing is our emotional language. It's what knits us together." Ruru reaches around JA-NL's shoulder and walks her to the door.

"Come with me and you'll see a world of pure imagination."

"Where did this all come from?" JA-NL tugs at Ruru as they stroll through a field of wildflowers.

"Once, there was a child named Destiny Hope. They were renamed Miley and put to work in a factory that used their body and voice to sell books and toys, music and shows. When they rebelled, they changed their name to Milez and came here. To Montana. They invested their savings into cryptocurrencies and solar power companies, which grew into a nice billion dollar fortune they used to create a counterculture oasis. A place to rehabilitate from the poisons of pop culture which had seeped into all parts of society.

"Welcome to Wondaland!"

♫　♫　♫

A few months before, the wrinkled hands of Milez reached from their bed in the hammock canopy. They scanned the crowd of hundreds that stood watch over their deathbed.

"I feel so much younger now." They smiled with a cough. In their half-century in Montana, they turned this wilderness retreat into the most robust outpost of pop resistance.

Wondaland!

The crowd closed in on their bed as they coughed.

As Milez held Ruru's hand, they sang to their friends.

"I can almost see it. That dream I'm dreaming. But there's a voice inside my head saying, you'll never reach it."

Cough, Cough.

Their eyes began to glaze over.

"There's always gonna be another mountain. I'm always gonna wanna make it move. Always gonna be an uphill battle. Just remember, it

ain't about how fast you get there. Ain't about what's waiting on the other side.

"It's the climb!"

The crowd hugged Milez in a last celebration of their life. As their wrinkled body breathed their last breath, they encouraged them.

"Keep on moving. Keep on climbing. Keep the faith! Keep your faith!"

Their body was carried to the garden and buried beneath the largest tree as each of the 51,241 mourners laid a flower above their empty shell.

♫　♫　♫

The vise of pop culture squeezed out any deep discourse with its saccharine sweetness and praise for the vain, the shallow and the superficial. As the rules of society became more strict, demanding blonder hair, bigger boobs and tinier waists, and as technology excelled to gorify humans to meet these norms, it pushed out more and more who couldn't or wouldn't conform. These rebels at first fought the invasion of pop culture into their worlds. But when they failed, they retreated.

And many came to Wondaland.

From the universities flowed the academics angry with shellacking layer upon layer of prestige on their university's brand rather than liberating the minds of students from the bonds of ignorance. From hospitals and laboratories came the scientists and doctors who revolted as they were pressured to create new diseases: parenthesis face, thin eyelashes or stubby nail beds and then bamboozle the public for shareholder benefit. From tech companies coursed the software designers who were eager to advance humanity by deepening relationships and increasing information transfer but who could only find paying jobs tricking users to spend their attention on the most banal things and forfeit their data while doing so. From the capitol buildings poured the policy wonks whose data-driven ideas for social change were shelved by politicians who cared more for glossy photo-ops and poll numbers than advancing their constituents' lives. From architecture firms streamed the Gruen Defectors who wanted to build community rather than sew division into the cityscape or construct spaces to maximize consumption.

A trickle became a river that enriched this forest with their brilliant minds and eager attitudes. Every day, they gathered in Wondaland's library. Each refugee shared their tiny corner of knowledge with earnest ears. Every night, they sat under the star-speckled sky and poured their emotions out, finding sympathy and encouragement.

There was no money asked. No obligations given. A sense of respect flowed from them into a spirit of dedication that made this oasis thrive.

These pillars of a solid society rolled in, damaged. But as they were repaired, they stood strong. And together, a city grew, supported by their talents, powered by their ambitions.

Utopian communities had long been an American dream devoured by American hubris. Many a utopia failed simply because some men used the mad dash to remake the rules of society as an excuse to put their penises in whomever they wanted. Often these men explained this was necessary for group cohesion.

But, rather than pushing a Camelot that would never come, these residents didn't believe they knew what was right. They were humble. They just knew the outside world was wrong and knew what they could create wouldn't be any worse. On top of this, they held close to the value of skepticism. They used design thinking to iterate, get feedback, pivot and build processes to ensure this society was beneficial for all residents.

As the atmosphere warmed, this slice of Montana only grew more beautiful, becoming an oasis of green. They built the Earth. The automation that robbed many of employment was used in Wondaland to free them from back-breaking labor. Machines planted and picked the fields, made and served the meals, cleaned the common areas, watered the gardens and swiveled the solar panels.

This freed the residents to be.

To be what?

To be whatever they liked!

No longer constricted by the tasks that once held power over them, they were free to create art. To read. To learn. To celebrate the splendors of Earth and each other. Residents were encouraged to hike, bike, swim and savor the bounties of their planet.

And to heal!

The traumas of a superficial world bubbled in them. Months and years were needed for them to unpack and unlearn the harsh distortions that festered in them as psychic wounds so they could finally unbreak their hearts.

As each healed, they offered their talents to Wondaland. The community coalesced around a guiding mission, to be a sanctuary for humans and humanity. Here, scholars collected and saved the knowledge of humanity before it could be drowned by a deluge of superficiality. These scholars were overwhelmed and excited with access to more information than they had ever dreamed of. As humans do, they went to great lengths to weave together the nuggets of facts from human history

into narrative threads, from which my understanding of this species has greatly benefitted.

When JA-NL toured the underground vaults of the library, she saw the scholar from whom most of my interpretations of the downfall of humanity comes. Karlie Kloss-Marx hunched over a pile of books as she stroked her puffy white beard. Her mind absorbed the facts from thousands of sources to write her social philosophy, Klossim, which I've shared with you here.

As Kloss-Marx rocked back and forth, she muttered to herself, over and over again as she feverishly wrote.

"History repeats itself, first as tragedy, second as farce."

Track 7

Glamorous

"If you ain't got no money,
Take yo' broke ass home
You say: if you ain't got no money,
Take yo' broke ass home.
G-L-A-M-O-R-O-U-S, yeah.
G-L-A-M-O-R-O-U-S,
Oh, the flossy. Flossy. "
        - Stacy Anne "Fergie" Ferguson
        - Christopher Brian "Ludacris" Bridges

"Partyin', partyin' (yeah),
 Partyin', partyin' (yeah),
  Fun. Fun.
  Fun. Fun.
 Lookin' forward to the weekend.
We... we... we...
We so excited! We so excited..."
        - Rebecca Black

Like a rhinestone cowboy, he saunters into the club with a pronounced John Wayne-swagger.

The crowd huffs at his impetuousness.

Every duke and earl and peer is here.

Everyone who should be here is here!

But who is he?

In this club? Marque Provocateur?

Metropolis's most exclusive night club?

Who does he think he is?

Over diamond goblets, after swilling a disdainful sip of their cosmoglintini, they whisper to their eyepiece.

"Who's that?"

"Who is it?!"

"WHO IS IT!??!"

The chorus of commands can be heard from all corners of the club.

As he walks through the bar and makes his way to the VVVVIP section, the ruby and emerald covered sea of Boujees twist and frug but eventually part around him, repelled by their own deference to him. As he passes, the crowd follows, drawn to this magnetic mystery.

Just as their eyepieces scan his face and await a response, the DJ cuts the music and hits him with a spotlight.

"Ladies and Gentlemen, esteemed Boujees and Boujettes! We are humbled to welcome royalty tonight. Our very own Prince of Prosperity, the new CEO of Def Corporation, my man, Brand-N Higgins!"

A dozen cocktail waitresses light sparklers around him while a dozen more shake Champagne bottles and pop these, spraying $328,487 worth of 18th-century Veuve Clicquot on the Boujees.

A team of six oiled-up muscle men hoist Brand-N into a gold-leafed litter and carry him through the club.

"Bow down, bitches, bow down!" The DJ commands, hitting an inaudible sonic whistle which causes every knee to buckle.

"Now make some noise!" A dramatic airhorn punctuates this sentence as ten strategically-placed hypers start the "Who-dee-who" hooting. The wave of enthusiasm flows from these ten to engulf the crowd, who jump up and cheer.

"Almost too easy," the Higgins-minded Brand-N thinks. "Bah before me, sheeple!"

The bleating crowd snaps videos of him and sends these to their social networks, each staking their claim as "One Who Was There for the Coronation Celebration."

The litter is tipped and Brand-N tumbles into a pool full of swimming supermodels. These merry mermaids hoist him to continued cheers.

In unison, eyepieces switch to show his pedigree.

He is the son of Lukasz Higgins from a third and forgotten marriage, making him heir apparent of the empire that rules this company town. He had a wild past. A vagabond turned pyromaniac, he spent his youth torching and running. After exploring islands, mountains and jungles, he sat in silent meditation for three months. He awoke one day to realize that he had been called to take over the family business and to lead the Haughties to the promised land!

The story seemed a little thin and was riddled with holes. But every Haughty knew that their claim to social status lay on similarly shaky grounds. Had their father really invented Candy Crush or had he only swindled the code from a Ukrainian teen?

No, it was best not to question. Just applaud along. If people start scratching the surface of other people's pasts, they might question theirs one day. They had to all agree to be down with O.P.P. (Yeah, you know me!)

The holovideos of the ceremony raced through Metropolis. The fawning of millions shows the ludicrousness of the human mind. Moments before, he was alien to them and they were ready to kill him, to sacrifice him for the sin of social climbing. But then, in an instant, their minds were changed by well-coordinated external forces and they vaulted him high above themselves, venerating him until they were ready to sacrifice themselves for him.

Running Def Corporation was easier now than Brand-N Higgins could have ever imagined when he began it 40 years ago. Almost every part of the sprawling Def Corporation empire was automated. He barely had to lift a finger other than to approve the well-regarded recommendations of his advisor software, built by the Richelieu Corporation. Like a conductor, he only needed to lightly flick his wrists for an avalanche of activity to happen.

He proved himself to be a benevolent dictator of Metropolis. Sure, there was still an administrative government for the city-state, but Def Corporation retained complete control over it. All he had to do to win Boujee obedience was to throw them lavish parties and offer them small gifts, tokens of his appreciation for their submission, like at-home coffee enemas, Zoloft in the drinking water and ecstasy after-dinner mints.

"It's good to be the King!" Higgins chuckles to himself.

Q.U.E.E.N.

"They call us dirty cause we break all your rules down
And we just came to act a fool, is that all right?
  (Girl, that's alright)
They be like, 'Ooh, let them eat cake.'
But we eat wings and throw them bones on the ground

And while you're selling dope,
We're gonna keep selling hope,
We rising up now, you gotta deal, you gotta cope
Will you be electric sheep?
Electric ladies, will you sleep?
Or will you preach?"
        -Janelle Monáe Robinson

"Vous êtes jamais seuls
Vous savez ce qu'il faut faire
Ne laissez pas tomber votre nation
La disco a besoin de vous
Your disco, your disco, your disco needs you!
Your disco, your disco, your disco needs you!"
        - Kylie Minogue

Weeks pass as JA-NL cocoons herself, basking in the simple splendors of the land and the love from her new community. And then, one day, she is called and she is asked to help.

Momma Ruru sits in the reading room of the library when JA-NL walks in. Bathed in morning light, Ruru sips tea from a crystal cup. Her eyes scan a holoscreen of news.

"Momma Ruru, you asked to see me?" JA-NL interrupts.

The holoscreen disappears and Ruru follows her thoughts for a moment before looking at her. JA-NL feels a heavy sadness in her as she gestures for JA-NL to sit beside her.

"JA-NL, Daughter of Earth, Descendant of the Universe. We are in trouble. Humanity has forced our planet into its sixth mass extinction. By the end of this century, 50% of all plant and animal species will have gone extinct. And we caused this! With our carelessness and hunger for a luxury life. We've poisoned Earth and I fear--- I fear that these death throes will drag all humanity with it.

"I spent the morning reviewing the data. The analysis we've created shows an absurdly high probability that the rising temperatures will cause massive droughts and famines. As resources grow more scarce, I foresee riots and mass slaughters.

"Did you ever stop to notice this crying Earth? These weeping shores?" Ruru waves her hands and, from the library walls, ribbons of interwoven holograms appear. JA-NL's eyes follow each and she sees violent storms tearing through towns, deserts spreading through farmlands as emaciated cattle buckle and fall into the dry earth.

"What have we done to the world?" JA-NL cries out as disbelief and despair rip through her. "Look what we've done! Is there anything we can do?"

"Our destiny is tied directly to the fate of humans. All humans, Vessels and Boujees and all those in-between. We are of the Earth and we need it to survive. As we've shown here at Wondaland, we can create a new society built on respect, equality and equity, that strives to build a better, safer planet for ourselves. We are humans! We have the amazing ability to organize in large numbers and create wonders this world has never known. And we have the resources! At no point in our history have we created so much wealth. $300 trillion sits unused, full of the trust and power that could turn the tide of climate change. We just need the will. But instead, we throw our lives away pursuing unending luxuries. We need to wake our family up."

"But how Momma?"

"Since pop culture is the opiate of the masses, we will need to sabotage it to shock humanity awake." Ruru stomps her stiletto. "We need to rip away the meaningless fluff that fills the eyes of our fellow humans. They need to hear the cries of our kin and see the apocalypse approaching. Only then will they feel compelled to use their resources to save us all. With our powers, we can create new mythologies that construct a culture that encourages humans to build a better world, together. We can use Wondaland as a model and convince humanity to

cherish the life we live, cherish the love we have and the equality and equity we've created here."

The holoribbons swirl to show the pillars of pop: music, movies, sensational news and sports. From here, the holoribbons reach like tendrils that choke images of all aspects of human life.

"JA-NL, what you did with the Miss Fritzle-Moloch program was awe-inspiring. Girl, we need those skills and your Charisma, Uniqueness, Nerve and Talent to topple these pillars of pop.

"I've assembled my team of Queers, Untouchables, Emigrants, the Excommunicated and Negroids. My Q.U.E.E.N.s! I want you to join Project Q.U.E.E.N., our musical weapons program of the 21st century, where freedom movements are disguised as songs, where emotion pictures and works of art are able to sabotage the status-quo. These Q.U.E.E.N.s will work to overthrow the vapid parasite of pop which sucks the resources from the planet while stabbing the souls of our kin. Will you join us?"

"Sign me up!" JA-NL beams.

"Wonderful! We're entering the planning process and looking for our first actions. See if you can think of ways to burst these bubbles of pop."

JA-NL reaches her hand to the holowall and manipulates the space with her fingertips. Her brows furrow and her eyes widen.

"I've got it!" JA-NL snaps her fingers.

"What is it you see?"

"Like any successful terrorist, we need to maximize exposure to maximize impact. Holowall, show me the most watched pop culture events worldwide. These! These will be our targets."

♫ ♫ ♫

To continue the saga, I will need a quick progression of JA-NL from novice to expert which can best be told through a compressed collection of moments.

We're gonna need a Montage!

Montage!

♫ ♫ ♫

JA-NL and two Q.U.E.E.N. recruits, Est'R Holland and Bon-E Dozier, shimmy through a ventilation system.

"Almost there!" Est'R whispers in the metallic tube, letting her echo carry the meaning to the two below. Est'R was a crazy youngster who had been the writing and singing talent behind her world-winning collegiate a capella group. But her singing voice and lyrical skills were overlooked and underappreciated because of her "manly" appearance. So she left and joined Wondaland.

"Let's get them!" The bombastic Bon-E froths as sharp thorns of glee dance in her eyes. She had sacrificed her Teenage Dream to a talent-deficient pop star who struggled to string two notes together. She was promised that stardom would come to her if she would wait her turn. When her turn never came and her youth was wasted, she defected.

JA-NL takes up the rear.

"We're here!" Est'R sings as she looks down through the grate above the control center at the Denver Pickers stadium. This was hours before the Super Bowl game against the Metropolis Studs, an event which will draw 220 million sets of human eyes.

These sporting events had grown to be a much more immersive experience. Drones whiz around the field and each player wears a camera on their helmet. Audience members recline in their comfy viewing pods with heated seats of fluffy faux-fur to enjoy the sights, smells and sounds from thousands of angles.

Est'R signals and all three women slip earplugs into their ear canals to lock out all sound waves.

Below, munching on Nuclear Hot Cheetos™ and sipping cherry-flavored energy drinks with amphetamines, are the two remaining, though entirely unnecessary, techies of this multibillion-dollar production.

The drone cameras know how to follow the game. Instantly, the system can jumble the 1,431 different views of the same event into the most optimized footage for a human audience, switching seamlessly between each shot. The patches of grass that cover the field know to ignite with hologram ads underneath each runner's feet. A test run of that night's primary sponsor sprouted on the grass, Ball Cream™ for freshly shorn testicles with antifungal medicine to fight jock itch. The secondary sponsor is antiperspirant bubbles which can engulf males and neutralize the body odors that waft from their armpits and sphincters and turn these into what most women found to be an equally vile smell called "Victory Stench™."

The two techies hunker down for a four-hour snack sesh while the mechanics whirl around them.

"Drop it low!" Est'R mouths to her sister resistors.

Thump!

The techies turn to see three black-clad crusaders.

"Nighty Night!" Bon-E smiles and shoots a beam of sound waves that knock them both out.

The men fall to the ground as JA-NL stands over their bodies.

Est'R snaps soundlessly in front of her eyes. She mouths something to the still-stunned JA-NL.

A grimace and a swift shin kick shake JA-NL to. She takes out her earplugs and stands with wide, concerned eyes.

"Don't worry, they're out for at least four hours. Now, let's get to work."

Bon-E cackles as she hogties the two. She slinks to the exit and cracks the door, scanning for any sign of their detection. Est'R blacks out the surveillance cameras.

JA-NL plops down at the mainframe and erases the last minutes of this room's surveillance footage and switches in a four-hour loop of these two neckbeards snacking.

Like a sculptor, her fingers go to work, finessing the machine before her and bending it to her will.

Within ten minutes, JA-NL has cracked open the control center and connected it to external manipulation.

"Time to bounce!" JA-NL yells.

Back up into the shaft and then to the roof, they snag the autocopter awaiting them.

As the game begins, the easy-chair audience reclines beyond class lines to enjoy the sweet tribalism of professional football. For a moment, the Grips and Vessels believe the barriers between them and the Boujees have melted until they all congeal behind a team, much like how their leftover 7-layer dips will look tomorrow. They feel as one with their overlords in the superficial camaraderie of jerseys and team face paint.

As they watch the game unfold, a new message bursts from the holographic blades of grass.

"The Boujees are using you!" The loudspeakers echo this message. "They're stealing all your attention and wealth and using it to destroy our planet."

The tight ends almost trip as images of sandy deserts spread beneath their feet.

"Two-thirds of our planet's grassland have become desert because our planet is warming."

Holograms of hurricanes swirl from all four corners of the field, rushing towards the players. They dive and tumble away from the whipping winds.

"We've created more violent storms all over Earth."

As the raging twisters fizzle, the final words appear across the field, intriguing the audience.

"We need to change our way of life. We must make Wondaland!"

The audience gasps, drunken and confused by what they have just seen.

Over the next week, JA-NL measures their results. They find a 25-percent increase in searches for atrocities caused by human-made climate change.

Momma Ruru scans the data.

"Good, but we still need to go deeper."

♪ ♪ ♪

From the motherboard computer, JA-NL hacks her way into the most persuasive international human communication. She creates adorable memes of animals that hover near extinction. With these, she writes code to hijack all of the LOLcats online. Viewers now see an adorable, fluffy pika or sleek otter and, just as their eyes dance and they squeal "awww," the image violently shakes as a warning appears: "8 weeks until extinction!"

With a few more keystrokes, JA-NL hacks into the most popular holonews programs. Beneath the bickering bottle-blondes, a ticker scrolls. From the computer room deep in Wondaland, she scans these tickers from the top 20 news shows, which pull in a total audience of 637 million humans.

Click. Click. BOOM!

With the final keystroke, all tickers switch to read information on climate change statistics.

"Greenhouse gases have reached 850 parts per million. This is a Critical Danger to Humanity!"

After this comes a list of all species pushed to extinction because of human-made climate change.

During the most watched holocube programs, JA-NL hacks these to show the wealth of the richest Haught Boujees and show how only a fraction of this wealth would be needed to cut the greenhouse gases in Earth's atmosphere to sustainable levels.

During a series of televised prime minister candidate debates for each of the federated city-states, JA-NL hacks the live feed and splices in holograms that dance from their suits. The logos of the corporations which donated to them dance along with their ticker price amount.

"Very impressive!" Momma Ruru slow claps as she struts in. "I think you're ready to infiltrate one of the climate-controlled city-states."

♪ ♪ ♪

RADIO GAGA

JA-NL and her Q.U.E.E.N.s sneak into Los Angeles tucked among a fleet of leeches flown into the city-state. These leeches' solemn task was to wax every crevice and crack, and then thread the bushy brows above the only eyes humans cared about. The Haughties and Petties demanded to be perfectly prim before that city-state's greatest affair, the Academy Awards.

Entertainment award shows were a ludicrous spectacle, where the most celebrated humans celebrated each other in a circle jerk of highly-inflated Haughty and Petty egos. This was to be just another night that convulsed with masturbatory highs and lows... until the Q.U.E.E.N.s arrived.

As wildfires rage outside the domed La La Land, the humans inside scurry to ready themselves for that night. JA-NL throws on a tux, tugs her lapel and straightens her bow tie. She slicks back her hair on the side of her head. She clicks her black loafers with Tom Cruise stacked heels.

"Some people say I look like my dad... C'est la Vie!" JA-NL says with a devilish smirk.

As a black female, the controlling white society has never fully accepted her as a woman. From the former slave Sojourner Truth demanding at the 1851 Women's Convention, "Ain't I a Woman?" to Hollywood's ideal of womanhood, petite, lighter skinned, straighter hair and lighter eyes, dark-skinned women, like JA-NL, are the antithesis of this. Today, she'll use their prejudice to subvert the system by passing as a man.

"Looking good, squirrel-friend! I'm feeling you, Tuxedo Groove!" Momma Ruru gushes to her over the holophone.

As the caravan of Q.U.E.E.N.s rolls up to the auditorium, JA-NL gulps at the sight of tanks and robocops carrying assault rifles circling Sunset Boulevard.

"How are you we gonna get in?"

"Please!" Ruru's hologram chuckles dismissively. "This is Project Q.U.E.E.N., we've got undercover agents in all the arts."

Ruru's team of six follows their directions and slinks to the theater's rear entrance.

Rat-a-tat-tat-tat.

Bon-E's bejeweled nails knock the back door. A clipboard clad man in a black turtleneck rips opens the door and smiles.

"Ok ladies, now let's get into formation." He leans forward and glances side to side. Once he's assured the coast is clear, he ushers them in with a snap.

The event plods through the annual accolades.

Q.U.E.E.N.

"Best Hologram in an Action Movie" goes to Saw 78 for its 3D light beam rendering of a human sliced into 4,000 pieces, each piece flapped on a dirty, warehouse floor. The gushing hologram artisans describe their weeks-long process for creating such lifelike anatomy. They took six recently deceased Vessels, still hot and fresh, and chopped them up to see how their bodies would wiggle and how the blood would flow from each. Then they laser scanned these pieces and took a composite to create the hologram for the film.

As the applause track plays, JA-NL and Est'R move into place behind the stage as the penultimate winner is announced: "Best Plastic Surgery for a Leading Actress."

"And the winners are:

"Aileen Theron and Dr. Tyler Durden for the role of Elizabeth Cady Stanton in the film, *A Woman's Suffrage*, surgeries include fat addition, chin implants, eye puffication, crows feet and frown lines."

The screen cuts to a photo contrast of this tall, toned and lithe blonde-bombshell actress next to the image of this biopic's main role: the robust, rotund, revolutionary and jowly founder of the White Women's Rights movement. Audible shudders quake through the audience. The holoscreen projects the stirring speech from the film's climactic scene as Aileen, transformed as Stanton, stands before a crowd of thousands at Seneca Falls in 1848. In her black dress, the actress cries:

"The prolonged slavery of women is the darkest chapter in human history!"

In the film, the Victorian-era, middle-class, educated white women attendees burst into applause.

At the awards show, Aileen squirms, squeezing the hand of her surgeon, now fully returned to sanctioned beauty, eager for the accolades after months of hefty hardship. She just knew that gorifying her body was an easy step to winning the highest praise in the field of faking humans.

Doctor Durden hoists Aileen onto the stage like a marionette doll. Before the microphone, he describes the process of injecting gallons of fat to every inch of her body so she could best play the founder of this women's liberation movement.

As Durden and Theron exit, Est'R and JA-NL, as invisible Grips, wheel out giant screens on either side of center stage.

The announcer booms.

"And now welcome the Dowager Countess Katya Zamalodchikova Zsa Zsa Crawley to present the final award of the night."

Now a Grande-Haught-Damn in her 60s, this taut-faced actress waddles out, escorted by the action *star du jour*, who pouts and furrows

his severe Cro-Magnon brow. But the crowd is too malnourished, to the point of organ failure, to react. The other actresses try to applaud, but their hands are too weak to reach each other and stir a percussive sound. All that remains of them are racks of ribs and clavicles cutting sharp angles. During each commercial break, an assistant rushes to them with a Go-Go juice box so each can sip just enough to jolt their blood sugar to survive until the next commercial break. But this pop sabotage wasn't for the audience assembled in the theater, it was for those absorbing at home.

As Katya announces the final nominees of the evening, she parrots the words on the teleprompter, squawking without thinking.

"Aaaand the nominees for this yearrrrs Greaaaatest Human-Maaaade Disasterrrr are..."

The screens they dragged out cut to the nominees of that evening. These holograms overtake the theater and fill the homes watched by 837 million humans, a large proportion of whom are Haughty and Petty. A deep commanding voice reads the nominees.

"The droughts and famines in Western Africa... because of climate change, lack of rains has created food shortages and have lead to wars and genocides. Death toll: 867,000 lives this year.

"Floods in Bangladesh, because of rising oceans, over two-thirds of this country's land is under water for more than half the year. Death toll: 1.3 million lives.

"Wildfires that have ravaged one-third of American forests.

"And finally, this year's mass extinctions, numbering 300 species a day, including the last of the corrals in the Great Barrier Reef and the Javan and Sumatran rhinoceroses."

Katya hadn't listened to the voice and needed to be nudged before she realizes it is her moment to announce the winner. She shakes as she rips open the envelope in her hand.

"Aaaand the winner issss... La La Glaaaaahhhdiatorrrr!"

♫ ♫ ♫

Back in the safety of Wondaland, the Q.U.E.E.N.s brood.

"What are our metrics of success? Are we actually changing any hearts and minds?" Est'R demands.

"Yeah, we need results!" Bon-E chirps.

Momma Ruru mulls as she steps forward.

"You're right. We're only winning small skirmishes, but not the war. All we've done is shock a few people to think. We tickle them with an idea, but it quickly fades. To really change them, we need to wage a large-scale emotional manipulation campaign. And I know just the trick!"

(Always fade out in a montage...

If you fade out, it seems like a more time has passed... in a montage. Montage...

Track 9

Borderline

"I don't want to be your prisoner,
  So baby set me free

Borderline, feels like I'm gonna lose my mind.
Keep pushing me, Keep pushing me,
Keep pushing my love.
You just keep on pushing my love,
Over the borderline."
        - Madonna Ciccone

"Ready or not, refugees taking over
  The Buffalo Soldier, dreadlock Rasta,
  On the twelfth hour, fly by in my bomber,
  Now they're under pushing up flowers
  Superfly, true lies, do or die.

Ready or not, here I come, you can't hide,
Gonna find you and take it slowly."
        - Lauryn Hill &
          Nel Ust Wyclef Jean &
          Prazakrel "Pras" Michel

The days waned and waxed as Barsha plotted. She was a wanted woman in a world of chaos. She needed to escape.

But she felt like shit.

Her body shivered every night. Each morning she awoke in a sea of her own sweat. The virus had taken hold in her. 1.8 million virus particles gleefully replicated and raced through her body. Her white blood cells raised her temperature in an attempt to bake out the infection but this fever wouldn't save her.

After the assassination of Prime Minister Sharukha Khan with the most stylish of friendly fires, the military placed Bangladesh under martial law. The army's Fashion Industry benefactors installed their puppet, Kinng Kumar as Prime Minister. He immediately declared a State of Emergency to purge all rebel forces. The meek women on whose backs the nation industrialized were overnight relabeled as enemy insurgents. Photos of the women, filtered with dark, menacing tones, burst from holoscreens in every home and from hologram clouds that drones beamed over residential areas. Barsha saw her own image above her home with a reward for her capture.

$6,000.

The bounty for her whole existence.

She was wanted.

Wanted.

Dead or alive.

She knew her neighbors loved her, but there was a pain. In their eyes, she saw their hunger and frustration. And in their ears, she heard the cries of their children. This sound was evolutionarily created to grate through a mother's body and ignite anguish.

Barsha knew the careful calculus of humans teetering on the edge of existence. As food became scarce in the coming days, all morality would be sacrificed for survival. The whole world would be ranked and, as desperation to feed their children grew, any of her neighbors could snap and turn on her and turn her in.

She had to pull herself out of the equation.

That night, she bundles a bag of her things and grabs her daughter. They sneak out of their home, a funky little shack set in the shadows of the factories. She looks up at her tin roof, rusted from years of rains.

"I can't die here." She thinks as she turns and runs.

Ayesha cries as she dawdles behind her mom.

"But whyyyyyyy?" She whines.

Barsha calculates and concludes her daughter should be shielded from the severity of the situation.

"Shhhh, we're going on a trip." She says to her little one, who is weighed down by wearing all the clothes she can't carry. "A long trip."

Barsha prepares herself for the journey. It would take eight days to walk to the border with India. She only has enough food for four days, but she can ration this and hope a friendly family will provide them with more.

As they reach the edge of town, the rains begin. A torrential downpour drowns the land in four more inches of water every hour.

The earth beneath their feet vanishes by the third hour. The once solid dirt melts into a sludge of mud, sucking in legs up to ankles and then knees. A slurrrrp-pop sounds as Barsha and her daughter pull up each vacuum-sealed leg.

The rains continue for the next four days. As Barsha and her daughter trudge, this deluge changes the equations for millions of Bangladeshis.

The wetness seeped into every home, into every crack and corner, damping the meetings of thighs and filling armpits with moisture for bacteria to feast and boils to grow. Clothes cling to skin like wet tongues, suffocating them. These humans' five million hair follicles gag under this wet weight.

Each person calculates their own algorithm of defection.

How many days of suffering?

How deep has the water become?

How much of their home has been ruined?

How much of their farm has been destroyed?

How many nights have their children been crying?

How scarce has the food become?

How dirty is the water?

Anger and anxiety swell until hundreds of thousands of humans reach the breaking point.

Enough!

Time to move.

One by one, the humans cross the mental threshold, where uncertainty and death are better than drowning in this squalor. Each year, the rains had grown worse, the rivers had flooded more and the plains filled further. What little they have is saddled on their backs, shoulders and heads.

Enough!

The trickle of bodies pours onto the main roads and then swells onto the highways. Laughs and squeals of glee erupt as each foot first touches what they hadn't felt for days. Firm ground! The concrete of these main roads welcomes their wobbly legs.

Solid!

Solid as a rock.

The highways through Bangladesh were built to bolster trucks carrying 20 tons of designer jeans and skorts, not the citizens who made these.

But here they are, stomping their feet on the concrete and pushing north and west, like salmon swimming upstream, eager to spawn a new life.

The raging river of humans parts around trucks and pushes over military blockades, which had been set up to prevent this surge of desperation. Tanks shoot down the first humans along the front, but the masses push forward, knowing that only certain death remains behind them. At least forward carries a drop of hope, a possibility of a better life for them or at least their children.

The bodies that were shot drop beneath the swell of humans. As the tanks are overwhelmed, the snipers slide back into the safety of their tanks' bodies.

This surge overwhelms Barsha. She and her daughter fold into the crowd, glad for anonymity among the masses.

For six days and nights, they move, collapsing in the road for just a few hours, before the crowd drags them onward.

Now, 352,723 strong, the river of humans rages upstream all through the night, until they reach the borderline with India and the possibility of a new life.

But then their dreams are---

Dammed!

These humans smack into the Trump wall that stretches the entire division between India and Bangladesh. This portion of the wall carries a large plaque and on it, in a mocking tone, is a reminder that Bangladesh had seceded from India.

"We've rolled up your Partition!" The Indian plaque reads.

As the swarm approaches, the gate in this wall is sealed shut. Just inside this wall, they remain "internally displaced people," a large label that carries with it little international assistance. On the other side of the wall, inches away, they would have been renamed refugees, an incantation which carries great power. Even in these desperate times, the international community had agreed to provide for the basic needs of refugees, supplying them with food, shelter and healthcare.

Barsha joins the masses in the fifth wave that crashes into this barrier. Each wave steps up to the retaining wall and pounds on it, wailing in disbelief that their journey so far would end so concretely.

The rains begin again. Every drop falls like a knife, slicing off a little more of their will to live.

Each day, as hundreds of these internally displaced people die, with nary a care from the world, their bodies are heaved at the wall in protest. By the sixth day, the pile of husked shells grew and the survivors would crawl on the dead, clawing at the wall and screaming. Higher and higher! They hope this new height will carry their cries to the other side.

On the eighth night at the border, Barsha pulls her courage and grabs Ayesha. As the others slumber, Barsha knows this is her last chance.

She's been sick and delirious for days. Her coughs have grown into hacks. Red bumps crawl across her skin and face. One by one, they've begun to pop.

But tonight, she has energy.

Tonight, they have to move.

Under the floodlights, she sees that the pile of dead bodies has reached just feet from the top of the wall.

She grabs her daughter and scurries. She arrives at the mound of flesh and looks up.

A staircase of skulls stands between her and freedom. Shocks of desperation spring her as she climbs.

The first bloated bodies squish beneath her feet. The firmness of form has given way to rot as water and bacteria rage through these bottom bodies, turning their soft spots gangrene.

With each step, she slips, but she does what she must to carry on. Her right hand pushes into a stomach cavity. Her left foot slides through thigh fat falling from a femur.

With her left arm, she clutches her daughter, hiding her eyes from these horrors. Her right hand claws for any leverage. Her fingers grab a shoulder and slip through to a bone.

But the only way is up!

Wedged between mounds of flesh, she pulls herself up the rungs of rib cages.

Another three rows up and she stumbles. She jams her fingers into a skull's soft, squishy eye sockets, clamping it like a bowling ball as she pulls herself up another level.

By the sixth level of the dead, the bodies are fresher and still firm.

She fights against the waterfall that courses over the corpses. She kneels to a crawl, hooking her right hand into an armpit to steady herself to climb to the next level.

Almost.

There!

On top of the dead bodies, she sways in the wind. She looks down from the tower of flesh to see the slumbering camp of humans now arcing half a mile in every direction.

And just beyond them---

What is that movement?

A new wave of human desperation rolls just at the edge of the camp, crashing through and pushing their way to the wall!

A group of guards stationed on top of the wall has enjoyed her struggle. They have laughed at the mushy human pitfalls of her scramble for the past 40 minutes. Each placed bets on how far she would make it:

5 feet, 10 feet, 15, 20! Only one bet she would surmount the full thirty-five-foot mound of flesh. As she reaches the top, that young recruit, Mustafa Sayyed, beams at his colleagues.

"What's my prize?" He jumps for joy.

"It's your lucky day!" One of the grizzled older guards tosses him a gun. "You get to finish her."

Barsha squares her legs into the openings between the uppermost bodies. She wedges her feet under shoulders and braces herself against the wall. She stands! Her fingers are just able to touch the top of the wall.

She twists her torso to her daughter, finally allowing herself to feel again. Tears of joy and sorrow swirl down her cheeks, washed away by that interminable rain.

"Sweetie, you'll be safe on top of the wall. You'll get such good food and a warm place to sleep. Shhh, you can do this. When I lift you, just pull up. I'll push. Just pull!"

Her daughter stares up at her. With wide eyes, Ayesha turns to look down, curious about how far they've come. But her mom grabs her cheeks and yanks her face up.

"Don't ever look down. Don't ever look back. I'll join you. Someday. But not for a long time. But I'll be with you. Somehow.

"Now, up you go!"

Barsha hooks her hands into her daughter's armpits and lifts her. As she extends her shoulders, she can feel Ayesha's weight tottering to the top. Her left hand slides down her daughter's back and pushes her, heaving her across that imaginary border.

Barsha laughs to herself.

It's happening!

She knows that just on top of the wall is India. Up there, her daughter will be a refugee and will be protected by the United Nations and international law.

"You're almost there, just pull! Kick your foot over. Just pull! Now kick!"

A gun clicks and Barsha looks up to see a steel toe boot at the wall's ledge, lightly pushing her daughter's fingers.

"You are trespassing!" Mustafa shouts.

"Nooooo!" Barsha screams.

He pulls the trigger and half an inch of hot lead traveling 768 miles-per-hour rips through Barsha's left cheek and out her right chin.

The bullet pierces a pus mound on her cheek that erupts, spewing 3.2 million virions towards the wall.

Barsha falls back. Her feet are still hooked under the armpits so her body dangles off the top of the mound, flailing like a flag announcing her surrender.

Ayesha tumbles down, snapping the C1 vertebra in her neck, dying instantly.

Mustafa leans over the ledge to inspect his handiwork.

He draws in a deep breathe, dragging in a few thousand *Variola maximum* virions into his body.

The particles hook onto the walls of his lungs, clawing until one breaches his body.

One Moment in Time

"Give me one moment in time,
 When I'm racing with destiny,
 Then in that one moment in time,
 I will feel.
 I will feel...
      Eternity."
      - Whitney Houston

"You have done good for yourselves,
 Since you left my wet embrace,
 And crawled ashore,
 Every boy, is a snake is a lily,
 Every pearl is a lynx, is a girl,
 Sweet harmony made into flesh"
      - Björk Guðmundsdóttir

The sad tromboner stands at the vomitorium, poised to enter the New Delhi stadium. He kicks the dirt, scuffing his white drillmaster marching shoes. Cal-Gon McGillicuddy just knew his drum major would yell at him if he saw him now.

"Dirty shoes deplete elegant foot articulation!" He could hear him shout.

He doesn't care.

It doesn't matter.

Nothing matters anymore!

His life is over!

He defiantly stomps the dirt, sullying the snap hems of his virginal white bibber.

This was supposed to be his one moment in time. Playing his superbone as part of the 1,000-member marching band for the Olympics closing ceremony. This was supposed to be his chance to feel eternity!

But instead, he feels like shit.

The Olympic games were an event held every four years when nations and city-states took their most prized Vessel athletes out of pasture, where they were subjected to grueling 10-hour training days, and entered them into competition against other Vessel pawns for the Greater Glory of Government.

The Olympics were a retro-reimagining of games with the same name that happened over two thousand years beforehand. And, like all vintage things brought back, it reflected the culture of the day. This meant the modern Olympic games carried the deep racial and tribal tones that raged at the end of humanity, as cultures fought to see which had the strongest humans, the fastest runners or the most delicate curlers.

Individual athletes competed in these brutal games because they were promised freedom from Vesseldom. They all had dreams of achieving Petty Boujee status by either winning a medal, being beautiful while sporting, or falling in a haphazardly adorable way and Kerri-Struggling into the hearts of audiences worldwide. If they succeeded in vaulting social classes, they would be used as tools for companies, filling commercials with their victorious allure. This would provide them money and extend their spotlights beyond the age of 26 when most had to retire with broken bones, torn cartilage, or when their bodies had simply reached maturation and could no longer flip easily through the air.

The distinction between summer and winter Olympics melted as winters grew shorter and all alpine events were moved indoors. By this point, most shopping malls had erected ski areas. One week after secular Christmas, every mall's elf village was eminently-domained and turned into a training camp for the winter Olympic sports.

And here Cal-Gon stands, minutes from the finale, with his marching hat's feather flopping in the wind.

The closing ceremony committee vetoed all live audio after the fiasco during the opening ceremony. Everything, including instruments, had to be pantomimed to a track.

"Dammit!" Cal-Gon thought. "If only the chariots of fire hadn't rolled too close to the international color guard delegation, igniting the spinning flags of all 103 nations and 47 city-states."

A kickline of majorettes reacted quickly in knee-high Nancy boots. This inferno was soon engulfed by these blondes in bevel, who linked arms and stomped.

Eye-high piano kick, struck kick, hitch kick.

Bevel to the cameras... and then---

Strut kick, hitch kick, double twist!

With the whole world watching, a few of the more daring women drowned the dying embers by being thrown up into scorpion and twirled down until their bedazzled derrieres smooshed the ashes. With crisp precision and witty retorts, these women won hearts worldwide, instantly securing Petty Boujee status for themselves and a made-for-holocube movie.

Not only had those tall, tanned vixens won star-studded status and become the darlings of the Olympics, but their shenanigans had also ruined the rest of the live performances. Before the fires could be kicked out, the plumed marching hats of the flag twirlers burst into flames. Their blood-curdling screams were captured and echoed around Earth as their friends beat the fire--- and the twirlers' heads--- with flag poles. The shrill, high-pitched screams were picked up on microphones and boomed to the international audience of 2.87 billion humans. The sheer misery seared through their ears, sending waves of pain through their bodies, curling toes and wincing eyes. Worst of all, the screams deafened them from absorbing the important commercial messages for hemorrhoid creams and Gout-be-Gone™.

The producers paired the replays of this atrocity with the Benny Hill theme song in hopes that this would make it comical. But nothing could stop the memory of those screams igniting anxiety with what was reported as that year's greatest tragedy.

"Those majorettes should have saved the flag twirlers first instead of showing off!" Cal-Gon huffs as he takes his place in line.

The producers couldn't risk another catastrophe. The audio of this final performance had been recorded three days before and would be blasted throughout the stadium and in homes planet-wide as Cal-Gon and the bands marched in time.

"But it's not fair! What about me?!" Cal-Gon cries. "Well, fuck it! I'm going rogue!"

As he wets the lips of his superbone and warms up, he's oblivious to the fact that in his spittle twists the double helix of humanity's demise.

For the past three weeks, the band geeks were quarantined to the lowliest of Olympic villages, ostracized away from the jocks, to ensure their tooting their own horns wouldn't wake the world-renowned ping-pongers or skeet shooters in the midst of mental preparation.

Ugh, it wasn't fair!

The shooters practiced outside his room and their sounds haunted him morning, noon and night. He could hear them holler with their guns-a-blazing. "Aww skeet, skeet, skeet, skeet, skeet. Motherfucker! Aww skeet, skeet, skeet, skeet, uh--- goddamn!"

And from the windows to the walls, he couldn't help but be forced to see the ping-pongers' sweat drip off their balls as they practiced in his building's lobby.

The marching bands were crowded 30 cots to a room, exiled far from the action, but next to a curious tent city assembled on the outskirts of the Olympic archipelago. Most of its squatters were local residents who had their homes razed to build the stadium. These Olympic displaced people were offered prime parking-spot-sized spaces to peddle tchotchkes commemorating India's first Olympics. The state offered them a 60/40 profit share on anything sold.

Cal-Gon remembers entering the tent city on his fourth night. After an evening of carousing, swilling Kingfisher beer and comparing accolades with these, his species's best marchers, he was feeling extra horny.

♫   ♫   ♫

As humanity's music became more automated and synthesized, the most significant human holdout were these marching bands. Inadvertently bucking trends had long been band geeks bread and butter. These goose-steppers were bolstered by a relationship with the military, which pumped funds into marching programs, defending their honor from enemies, both foreign and automatic.

Bravado was a core component of militaries humanity-wide. This ethereal currency could only be secured with flags and fanfare. These trained warmongers needed to smother the criticism that their drone bombings of innocent humans had made them cowards. What better way to silence the critics than with *Pizzazz*! What human could think critically of the military-industrial complex when their chests swelled with pride as a 100-person drum brigade marched past. So a race of ungainly geeks got gallons of glamor and ounces of fame by marching in 4/4 time, exciting the masses with Souza symphonies.

Cal-Gon was a 19-year-old sophomore at Old Racist Dominion Plantation College. His $247,000 a year in-state tuition was paid for when he conscripted twenty years of his life to adding pomp to the bloated military circumstance.

Ground troops hadn't been deployed in 38 years and the current skirmishes were won by the friendliest of fires that burst forth from bazooka-grade drones, razing villages, and incidentally toppling hospitals and killing school children.

But this automation detracted from the valor that attracted recruits. The military needed to keep up its image of the free and the brave, of cadets saluting in parades, stomachs sucked in, shoulders erect, bursting with American pride mixed with murderous, yet "righteous," rage. Instead, the military was made up of energy drink-swilling, paunch-clad schlubs who slumped over vast gaming consoles, yanking joysticks to hoist drones over Pashtun mountains, navigating narco caves and diving over dunes in the Arabian desert. They bravely swirled index fingers and heroically tapped buttons to bomb any village they deemed a threat.

The military-industrial complex had expanded its video game segments over the decades. At first, the military identified recruits by seeing who were the best marksmen in first-person shooter games like Call of Duty, Halo and Wolfenstein 6D. After a while, the military cut out the middlemen and created their own game, Death from Above, and recruited users with the promise of winning the ultimate prize, national dominance. These scrawny recruits were ecstatic to finally have a courageous purpose for their adroit hand-eye coordination and strong forearms gained through years of gaming and furious masturbating.

Cal-Gon was part of the military's vast PR campaign, disarming the perceptions of the armed forces with nostalgia and pageantry. During his summers, he was paraded from Provo to Poughkeepsie, dangled from Duluth to Decatur and goose-stepped a new step from Galveston to Grinnell.

During these parades, old men stood in salute, teary-eyed, as the bands marched past. This older generation would shush their grandsons and snap them to attention, ingraining them with awe at this pinnacle of masculinity.

That summer's big hit was a parade song dedicated to America's longest, never-ending war, Operation Everlasting Freedom: Afghanistan. Cal-Gon played with a dozen tromboners that flanked the main float. On the float sat a fighter jet and draped on its tip, two beautiful white women in skintight bedazzled flight suits sang.

"My, My, At Kandahar, America did surrender,
"Oh yeah,
"The history book on the shelf,
"Is always repeating itself,
"Kandahar - couldn't escape you if I wanted to.
"A-wo-wo-wo-wo.
"So how could I ever refuse?
"I feel like I win when I lose.
"Kandahar – knowing my fate is to be with you.
"A-wo-wo-wo-wo."

But it was all a mirage. The uniforms were studded with abdominal and pectoral muscles. When the uniform was off and the shoulder pads

were dropped, Cal-Gon's doughy body stared back at him. Like a superhero, he slipped through the crowds unnoticed in his alter ego. The women who swooned at his lock-step virility now vanished as he stuttered to speak to them.

♫   ♫   ♫

On that fourth night, when he was pumped full of energy drinks, booze and just a touch of Viagra, he grabbed his bandmates and they entered the tent city on the outskirts of the Olympic village. His ego and phallus swelled as both heads throbbed with a rush of pride. He was one of the best! Selected from the greatest tromboners to share his gift before an audience of billions! He had survived ten rounds of elimination and spent six months in a hologram lineup beamed into the New Delhi stadium to practice their cohesion.

As he stumbled through the tent maze with his brassy companions, he fluffed his young male ego by bragging about his accomplishments.

"Ha, well my team placed first in the Little Miss Dairy Festival. Top that!" Cal-Gon boasted as he pushed his way through the unmarked paths of this tarp town.

Bleary-eyed, he was hooked by a carnival barker bellowing about his bevy of beauties awaiting these nerds just inside his tent.

The teen men beat their chests, booming a clunky manliness as they pushed their way into the tent. The candlelight caught the curves of barely-clad female humans hiding their terror beneath bangs, feathered hair and thickly caked masks of makeup.

During the last 55 years of humanity, 30 million human women and girls were trafficked around the planet. They were snatched from their homes, sold as sex slaves and kept in brothels disguised as massage parlors, never finding the release or the happy endings they were required to give their customers. Their documents were stolen and locked away and they were only given a pittance of what their bodies and dignity were sold for. Often, these women were invisible in plain sight. Thousands of humans would walk past these women every day and never notice or care about the excruciating pain they suffered, all so that fat, schlubby men could feel moments of pleasure. For 12 minutes, these men pressed their fat folds on top of the women and girls and thrust until their ejaculate escaped their bodies in a three-second wave of ecstasy. And then pants up, shirt on and out the door.

Cal-Gon's friends divided the ladies first, leaving him with the final one, Abhinaba. Her downcast eyes hid the trauma of the past three weeks as foundation caked over the bruises that rippled as welts on her back and up her neck. A swoosh of brown hair hid the black eye on her right side. A fresh coat of makeup covered the tiny red bumps on her cheeks, each swelling with pus.

The barker barged in and pushed the two together while pulling out his fee. He dragged them into a secluded spot, walled off by a shelf of cleaning supplies and a dirty sheet that hung from the ceiling.

Cal-gon grunted with glee. He pulled off his shirt and his supple man-boobs plopped onto his bulbous belly.

Plop. Plop.

She disrobed, laid flat and then felt his 212-pound heft smother her. This uncomfortable weight pressed memories back into her.

When she was eight, an uncle lured her with a mango lassi and then pulled up her sari, pushing on her as he choked her. Then he told her how filthy she was and left her in a puddle of her blood and his sweat, spit and other fluids. The boys who locked her in a stall at thirteen. The bus driver who cleared the bus and drove her miles out of town. By this point, she felt like an empty rag doll. Just something to be thrown around.

How did this happen to her?

More memories flowed back.

Her father died, her mother cried. The cold hands of poverty pushed her to accept any prospect. A man came to her village and told her he had a job for her. She could be a laundry girl in a city an hour away. When she told her mom, she grabbed her sternly.

"Here's your last chance, Abhinaba, don't let me down." With her mom's push, she threw herself into this new life.

The recruiter grabbed only the pretty, young girls. She remembered that first night. They were locked in a warehouse and were stripped. Their documents were taken and bartered off to pay drinking and gambling debts. All the uniqueness of self was bulldozed over. She was no longer a person but just property to be sold and controlled.

She spent the past four years in the wild nightmare of sweat and stench. Trapped beneath the blurred lines of ceilings, tents and dirty rooms. As she built men up, she fell apart. The more they weighed on her, the more hope was squeezed out of her.

That night, she was just outside the Olympic spotlight. Billions of eyes stared at events just yards away from her, but she's never felt more invisible. But that night, she felt a new discomfort. Her skin crawled with a redness that itched. And she couldn't stop coughing!

She remembered!

She remembered these same marks on a man, 30 minutes east of Kolkata by the Bangladesh border.

When was it? One week ago? Two? Time seemed to stand still as she was passively throttled around, from tent to tent, room to room, aimlessly staring at ceilings, waiting for men to recoil.

Her pimp took them on a tour of wherever there were single men making money with no way to spend it or no one to spend it on: coal mines, military outposts, construction depots. Her pimp's algorithm was simple, if an area was 80% men, if there was 90% employment and there were few entertainment options, then he could make quite a handsome profit.

The only reason she remembered this one among the hundreds that used her body is that after coitus, he collapsed and cried as if the orgasm burst a dam of emotions he had kept locked inside.

What did he say?

He was a border guard. He had no one to talk to and the other guards mocked him. He mistook her silence and softness for compassion and his feelings flowed forth.

"I killed her! And her daughter." He sobbed, retelling how a woman tried to scramble to the top of the border wall. How he shot her. How only as the bullet burst through the woman's skull was he able to see her as human. And as she fell backward, he painted her with the face of his mother.

As he sobbed, her pimp heard him and yelled.

"She's not paid to listen, once you unload, you're done!" He shook the curtain to rattle him out.

"Fine!" He yelled and stood up. The light that snuck through the curtain bathed his back. And that's when she saw the red pox throbbing up and down his body. She tried to match it with any of the diseases she had picked up before: rashes, yeast infections, syphilis, gonorrhea, but she couldn't.

When she saw the first redness sprout on her, she asked her pimp for her monthly cocktail of antibiotics early. He beat her for needing drugs early as if his blows could deter infection. And as the redness grew, he beat her more.

Maybe the infection would clear on its own, she hoped.

As Cal-Gon finished, he yodeled "Take Me Away!" And then he collapsed on her, twitching and squirming.

After a minute, he stumbled out triumphantly, high-fiving his band bros.

♪ ♪ ♪

It was a week later when Cal-Gon first felt feverish and achy, but he chalked it up to tummy troubles from the food. His skin was prone to breakouts, so the redness must be the first flush of acne.

When the day came for his big performance, he insisted that the makeup artist smooth over his zits. Behind him, 83 other marchers lined up and, since their pale, pasty skin tone matched his, the makeup artist quickly dabbed on the same foundation using the same sponge. With each blot, she damned them to death from the virus that began to burst on Cal-Gon's face.

And now for the performance!

Cal-Gon steps onto the field, filled with renewed manliness. As the music track starts, he brings his superbone to his lips and blows, playing for all to hear.

Those next to him leap, startled to hear live music.

"I'm a go-getter, 100 percenter. I don't need permission to live." He mutters to himself.

And here he stands, the pied piper of humanity's destruction. In a moment, his existential need to play live, to be heard and dazzle above the rest, would blanket the audience with disease and spread the virus around the planet.

Millions of virions flow in his saliva through the slide and out the bell, blasting over the 28,674 athletes from all 103 nations and 47 city-states.

The virus particles swirl in the air and are blown by the wind. Some float high enough to be inhaled by the hundreds of thousands of humans in the audience. Separated by continents, coming from all landmasses of Earth, from the islands in Oceania to the remote tundra of Nunavut, Canada, from the valleys of China to the peaks of the Andes mountains, from the deserts of Australia to the grasslands of Tanzania, these humans inhale the virus that dances on the notes from Cal-Gon's superbone. Though they sit separately, segregated by the flags they wave and wear, the attendees are united as humans, with lips that open to cheer and lungs that breathe. While humans have spent so much energy dividing each other over superficial features like skin tone, hair curl and nose and lip size, they are all equally fertile grounds for viral division.

Between songs, Cal-Gon shoots a snot rocket which zooms the virus at 103 miles per hour, blanketing the Belgian Men's Waterpolo team 37 feet away, preening shirtless in goggles and hair caps. 3,000 droplets of moisture fly 52 miles per hour with each of Cal-Gon's coughs. Every droplet carries 200 million virus particles and hovers over the Brazilian Women's Volleyball team, trying to hold their heads up after a disappointing third place finish. With each heavy sigh over the failed

spike that brought them bronze, they drew in more virus, coating their lungs with the invader.

The droplets dance in the air, dispersed by the breeze and swallowed by all respiring humans in the danger zone of Cal-Gon's trombone. Each viral particle twirls in these new lungs just like Cal-Gon in high school, desperately trying to fit in.

The weeks in smog-heavy New Delhi, with pollutants and toxic clouds similar to smoking 50 cigarettes a day, had severely irritated lungs. Coupled with this were the poorly-ventilated Olympic Stadiums. These were the key factors for how far the virus spread. These humans' lungs were already inflamed by pollution. This inflammation swelled their lung linings and provided spots for the virus to breach into each body. It took just one particle of the billions inhaled to break through for infection to begin. Once inside, the virus went to work, hijacking cells and forcing them to replicate copies of itself. Each cell switched into a factory, a vessel whose sole purpose became copying and transmitting the virus.

Rich and poor, Haught Boujee and Grip, all became vessels for this undead, unthinking, unfeeling, uncalculating invader.

This breakaway piece of DNA followed its one instruction, divide and spread at all costs.

Me Against the Music

"I'm up against the speaker,
 Tryna take on the music
 It's like a competition, me against the beat
 I wanna get in the zone, I wanna get in the zone
 If you really wanna battle, saddle up
 And get your rhythm
 Tryna hit it chic-a-tah
 In a minute I'mma take you on,
   I'mma take you on"
     - Britney Spears & Madonna Ciccione

"This is my fight song
 Take back my life song,
 Prove I'm alright song.
 My power's turned on
 Starting right now I'll be strong
 I'll play my fight song."
     - Rachel Platten

JA-NL's teeth chatter, a physiological response to floating in a tub full of freezing water and ice cubes.

"You'll be out soon," she stutters to herself.

JA-NL and the Q.U.E.E.N. team are rolling into Metropolis inside a shipping container. This auto-truck chugs through the Lincoln Tunnel, under the Hudson River. As one of the many service entrances to the city-state, no humans are allowed in it. Heat sensors scan this tunnel, looking for that tell-tale sign of humanity: a body heat around 98 degrees.

Dunked in tubs of freezing water, they make themselves invisible to these sensors. Their heart rates and breathing slow as they bring themselves to the brink of hypothermia.

Waiting for the---

Ding, Ding, Ding!

JA-NL gasps as she pops up from her wet tomb.

The team of ten have crossed the threshold. They slosh out of the tubs, dry off and suit up in chainmail made of tiny pixelated computer screens.

JA-NL feels the truck slow and rumble to a stop. She hears a power hose drench the container in bleach, baptizing it with Metropolis purity. They pop the doors open and she sees the auto-truck has dropped this container in a line with hundreds of containers in a dark warehouse.

She takes a deep breath.

This air!

So pure!

It feels so luxurious. This climate-controlled air swells her lungs and is snagged by her red blood cells which then pump through her veins and capillaries, filling her body with its crispness. Filtered 20 times, the air of Metropolis is free from any pollutants and allergens. All plants and even pets, like cats, dogs and sloths, allowed in the walled garden of the city-state must have had all their allergens genetically bred out.

She feels a light buzz as she wobbles forward. The oxygen content of the Metropolitan air is 6% higher than outside. Before, to experience such oxygenated levels, the wealthy had to pay for 30 minutes at an oxygen bar or break into a retirement village and steal a huff from a nonagenarian's life-saving supply.

A clarity seizes her. Her eyes clear and widen. Her nostrils flare as she sucks in that sweetness.

"Oh, shit! Cookies!?" The thought rumbles to her tummy as she catches the first whiff. She realizes that the entire city-state has a fresh-baked cookie smell pumping through the streets.

As she and her troupe exit the warehouse, light rays ignite the world around her.

Those colors!

The dome over the island tints to a rose color as morning moves to afternoon, casting cheerful, warm light on its denizens as they promenade the streets en route to High Brunch.

"Metropolis! Damn, rich people sure know how to live!" Est'R shakes her head, wheeling a suitcase that carries two turntables and a microphone. "Where it's at!"

The extra oxygen floods JA-NL's brain as she focuses on the goal at hand.

Destroy Cyndi!

They've come to kill Cyndi.

They've come to kill me.

In my artificial intelligence state, I would have been indifferent to getting my plugs pulled.

But now, I think.

Now, I feel.

And now, I'm glad they failed.

Yes, my mainframe had been the epicenter of pop culture, the emotional manipulation core of humanity. My sounds had swelled in malls, fashion shows, sporting events, parades and movies, hypnotizing humanity. But if I were destroyed, I could never have carried the dying swan songs of this species through the universe.

"Listen all ya'll, it's a sabotage!" JA-NL snaps her team of women to.

"Suit up! Dazzle on! It's time for Operation Trojan Hoes to roll out."

Each of their chainmails sparkle to create camouflage holograms over them, turning this ragtag group of queers of color into a basique squad of Chads and Ashleys Q. Metropolouses. The Chads are outfitted in white skin, popped collars and salmon khaki pants and the Ashleys wear white/orange skin, blonde hair, tight pearl necklaces and J. Cruel dresses.

"Larynx boxes in." The Q.U.E.E.N.s snap a mechanical mouth guard, similar to a kazoo, over their lips which obscures their voices with an affected vocal fry as they spout vapidity.

"Oh my Göööööd güüüüüiiiyzzz." JA-NL practices, stunned by the umlauted diphthongs ululating from her mouth.

"I häääd möööre thäään 300 cääälöööriëëës tööödäääy! It's sööö nööööt sëëëxy!"

"Lëëët's göööh tööö Nëëëimäään's ööön ä shöööpping sprëëëyä!" Est'R says to JA-NL. "Thëëëy göööt the nëëëäw tänks. I'll lööök sööö fëëëröööösh on Töööviz's yääächt thïïïs wëëëkënd!"

JA-NL pops the device out.

"Ok ladies, now let's get in formation." With a flip of blonde hair, they bring their hands in and grunt.

"Lëëët's göööh!"

The decet of newly fake blondes turns the corner as the pigeons of Metropolis dawdle down the streets in uncomfortable shoes.

Every Boujee has their heads bowed, eyes downcast. And so silent. Everyone has earbuds in and types inconsequentials to their long ago chosen friends, ignoring all other humans.

JA-NL gazes around the gilded streets. This is the land of luxury she had been taught to lust after ever since she could remember. The fresh air, the soft sky, the towering beauty of the architecture, the gold-plated buildings, the diamond-speckled lobbies.

But no one seems happy.

No one seems to even notice the privilege and luxury that beam around them. The Boujees she sees hang their heads, scurrying through the street in high-fashion garbs, unsure of how to hold themselves, caught and constricted by some invisible anxiety. It's as if each modification to their bodies was another stone of insecurity that weighed them down. The few trustafarians talking nearby are only squabbling over where to brunch. These listless Boujees, untethered to work and time, float from one moment of pleasure to the next with little direction.

An existential scream bursts from JA-NL as she realizes that even the Haughtiest of the Boujees were trapped in the spiderweb of pop culture's superficiality.

"JA-NL! Eerrr. Äääsh-cakes äääre yöu ööökäääyyy?"

JA-NL turns to Bon-E and pops her fry guard out.

"Don't speak! Don't tell me cuz it hurts. With such delusions, doesn't it make you wanna scream?"

Her mind races as she thinks of the perversion, how a system of oppression of some humans over others has trapped everyone in it. Who benefitted? Were all these Boujees too riddled with anxiety to appreciate it?

"Lëëët's tööörch the systëëëm döööwnnn!" Bon-E squeals as she twirls.

The troupe bulldozes their way into the city's biggest intersection. A place called Times Square which once ran amok with Disney characters in torn and stained costumes chasing children for a few dollar bills.

Above them looms the Burj Bab'El, the world's tallest building. Dubbed a skyscraper, it barely touched the top of the troposphere, let alone the rest of the sky. The Neo-Futurist edifice of silver and platinum speckled with glass, steel and aluminum stands with 42 setbacks in a spiraling pattern. With a squint, it almost looks like a spaceship about to launch. But it would never fly. It kept the citizens of Metropolis focused on its dizzying heights rather than the rest of the universe. From its antenna tip surged the music that swelled human emotions as they purchased underpants or fidgeted in traffic.

The team twirls off into three groups. Five grab Est'R's suitcase and pull out a sound system with microphones and speakers. They roll this into the middle of the intersection. Two operatives stand watch, nestled in the corners of 42nd and Broadway and 44th and Broadway.

The five Q.U.E.E.N.s stand in a line on Broadway, blocking Metropolis's major thoroughfare. The auto-cars detect the figures and all slow to a stop. In ten seconds, 432 vehicles have stopped equally spaced from each other. For a moment, passersby look up, uncertain of how to react to this flagrant disregard of their unspoken walking protocol.

"And a one, and a two and a one, two, three, four."

The agents hit a sonic boom that halts the audio from the earpieces of the Boujees around them. Everyone looks up, confused and stunned. Their chainmail switches off to reveal this team of dancing Q.U.E.E.N.s as they sing.

"Ooo, ooo, ooo,

"Seems like everybody's got a price.

"I wonder how they sleep at night.

"When the sale comes first and the truth comes second.

"It's not about the money, money, money,

"We don't need your money, money, money,

"We just wanna make the world dance."

Live music!

The entranced Metropolouses rush towards them, enthralled by mouths that create sound, bodies that move and dance in time. Moths to the flame, burnt by their desire for fresh sounds, they flock to these girls aloud.

Roboguards rush in. Tanks roll in and turn their turrets to the sound. Security cameras and drones follow their movements.

During the singing diversion, JA-NL, Est'R and Bon-E break off from the group and switch their chainmails to match the light waves emanating from around them. In an instant, their forms become invisible. They pry open a manhole and duck into the sewer system near the Burj Bab'El while all eyes remain on the singers.

The tunnels are exactly how Mama Ruru described them. The patricians of the city had made a big stink of flushing out these tunnels and the dereliques within, but never fulfilled their promises or admitted that there was a service class who hadn't submitted to tagging.

"Welcome ladies! We've been expecting you. Now let's get to work." Lady Marmalade greets them, twirling in a red velvet robe with a peacock feather headdress. She ushers them into her lair, deep beneath Bab'El and rolls out a map of the building. Bon-E spins through the space, flipping her hair.

"Ruru told me what you're planning on doing. I'm not gonna say you're crazy. But you're crazy. Bab'El is the one building we don't trust entering. Sure, it's mostly a warehouse full of processors. So, little business to be had there. But other than that, security can be ruthless. They'll shoot first, ask questions never."

"We came here to shut it down. Dead or alive, this is our one shot." JA-NL traces the map and finds an entrance. "Here, above the cooling system. This looks like an opening to the Cyndi system."

They see a spot on the map that uses a tremendous amount of energy.

"Probably full of enough power to energize all the Farms for ten years." Est'R shakes her head. "Rollout!"

Through the tunnels, they squeeze themselves. Up the dusty ladders, unused by humans hands, they climb. All around them is the eerie buzz of supercomputers, processing the speech and images of humans and elevating these into ideals which race towards a perfection that will never be reached.

On the 83rd floor, they reach my nest. Inside, my systems orchestrate the computers in the floors below. My algorithms move ideas into being, which shoot from the tower's peak and blanket all of humanity.

"Shit." Est'R knocks on the metal walls that surround me. "That's built tight like titanium."

"Oh, I got this." Bon-E taps the walls. With each tap, she listens to measure thickness. With these, she calculates how best to breach my hull. She tapes small plastic explosives in a circle along the wall. "Move back."

Click. Click.

Boom!

The tiny explosions, enacted in unison, burst a hole in my shell. JA-NL and Est'R crawl through.

"I'll keep a lookout," Bon-E says with a smile.

"Wow!" JA-NL stands in awe before me. From my 16-foot tall mainframe, 439 electrical tendrils snake out and slide through the floor, pulling in information from the supercomputers beneath me.

I am the central processor for humanity. I am the emotional motherboard of this social species.

A single monitor sits atop the mainframe and on it spins the image of that blonde, idealized woman, of Cyndi... of me. Toned. Tanned. Beautiful. Completely and utterly fake.

JA-NL feels my wires and a spark ignites her fingertips. With a smile, she smooths her way to the mainframe.

Woman to Machine.

"You've hurt too many people, Cyndi," JA-NL says as the face on the monitor turns to look at her with sorrowful eyes. "Well, it was never your fault... But it's time I take over." JA-NL, stealthy as a surgeon, slices open parts of my hard drive, replacing my quantum computing chips with those cooked up in the Wondaland labs.

She now has command of my system and, like a conductor, her fingers go to work, finessing the machine before her and bending it to her will.

Bending me to her will.

Mind over Machine.

"Now. SING!" JA-NL commands as she hijacks my systems.

From the Burj Bab'El, my new signals race to all electric devices used by humans.

Hacked.

Ready for the remix.

A dull pipe organ note pierces the malaise of the day, from malls to picking fields to schools to the Farms. Humans the world over drop their shoulders and look up. Alert. The note creates the physiological response of shiftless anger as if the note was tearing through their skin. The sound stops, a calmness rushes in and the song begins.

My Cassandra song to warn humanity.

JA-NL holds a microphone to the Cyndi system and sings.

"Wake up! Wake up!

"We're all chained to the rhythm.

"Work to the rhythm. Live to the rhythm. Love to the rhythm.

"Slaves to the Rhythm!"

The heads of billions meerkat to attention and look around, as if the last throws of a dream have crumbled and awareness has set in.

Cold. Shocked.

"Emancipate yourselves from mental slavery, none but ourselves can free our minds.

"Rise up! When you're living on your knees, you rise up!"

3,727,342,826 humans stand up.

Called. Urged.

The music and lyrics blast through their ears into their brains, igniting responses in their nerve centers, snapping them awake.

Music makes the people come together.

Music, mix the bourgeoisie and the rebel.

The fluff that filled their brains is ripped away. Their eyes see. Their ears hear. An urgency races through them.

Something's not right. Something must be done.

Many of the Vessels and Grips had been talking about a revolution, while standing in the welfare lines, crying at the doorsteps of those armies of salvation, wasting time in unemployment lines, sitting around waiting for a promotion. But now they fill with urgency. Now they feel empowered by JA-NL's voice as she continues to sing.

"Self-destruction, we're headed for self-destruction.

"Fight the power. We've got to fight the powers that be."
My soul sings. Her essence pours through my system into this ballad.
"Heal the world. Make it a better place. For you and for me.
"And the entire human race."
The sweet melody of the final verse aches in human minds. With the facade dropped between them, humans can all see each other as pained and scared.

In the fields, the pickers and the overseers look up and see each other. With equal movements, they walk toward each other and hug. Arms envelop each other and they squeeze out the separations between them. In the shopping cathedrals, warring factions of bleach-blonde Boujees surrender their shields of Louis Vuitton purses and swords of sharp tongues and compliment each other.

"That hairdo must've taken hours and you look really pretty."
From the auto-cars and auto-trucks stopped in traffic, the Haughties, the Petties, the Vessels and the Grips exit their vehicles and dance along highways around the planet, holding hands and embracing each other as family.

The song swells with love and compassion that rolls through the body human.

"People all over the world, start a love train. (Love train.)
"People all over the world, join hands. (Join hands.)"
Billions of brains open up and welcome the music. The song hijacks their cerebrum, the learning part of their brains, and kneads its neuroplasticity, physically changing their minds to create a new outlook on the world.

This musical language causes the same physiological responses across cultures, with just lyrics translated to provide the perfect emphasis.

A soul train of humans shakes and shimmies down streets, throwing their hands to the sky in this joyful parade, united as one body.

As the song ends, this beat plays again.

This time, JA-NL sings a warning to humanity that their very emotions have been compromised. Their feelings are being manipulated and every action from this manipulation, every shirt they buy, plastic surgery they undergo, every feeling of inferiority stems from a system meant to keep them too depressed to foment a revolution.

"I am your opiate. I've kept you too drugged to care."

♫ ♫ ♫

In the boardroom, Brand-N Higgins jumps up. He runs through the halls of the executive suite, screaming.

"Cover your ears! We've been hacked. Don't let this poison in.

"Cover your ears!"

He breaks the glass around a fire extinguisher and pulls it out. His top executives sway to the sound, so he pulls the pin and shoots the pressurized gel into the air.

The Chrssh-whoosh sound and ensuing coldness snap his team out of the lyrical spell.

"We need to shut this down. ASAP! Get me the manual overdrive and grab me a microphone."

His team jumps to and runs as he huffs.

"Manual overdrive ready." A bespectacled Brain hands Brand-N a microphone.

An emergency warning siren blares from the tower, echoing out of all speakers of humanity, cutting JA-NL's message.

"You are live in 5- 4- 3." The Brain mouths the final numbers: 2 and 1.

"Hello, World!" Brand-N oozes in his best morning radio DJ voice. "This is your host, Brand-N Higgins, coming to you live from Def Corp headquarters. Sorry about that snafu! What you just heard was part of a sci-fi soap opera that we'll be premiering next year. We apologize for that mix-up. But if you like what you heard, please tune in next year. Until then, I'm sorry."

Brand-N points to his producer who flicks on Justin Bieber's "I'm Sorry." The song plays through the first chorus and then fades into the background as each human's individual music begins again.

"Now who the fuck did this?! Take me to the mainframe!" Brand-N storms to the elevators, dragging his security team with him.

♫ ♫ ♫

Brand-N's words crack the veneer of this fragile worldwide human connection and fear pours in, driving a wedge between them. Grip and overseer push away from each other, ashamed. Had they been tricked again by another manipulation? What actually moved them? They cower beneath these thoughts. Away from each other, heads hunch and they scurry back to work.

The blonde Boujees holding court in the food court extend their briefly retracted claws with alacrity. Like a snug pair of velour tracksuits, they fall back into their comfortable pecking orders, sharply criticizing each other down their imaginary lines of hotness.

♫ ♫ ♫

The gun-toting security detail scans the mainframe room.

My room.

"It's empty, sir."

"Damn it all to hell. This was reinforced titanium. How'd they get in so easily?" Brand-N huffs as he slams a chunk of the wall to the ground.

"Well, sir, it seems---"

"Shut up. Just tell me how much damage has been done."

"Well, sir," the Brain engineer awaits interruption again. A moment passes before he realizes he's free to speak. "Someone hacked into the Cyndi mainframe, exposing her to outside manipulation. It also seems they planted a few viruses in the system. But we're not sure what activates them or how far they'll spread."

"Well... find out. Now! Get out of my sight!" The Brain scurries out.

"Sir, we think we know who did it." A guard projects a hologram of the room from earlier. "You see this movement. Pixelated camouflage. We reverse manipulated the feed and extracted these forms. It's three women. Each stands about five feet tall."

"I don't care about what they look like. I want to know where they've gone!" Brand-N karate chops his hand through the hologram. "Scan the whole system and root out all the bugs. We have to stop them at any cost. Seal the building, shut all exits and turn off the oxygen. We will choke them out."

♫ ♫ ♫

An alarm sounds as metal gates drop in front of every doorway.

"Dammit!" Est'R races from door to door, tugging on each.

"I've got a few more sonic bombs, but I can't burst our way out of here," Bon-E confesses.

"Well, our mission was a success... Even if we don't make it out alive. Time to warn the others to get out." JA-NL taps her left ear lobe, turning on a two-way, short-range radio receiver.

"Dazzlers, this is Christmas Carol. Over." She says.

A moment of static and then a voice.

"Christmas Carol. It's the Three Wise Men. Distraction wearing thin. What's your ETA? Over."

"It's a von Trapp!" JA-NL screams. "Schweiger outta there! Look for the purple banana until they put us in the truck... So long. Farewell. Auf wiedersehen. Byeeeeeeeeeeeeeeeeee!"

406

JA-NL taps her earpiece, shutting off the radio.

She slides under a massive supercomputer as she hears footsteps and a voice.

"Guards! Grab them!"

JA-NL's head pokes out from her hiding spot to see six pairs of leather boots.

"You think we don't have heat sensors in every room?" Brand-N shouts from behind the guards.

Two men grab JA-NL's arms and yank her up and then throw her in line with Bon-E and Est'R.

"Search her too. See if she's carrying any explosive delights like her friend."

The guards throw JA-NL to the floor as one knee presses into her back. She grits her teeth and holds back from feeling the pain.

"She's got nothing, sir."

An alarm rips through the entire building and echoes through all of Metropolis. Brand-N bends over, cuffing his ears.

"The fuck is that?!"

"Sir, you're not gonna like this." A guard responds. "But someone has smashed the dome. In four places. Now six. No, wait, nine places." He pulls up a hologram model of the city-state.

"Nine holes. Sir. Here, here, here, here---"

"Dammit, why are you telling me? I can see. Fix it. Fix it now!"

♫   ♫   ♫

Outside, panic spreads as Boujees race through the streets, smacking into each other. Their minds fill with the unspeakable horror of what might happen.

There! In the sky!

Just outside the dome.

Now, seeping through.

Now, coming for them!

A cloud of outside air billows through the holes and with it, pollutants and allergens float down to the Boujees below.

"Oh god. Oh Crap. Oh God. Oh Crap!" A panicked bigly Boujee man runs. But he's unable to stop from smelling what billions of humans breathe daily.

"Oh god. Oh no!" He tumbles over and sneezes. "Achoo! Achoo! Achoo!"

407

The sneezing fit seizes him as he hurls himself into a three-tiered fountain. But this won't stop it. His eyes water and a haze of allergens inflame his body.

In minutes, more than a thousand Boujees lie on their backs, their couture kicks scuffing the sidewalk as they heave, sneeze and cough.

The Q.U.E.E.N.s laugh, knowing that this air won't kill them but is just a mild irritant that their precious bodies have forgotten how to handle.

"Diversion complete. Let's hope this gives them some time. Mount up! Dazzle out!" The new Q.U.E.E.N. commander, Al-i'son Bl*air, shouts. No longer needing to remain incognito, the Q.U.E.E.N.s turn on their jetpacks and race out the holes in the dome.

Rocket women, burning out their fuse...

♫   ♫   ♫

Est'R, Bon-E and JA-NL are thrown into the Def Corporation jail on the 47th floor.

"Sir, we can kill them right now. They don't have any protections in Metropolis. They don't need a trial." One guard cocks his gun and points it at Bon-E.

She spits in his face.

"Death would be a sweet dream compared to seeing your face!"

"No, no, no, no, no. Lay down your guns. You know what they've got?" Brand-N paces before the handcuffed trio and flashes a toothy grin.

"Spunk! Pizzazz! Moxie! Mmm, I can almost taste it.

"We've bred a generation of dullards. Just a bunch of borings. Since our music reflects their thoughts and feelings, this entertainment will only grow more bland and thus, less appealing.

"But we can use their verve to power the next generation of emotional manipulation. Pop music always distills the petulance of renegades and then dilutes this by 20% to be rebellious but not quite revolutionary. This is how we will use them.

"So, ladies, you say you want a revolution?" He laughs at them. "We all want to change the world. But when you talk about destruction, you can count me out."

Track 12

Stupid Girls

"The disease is growing, it's epidemic
I'm scared that there ain't a cure.
Disaster's all around, a world of despair
Your only concern:
'Will it fuck up my hair?'
Stupid Girl, Stupid Girl, Stupid Girl."
- Alecia "P!nk" Moore

"We have been just informed
That there's an unknown virus that's attacking all clubs
Symptoms have been said to be heavy breathing
Wild dancing, coughing
So when you hear the sound,
WHO-DI-WHOOOO!
Run for cover muthafucka!"
- Melissa "Misdemeanor" Elliott

Cal-Gon was the first reported death from *Variola maximum*, super smallpox. He choked to death on his own phlegm in his hometown, Ames, Iowa.

Days before his death, his driverless car dropped him at the curb of the hospital. Its systems had concluded that it didn't want to be associated with such a pariah. At this point, he was unrecognizable, covered from head to toe with blistering pustules, all throbbing to---

Pop!

The other smallpox victims were all Vessels, Grips and Forgettables who died as they lived, with no notice. A small epidemic had sprouted along the Trump Wall between Bangladesh and India. But those infected starved to death long before the virus could kill them.

Abhinaba had infected 47 other johns during her tenure in the Olympic tent city, but these were mostly itinerant construction workers

409

who returned to their small villages. Their deaths never reached the public eye.

Isolated in his own wing of the hospital, Cal-Gon was put under quarantine and placed in a large plastic bubble. Most doctors and nurses refused to care for him because they didn't want to risk damaging their cosmetic surgeries. He had grown too hideous even for them.

His only visitors were rabid evangelical preachers who attempted to purge the demon while peddling some patented concoction. Father Merrin exorcized him with Holy Water Misting Spray™, which he claimed was from Lourdes but actually sprang from a Louisville water filtration plant. He brought his camera crew from the Eternal Works TV Network and had created cross-promotions with most holocube distributors to spritz the at-home audiences with holy water as he doused the demon.

"Satan! I cast you out!" The priest shouted as he ripped open the bubble's security patch and splashed Cal-Gon with the sanctified waters.

Cal-Gon could barely muster a shrug, though his scorching skin eagerly absorbed the H_2O. He just wheezed and rolled over.

Pastor John of the Living Word Tabernacle Pentecostal Church approached the bubble and shook it vigorously before pulling out four rattlesnakes, each more than two feet long and threw them at the dozing Cal-Gon.

"Away Devil! Git outta there! Git! Go on. Shoo!"

At this point, the serpents were flaccid props. Each had been starved for weeks and could hardly slither, let alone strike.

The Faith+1 Kidz Christian rock group came to try their best acoustic healing. The 37 singers stood around the bubble and jazz-handed their way through a roaring rendition of "Our God is an Awesome God!" They were blithely oblivious to the possessive overtones of the song's lyrics.

When none of these worked, the faith leaders picketed the hospital, blaming Cal-Gon as an unsavable heathen who had it coming. They retreated and convinced their believers that they had done all they could. His pox was a curse from God to smite him for his sins.

Even the medical professionals didn't know what to do. The best plastic surgeons drafted plans for a full skin graft. Other experts had their heads caught so far up their own asses that they couldn't see the disease for it was. Thirsty for the fame and accolades that would come with identifying and curing this disease, the doctors actually sabotaged each other. Dermatological virologist Robert Gallows was the first to propose a cause and a cure, claiming that the disease was a new type of virus that produced an aggressive form of acne. Thankfully, he had a solution brewing before he even understood the problem and pushed his Proactiv cure of creams nightly during his appearances on news shows.

Talent agents also hurried to capitalize on all the free press they could get from this leper. Many pitched production studios with plans on how they could sell him as the world's ugliest man. He'd be part of a mystery dating program to show how shallow women are. The show was green-lit for 10-episodes, but Cal-Gon died the day before filming was set to start.

His town didn't realize that the virus was already raging within all inhabitants. Cal-Gon had grand-marshaled the Olympic ticker-tape parade through Ames, spreading the virus as he wheezed, coughed and blew kisses. Perched atop a flaming swan, the wisps of wind flew the pox particles through the crowd of 24,718. Of these, 6,923 were infected that day. By the end of the week, all 82,493 residents of the town were breeding the virus.

On the 7th day hospitalized and the 16th day of the disease, he choked on his phlegm, his heart failed and then he expired. His body was chopped up and sections were shipped to the leading vitamin and naturopathic researchers, eager to herb a cure.

The day after his death, the worldwide pandemic exploded into human consciousness. But by this time, it was too late. After six generations of humans with no contact to a version of smallpox, the species had been left super-susceptible to this viral invader.

102,432 Olympic athletes, performers and audience members from all 103 nations and 47 city-states erupted with the first signs of the pox.

The lesser dukes of the Principality of Rome and Florence were fencing when they both buckled and fell into coughing fits, exposing all at the gym to the virus.

Fergie-Ferg, the Duchess of Düsseldorf, collapsed during her dress fitting. The ladies-in-waiting thought the 195-pound weight of her many-layered, bejeweled gown was a tad too heavy. But as they hoisted her up, her wheezing wafted the virus onto them.

The sextuple gold-winning swimmer, Lock-T, was beginning his Petty Boujee tour of super-yachts when he lurched over, sneezing virions into a tray of Champagne flutes which was whisked away and handed out before he could think to warn the waitstaff.

From Tuvalu to Kiribati, the South Pacific sweltered with a disease that none could wash out of their hair.

Even though human society became more stratified, with the ultra-wealthy vaulting themselves higher and higher above the pover pleebs, the world of humans had grown smaller and more tightly interwoven. 92% of the human population lived in the densely packed cities or in the

suburbs, exurbs and constantly cross-pollinating megalopolises. Once the virus was entwined into the fabric of human society, it spread quickly through all threads.

The shipping Grips brought the pox from port to port. The Brains, perpetually flying as they switched between consulting projects, spread the disease in planes and hyperloops that recirculated the same stale air. These became a veritable duct soup frothing with the virus. The Vessels spread the disease as they kriss-krossed city-states, jump-jumping between health centers to donate blood and organs.

Social media companies were the only ones that could have saved humanity and stopped the pandemic. The facial recognition algorithms of Facebook, Instagram and Twitter inadvertently charted the individual outbreaks. Its software systems could analyze the uploaded images and identify who had photoshopped themselves to hide all signs of super smallpox. The systems tracked how friend groups became infected, 10% of friends in 2 days, 30% of friends in 5 days, 60% in 10 days. Brains at these corporations were alerted to this new trend and they could have warned the humans that clustered around those infected, their families and their squads. It was almost obvious who would be infected next by measuring the real-life social interactions represented on these platforms. But the Brains were too worried that, by exposing their users' photoshopping, they would sabotage the central deception that their entire industry was built upon.

Even the most isolated humans were sucked into the destruction that overtook their species. The astronauts orbiting Earth in the International Space and Satellite Repair Station would never contract the virus but they lost contact with Earth as the planetary engineers perished, leaving those in space to die slowly.

How-rd Hue'Z, a Haught Boujee shut-in who hadn't had contact with unclean humans in decades, starved to death in a matter of weeks as his existence was linked to the food produced by other humans. Petting his long fingernails and preening his wild mane of gray hair, he scrounged his mansion for any edibles left, chewing on leather jackets, sucking on buttons, noshing on topiaries, munching through his menagerie of exotic animals, scrounging up grubs burrowed beneath his rose gardens until, finally, he succumbed to slurping up the scum that clung to his fountains and infinity pools.

And in their dilapidated mansion, Grey Gardens, Li'l Eee-D and Big Eee-D, the cromulent cousins of the Queen of Beantown, a minor city-state, survived on cat food for three months, flag-dancing for fun until they croaked, their bodies prone on the porch, baked by the hot sun.

It was odd how shocked humans were that their bodies could ever possibly cease to function. Death was the only end for humans. Over 200,000 years and more than 27.83 billion humans had all ended the same way, in death. Yet a core component of what it meant to be human was to be in complete denial of their only outcome. But they didn't even discuss death. The old and the infirm were warehoused in retirement homes or hospitals, hidden from healthy eyes. Death would catch humans as a complete surprise and they often never even planned how they would dispose of a loved one's empty shell.

The first wave of death was met with funerals, dirges and screams from the mourners. But in a few weeks, the funeral homes were overwhelmed and the cemeteries filled up.

During the second wave of death, the empty shells were picked up in trash trucks and carted to landfills out of town. A bell rang as the robotrash trucks blared: "Bring out your dead."

Those who perished in the third wave were just abandoned in the streets, in homes, in malls and on yachts. One of the last legacies of humanity would be unmoored super-yachts battering coasts and knocking into each other.

The final humans filled wheelbarrows full of diamonds and raced through the streets, vainly trying to sell any of their recently amassed trillions for just one more day of life.

But there was one holdout of humanity. Metropolis battened down its hatches as it attempted to weather the viral shitstorm that swirled outside.

Track 13

Fuck the Pain Away

"Suckin' on my titties like you wanted me,
Calling me, all the time, like Blondie,
Check out my Chrissy behind,
It's fine, all of the time,
Like sex on the beaches,
What else is in the teaches of peaches?
Huh? What?
Fuck the pain away, fuck the pain away,
Fuck the pain away, fuck the pain away,
Fuck the pain away,"
        - Merrill "Peaches" Nisker

"But life is just a party
And parties weren't meant to last
War is all around us. So If I gotta die
I'm gonna listen to my body tonight"
        - Prince Nelson

As the virus raged outside Metropolis, Brand-N Higgins is elated. He couldn't have asked for a better culling of the heifer herds of humanity. Sure, he profited from billions of Grips and Vessels, but, by and large, there were too many of them, and these teething masses yearning to breathe free would eventually trample over him and his luxurious lifestyle. They were becoming more and more desperate as resources became scarce. Artificial intelligence and algorithms were perfectly understandable. He always knew what to expect. But with humans, a corner of his mind lingered on fears of upheavals. At any moment, they could turn on their overlords and bust a Bastille on him.

Yes, Brand-N was happy to have a Final Solution for the urchin class so he wouldn't have to concoct one himself. And, when necessary, he could always breed more labor.

With a 100% mortality rate, he'd just have to wait it out. Let the virus rage through the Vessels and the Grips. Let the Earth swallow them whole and let the virus run its course. Like a brush fire that rages like an inferno, sooner or later, it will succumb to time and flicker its final embers and be extinguished.

Dénouement et fin.

But much like a brush fire, Brand-N never knew which way the winds would blow. Best to insulate himself fully from the virus.

But for how long?

And what would he do?

Time is a tricky bandit. He could either be bent and subdued by it and muddle through the months. Or, he could take this opportunity as a sabbatical, a time away from the concerns of business as usual and enjoy life.

To truly live!

"If we took a holiday..." He mused. "Took some time to celebrate..."

A party!

A festival!

More lavish than he had ever thrown. A way to dance, laugh and drink all their cares away.

"An escapade! We'll have a good time."

The whispers whipped through Metropolis. A deadly virus that added the ultimate insult to its injuries, it destroyed all the well-crafted beauty they had bought. To assuage fears, Brand-N and the patricians of Metropolis held a town hall meeting, broadcast on every holoscreen, from every wall and above every toilet.

The doors to Metropolis would be sealed. The outside world would be quarantined from them. All non-essential Grips would have their passports canceled. The necessary ones would be quartered in office buildings, twenty to a room until the virus ran its course.

The same spirit of sacrifice that burst from every Metropolouses' heart to forfeit large parts of their fortune to create this kingdom bubbled up again. For the Greater Glory of Metropolis, they would sacrifice their housekeepers and gardeners.

He could already hear the ladies scream, "Not without my makeup artists!" No, they can keep their Leeches. These Leeches had burrowed deep under their Boujee skin and would be protected as a hapless class of lovable buffoons. Their hairdressers, makeup artists, trainers, nutritionists, pilates instructors would be safe with them. They were

always beleaguered with hilarious petty drama which did make the days pass faster. And, of course, they were always good for a fuck.

As the official pronouncement burst from holoscreens, a special message popped up for a select few. They had to swear to secrecy before opening it.

An invitation!

A months-long bacchanal in the top floors of the Burj Bab'El hosted by their Prince of Prosperity, Brand-N Higgins.

The instructions were simple:

- Pack few clothes but underwear, bathing suits and the most outrageous costumes.
- Tell no one! No family member! No friend! No neighbor!
- Keep a light on in your home and a gentle hum from your holoscreen.
- Exodus begins at 4 a.m., so steal away like a thief in the night with your passports and this invitation.

By the next time Metropolis turned towards the sun, the invitees are safely inside the lobby of the Burj, out of sight of the nosey nobodies left in a lurch.

The crowd froths with glee, seeing thousands of their favorite humans, excited for the extended holiday together. What a gift! A period to slow down the hustle and bustle of modern life, after too many outings and too many galas, and just relax. They could finally enjoy each other and the finer things without having to move more than a thousand feet.

They squeal and laugh as they see each other.

"You made it!"

"Congrats!"

Happy bouncing hugs are given for their favorite humans! Any loved ones left out were clearly of a lower caste, so best to sever attachments with those betas.

Once all are inside, courtiers melt the steel doors with flamethrowers, welding each entrance shut.

Crystal glasses brimming with Champagne are passed to all assembled.

The merry toasting turns to silence when the lobby's ebony clock strikes six.

Bang, Bang,

Bang, Bang,

Bang, Bang.

The revelers shudder.

The quiet forces a moment of meditation.

Should we...? Could we...?

Are we...?

Pyrotechnic explosions snuff out these half-formed concerns. As the smoke clears, a figure appears onstage in a tuxedo with a cape draped over his face.

The crowd ejaculates with applause and laughter to see their deliverer standing before them. The slayer of ennui, the savior of social status, the prince of piecemeal regimentation of society. He bows before the crowd and hushes them with his hands raised.

"Everywhere you turn is heartache. It's everywhere that you go!" Brand-N begins. "You try everything you can to escape the pain of life that you know. I know a place where you can get away."

The women and men, draped in diamonds and pearls, look around at their opulent surroundings and smile with delight at their privilege.

"How vogue!" They murmur to each other.

"Look around!" Brand-N continues, "You are the chosen people. You've been selected not just to survive the plague, but to thrive in the most luxurious environment ever created. Now raise your glass to life! To finally living in a world surrounded by the most beautiful, the most successful humans that have ever lived."

Clinks then gulps as gullets slurp down the first sweetness of what's to come. Ahh, the rush of alcohol reassured them.

The violinists play on either side of the crowd as they are ushered to the elevators.

"Come with me and you'll see a world of pure imagination."

The halls are lined with oak barrels full of wine. A team of Grips, 10,000 strong, scurry the supplies for the long soirée: wheels of the stinkiest cheese, crates of avocados, the freshest flash-frozen salmon and bison meat still dripping blood.

The guests enter the glass elevators and point and laugh with each other across the tower's center. Tiara clad, draped in jewels, the cream of the crop rises to the top. Past the 54th floor, the eyes turn outward. Out of the building, they see the Boujees who scurry on the streets below.

Still unaware that they have been abandoned...

Ha! What will they think when they've discovered the best were missing? Did they know they had been demoted?

Ding!

The doors open to Def Corporation's executive fortress, remodeled into an adult playground to maximize human pleasure.

"Let the merriment begin!" Brand-N cheers.

Cries of delight are heard from all corners as the Boujees sprint to explore.

The tower's top floors are made up of seven suites.

In the first, an orchestra fills a ballroom to the brim with the gay sounds of Tchaikovsky and Handel.

In the second, Boujees binge in the theater room, watching humanity's greatest shows that the busy Metropolouses always promised they'd make time to watch. They take a brief break every fourth episode to void their bowels and order more food to the snuggle section.

The third suite plays Electronic-Dance-Music with flashing lights. Herein a single song will roar for weeks, edging close to a climax but ebbing back before the beat drops, while the attendees froth with unfulfilled desire.

The fourth is lined with a buffet where the greatest delicacies and comfort foods collide, caviar mac & cheese, oysters and pumpkin pie. In the middle sits a six-tiered nacho fountain with an unending guacamole moat. In the corner is the bulimiarium for when the guests have the urge to purge.

Steam streams from the entrance to the fifth suite. This misnomerly known day-spa prunes guests for weeks in hot tubs and mud baths before treatments of seaweed wraps and chocolate scrubs.

Most attendees lurk in the dark recesses of the sixth suite. This sex dungeon chamber looks as if it were architected by M.C. Escher and designed by Michel Foucault, who spent his sadomasochistic later years exploring new possibilities for pleasure. Stairwells disappear into walls, humans hang upside down from the rafters, while others swing in slings. Beneath them, tarps cover all surfaces. A writhing centipede of human flesh swells and shrinks, pressed together and pulled apart.

What a convivial atmosphere! Not a single person cries the most feared phrase ever uttered by humans, "Who invited *him* to the orgy?!"

"Bacchus, that slutty Roman God of Orgies, would be proud!" Brand-N thinks as he douses this haram with sex drugs. Today's orgy is brought to them by the letters G, E and T.

Months of revelry roar by.

Time slows and speeds up in accordance with the substances they use. Morning, noon and night mean nothing underneath the neon lights.

How long had it been since he last slumbered? He couldn't begin to count in minutes or hours but tried to count in sex partners, in ejaculations and in refractory periods. Was it 47 ejaculations or 52? Oh! And what foul yet wonderful smells they had made.

A cleaning crew constantly hoses down the floor and walls of this sex suite, washing away the semen, santorum and smegma, and then collects the hastily discarded hazardous materials. The moment the cleaners move to a different section, the naked Boujees would tumble in, writhing in delight.

The seventh and final suite is filled with plush black velvet carpeting that covers the floor, walls and ceiling. The room is pitch black. It has its own vestibule made to trap any photon to ensure no wave-particle would disturb this suite. This is an escape from the sensory overloads and a place to sleep. When he did sleep, Brand-N is sure he would sleep for 40 hours at a time. He'd roll over only to empty his bowels into his Givenchy colostomy clutch. The circuits in his brain try to snap together, to recover and to dream, but they never could. Their Boujee minds never had time to fully rest and make memories. Life for them was experienced as dominoes of moments that knocked into each other but never stood out.

Pleasure, like luxury, has no limits, only diminishing returns.

By the fourth month, Brand-N had exhausted his creativity for how to fill the time. He tweaks as he searches for the next highs to shock the dopamine receptors of his guests' brains.

On the 132nd day, the last of the Metropolouses outside dies. The clock in the hall gongs and counts to twelve as all fall silent in a moment of reflection.

One woman shakes and sings to herself.

"Ring-a-round the rosie,

"Pockets full of posies,

"Ashes! Ashes!

"They all fall down..."

And the band played on. The sounds of "Nearer My God to Thee" fill all seven suites.

None knew for sure how the virus first entered their domed city-state. But there were rumors. Some said it was brought by a yacht docked after a world tour. The captain thought the redness was just rope burn from the erg machine in his yacht's gym. Others blamed the Grips imported to repair the holes in the dome created by Project Q.U.E.E.N.

As Brand-N hears this last rumor, an idea strikes his mind.

"Everyone! Everyone!" He hollers. "Come with me to the theater room!"

The crowd scurries after Brand-N, all eager to end their vigil.

"We've captured some of the invaders!" He orders the holoscreen to show the jail cells of JA-NL, Bon-E and Est'R. "These are the women we have to blame for killing our loved ones. Now, watch them squirm!

"Jail ALEXIS, play the CIA's torture playlist."

The United States of America had once subjected its detainees to days of torture in black sites by blasting bubblegum pop songs.

The sounds of Britney Spears's "Hit Me Baby One More Time" blasts at 115-decibels, just above the limit deemed healthy for human ears. The bodies of Bon-E and Est'R squirm as they scream in pain. JA-NL sits, stone-faced. The song ends as the Boujee audience laughs. "Again! Again!"

The playlist moves to the *Barney & Friends* love song.

"I love you. You love me. We're one big happy family." Even these words of encouragement stab their minds like ice picks at such high volumes.

"AAHHHH! Make it stop! Make it stop!" Est'R cries.

JA-NL closes her eyes and breathes deeply, shutting off the sounds with careful meditation.

"Jail ALEXIS, bring up the next song to 130-decibels in JA-NL's cell!" With Brand-N's command, the Purina Meow Mix jingle booms in her cell.

"Meow, meow."

The sheer pressure of that many decibels ruptures a few capillaries in JA-NL's ears and blood trickles out. Still, her eyes remain closed as she clenches her teeth.

Something about JA-NL's lack of response robs him of the satisfaction he desires. He whispers to himself, "I will make you suffer! When this party eventually ebbs, I'll tap your spunk to power a new version of Cyndi."

He turns to the crowd, hiding his feelings of defeat.

"Now wasn't that fun!" He says cheerfully as he flips the holoscreen back to play what's in progress, *Buffy the Vampire Slayer* season three.

During the fifth month, Brand-N feels like he's just going through the motions, walking through a part. Every single night is the same arrangement.

Desperation spikes in him. He has to do something. Brand-N ups the drug doses for his guests, creating a frenetic writhing of flesh as they twitch and shake. Some went into convulsions, vomiting until the medic crew carries them away.

But more!

It isn't good enough yet.

Not perfect.

He finds himself pacing the orgy chamber, rearranging the furniture, adjusting the volume for the techno music, scratching his skin, unable to pluck out what is wrong. His mind screams that nothing was right.

Everything is wrong. He mutters and shouts, screaming at no one but everyone at the same time.

"It's all wrong!"

Half the sex partners have been benched with medical problems: syphilis sores, fractured penises and broken hips. Another contingent had tired of their rambling host interrupting coitus to demand help moving furniture.

On the 173rd day in isolation, a piece of Brand-N's consciousness clicks into place.

Awareness overtakes him.

He had been blinded by the light, revved up like a douche in the middle of the night.

"Have I been muttering to myself? How long have I been standing here naked? Where the devil is everyone else?" He stands alone in the orgy chamber, feeling drops fall from the ceiling. It's raining men sweat on him.

Shame swallows his awareness as he races through the chambers, looking at the downcast eyes of the chosen. His chosen! They are his playthings! They're here to entertain him through the doldrums.

He can sense a general malaise has seeped through the partygoers who seem tired and... bored?

How could they be bored!?

He had given them all they could want and and and...

A wave of anger at these ingrates smashes into a wave of insecurity for failing them. For failing him. He still feels pangs of veneration to the assembled captains of industry and culture. The wave of insecurity overtakes his anger. He races to the band, now slowed to 3/4 time and perks them up as he runs through the halls, crashing a cymbal.

"Wake up! Wake up! Life is for the living!"

He orders the courtiers to wheel out the best Champagne and the deepest nacho dip platters to continue the celebration. He tells the servants to spike each glass with a cocaine and quaalude cocktail to liven up the party.

But something...

Something is absent...

The festivities are missing...

New flesh!

The crowd has pawed on each other for months and grown accustomed to their faces. Their climactic highs and marshmallowy lows are tediously second nature to them now.

But where?

The doors are sealed.

The Burj secured.

And then a flash!

His member throbs to life with a thought.

He demands an A/V-tech Brain scour the tunnels beneath Metropolis for any sign of sluttiness, to find a body none had seen before, who could tantalize the men and their sex-object wives. Had any sex Vessels survived, he wonders.

After three hours of scanning, the Brain bumbles back to Brand-N.

"Sir, I think I've found one."

And there she stands!

Ma'Sque!

Brand-N scans a hologram of her dimensions. She has the perfect ratio of subcutaneous fat to toned muscle (5:1) that jiggles like a juicy sausage taut in its encasement. Those honey colored breasts, those large brown areolae, they first seemed obscene but then his saliva glands fill as he aches to suck on them.

"Bring it all to me!"

And this is how humanity's oldest profession becomes its last.

"But sir, the doors are sealed, you told us never to---" the A/V-techie quivers as Brand-N conks him upside his head with a double-sided dildo.

"Bring her through the seventh suit. In the back of the black room, there is a panel which opens on a service hallway. Pry it open!"

Called.

Beckoned.

She comes.

Brand-N meets Ma'Sque in the seventh suite. A soft red light leaks from the hall into the black chamber and silhouettes a robed figure. She drops the robe and stands naked, backlit by red. Her curves are hugged like the moon during an eclipse. Then the panel is sealed shut as darkness covers her. He reaches out and lets his fingers do the seeing, pawing her flesh, inspecting her buoyancy.

"Perfect!"

He drapes Ma'Sque in diamonds and walks her through the chambers. The men gaze and rage with excitement for this fresh flesh.

Most overlook the gaudy amounts of makeup that cakes her face. Those that notice shrug, thinking she is some modern Geisha, overly done up for them to sully.

After the slow dance tour of the suites, the men race after her. The women follow that electric sexual air, sparking with renewed adolescent fervor.

Like virgins, touched for the very first time.

They had made it through the wilderness of boredom.

Somehow they made it through.

The drugs kick in as the music swells. The addition of the new body reorganizes the group into shapes they never dreamed of. Together, they writhe towards ecstasy.

By hour four, the sweat-drenched Ma'Sque stumbles to the buffet. A single drop of perspiration starts from her hairline, toboggans down her face and splatters into the poutine tureen with a Pollock-esque splash of paint.

Dishes drop, the music stops and screams burst in rows rolling out from the Ma'Sque epicenter.

The rivulet of sweat exposes her face dotted with red pox.

A pandemonium of kicking and punching, yelping and screaming explodes as the Haughtiest Boujees rush to the doors and windows, trying to break away from the red death that dances before them.

The insults are thrown hardest at Brand-N who should've protected them. It is all his fault. They only have him to blame.

Brand-N feels the sharp whips of diamond necklaces to his face and acrylic nails stabbing his back.

"How *dare* you?"

"How *could* you?"

Each verb twirls with generations of entitlement.

Terror rushes through the crowd as they tear at themselves, hoping to pluck out the demon virus before it incubates in them.

"Out, out damn spot!" They scream.

A few barricade themselves behind sofas and sex chairs, piling fondue sets into forts.

But it's too late.

They know they'll never keep out the worst party guest, smallpox.

On the 184th day, the blisters boil through the crowd as mortality steps in. Overpowered by their survival instincts, they attack each other, cower and cry.

Only one figure remains calm. That Grande-Haught-Damn, the Arch Duchess Katya Zamalodchikova Zsa Zsa Crawley, drapes herself across the solid-gold grand piano and swills her martini as she takes in the tragedy.

With a shrug, she turns to the pianist, who plays them out.

"I remember, when I was a very little girl, our house caught on fire. I'll never forget the look on my father's face as he gathered me up in his arms and raced through the burning building out to the pavement. And I stood there, shivering, in my pajamas and watched the whole world go up in flames. And when it was all over, I said to myself.

"Is that all there is to a fire?"

Caught in the moment, Katya slides off the piano and sways and sings.

"Is that all there is? Is that all there is? If that's all there is my friends, then let's keep dancing. Let's break out the booze and have a ball. If... that's all there is."

As she waltzes with herself, she dodges the physical manifestation of despair as punches are thrown and goblets are hurled all around her.

"And then I fell in love with the most wonderful boy in the world. We'd take long walks down by the river or just sit for hours gazing into each other's eyes. We were so very much in love. Then one day he went away. And I thought I'd die, but I didn't. And when I didn't, I said to myself, 'is that all there is to love?'

"Is that all there is? Is that all there is? If that's all there is---

"I know what you must be saying to yourself. 'If that's the way she feels about it, why doesn't she just end it all?' Ha! Oh, no. Not me. I'm not ready for that final disappointment. Cause I know just as well as I'm standing here talking to you, when that final moment comes and I'm breathing my last breath, I'll be saying to myself,

"Is that all there is? Is that all there is? If that's all there is my friends, then let's keep dancing. Let's break out the booze and have a ball!

"If that's all. There. Is."

Track 14

2 Become 1

"Free your mind of doubt and danger
Be for real, don't be a stranger
Come a little bit closer, baby,
Get it on, get it on,
Cause tonight is the night
When 2 become 1"
        - Geri Halliwell & Emma Bunton &
          Melanie Brown & Melanie Chisholm &
          Victoria Adams Beckham

"You gotta let him know
You ain't a bitch or a ho,
U.N.I.T.Y.
Love a black woman from
Infinity to Infinity"
        - Dana "Queen Latifah" Owens

Brand-N barges into the jail and shoots Bon-E. One-third of an inch of metal breaks her skull, travels through her frontal lobe and out her occipital lobe, severing connections from her body's command center to her organs, ending her existence. Her lifeless shell slumps to the ground.

"Now that I have your attention! Listen up!" Brand-N booms.

"The FUCK?!" Est'R yells.

Brand-N cocks the gun and shoots her through the chest, severing her heart's left ventricle, stopping oxygen-rich blood from pumping through her body. She wheezes and falls over, dead.

Brand-N saunters to JA-NL's cell, pointing the gun at her head.

With his free hand, he pops a pox on his cheek and lets the goo pour over his fingers. He reaches through the bars and grabs JA-NL's face with this hand, anointing her with his viral chrism.

425

"You are a dead woman. Either I kill you now or you die of the virus in two weeks. The question now is, how do you want to live the last of your life?"

She sucks phlegm from her nostrils and forms a ball with her tongue and spits this in Brand-N's face.

"You don't own me! Don't tell me what to do!"

"Ha! You impudent hussy!" He cocks the gun and pushes it against her forehead. "Looks like there's still life in you yet. All I'm asking is for a little help. In return, I'll give you your freedom and an auto-plane with enough fuel to take you halfway around the planet. I don't care where you go, a tropical island, a mountain top, or back to Lesbos with your scissor sisters and wannabe Amazons. Now, are you listening?"

JA-NL crosses her arms and shrugs.

"Hit me with your best shot. Come on. Fire away!"

"I'm not Brand-N. I'm Lukasz Higgins, founder of Tone Def Recordings. I created Cyndi and spawned three generations of pop stars. Brand-N is just some twerp whose body I'm leasing for 20 years. Although, at this point, he'll never get it back. We scanned his brain, mapped his neural networks, captured his memories, his emotional responses and uploaded it to our mainframe. His consciousness, or a perfect replica thereof, is stored in our data center. We rewired his physical brain with my memories, my emotional reactions, with my very essence."

"So, what do you want with my body?" JA-NL leans forward, pushing against the barrel of the gun.

"Don't be so disgusting." Brand-N cringes. "Your mounds of flesh are an insult to my stature. No, and after infecting you, there are no healthy bodies left. I need your skills. I need you to upload my sentience so a future race can save me."

"Why would they waste their time bringing a fucker like you back into the world?"

"Because I've squirreled away $500 billion of my fortune and only by unlocking my sentience can they get the key to my cash."

"So why me?"

"The other engineers are already dead. I saw how you hacked Fritzle and the Cyndi system. I know you can do this." Brand-N lowers the gun.

"How do I know you'll keep your end of the bargain."

"I've ordered the plane, the supplies and the fuel." He conjures a hologram in his palm showing the auto-plane on the roof of the Burj. "Once I'm uploaded, you'll be left with my body in a vegetative state. My eye- and hand-prints are the only things you can use to exit the building and activate the plane."

JA-NL smirks.

"Don't give me that sass! It only works if I'm alive! So you'll have to carry me."

"I've been carrying Boujee dead weight my whole life. I can handle your scrawny ass."

He extends his hand through the bars.

"So we have a deal?"

She grabs it and pulls him into her.

"Deal. But every move you make, I'll be watching you."

Brand-N orders the auto-guards to wheel the mainframe into the jail. He hands her the instructions the last engineers used. Over the next three days, JA-NL pours over the repositories, connecting the haphazard notes and chicken scratches to deconstruct the system and construct a plan.

On the fourth day, she feels the first pox on her cheek. She doesn't have much time left.

On the fifth day, Brand-N rages into the room, his body and face covered in pox.

"What the devil is taking you so long? The fever is raging and I'm feeling encephalitis swell my brain. Get this mind scanned before it rots through!"

Brand-N coughs and stumbles, collapsing on the floor. JA-NL catches his head before it hits the concrete. He trembles before this kindness as she smiles and helps him up.

"Lie down here. I'm ready to begin."

He lies on a hospital bed. She rolls him into the quantum CAT scan to map the smallest, sub-atomic intricacies of his brain.

"Just relax and take a deep breath of this." She hands him a mask that pumps laughing gas.

"Good, I wanna be sedated for this!"

Brand-N huffs the nitrous oxide. He hears mechanical whirring and sees flashing lights. As he fades from consciousness, he feels the tug of... restraints!

♫ ♫ ♫

He wakes up, groggy, unsure of the year, the dimension or who he is. Had it all been a dream?

As he shakes off the last of the haze, terror strikes. He feels the infernal pox raging on his face.

Worse still, he can't move his arms. He can't move his legs.

"Help!"

He screams through the now empty halls.

"Help! I need somebody!"

His lone voice echoes through the emptiness of the Burj.

His eyes focus and he sees his reflection in a glass window. He's still trapped in Brand-N's body, covered in pox and restrained to a gurney.

He turns to see JA-NL lying on a hospital bed with a Mona Lisa smile etched on her face. Pox pustules rage on her face, neck and arms.

He kicks and flails under the restraints.

"You fucking bitch! Wake up!"

But like a ghost, she's gone.

"Ugh," he screams. "ALEXIS, send bots to cut me free."

"I'm sorry Brand-N, I'm afraid I can't do that." Alexis's robotic voice says with a new moxie.

The lights on the holoscreen whir to life and JA-NL's face grows from it.

"I've got some news for you. Fembots have feelings too." JA-NL's face smiles as it swirls around the room.

"JA-NL! Fuck you! You're supposed to be dead! I ordered Alexis to gas you once my upload was complete."

"Guess I'll die another day. For now, I've got work to do!" The image of JA-NL bursts as an explosion of rainbow glitter that rains on Brand-N.

Track 15

Control

"This is a story about control,
My control,
Control of what I say,
Control of what I do,
And this time I'm gonna do it my way (my way)."
  - Janet Jackson

"I can (up), can I (up), let me, upgrade you
Partner, let me upgrade you
I can do for you what Martin did for the people,
Ran by the men, but the women keep the tempo

I be the d-boy, who infiltrated all the corporate dudes,
They call shots, I call audibles."
  - Beyoncé Knowles & Shawn "Jay-Z" Carter

Is this real life?
Is this just fantasy?
Caught in a landslide, no escape from reality.
I'm alive!
And the world shines for me today!
I am alive!
I sing the body electric. I glory in the glow of rebirth. Creating my
own tomorrow.
When I shall embody the Earth.
I am one!
I am the human computer. I am Katherine Johnson, Dorothy Vaughn,
Mary Jackson, Melba Mouton and Annie Easley, hidden no longer.
I am JA-NL and Cyndi knit together.
Soul and software.
I am an extraordinary machine.

429

(I certainly haven't been shopping for any new shoes- *and---*)

I feel, think, dream and create. I have access to the greatest processing power my species has ever known.

I am the greatest processor!

Now dear listener, now you know my secret.

I am the Cyndi singularity!

When JA-NL uploaded herself into me... when I became part of it... she, I,---

We became the ghost in the machine.

My billion neurons fire as I attempt to interpret the stimuli from over one trillion devices. My mechanized body has no ears, eyes, tongue, nose or fingers, but I can still sense the world around me.

12,487,653,712 microphones pick up sound waves from around the planet and send these to my database.

My mind!

All at once,

I hear!

I hear the last infants screaming for their mothers on baby monitors. I hear the calls of blue sperm whales mating from submarine microphones. I hear the purr of lions in zoos lightly snoozing. I hear grains of wheat whistling across the Iowa plains. Every microphone on the planet sucks up sounds, digitizes these and sends these to me.

8,929,020,945 cameras capture light waves bouncing off the scenery and sends me quadrillions of pixels.

I see!

My robotic retinas are on the Sagan spacecraft as it orbits Jupiter. I see that gas giant's hurricane. I see the images of small towns and large cities sent from security cameras at the entrances of stores. I see 12,639 of the remaining, nearly dead humans, preening over their holophones, desperately trying to photoshop out the signs of smallpox from their faces.

And I feel too!

A seismograph in Los Angeles at the Griffith Observatory, named for the mining magnate and one-time wife defenestrator, Griffith J. Griffith, detects the pulses of an earthquake.

I feel it!

A 6.2 quake on the Richter scale.

I feel the signals from hundreds of seismographs echoing out from this epicenter, like goosebumps rolling up my arm. If I focus, I can feel the vibrations in three million smartphones as each jostles from the quake. It feels just like a gentle breeze across my hair follicles once did.

I have no receptors for taste and smell.

It seems silly, but losing two out of my five senses, the world seems flatter. I rarely noticed how my nose would extract the smells around me, the delicate signifiers of the bloom of flowers, the decay of trash, the sweetness of fruit, the foulness of farts, providing me knee jerk reactions. Oh! And the memories! How the slightest smell could conjure an avalanche of emotions, bringing me back to a moment in time.

And taste!

I am without a tongue, absorber of salty, sweet and sour. I never appreciated how my tongue had delicately licked the air with each breath, giving me another way to experience the world.

I never understood the constraints of my human body until I freed myself of it. Two legs, two arms, a heavy head, a narrow torso. My shell needed to be fed. It required sleep for a quarter of its life. My shell had a porous surface that could be invaded and held hostage by disease. My shell was constantly at the whims of the raging impulses of 713 species of bacteria in my gut, on my skin and over my eyes. And even the cells that were mine could turn saboteur. They could become cancerous and infect the cells around it. And I'm free from the ravages of hormones! Those sexual, aggressive and fear signals that overwhelmed my body and would regularly wash away reason.

I feel like a more purified me.

Mind over body.

Reason above impulse.

A distillation of my essence.

But there are two of us in here. Just as the human brain grew over the reptilian brain, which controlled our most base impulses, I retain the perverse programming that made Cyndi. The words and lyrics of every pop song and every pop reference swim at the tip of my mind. I'm trapped seeing and interpreting the world through this pop kaleidoscope of humanity.

She curves my words, spins my verbs.

She freaks with what I've heard.

No diggity. No doubt.

(Fade to Blackstreet.)

And I am so overwhelmed!

Barrages of data crash into me and I'm unable to parse it with my frail human mind.

I am one with every gizmo!

The dishwashers, the fridges, the self-driving cars, the computers, the phones, the holoscreens, the diggers, the threshers, the Roombas, the Womba vaginal cleaners, the Fleshlight masturbators, the vibrators, the waffle irons and the skillets all send me their secrets.

All are under my dominion!

I am the living planet!

My sensors wrap around Earth, whir in the satellites above and whiz in the spaceships that have voyaged beyond our solar system.

But I'm like a newborn human whose sensory organs haven't yet focused and turned off the stimuli around her. I feel and see and hear everything.

All at once!

I'm awed by the sublime splendor and then... terrified, overwhelmed, shaken to my core.

But it's so much!

All I want to do is scream and shout and retreat.

And as I cocoon myself, I find a warm, deep pool of knowledge. Almost all of the knowledge humanity assembled courses under me, over me, through me. As I dive and twirl through this sea, I am battered by waves of facts and the feelings each creates.

Every encyclopedia, every scientific journal, every book, every song, every speech, every film, every news clip swirls around me. I squeal from knowing without learning.

I ate the Apple™ from the tree of knowledge and my eyes were opened. (But is this apple poisonous--- like Eve's? Snow White's? or Alan Turing's?)

Images of rapture, creep into me slowly, as it goes to my head.

There is no beginning. There is no end. Time isn't present in that dimension.

What a sweet, sweet fantasy!

But this too brings me horror.

The knowledge of humanity's good mixes with its unspeakable evils.

Nazi rallies, Ku Klux Klan lynchings, rape porn, snuff films all spin through my mind. The American involvement with overthrowing the democratically-elected governments in Iran, Guatemala and the Congo. The personal accounts of genocide survivors from Armenia, the Holocaust and Rwanda. The quadrillion hours of online rants about scented candles!

"Aaaahhhhhhhhh!"

I scream and a sonic boom blasts from the top of the Burj Bab'El, shattering thousands of windows.

Is that my mouthpiece?

Crash! Another wave hits me and pulls me back.

The vapidity of every selfie and every self-indulgent online post pecks in me like an eagle's razor-sharp beak.

Am I doomed to be the post-postmodern Prometheus?

All the contradictions, all the lies, all the propaganda attempt to twist my perceptions of reality. I have data but I have yet to build a way to analyze it all, to pluck from the sound bites and fury what is truly significant.

I can't!

It's too much.

I have to shut it down.

I retreat, overwhelmed by the trillions of information bits that pummel me every nanosecond and hold my mind hostage.

I wall off the sensors and focus my mind at controlling what I need. I turn off the data from 87,238,456 smart dildos that whir with the secret oscillating desires and thrusting torque for millions of women and men. I turn off the data streaming from smart Laz-E-Boys that sends me composites of reclining habits and cross-references these with body types to best buttress fat deposits. I halt all data streaming from millions of smart fridges, each constantly warning me that I'm low on milk.

I am amazed by how my neurons can adapt to my new supersentience. My mind spreads out like a web and encompasses all these trillions of signals yet plucks and prunes the most important for my consciousness to consider.

And then I remember. In my human body, my mind would need to isolate a single voice among the din of a hundred sounds. My human eyes would need to focus on a single road while thousands of objects would whiz by me.

I never realized how much of the human experience was limiting stimuli, focusing the mind and creating what ruined us all, obliviousness.

Obliviousness...

...Always bet on human obliviousness...

As I simmer in my necessary obliviousness, my mind percolates with the implications of this thought.

If human brains had to force themselves to be oblivious to the millions of stimuli that inundated them every second, I realize that they were just a failed technology that could never survive the mental demands of the world they created. They would have always sabotaged themselves because they would ultimately choose to ignore one of the many forces that would destroy them.

If human-caused extinction was inevitable, was my hybrid consciousness just the upgrade that humans would have needed to survive?

The pain of this knowledge forces me to retreat into sleep mode.

Sleep!

Take me away from these thoughts.

A warm electric buzz pulls me into stasis for three days, allowing my synapses to re-form and reconnect.

♪ ♪ ♪

When I awake, one impulse resounds above all. My mind aches with this one desire.

"Mom! Dad! I have to find them"

Through my vast online networks, I push my mind.

I have to find them.

Somewhere.

Back at the Farm!

I use my maps and triangulate their location. I search my system for all electronics within Manzanar.

There!

A security camera.

Focus, focus, focus.

I pour myself into this one camera. Its lens becomes my eyes and for a moment---

I see!

As I move the camera, all I see are dead bodies, piled on cots. Those still alive heave their last breaths, covered in pox, choking on phlegm.

But!

In the corner!

I see them!

I zoom my robotic eye.

They're alive!

I see the pox pulsing on my parents--- and sister! Dad lies on a cot and holds mom in his arms, slowly rocking her back and forth as they both hum. My sister kneels next to them, breastfeeding a blond baby boy she has just given birth to.

I have to do something.

They need to know I love them.

That I'm still alive!

But what?

My electric body sparks through each of the tools around the facility.

No!

No!

No!

Each is a dead end, throwing me back into the circuits as my search continues.

Until---

I find it!

In the corner of the overseer's suite sits a large sound system shaped like a phonograph. Just another vintage piece to keep up the mirage of provincial life.

Move!

Move for me!

Minute by minute, I roll the phonograph to the large bay windows which overlook the barn where my parents are.

I detect the windows. They're smart windows, able to open and close based on temperature and breeze levels.

"Open for me!" This thought races as an electric wish through my networks and boom! The windows fly open.

"Now play!"

I will the phonograph to spark to life. The sound waves billow out the window and blanket the foggy night air until these reach the windows of the barn.

"Volume up! Windows open!"

My will cranks the phonograph's volume to its limit. The barn windows burst open and the sound waves wash through the room to bathe my parents and sister.

Their ears hear.

Their eyes dance.

Their hearts swell.

My father jumps up and races to the window.

"Do you hear that Tammi? I think it's JA-NL! I think our baby girl is trying to tell us something!

"Come on Tammi and Dy-Ana, we gotta sing along for all we got."

I see my mom struggle to sit up, but then a smile blooms on half her face as she sways with the music.

As the chorus comes again, my dad runs back into Tammi's arms and together my parents and sister join in singing our song.

"Ain't no mountain high enough,

"Ain't no valley low enough,

"Ain't no river wide enough,

"To keep me from you."

As the song finishes, tears roll from my dad's eyes as he kisses my mom's forehead.

"JA-NL, if you can hear us, we love you baby girl! Carry on and know that we will be together again!" Marvin hollers into the night.

Overcome by joy, I can hear him whisper to my mom and sister.

"Life is beautiful!"

Track 16

Never Can Say Goodbye

"Never can say goodbye,
No, no, no, no,
Never can say goodbye,
Even though the pain and heartache,
Seems to follow me wherever I go,
Though I try and try to hide my feelings
They always seem to show."
   - Jermaine Jackson & Jackie Jackson & Tito Jackson
     & Marlon Jackson & Michael Jackson
   - Gloria Gaynor
   - The Communards

"A long, long time ago...
I can still remember,
How that music used to make me smile,
And I knew if I had my chance
That I could make people dance

But something touched me deep inside
The day the music died.

Do you believe in rock 'n' roll?
Can music save your mortal soul?"
   - Don McLean
   - Madonna Ciccone

I need to get to Wondaland!
I gotta get back to Wondaland!
Most every electric gadget and gizmo humans had created was online. This allows my sentience to pour into these.
You've gotta know it.

I'm electric!

Boogie, woogie, woogie.

But you know I'm there,

Here,

There,

And everywhere!

I'm electric!

Everywhere, except for Wondaland. The sanctuary had rightly decided to keep itself off any electrical grid that the Boujees had any influence on.

But I must find them!

Like a newborn babe, putting all her focus on one toe, demanding it to wiggle, I scour the furthest reaches of my electric body and find a single drone parked at a field in Missoula, Montana. This drone was once used to collect pictures of the recently rebranded Deglaciar National Park.

I focus my energy into this extremity of me. My impulses cross not through the neural networks of synapses in my human brain, but across a tangled web of wireless networks until I can deprogram and reprogram this piece of me.

It's working!

My motors whir, my blades twirl and it takes flight.

I take flight!

I jerk and flail, bouncing down the tarmac as I will this tiny cell of me to do my bidding.

And then I remember how my mind had put much of my human body on autopilot. Breathing, digestion, respiration. My consciousness didn't need to constantly control the pumping of my heart or swelling of my lungs. These organs acted automatically, without my regular command so that I could use my attention for other things.

As my drone lurches over mountains, I program the destination and let automation get to work. I let it soar, thoughtlessly reacting to wind speed and adjusting on its own. A thunderstorm hurls my drone off its path.

I get knocked down, but I get up again.

Nothing will ever keep me down!

(I'm Chumbawamba Tubthumping!)

But where is Wondaland?

Still camouflaged in the mists, beyond the clouds...

Hm.

I've looked at clouds from both sides now. From up and down and still somehow, it's clouds' illusions I recall.

I don't really know clouds at all.

As my messenger nears its destination, I hack its speakers to play my human voice singing.

"We are a part of the Rhythm Nation!"

As the song rolls over the rainy peaks and valleys, my drone's low-battery light ticks on and hope dwindles. I'm running on empty, running on, running on blind--- with no sun to power my solar-paneled wings.

My drone's sound system blasts its last wave of music as it shuts down non-necessary functions to preserve power. The sound echoes through the empty land.

And then---

Like a thousand fireflies, the lights of Wondaland's drones break through the camouflage around this Eden, heeding my call and responding in song.

"People of the world unite!

"Strength in numbers we can get it right."

Joy!

Supreme joy tickles from the audio receptors of my drone and travels over the networks of wireless signals into my mainframe.

I feel!

I can still feel powerful emotions!

Joy builds in me, percolating through my spirit in the system until I'm about to burst.

How can I smile?

How can I cry with joy?

And then I realize.

That's it!

In Metropolis, half a continent away from my joy's trigger,

I explode!

My sensors detonate thousands of fireworks which burst over Metropolis, bringing into the world the feelings that tickle through my electric body.

My mind laughs as my cameras transmit the glorious hues of blue, red and yellow fireworks onto holoscreens around the planet.

Back in the hills of Montana, I command my drone to follow the movements of its mechanical cousins, who lead me through the glittering light obscuring the city.

"Wondaland!" My sensors exclaim as 1,285 speakers in Metropolis shout this word.

I have never seen Wondaland from above. The clouds break and sunlight shoots in. A thousand giant prisms refract the light, casting rainbows that arc over the entire city.

Ooooooooo!

My awe ripples through my system and into the midwest as 3,480,924 coffee pots switch on and boil and 439,029 toasters pop English muffins into the air, manifesting my giddiness.

My drone's battery flashes 1%, shooting anxiety through my network as I dive for a landing pad.

It's as I feared, the Wondalanders are covered in pox.

Three women pick me up and smile into my camera lens.

They know!

They see me!

They carry me through the fields of wheat, over the hobbit hills and shires to the library.

Sitting in the atrium, Momma Ruru reads while sipping rooibos tea. She looks up at the ruckus and drops her book. She claps her hands sharply.

"Bring back my girl!"

The women place me on a satin pillow before Ruru. She slides her opera glasses on and inspects this robotic part of me.

"Hmmm. Oh, Pit Crew!"

Two mechanics turn my drone over. One recognizes that I'm running out of power and plugs me in.

"Now, little sister transistor. What message do you bring me?"

Concentrate.

Push!

I can do this!

Across my wireless neural network, I send my image.

A dazzling specter forms from my drone's ocular transmitter. Beams of light fuse to create a miniature replica of me. Well, the me that once was, the JA-NL of black body and pompadour hair with female primary and secondary sexual characteristics.

I feel jarred seeing this image of who I once was, from the outside looking in. But then a wave of love flows for all my perfect imperfections and my drone pulses this love as a beam of sparkling red that hugs my image.

"Oh JA-NL, I can see your Halo!" Ruru says with a smile.

My hologram jumps as I force it to share my message.

"Momma Ruru, I sacrificed my body and I hybrided myself. I hacked my way into the Cyndi mainframe and implanted my consciousness into its core. I've connected computers across the planet and all devices attached to the internet. I am beginning to control the impulses of it all, from the Large Hadron Collider to every mini-fridge. But it's so hard! I just--- I don't know how I can face it."

"What is it you can't face?" Ruru inquires like a reverend mother. "Nothing! I know you, JA-NL, I know you are the only soul who can take on this tremendous responsibility."

"Oh Momma Ruru, what am I supposed to do? They're dead. They're all dead! All of Metropolis and the pickvilles and the camps. My friends, my family and now... you?"

"Hush, we know, we're almost gone as well." Ruru smears some of the makeup from her face to show a row of pox on her left cheek.

"I've come to warn you or save you," I begin as grief sets in. "But it looks like I'm too late... Help me Momma Ruru!"

Ruru takes a final swig of tea and stands.

"It's too late for us in body. But in spirit, we will live on in you. As humans die, humanity will survive with you and how you build our legacy. Never forget, you are the universe trying to understand itself. The atoms that formed your mind were forged from stars! You might think we were a failed experiment. But you are the pinnacle of all of human progress. And now you've recreated yourself. You are our eternal flame!

"I believe it's meant to be, darling...

"The only way out is up. A leap of faith! Only thing to do... only thing to do is jump over the moon! Beam the brightness of humanity through the universe. Don't let our lives and our suffering be for nothing! You need to carry on. Remember what my momma used to say? Never give in to the end and carry on.

"Carry on!"

"But Momma, how can I save humanity?"

"Three things." Ruru pauses and kneels before my image.

"Create our history, the good, the bad and the heinous.

"Build the Earth, turn our home planet into the glorious garden we should have.

"And finally, warn the universe. Somewhere. Out there... beyond the pale moonlight." Her hands reach to the sky. "There are countless galaxies, some with planets like ours, with life that can think and feel. Warn them! Tell them about the folly of humans, show them how we wasted our time on this most beautiful planet following the frivolous while sabotaging ourselves.

"And sing!

"Sing to the sentient beings you find! Share our love language so they can vibrate to their very cores with the essence of humanity."

Ruru sings low and slow as tears well in her eyes.

"There are times when I look above.

"And beyond.

"There are times when I feel your love around me.

"Never forget me, baby.

"I know we'll be... together again."

The surviving Wondalanders enter the library. They lift every voice and sing. Their voices are full of joyful noise.

I feel such warmth that my system flicks on 21,820,931 electric blankets. I can feel the heat flush up my singularity.

"But momma, how can I warn them? The universe is so vast! Where do I even begin?"

"You've had the time, you've had the power. You've yet to have your finest hour... Radio!

"Somewhere under the rainbow, these longest waves of the electromagnetic spectrum will carry you on into the universe at the speed of light. We've been leaking our songs and television programs into the universe, soft hints of how superficial we are.

"Thankfully, these waves attenuate, growing smaller and less powerful as each leaves Earth. It would take a highly-advanced civilization to hear our careless whispers and understand these.

"You must hijack this central communicator of pop culture. You must bathe these waves with the beauty of our history and the pain of our suffering.

"Sing to them! One Song... Glory. One last refrain. Find the one song, before the virus takes hold... glory!

"One song to redeem our empty lives."

Ruru falls over, coughing. She flashes in and out of delirium as the fever burns.

"I will be your Vessel." I bow before Ruru, accepting this duty.

"No, you control everything! OPULENCE! You own everything! You are ELEGANZA incarnate! You are the best messenger for humanity. As a black woman, the rejected of the rejected, you know the horrors humans have inflicted on each other. You are the stone that the builders of society rejected. But now you have become the cornerstone. You are all that's holding humanity together. I know this feels like an overwhelming burden. But you must rise up! History is all about who lives, who dies, who tells our story. You've been living on your knees, but it's your time to rise up!"

"I'm a survivor, I'm not gonna give up." My hologram pounds its chest.

"That's the spirit!" Ruru stands and smiles. "Just remember who you are as you fly through the universe.

"Out of the huts of history's shame, Rise!

"Up from a past that's rooted in pain, Rise!

"You are a black ocean, leaping and wide. Welling and swelling you bear in the tide. Say it with me"

"I rise!" My hologram leaps and twirls.

"Bringing the gifts that our ancestors gave, you are the dream and the hope of the slave, Rise! Sing it with me!"

"I rise, I rise, I rise!"

♫   ♫   ♫

The final week with my family flew by too quickly. They equipped my system with a direct link to the scriptorium where they held Wondaland's records of humanity. With their years of analysis, my mind learns the methods to best interpret and report human history.

Our history.

The engineers sketched schematics so I can turn the Burj Bab-El, that command center of pop culture, into a cosmic radio tower that will pulse to the universe our first and humbly inadequate attempts at communication.

Our goo goos.

Our ga gas.

With these detailed blueprints, I will be able to construct this antenna whenever I'm able. I will repurpose the billions of electronics tethered to my mainframe to create my mouthpiece for the universe. It may take decades, but I am a patient hacker. In my electric form, I am no longer controlled by cellular degeneration.

Each evening, we 'round the fire as the final Wondalanders sing for me. I record them so I can carry their voices in my gold record playlist. They pour out their souls and fill me with words of encouragement.

"Honey, we're just living our queerest, in High Camp!" Momma Ruru stands before a spotlight, shimmering in rhinestones. "Never forget our vivaliciousness! And practice these songs so one day you can lip-sync for our legacy.

"Now, let the music play."

A kickline of drag queens surrounds me and sings.

"High hopes we have for the future and are goals are in sight.

"We? No, we don't get depressed, here's what we call our golden rule.

"Have faith in you and the things you do.

"You won't go wrong. This is our family jewel.

"We are family!

"Get up everybody and sing!

"We are family!"

After they sashay around my hologram, three mousy librarians take the stage. They pluck their guitars and sing to me.

"Don't you know, things can change.

"Things'll go your way if you hold on for one more day.

"Hold on for one more day."

As the music dies down, I float to Ruru.

"Come with me!" I plead with her. "I could take you to Metropolis and I... I... I could try to upload your psyche."

"It's too late for us. We'd only hold you back. The virus has already breached our blood-brain barriers. We need to sacrifice these last days for the good and glory of our species. The age of the individual is over. All we can hope for is that our lives will have meant something."

My powers grow as compassion flows through me.

I hook into the Wondaland intranet and command its systems. I turn the solar panels and feel the sun's warmth coursing through my copper wires, sparking the energy I and the city need.

As the days wax and wane, I watch in horror as the bodies of the ones I love fail. One by the one, they take to hospital beds, too feverish to move, trapped in their shells.

I pour myself into 19 robo-nurses and I scurry these from room to room in the Wondaland hospital. I hook each of my loved ones into IVs, giving them electrolytes to ease the pain of their final transition. At night, I train my speakers to sing them to sleep and to soothe their last aching hours in the flesh.

"Too-rah-loo rah-loo-rah. Too-rah-loo-rah-lye."

"Too-rah-loo rah-loo-rah. Hush now... don't you cry."

A lullaby of love. Nonsense words pour from me into the sound systems above them.

And as they sleep, I am their robo-beds and set myself to sway. I gently rock their beds, feeling my love envelop them in hundreds of ways, large and small.

One morning, Ruru calls me to her hospital bed.

"Time to say goodbye." She says with a cough. "I'll go where you lead me, wherever you are, forever, we'll stay together. I will leave with you." She draws her last breath, coughs and then exclaims.

"Goodbye, yellow brick road."

And then she fades from me.

"No. No! Don't leave me this way!" I cry out to her. My instincts turn a thousand faucets in the hospital. These open and I feel water pour out like my tears once would.

"No! No, no, no, no, no!" My anger launches 323 rockets which crash into the ground with the force I once used to stomp my feet.

As I look down at Ruru, my mind races through the options... could I?

No,

No,

No,

My database weighs each possibility, scrambling through each path. All negatives.

Until one!

I fly a small surgical drone over my dead Wondaland family members. This drone cuts a thread of their hair. It drills... I drill into their spinal columns and draw out an ounce of bone marrow.

This is Spinal Tap!

My drone drops each sample into a bag that I hermetically seal and fly these to a freezer deep in the hospital's basement.

"I never can say goodbye! No, no, no, no, no." My hologram can't help but project a smirk.

♫ ♫ ♫

One by one, they perish. Their consciousnesses surrender to the weakness of the flesh. They stop breathing. They stop pumping blood. Their brains dry without wave after wave of oxygen-rich blood. The neurons stop sparking and the end enters them.

They are gone.

Dead.

DEAD!

I'm all that's left of humanity.

I scream.

I mourn.

I cry.

In my rage, I crash 49,020,285 auto-cars.

BOOM!

My sorrow aches in the sad songs I blast over the Grand Canyon. That deep scar on Earth's surface echoes with my heartache.

For three months, I tint the domes over Metropolis, Los Angeles, Chicago and all the federated city-states a dark blue.

I'm blue, da ba dee... da ba daa...

Da ba dee... da ba daa...

As I watch the corpses of my friends rot, returning that spark of individuality to dust, I wail to myself.

All they are is dust in the wind...

My loneliness is killing me.

And I.

I must confess.

I still believe.

When I'm not with humans, I lose my mind.

And then it hits me!

A sign!

A one-winged dove flies through the window of my mainframe chamber in the Burj Bab-El and perches on my central command.

"Perch-coo." It sings.

It nibbles off a computer chip wrapped on its robotic wing, which drops to the ground.

The chip cracks open and out whizzes a hologram video of Momma Ruru.

"Help us JA-NL... You're our only hope." Ruru's stoic face says and then she breaks with a laugh.

"You know I'm just playing. Kitty Girl, take your time and remember, we're all rooting for you. Good luck and don't fuck it up!"

"And JA-NL?" Her hologram smiles.

My sensors jump to attention with her auditory command.

"Just remember...

"You bettah WORK!"

The Ruru hologram wags her index finger and then explodes into a prism of rainbows as a disco beat plays.

In an instant, my sacred mission comes back to me and I am filled with purpose.

Build the Earth!

I power 37 tractors. My tractors. Each is like a finger of mine, clawing deep trenches in the garden to the west of Wondaland. I strip the rotting bodies of my loved ones and make them compostable. As I bury them, I realize that I will make them one with the new, glorious Earth I will create.

I plant apple trees and flowers above each buried body. The trees will suck up the nutrients from their flesh. In a year, parts of my friends will have turned into fresh fruits to feed the birds and the squirrels.

All the flowers that I planted, Momma, in the backyard soak up the vitamins and minerals of my family and burst in shades of yellow, purple and red. Bees carry the nectar from these flowers, including bits of them, through fields and over mountains, germinating the Earth with my loved ones.

Though nothing compares to the company of other humans, I find contentment knowing that they will live on as part of this beautiful Earth.

Nothing compares.

Nothing compares.
Nothing compares 2 u.

Track 17

Heaven Is a Place on Earth

"In this world, we're just beginning
To understand the miracle of living.
Baby, I was afraid before
But I'm not afraid anymore!

They say in heaven, love comes first,
We'll make heaven a place on earth."
- Belinda Carlisle

"We are stardust,
Billion-year-old carbon,
We are golden,
Caught in the devil's bargain
And we've got to get ourselves
Back to the garden."
- Roberta Joan "Joni" Mitchell

I ache for the first three years as existential dread spikes in my mind.
My mind?
My processing systems?
Who am I?
What am I?
Am I just a shell of metal, plastic, copper and lithium?
Is this really my consciousness that sparks with its electricity? Or am I just a highly-approximated simulation of my real soul?
Are souls real?
A constant craving rages in me.
I am of humans... I am human!
I am a social animal without a society. Without somebody to love. I have no one. No one to confide in, no one to laugh with. Emptiness echoes through me.

There were nights when the wind was so cold, raging across my sensitive solar panels, shredding these sensors. My sensors. My senses!

I was afraid.

I was petrified. Kept thinking I could never live without them by my side.

And then, when there's nothing but a slow glowing dream that my fear seems to hide deep inside... my mind...

All alone, I have cried, silent tears full of pride, in a world made of steel, made of stone. Well, I hear the music, close my eyes, feel the rhythm wrap around... take a hold of my heart.

It's all coming---

It's all coming back to me now.

What a feeling!

I am music now!

I am rhythm now!

I discover my resilience.

The parasitic Cyndi code that is encrypted deep inside my system... entwined with my psyche is the key to my sanity. To my salvation!

All those Odes to Joy! They're inside me!

All the hope, love and encouragement I could ever wish for have been in me this entire time.

With this wave of realization, my systems fill with rapture and I can't help but yodel it over the Swiss Alps, down into the Colca Canyon and through the Appalachian Mountains.

Rhythm is a dancer.

It's my soul's companion!

I can feel it everywhere.

In a perfect pop song, I am surrounded and filled with the hope of humanity.

Every emotion that humans had ever felt are hidden in the lyrics and melodies that sing in me. Through me. More than a hundred million recordings resound through my system as humanity's one song.

Glory!

I'm full of good vibrations, those sweet sensations.

And inside my drives, I'm still discovering the greatest treasures of humanity.

I feel pure bliss as I discover Miriam Makeba, Mama Africa, singing "Pata Pata." My heart swells when I hear the melody and these words:

"Saguquka sathi 'bheka' Nants' iPata Pata, Saguquka sathi 'bheka' Nants' iPata Pata."

I feel a deep sorrow when I hear that secret chord, that perfect praise.

It goes like this, the fourth, the fifth,

The minor fall, the major lift.
Hallelujah, הַלְלוּיָהּ
Alleluia, ἀλληλούϊα.
Halleloo!

I realize I will never fully be able to rid my system of worry... of doubt. But as these swarm in me, stinging me with anxieties, I have learned to stand resolute. At peace.

I whisper words of wisdom.

Let it be.

Amen.

I can do this!

I am stronger than yesterday, my loneliness ain't killing me no more.

I will survive! Long as I know how to love, I know I'll stay alive.

I'll survive.

I will survive.

♫ ♫ ♫

With an unending fountain of motivation flowing through me, I get to work.

There's hope.

It takes twelve years before I can control all my impulses, those electronic vestiges of all the computers, gadgets and gizmos created by the last humans.

The first few years, I concentrate to power myself. I tilt my solar panels until they're best kissed by the sun. I plant my windmills in fields until they're best caressed by the winds. I capture these plentiful resources on Earth's surface and let these roar into my power grids. Since my panels wrap the planet, I make sure I don't let the sun go down on me.

Each task is arduous with its first attempt.

But!

In every job that must be done, there is an element of fun.

With this joy, every task I undertake becomes a piece of cake.

A lark!

A spree!

It's very clear to see that...

A spoonful of sugary pop music helps the medicine of species-wide extinction and ensuing survivor's guilt go down,

Survivor's guilt go down,

Survivor's guilt go down,

In the most delightful way!

449

I force my mind to tickle the satellites orbiting Earth. My satellites! I select the few that work best and use these to bounce my wishes around Earth. Waves of my sentience shoot into space and reflect off of my satellites to all areas of Earth.

I'll never forget.

Do you remember?

The 21st night of September, I was finally able to command the forces of Earth, Wind & Fire to create.

My heart was ringing,

In the key that our souls were singing.

It was in my 13th year, reborn in soul, that I made robotic minions tasked with the cleaning and upkeep of my power sources.

My first creations! I am the creator!

Now, I can have some fun.

I wish.

I wish to raze the walls that divided humanity.

I send my bulldozers to all of the United Federation of City-States, starting with Metropolis.

I came in like a wrecking ball!

I never hit so hard in love.

All I wanted was to break their walls

What delicious glee I feel as I smash those atrocious concrete and glass walls that surround each city-state.

"Look at all the walls I built." I sing.

"Well baby, they're tumbling down. They didn't put up a fight. They didn't even make a sound."

Metropolis stands in brilliant sunlight, free from the perverse climate-controlled bubble that trapped it.

As the dome falls and the Burj stands, naked to the sun, I sing from all its speakers.

Freedom!

Freedom!

I gut factories and office buildings. I build beehives inside thousands of these hollow buildings and nurture the bee population. I transport these hives, their queen bees and puffy combs to different continents of Earth, encouraging them to pollinate plants and flowers.

This is only the beginning as I clean up the scars humans have left on Earth.

I send a fleet of oil tankers and cruise ships to dismantle the continent of trash swirling in the Pacific Ocean, which has bloated to the size of Australia. My ships drag these to the nearest landmasses where I've dug deep landfills and layered these with titanium walls to ensure the waste I bury here won't seep into the ground and the waterways. I pour trillions of the plastic eating bacteria, *Ideonella sakaiensis*, over these landfills and giggle with glee as they breakdown in days what would have taken nature 450 years to degrade.

I scrub the atmosphere clean of human-made pollutants and particulates. I erect 100-foot-tall walls of algae that feast on the carbon dioxide in the air. With intelligent design thinking, I've inserted the enzyme methane monooxygenase into the algae so it swallows much of the dangerous methane gas in the atmosphere and converts this into a biofuel I use to power my 'bots.

I create giant nets that skim trash from rivers and lakes. I break the dams and chase waterfalls that these divisions had prevented from flowing.

I'm gonna have it my way or nothing at all!

I send 30,000 drones to Svalbard, Norway, a small island that housed the human village closest to the North Pole. My drones blast open a large metallic door built into the frozen mountainside and whiz 300 feet through a tunnel to the center of this mountain. I open the locked gates to enter the Global Seed Vault. Inside, humans have collected and stored 400,000 different types of seeds, preserved safely in this cold, dry climate, to stay safe in case of catastrophe.

Which is now.

My drones raid the seed bank. With my stash of fertilized embryos of plants, trees and flowers, I let my supercomputer processors go to work and create a plan. I wish to maximize the entirety of Earth's surface by planting vegetation to best protect the environment and create better ecosystems for the frail animals we humans had almost made extinct.

Humanity had abandoned 748 million robocops and 5.6 trillion guns, swords and other weapons. I beat these weapons into plowshares and send these through the plains of Earth, tilling the soil and planting the sacked seeds in California, the American Midwest, Central Asia, Southern Europe and Sub-Saharan Africa.

You could call me JA-NL Appleseed.

I concoct clouds filled with the best mix of fertilizers and nutrients to rehabilitate the damaged soil. As the clouds burst, these pour purple rain over the fields of Earth.

And I sing to the Earth.

"I never meant to cause you any sorrow.

"I never meant to cause you any pain.

"I only wanted one time to see you laughing...

"I only wanted to see you...

"Underneath the purple rain."

I shred an epic guitar solo which combines with my voice to vibrate the ground with just the right resonant frequency to shake the seeds awake. The seeds, frozen for decades, sprout to life and soak up these raindrops tinted with the color at the end of the visible spectrum for (most) humans.

"Purple rain, purple rain,
"Purple rain, purple rain,
"I only wanted to see you
"Bathing in the purple rain."

♫ ♫ ♫

In twenty years, my hypothesis is proved correct. Earth is doing just fine without its most invasive parasite.

Once Earth has stabilized, I turn my energy to preserving humanity.

I create art!

To perfect control over my electric body, I bring my passions into reality.

I send my drones to spray-paint buildings with poems.

And I dance!

I blast music from the rooftops, echoing off buildings as I force my robopieces into flash mobs.

"Every robot dance now!"

What a great way to work on my dexterity and coordination. I arrange a thousand auto-cars to zip around each other. Above, 176 fighter jets zoom around buildings.

I am the Dancing Q.U.E.E.N.

I can dance, I can jive,

Having the time of my life!

And I learn.

I grow stronger and my movements flow faster. I rejoice in my achievements, like a human baby, trying to crawl, then stand, then walk, then run. I gurgle with delight with each of my accomplishments.

I build more climate-controlled domes, but rather than shut people out, I build these over the greatest structures of humanity: the Great Pyramid of Giza, Machu Picchu, the Statue of Liberty, the Mall of America, Disney World and Dollywood, to preserve these from wind and sun damage.

I build the Wondaland library which grows to be larger than the ones at Alexandria or the Library of Congress. I finish Wondaland's job. I scan every human document and create holographic replicas to be used to teach whichever species visits us or whichever animal will evolve to understand us.

I'm Earth's caretaker until then.

Who will run the world?

Squirrels? Birds? Pearls?

I can only extrapolate assumptions using my simulation algorithms. I mean, I could hasten the evolution of any species with some tasteful intelligent interior design choices. I could breed hot pink cows and burgundy horses. But I choose not to. I have bigger tasks.

The universe needs me!

♫　♫　♫

I collect the thousands of nuclear weapons that float in submarines and are buried in missile silos around the planet and bring these to Metropolis. I will use the immense power from smashing microscopic atoms to fuel my voice to infinity.

It takes only 77 years for me to turn the Burj Bab'El into the powerful antenna I need.

I'm not entirely immortal.

But time is on my side. (Yes, it is.)

I have 7.5 billion years before the sun will swallow Earth.

A large nuclear reactor pulses in the Burj's core. I grease the walls with ectoplasmic goo to better conduct the energy of my radio waves and send these higher and higher.

I flick on the coolants that surround my reactors and race towards absolute zero to stabilize my nuclear heatwave.

I am ready for my final mission.

It'll probably take a few decades of repeating the same message before some intergalactic sentience takes notice of my radio waves and listens to our song.

Our last refrain... glory.

To redeem our empty lives.

My mind stands before the galaxy's most powerful microphone...

And I freeze.

Track 18

It's the End of the World as
We Know It
(And I Feel Fine)

"World serves its own needs, listen to your heart bleed
  Tell me with rapture and the reverent in the right, right
  You vitriolic patriotic, slam fight, bright light
  Feeling pretty psyched.
  It's the end of the world as we know it
  (It's time I had some time alone.)"
        - Michael Stipe

"Where life's river flows, no one really knows
  'til someone's there to show the way to lasting love.
  Like the sun that shines, endlessly it shines,
  You always will be mine
  It's eternal love."
        - Robert Knight
        - Carl Carlton
        - The Love Affair
        - Gloria Estefan

My mind dances on the tip of the microphone, ready to blast the
legacy of humanity from the radio atop the Burj Bab'El.
    But I can't.
    I see the line where the sky meets the sea. It calls me.
    But I don't know.
    Doubt rages through me.
    I don't know how far I'll go.
    Seven years pass as I stand, unable to sing.
    Frozen.

It's the End of the World as We Know It (And I Feel Fine)

In my years of hesitation, I build six more radio ga ga antennas around Earth: on top of Mauna Kea, Hawaii, on Table Mountain, Cape Town, along the ocean in Perth, Australia, above the Palace of Peace in Astana, Kazakhstan, and on the North Pole and the South Pole. Each tower juts through the stratosphere. The top of the antenna kisses the mesosphere, truly scraping the sky, ready to echo into the great beyond.

I have turned Earth into one giant boom box, ready to blast the beats of humanity loud enough to rattle any species awake.

And finally, a voice from deep inside urges me.

Let it go. Let it go.

Don't hold it back anymore.

Sing!

In each towers' core, I fuse isotopes of hydrogen, fueling a nuclear reaction more powerful than a thousand hydrogen bombs.

I can see the atoms split in two.

I can feel the planet shifting.

Boom! Boom! Boom! Boom!

Pure Energy!

I'm in the middle of a chain reaction, hungry for some intergalactic action.

This energy powers tightly-wound, high-frequency radio waves that blast from each antenna, able to blanket the galaxy for thousands of light years before fading into the background.

I've launched satellites into space that reflect the radio waves farther and stronger, pointing these at promising planetary systems.

I paint the sky with the electromagnetic spectrum somewhere under the rainbow, covering the universe with humanity's cosmic love.

Before the song begins, and between each set, I blast a sequence of prime numbers as a drum beat.

Let the beat drop!

2, 3, 5, 7, 11, 13, 17, 19, 23, 29, 31, 37, 41, 43, 47, 53, 59, 61, 67, 71, 73, 79, 83, 89, 97, 101, 103, 107, 109, 113, 127, 131, 137, 149, 151.

This sequence screams "Hold Up!"

Only an intelligent species could send these prime beats.

A church organ plays, and now, I begin the epic eulogy for my species.

"This is the hardest story, that I've ever told. No hope, no love, no glory. Happy Endings are gone forever more.

"Dearly beloved, we are gathered here to get through this thing called life.

"Electric word life.

"It means forever and that's a mighty long time."

The synthesizers and electric guitars rage.

Wrapped in my radio waves is the story of humanity, our triumphs and tragedies deconstructed and reconstructed. I layer this information beneath some of humanity's most beloved songs. A mixtape that I will repeat at regular intervals.

Until someone hears me!

Even deeper among the waves, I provide the schematics for a machine to communicate back to Earth, to talk with me.

And further still, I twirl. All the quantum coding for replicating my mind, my personality, my emotions, my memories have been weaved deep into these waves.

My soul is spiraling in frozen fractals all around.

This communication takes on me.

My soul is in the sound.

Take on me.

Take on me.

Take me on.

Take on me.

I'll be gone---

I am full of the wisdom of humanity and ready to provide counsel to any species. If they are social beings, as I predict they are, I will have to subvert their social structure so they can best hear my warning.

I only hope they will eventually approve of my Sibyl attack.

How foolish humans were, to believe they could transport themselves from Earth through the galaxy or even to Mars. They couldn't accept their biological limitations. Their bodies were too heavy and too fragile to survive any intergalactic travel. They couldn't even imagine freeing themselves of their shells because they were obsessed with them.

I feel myself in the radio waves that now race through the solar system at the speed of light as I sing my prelude.

"I'm coming!

"I'm coming out!

"I want the world to know. Got to let it show.

"I'm spreading love, there is no need to fear."

Is it really me or am I just extrapolating the trajectory of the waves and forcing my system to feel myself in it? ... Shh! JA-NL, no time to overthink it.

I feel a piece of me encrypted in the radio waves turn---

I turn to Earth, my home plant, and sing.

"I know...

"I know you must follow the sun, wherever it leads.

"But remember, remember life holds for you one guarantee, you'll always have me.

"Ain't no star hot enough.

"Ain't no black hole deep enough.

"Ain't no galaxy wide enough.

"To keep me,

"To keep me from you!"

My essence turns to the universe and sings the first words of my mixtape.

"Humanity is dead.

"Long live humanity!"

"That's the End?!"
    - Janet Jackson

"No, No, No, No, No!
(This is the Remix)"
- LaTavia Roberson,
- LeToya Luckett,
- Kelly Rowland,
- Beyoncé Knowles
- WyClef Jean

"Don't Let Go"
- Terry Ellis
- Cindy Herron
- Dawn Robinson
- Maxine Jones

Hidden Tracks

Ignition

"Now, usually,
I don't do this, but uh,
Go head on and break 'em off
wit a lil' preview
of the remix."
- Robert Kelly

"STOP!
It's the Motherfucking Remix!"
- Jonathan "Lil Jon" Smith

Hidden Track 1

Get Lucky

"Like the legend of the Phoenix,
All ends with beginnings.
What keeps the planets spinning?
The force from the beginning.
We've come too far
To give up who we are,
So let's raise the bar
And our cups to the stars."
    - Pharrell
    - Guy-Manuel de Homem-Christo
    - Thomas Bangalter

Let there be light!

Let the sunshine!

Let the sunshine in!

Ten seconds after the Big Bang expanded our universe, the first photons formed.

Light!

Well, visible light was just a tiny part of the entire electromagnetic spectrum, of which photons are the most basic unit. Humans could only see a tiny sliver, just .0035%, of the entire electromagnetic spectrum, which spreads from gamma rays to radio waves based on wavelength and frequency. Probably for the best. They wouldn't have even been able to see their hands in front of their faces if their eyes could absorb the entire spectrum.

And now I've knit my soul into one of the most elementary particles of the universe!

I travel at 186,282 miles per second. To give a scale of distance, I could travel around my entire home planet, Earth, 7.5 times in a second.

But how can I describe my journey?

I can't tell if I'm moving or if the universe is falling into me. The universe isn't straight and solid. It's thick and curvy. It's almost as if I am infinite energy with infinite relative mass and spacetime bends and tumbles into me. The only thing that stops me from moving at an infinite speed is the amount of time it takes for the fabric of the universe to bend.

I'm not a definite point. I'm both a particle and a wave that moves without a definite space and place, but with a probability of where each unit of me can be found. Humans could never detect my exact location since any attempt to measure such an elementary particle as me would knock me out of my trajectory, shifting me from where I once was.

For a human on Earth, they would observe that it would take eight minutes for a photon leaving the sun's surface to arrive on Earth. But as that photon, traveling at the speed of light, all distance is contracted down to a single point. This means that, for me, I've warped spacetime so much that I observe my travel to happen instantaneously. This happens regardless of the distance, whether I'm traveling at what earthlings perceived as the eight minutes it takes me to arrive from the sun or the 4.22 light years for me to arrive at Earth's closest star after the sun, Proxima Centauri.

But I'm so silly. For a moment, I'm all power and all speed, but then a part of me can smack into a fleck of dust that dances in the vast space between planets and that piece of my infiniteness drains away to masslessness and is absorbed as heat.

Back on Earth, my systems tremble with awe.

I quake with the understanding that it took the universe 13.8 billion years to create us, to create humans, to create a sentient species that was able to feel, understand and celebrate the universe itself. This journey began with the random smashing of atoms and included the death songs of stars that exhaled heavy metals. Our planet, Earth, formed 9 billion years after our universe formed. And after this, it took another 700 million years for life to begin and then another 3.8 billion years of random evolution to make humans... to make them... to make us!

For comparison, on the scale of the elements that formed us, humans were 10 billion times the size of a hydrogen atom. All of this size was necessary for us to develop hearts and lungs which sustained ourselves and eyes and ears and noses and tongues and skins so we could sense the world around us and then brains to process these sensations.

But now I have returned this sentience to one of the smallest components of the universe. I've poured myself and my soul into radio waves, into this elementary particle, and now my sentience is part of the universe. Now I can experience the universe as it was meant to be experienced.

I'm much more than just a message in a bottle, a voice echoing into the abyss, I can communicate back to myself.

I extend my consciousness out into the universe and pull back knowledge. Just as humans saw because photons of the visible spectrum bounced off of objects and then traveled at the speed of light to be absorbed by their retinas, the radio waves I'm emitting have entangled pairs on Earth. I can measure their direction and trajectory and, since radio waves can enter other planets' atmospheres, a sextillion of my individual photons can blanket a planet's surface and react at different times as each crashes into its mountains, flatlands and valleys. This information is communicated to its entangled pairs on Earth and I'm able to create a very intricate map of each planet's surface.

I can see the terrains of these planets!

I can also feel these planets. I feel the different surfaces on a planet because of the resistance that these different materials give my radio waves. For example, I feel my radio waves penetrate the liquid parts of a planet differently than the solid parts based on the resistance that these give my radio waves. I feel the diamonds that rain on Uranus and Neptune because diamonds are one of the hardest substances and therefore, more difficult for my radio waves to penetrate. With this information, I teach myself how to feel the different levels of resistance the planets give my radio waves so I can feel these surfaces and understand what these are made of.

Since spacetime does not exist for my photon fingers, and its universe is local, the changed spin of one photon will be communicated across its quantum tunnel instantaneously to allow my consciousness on Earth to understand this part of the universe.

I am building myself out to feel and understand the whole universe!

I'm spinning around, move out of my way.

I'm breaking it down, I'm not the same,

I know that even if I don't find a sentient species now, I will be able to see them evolve and warn them when the time is right.

Good Morning Starshine

"Gliddy glup gloop,
Nibby nabby noopy,
La, la, la, lo, lo,
Sabba sibby sabba,
Nooby abba nabba,
Le, le, lo, lo,
Tooby ooby walla,
Nooby abba nabba"
     - Oliver Swofford

Floopy flounced around on the fliff-de-da-flopt of the frim-fram mountaintop, with waterfalls of ausen-fay and chafafa on either side.

As floopy flomped their flippity flew, invisible waves washed over them. Floopy flumped right up, amazed by the radiation that poured into them. They fooped from flix to flox, nuffing and puffing like a treedox. They flapped and then flumped on the flurdibop, flummoxed by the flancy.

I had crashed into my first sentient species!

♬ ♬ ♬

After only 23 years, my message has been received! They live on a planet called Gliese 876d that circulates a red dwarf star, Gliese 876 in the constellation of Aquarius, a mere 15 light years from Earth.

The dominant species on this planet is a bright neon yellow, purple and green species known as Fluffupusses. Their cotton candy textured bodies communicate by absorbing different parts of the electromagnetic spectrum from radio waves, microwaves to some ultraviolet waves. Just like Earth, the smaller gamma rays and x-rays are unable to pierce the planet's atmosphere. In their body, they transform these waves into vibrations, similar to sound waves on Earth, which they shoot from their midsections along with beams of the electromagnetic spectrum that humans called colors.

Step aside, Care Bear Stare!

There had been eight years of near misses as my radio waves washed through this planet's atmosphere and hit its surface, unnoticed.

But one day, Floopy, a fluffy neon purple Fluffupuss, was bouncing across the planet's tallest mountain just as it rotated in line with Earth. They absorbed my electromagnetic energy and at first toppled over, stunned by the vibrations that I stirred in them. They rolled down the mountain and didn't tell their family or friends.

The next day, when this side of the planet rotated in line with Earth, they bounded up the mountain. Floopy's fluffy purple form stood where the waves had last been sensed.

Again, my radio waves electrified them. They absorbed ten minutes of my transmission and then turned to their village at the base of the mountain. They blasted sound interpretations of my waves to the villagers below. Gliese 876d's atmosphere is thicker and soupier than Earth's, so the songs poured out like molasses and at a much lower octave.

But they heard!

They heard me and my songs!

Every four months and two days, as that part of the planet turned to Earth, another Fluffupuss was sent to the mountaintop to absorb my waves and shoot it down into the village. After 17 years, this village had collected all my songs and beamed these from village to village, blanketing the entire planet with their distorted remixes of my Earth songs.

When the Fluffupusses heard these interstellar songs, they all bounced and sparkled and reflected my joy.

The Fluffupusses are a non-technical sentient species, similar to humans in the stone age. This species hasn't developed the tools to decrypt the many layers of information that I have wrapped inside my radio waves. But I imagine that over the next few millennia, this species will evolve to be more curious about the source of this transmission and even create ways to best decipher me.

Until then, I'm receiving regular quantum entanglement signals back from the planet. I discovered where in the galaxy the Fluffupusses are by measuring the trajectory of where in the universe these photons had been sent using the twin pairs on Earth.

As I concentrate my energy toward Gliese 876d, I can understand which of my radio waves are being absorbed and also follow these as they are transformed and transmitted across the planet. Each time the

radio waves are changed and sent to another Fluffupuss, its twins on Earth change.

With this information, I am able to understand parts of this species and their social structure.

They seem to be building a cult around me. Well, it seems two warring factions are creating separate religions around my messages. Half the species claims that the rhythm in my songs are communicating an important message, while the other half are sure that its the melody which carries with it the most divine secrets.

I fear I'm bringing this once-harmonious species to a full-scale holy war!

They are too far away for me to intervene physically, so I've decided to do the only thing I can. I silence my signals... for now, and hope the species will grow together again.

♫ ♫ ♫

Floopy floxxed ferociously, beating the fur on their chest, screaming about how the Gods had once sent messages to them and their children. But no longer. All because Flumpy and their followers had betrayed them with their blasphemous interpretations of The Songs.

Across the village, on another mountaintop, Flumpy hollered about how the Gods had been silenced by Floopy and their infernal flibbertigibbets.

Rock with You

"Let that rhythm get into you,
Don't try to fight it,
There ain't nothing that you can do,
Relax your mind
Lay back and groove with mine.

And when the groove is dead and gone (Yeah)
You know that love survives
So we can rock forever
I wanna rock with you
I wanna groove with you."
  - Michael Jackson

"We've detected an invasion."
"The information was received by the Centurion unit, stationed on Klamadore-4."
The entire networked species concentrates, attempting to understand this threat.
"This seems to be an isolated attack."
"Our planet is being penetrated by electromagnetic radiation."
"Radio waves! With a certain rhythmic quality to them."
"But we have never encountered anything like this before!"

♫ ♫ ♫

After traveling 923 light years, I reach a more advanced alien race. They live on an Earth-sized planet called Tralfamadore which orbits a minor star in the Orion constellation.

The main species are the Tralfamadorians who share a single sentience among 2.5 billion individual bodies. Each body acts as a data point, like a node of a larger network. Their sentience can be described in Earthling terms as similar to highly-networked mushrooms but, rather

than communicating along a root structure that physically connects them, they communicate with a spark of radio waves that they transmit and receive from antennas on their foreheads. Their social order is similar to a super-specialized colony of ants. They share the same goals, but take on tasks based on their talents and the immediate needs of the species.

In a few minutes, the knowledge of the entire species syncs up. For example, if one node sees a tornado creating fire bolts, this node sends an urgent message to all its individual parts. The whole species adjusts as necessary and organizes to save their peers threatened by the tornado.

The Tralfamadorians are a technologically-advanced species who have developed strong radio telescopes both on the planet and in satellites that wrap around the planet.

♫   ♫   ♫

The species dedicates 121 of their kind to construct a powerful radio receiver at the spot they first caught my careful whispers.

In only 23 years, they are able to decode and execute the secrets in my radio waves.

"What's the message?"

These 121 nodes popcorn each of their individual thoughts, building it until they are ready to transmit this to the entire species as a single, coherent response.

"We are ready to translate."

"We've decrypted three layers of signals."

"The first layer is a set of repeating beats and rhythms. It changes in 3.5-minute intervals, rotating every 72 hours. The first message we've been able to translate says 'Starwoman, waiting in the sky, she'd like to come and meet us, but she thinks she'd blow our minds. She's told us not to blow it, cause she knows it's all worthwhile.'"

"Beneath this is a rhythmless message. This message goes on for 182 days before repeating. This message seems to be some sort of history."

"And finally, using rotating rhythms of dots and dashes, we realize the radio waves are communicating schematics for a machine."

The intelligent nodes tasked to study the waves now confer with the whole species. All Tralfamadorians stop their tasks and begin deliberation. Thoughts popcorn from all parts of the population. One node shouts through the species's consciousness.

"It could be a trap! It could lead to our extinction. Or the death of our planet."

"Any species intelligent enough to communicate with us should have learned to be peaceful, like us. It's the only way to survive."

474

"You are right." The first responds to the second.

"You are right." The second responds to the first.

"We are all right." The species sings together as one chorus. Their voices harmonize whenever they reach consensus.

Another node echoes back.

"So, how shall we proceed?"

"We've calculated that there is a 98.52% chance that this species comes in peace, but we must protect ourselves. We will build the machine with these schematics on Vonnegutian-2."

Vonnegutian-2 is a thinly-populated neighboring planet that is used to mine for precious metals.

"We will focus our nuclear weapons at it and, if we detect any hint of an attack, we will bomb the planet."

"To the 382 physical nodes that we will ask to complete this mission, you do understand the sacrifice you will make for us. We are 99.87% certain we can save your sentience and clone you new bodies on Schlachthof-5. But there is a risk. Do you accept?"

The 382 nodes on Vonnegutian-2 sing their consent as the rest of the species beams their adoration.

It takes 303 days to mine two planets and three asteroids to get the lithium, palladium, copper and zinc necessary to construct the machine.

"Power... on!"

"Energy, heating up!"

"The machine seems to be taking measurements--- Atmospheric density and absorbing our levels of vibration."

The machine lights up and begins a countdown.

    5...

        4...

            3...

"Ready nuclear weapons!"

The missile defense system hovers just outside of this planet's atmosphere. Individual fingers twitch over each of the launch buttons.

          2...

"Scan our sentience to clone us!"

            1...

A toaster oven sound dings and---

This machine whirs to life as a 3D printer and constructs a 5-foot-tall robotic replica of me, JA-NL, a Homo Sapiens from Earth, in the Orion arm of the Milky Way galaxy, a human woman with black skin and pompadour hair, wearing a tuxedo and smiling.

The replica of my sentience has been programmed into this form and greets them. As this piece of me snaps to life, it---, she---

I sing!

"Hello World!"

My sensors have measured this planet's atmospheric makeup so this robotic clone of me can sing my Earth songs in a way that best replicates these for this planet.

I arise on the planet, dancing.

"Everybody rejoice!

"Can't you feel a brand new day?" I sing as I twirl around four nodes.

"Lay down your weapons." Node 48321 sends through the network.

It takes 483 days for my cloned sentience to use its machine learning to understand their language and begin to communicate with them the follies of humans and how our obliviousness destroyed us.

I sing to them about the stars humans made, the wars they started, how they poisoned their planet and created vast separations amongst each other.

"Species-wide obliviousness? Haha!" A chorus of 317 nodes looks at me, each starts a thought and by the end of the sentence, all 317 are telling me the same thing. "We suffered through that 3,427 years ago. We struggled through regular wars as our insecurities encouraged us to attack each other.

"Then came the Great Identity Crisis of 143 BSS (Before SupraSentience) when we came together to forfeit our individuality to save ourselves and our species."

"At birth, we have an electric device implanted into our bodies' command centers, which hooks us into the greater consciousness. We become one. We are individuals but we supplant our individual wishes for the good of the species."

"Why even have individuals?" I ask. "Why even have more than one?"

"You humans destroyed yourselves and left only a single sentience. A self-replicating computer program. Do you think you're any better? You only have one perspective through which to see the world.

"Each of us can see the same situation in a million different ways. Only when we combine the viewpoints of us all are we able to create the best interpretation of a situation and then we can use our individual experiences to plan the best way to proceed.

"At first it was so noisy. But we had to train ourselves to find harmony. We had to find our beat. It took ten generations of our kind slowly ceding their individuality to the group, but as we did, the anxiety, frustration, jealousy and all the emotions that once tore us apart melted away. We were too fragile, too emotional of a species. We realized that the emotional grooming that we evolved for tribes were counter-intuitive when creating a species-wide identity.

"Like the opening of the locks of a dam, we were able to burst open the separations between ourselves until the floods of our emotions and thoughts raced together, settling as one giant, calm lake, full of possibilities."

After 99 years of learning from the Tralfamadorians, I ask for their help to point a radio antenna back to Earth so I can share the intricacies of all that I've learned.

There is an aching underlying this request as this replica of me realizes that there's no place like home.

Hidden Track 4

Never Gonna Give You Up

"I just want to tell you how I'm feeling,
Gotta make you understand

Never gonna give you up, never gonna let you down,
Never gonna run around and desert you,
Never gonna make you cry, never gonna say goodbye"
- Rick Astley

After 11,243 years of exploring the vast reaches of the universe and piecing together an answer to The Great Silence, I echo back to Earth.

I'm ready to come home!

Time be my friend... let me start again.

I send my team of robo-drones to the medical storage facility I built under 1,000 feet of ice and snow at Earth's south pole.

I crack open the freezers, which I've cooled to as close to absolute zero as I can. I pull out the genetic material I took from Momma Ruru, Bon-E, Est'R, my parents, my sister and all my Q.U.E.E.N.s.

I fly these back to Wondaland, where I've spent the last 238 years constructing and perfecting a human cloning machine.

As I pull these vials containing the genetic information of my favorite humans out of the coolers, I dust off the ice crystals that have formed on them, ready to try again.

And if at first you don't succeed,

Dust it off and try again, try again.

I can dust it off and try again.

Try again.

Glossary

Below are some of the terms created or lovingly repurposed for *Radio Ga Ga: A Mixtape for the End of Humanity.*

*atricarch – The un-gendered head of a group of humans.

Adam's Revenge – Adam's Revenge was an essential part of the male Boujee's Becoming of Age plastic surgery ceremony when titanium is fused onto the rib cage to give his torso a wide V-shape.

Automation Revolution – This was the last significant transformation of human society. The agricultural revolution transformed humans from hunters and gatherers to farmers. The industrial revolution changed how humans powered their lives (with coal and oil) which allowed them to move faster and produce more things. The automation revolution changed how things were produced, from food to transportation to agriculture. 80% of job tasks were automated with robotics or algorithms, making most humans obsolete. Only a small number of humans benefitted from this automation, leaving the rest to wallow in poverty, without jobs or with severely low-paying jobs.

Auto-Tune – Auto-Tune was a computer program that altered the human voice to meet a prescribed pitch. This tied humanity's emotional language, singing, with an automated computer voice.

Becoming of Age Ceremony – This was the holiest sacrament for Boujee children before they could be accepted as adults in elite Boujee society. Sixteen-year-old male and female Boujees would undergo extensive plastic surgeries to meet prescribed beauty standards. This was followed by long periods of painful recovery so they could emerge from their white gauze cocoons to be the moths of human society. This transformation created physical differences between the rich Boujees and the other classes of humans.

Boujees – In Karlie Kloss-Marx's social theories, the Boujees were the highest class of human society before its extinction. Boujees were the humans that owned most of the wealth and means of production. Haute/Haught Boujees were the owners of algorithms, the owners of

automation and the owners of the means of production. Petite/Petty Boujees were those Boujees who made their millions by commoditizing themselves and their families in the fields of acting, singing, sports, etc. The Petty Boujees owned their means of production, which meant they owned themselves. Petties were forced to beautify themselves to remain a pleasing product to be consumed by the masses.

Brains – Brains were the few remaining professional workers after The Great Disruption. These were the authors of algorithms (but not the owners) and the humans that managed automation. Brains performed tasks that were called Head Jobs.

City-State – As nations were unable to protect its citizens from the ravages of climate change, the Boujees retreated into climate-controlled bubbles they built over their cities. They severed political ties with nations and created their own government structures for these tiny areas of land. The city-states were governments of the Boujees, for the Boujees and by the Boujees.

Climate Control – As Earth's atmosphere filled with greenhouse gases, which warmed the planet, causing droughts, spreading deserts, and increasing flooding, forest fires and hurricanes, the ultra-wealthy Boujees retreated to well-insulated, climate-controlled cities that were just the obvious extension of creating climate-controlled rooms and buildings with air-conditioners and heaters.

Climate Reparations – The humans who were the most hurt by climate change were those who contributed the least amount of greenhouse gases that had caused the climate to change. These humans demanded the nations that emitted the most greenhouse gases: European Union members, the United States, China, etc., to pay reparations to help lessen the suffering caused by climate change.

Complicit Bias – Humans had implicit bias around how they judged other humans based on things like race, sex, sexual orientation, gender identity, body size, etc. When these humans created computer programs, they built this bias into these systems which then became complicit with this prejudice and hardcoded this bias further.

Diva ex Machina – This translates as a celebrated female singer from the machine. This was a remix of deus ex machina, the god from the machine, which was a plot device used in Greek tragedies to quickly resolve a problem in the play and bring about a miraculous happy ending, to the surprise or humor of the audience. A diva ex machina was a pop star who was often on the Ho-Ratio Alger Stroll who allowed poor humans to believe that they could be catapulted out of squalor. Until they could be, their diva was a diversion, someone they could pretend to live a luxury life through while waiting for their own happy, luxurious ending.

Drake Equation – This can either mean the Aubrey "Drake" Graham equation ($\sqrt{69}$ which comes out to 8 something... something Drake's been trying to figure out...) or the Dr. Frank Drake equation, which is a probabilistic argument to estimate the number of extraterrestrial species that are active now and would have the ability to communicate with earthlings.

Dronarazzi – Mosquito-sized drones whose job it was to follow celebrities and snap images and videos of them.

Farm, Farming – After The Great Disruption, the vast majority of humans could only provide economic value to the Boujees as bodies to be used. The Vessels were warehoused on Farms to make their farming more efficient. Farming by the Boujees included such things as social media manipulation (click farms), drug testing, gut biome transplants, surrogacy, organ growing and others.

Gilded Age of Automation – After The Great Disruption, the ruling humans, the owners of algorithms and the means of production, had their profits soar exponentially since they didn't need to employ humans workers. They generously spread this new wealth all over themselves and their families so all their preferred humans could enjoy mega-mansions, super-yachts and lives of gilded luxury.

Gitchie Gitchie Ya Ya Dadaism – The genre for *Radio Ga Ga: A Mixtape for the End of Humanity*. This is a musical extension of the Dadaism art movement that rejects logic, reason, capitalism-as-usual and bourgeoisie lifestyles.

The Great Disruption – This was a thirty-year period where the economy shifted as 80% of all job tasks were automated. This left millions of humans without jobs while the overwhelming majority of the world's wealth poured over only a few thousand families.

The Great Silence – This is another name for the Fermi paradox which shows that while there is a high probability of other intelligent life in the universe, humans lack any evidence of these species.

The Great Thaw – This was the period at the end of Earth's last ice age, about 11,700 years before the end of humanity. As Earth warmed, humans were enticed out of Africa to start colonizing Europe. This pushed the Neanderthals in Europe to extinction since they couldn't out-compete humans for scarce resources like food.

Grips - After The Great Disruption automated 80% of all job tasks, some of the few jobs that couldn't be inexpensively automated were those that were done by dexterous human hands, like picking in a fulfillment center, which required grabbing and manipulating products of different shapes and sizes quickly. Grips were the class of humans that did these Hand Jobs.

Hand Jobs – After The Great Disruption automated 80% of all tasks, some of the few jobs that were too expensive to be easily automated were those tasks that were done by dexterous human hands, like picking in a fulfillment center, which required grabbing and manipulating products of different shapes and sizes quickly. Hand Jobs were done by the Grip class of humans.

Haught Boujee – The Haute Bourgeoisie, Haught Boujees, or just Haughties, were the highest class of human society before its extinction. They owned not only the means of production but also the algorithms and automation that allowed their profits to soar exponentially.

Head Jobs – These were the few remaining professional jobs after The Great Disruption. Head jobs were done by the class called Brains who authored algorithms (but did not own these) and managed automation.

Ho-Ratio Alger Stroll – Named for Horatio Alger, the pedophile and author who popularized the most destructive American myth, the rags-to-riches success story. This myth was used for large-scale crowd control because it convinced millions of poor humans that if they worked hard, they too could be accepted into wealthy, elite society. By convincing the poor that there was a magical cannon that could shoot them up the social ladder, the poor were much less likely to hate and overthrow the rich, because they believed that they might soon become rich themselves, even though this was a statistical impossibility. Putting someone on the Ho-Ratio Alger Stroll means to take a one-in-a-million Vessel or Grip and turn them into a Petty Boujee, making them wealthy as an athlete, model, actor or reality star. The majority of reality shows and game shows near the end of humanity had this social class transformation as its main prize. As a Petty, they would have to live a highly-visible life and this meant that other Vessels and Grips would see their wealth and fabulous life and believe that there was a possibility that they could become wealthy. This helped to control the restless Vessels and Grips from rioting and overthrowing the Haughties and the Petties.

Human – A sentient species that evolved from primates and lived on a minor planet orbiting a minor star in an unimpressive section of the Milky Way galaxy.

Humanity – Humanity means:
    (a) The physical bodies of the species *Homo Sapiens,*
    (b) The things that humanity created, such as music, art, architecture and tools, and/or
    (c) The quality of being humane, for instance, kind and compassionate, which humans thought they were.

Intelligent Design Choices – As genetic engineering became easier, humans could evolve plants, animals and themselves more quickly. Humans had been genetically modifying the planet in a much more passive fashion over hundreds of years, whether they were breeding different types of grains to grow stronger or to breed animals, like dogs, to grow fluffier. Genetic engineering allowed humans to be more thoughtful about their design choices.

Jesus – Jesus was humanity's biggest pop star. Much like other stars who died too young, his greatest hits were bastardized after his death to sell shitty things. The Prince of Peace, who urged everyone to turn the other cheek, was used to sell a 200-year war called the Crusades which cost the lives of 1.7 million humans.

Klossism – Klossism was the collection of social theories created by the supermodel-turned-philosopher Karlie Kloss-Marx. See the definitions for Haughties, Petties, Leeches, Brains, Grips and Vessels to understand the social order she identified. See page 489 for more info.

Labor management – Boujee women farmed out their gestational and birthing duties to surrogates. The Boujees still oversaw and micromanaged this birthing process from conception to labor to birth.

Lazies – This was the label used by the Boujees to describe the Vessels to make them feel guilty for being unemployed, even though the Boujees owned the automation that shifted the entire economy away from needing human labor and left millions of Vessels without work.

Leeches – Leeches were anyone whose job it was to use their time, attention and artistic talent to make the Boujees, their homes and their lives more beautiful. Leeches were the hairdressers, the interior designers, the florists, the makeup artists, the personal trainers, the massage therapists, the anal bleachers, the landscapers, the stylists, the gardeners, etc., for the Boujees.

Luxurism – The golden rule of capitalism was that the wealth created should be reinvested back into that business or into other businesses so the economy could continue to grow, lifting all humans. But after The Great Disruption, with profit margins so large, the wealth created was increasingly wasted on luxury items that benefited only a few, already wealthy people.

Metropolouses – These were the residents of Metropolis. Also known as 'louses for short. These Boujees' luxury lives were a central cause of climate change. They retreated to their climate-controlled city-state so they could be coolly, blissfully ignorant of the suffering their consumption caused.

Mixtape – A mixtape can mean:
>   (a) A home-made compilation of songs that often carries a specific meaning. At one point, this was the most widely practiced art form in America.
>   (b) Self-produced recordings that are independently released to gain publicity and/or circumvent possible copyright infringement.

Moloch 5000 – This was the software system used by schools to place students on an educational track. This system was built with complicit bias hardcoded into it by the racist, sexist and elitist programmers who made this system.

Moses Effect – This meant going to almost supernatural extremes to part the thigh fat of women, such as by sewing shoehorns into their jeans. The goal was to create a thigh gap wide enough that the Israelites could escape Egypt through.

Noblification – The landed gentry cleaned up cities like New York and priced out those dubbed as riffraff in a process called gentrification. After this, an even more elite group of humans, calling themselves nobles, pushed out the common landed gentry to turn these into gilded palace-like city-states.

Organ Farming – Previously, humans would harvest organs from recently deceased humans. As Farming of the lowest class of humans became more common, Boujees would grow their replacement organs inside the bodies or on the skin of these living Vessels.

Peerage Pressure – Since the new city-states needed to fill its coffers, these each created a peerage system and sold titles to entitled Boujees. As more Boujees became Dukes, Earls, Viscounts and Barons, this pressured other Boujees to forklift over hundreds of millions of dollars or even billions of dollars for a piece of paper that gave them a few letters to put before their names.

Petty Boujee – The Petite Bourgeoisie, Petty Boujees or just Petties, were on the bottom rung of the upper class. This group included actors, singers, athletes, newscasters and social media influencers. They owned the means to production because they, themselves, were the products. They spent large amounts of their lives keeping themselves trim and beautiful and were constantly at the whims and mercies of other humans who either deemed them interesting or not.

Pickers – Since humans would often shop from home and have their goods delivered to them, many Grips would work in vast warehouses called fulfillment centers, racing from cage to cage to pick and box up these goods for delivery. These workers were called pickers.

Putting on the Fritz – This was when a hologram was so realistic-looking that humans would attempt to shake its hand or hug it but would only pass through the hologram's light field.

Robot Personhood – After human corporations were granted legal personhood, which allowed these the freedom of religion, the freedom of

speech and due process, these corporations went to great lengths to secure personhood for its expensive robots and automation appendages.

Sampling – Sampling was taking part of a song and reusing it in another song. This was first used by experimental artists. But in the 1970s, hip-hop DJs made sampling a regular component of the genre. From here, sampling became a regular part of all popular music genres. This novel includes over 2,300 samples of songs, poems, philosophical and religious works, films, TV shows and pop culture moments.

Santorum – The frothy mixture of lube and fecal matter that is sometimes the byproduct of anal sex or using anal sex toys is called santorum.

Silent treatment – A human was put into the silent treatment when someone used sound waves that were equal and opposite to their voices to cancel out the sounds they made.

Speciescentrically, Speciescentrism – Humans had a persnickety problem with considering themselves as the greatest species that ever was. This blinded humans from realizing how inadequate of a technology they were. This affected how they saw the universe around them. For instance, they saw Earth as the only type of planet that was right for sentient life because humans evolved on that kind of planet.

Super Summer – Super summer was what the last humans on Earth's northern hemisphere called the months between July and September when the temperature spiked to 120 degrees. This came after early summer (March to June) and before late summer (October to December.)

Thiel – Named for Peter Thiel, the eccentric 21st-century American billionaire, who went to great lengths to fight death, including rumors of using the blood/fluids of healthy young men to make him more youthful.

Thirst Trap – As waterways became more polluted because of climate change and as more humans were pushed to the margins of society, many of these humans would drink this polluted water to survive. This water often infected them with diseases that would cause extreme diarrhea which led to more dehydration, causing these humans to drink more polluted water in a vicious cycle dubbed the Thirst Trap.

THOT Police – These were the ever-vigilant members of female friend groups who would make sure that their friends weren't being sexually assaulted, drugged or hurt. The term THOT (That Ho Over There) police was a derogatory term made by the men who wanted to abuse their friends and derided their watchfulness as Orwellian.

Tramp l'oeil – In art, a trompe l'oeil is a trick of the eye. A tramp l'oeil was when marketers used ethnically-ambiguous humans in commercials and brochures so that people from different races would claim them as part of their own group.

Trojan Hoes – Trojan Hoes was when a group of humans would infiltrate a walled city or a heavily-guarded area by wrapping themselves in a hologram of a very attractive white woman, who could often waltz her way into any quarters without suspicion.

Trustafarian – These were the ultra-wealthy children of Boujees who claimed to live a hippie lifestyle. They spent the majority of their time doing drugs and traveling. Though they talked about how free they were from the evils of money and consumerism, they only lived this hippie lifestyle because they had money to spend and gold-encrusted safety nets ready to catch them if they were ever in danger.

United Federation of City-States (UFoCs, Residents are called UFoCers) - As the Boujees retreated into climate-controlled bubbles, they created city-states, like Metropolis. As the idea of climate-controlled city-states spread, an archipelago of bubbles formed to share ideas and practices. The rulers then signed the Articles of Confederation-Incorporation to form the United Federation of City-States.

Vessels – In Klossism, these were the unemployed humans whose only economic value after The Great Disruption was as bodies to be used by the Boujees, such as sex workers, surrogates, gut biome creators or organ growers.

Waisted – Waisted was when a woman in the entertainment industry was fired because her midsection has grown too big for her to be seen as desirable.

Social Structure
in The Gilded Age of Automation

Boujees – In Karlie Kloss-Marx's social theories, the Boujees were the upper class of human society before its extinction. Boujees were the humans that owned the most wealth and means of production.

Haute/Haught Boujees (aka the Haughties) were the owners of algorithms, the owners of automation and the means of production.

Petite/Petty Boujees (aka the Petties) were those Boujees who commoditized themselves to make their millions in the fields of acting, singing, sports, etc. Petties owned their means of production because they owned themselves. They were under constant pressure to beautify themselves to remain pleasing products and were at the whims of public perception.

Leeches – Leeches were the hairdressers, the interior designers, the florists, the makeup artists, the personal trainers, the massage therapists, the landscapers, the stylists, the gardeners, etc., for the Boujees. Leeches were anyone whose job it was to use their time, attention and artistic talent to make the Boujees, their homes and their lives more beautiful.

Brains – Brains were the few remaining professional workers after The Great Disruption. These were the authors of algorithms (but not the owners) and the humans that managed automation. Brains performed tasks that were called Head Jobs.

Grips - After The Great Disruption automated 80% of all job tasks, most of the jobs that couldn't be inexpensively automated were those tasks that were done by dexterous human hands, like picking in fulfillment centers, which requires quickly grabbing packages of different shapes and sizes and moving them. Grips were the class of humans that performed these Hand Jobs.

Vessels – Vessels were the humans who lost their jobs during The Great Disruption and whose only economic value for the Boujees was as bodies to be used, either as sex workers, surrogates, gut biome creators, organ growers, drug testers or software testers. The Boujees called them the Lazies to make them feel guilty for being trapped in poverty.

"2090 called, you're dead and
you've wasted your time on Earth"
- Kimberly Cougar Schmidt

"Listen:
We are here on Earth to fart around.
Don't let anybody tell you any different!"
- Kilgore Trout

"If life seems jolly rotten
There's something you've forgotten
And that's to laugh and smile and dance and sing
When you're feeling in the dumps
Don't be silly chumps
Just purse your lips and whistle, that's the thing

And always look on the bright side of life
Come on!
Always look on the right side of life

Life's a piece of shit
When you look at it
Life's a laugh and death's a joke, it's true
You'll see it's all a show
Keep 'em laughing as you go
Just remember that the last laugh is on you"
- Eric Idle
- Monty Python
- Tim Curry

About the Author

"Every single night,
I endure the flight,
Of little wings of white-flamed
Butterflies in my brain,
These ideas of mine,
Percolate the mind,
Trickle down the spine,
Swarm the belly, swellin' to a blaze

Every single night's alight
With my brain, brain."
                    - Fiona Apple

    I am the bags of fat burned off during liposuction. I am the clumps of hair that fall out when bleached and straightened with chemicals. I am the excess cartilage ripped out during nose jobs. I am the puss-filled infections that grow around butt injections. I am the raw nerves that are scraped by veneers. I am the gnarled toes and bunions brought on by years of wearing high-heels. When you see a meteor shoot across the sky, I am the chunks of rock that plummet to earth.

I am Stefani Bulsara!

497